SACRAMENTO PUBLIC LIBRARY
828 "I" Street
Sacramento, CA 95814
03/16

# THE PHOENIX DESCENT

D0972912

## ALSO BY CHUCK GROSSART

*The Gemini Effect*

# CHUCK GROSSART

## THE PHOENIX DESCENT

47NORTH

This is a work of fiction. Names, characters, organizations, places, events, and incidents are either products of the author's imagination or are used fictitiously.

Text copyright © 2016 Chuck Grossart

All rights reserved.

No part of this book may be reproduced, or stored in a retrieval system, or transmitted in any form or by any means, electronic, mechanical, photocopying, recording, or otherwise, without express written permission of the publisher.

Published by 47North, Seattle

www.apub.com

Amazon, the Amazon logo, and 47North are trademarks of Amazon.com, Inc., or its affiliates.

ISBN-13: 9781503945753
ISBN-10: 1503945758

Cover design by Cyanotype Book Architects

Printed in the United States of America

*To Goofy, Tiger, and Boo.*
*And a certain brown-eyed girl who*
*still makes my heart skip a beat.*

*Excerpt from an interview with Dr. Johannes Mattis*
*Director, Life Science and Technology Division*
*Phoenix BioLabs, LLC*
*May 23, 2021*

". . . the most remarkable life-forms on our planet. Some are incredibly specialized, and to be honest, a little terrifying from a human stand-point. Take, for example, *Ophiocordyceps unilateralis*, an entomopatho-genic fungus that infects one particular species of carpenter ant. It forces the ant to leave its home, attach itself to the underside of a leaf, and become a breeding ground for more spores, which eventually erupt from a pod that sprouts from the ant's head."

"That sounds painful."

[Laughing] "I suppose so, but the ant is dead by that point. It's really quite amazing, though. The fungi kingdom continues to surprise us, especially when we find species thriving where life—as we've pre-viously defined it—shouldn't exist. In the early nineties, a robot sent into the ruined Chernobyl reactor found a black growth on the walls of the containment unit—a radiotrophic fungus—using melanin, the same melanin pigment we find in our skin, to convert gamma radiation into energy, in much the same way a plant uses photosynthesis. In fact, the anabolic pathways are similar enough that we believe this species may be able to use energy from sunlight, as well, which would be a remarkable discovery. What I'm saying is, the possibilities are endless—with the right amount of funding, we could learn how to harness, or alter, the functions these simple organisms perform, opening up entirely new bioengineering applications for the betterment of the human condition . . ."

*Statement by the president of the United States*
*Associated Press*
*May 15, 2025*

"My fellow Americans, we've accomplished great things throughout the history of our manned spaceflight program, but it has not been without risk, and at times it has incurred a great cost. Tonight, it my sad duty to report to you that we have paid that terrible price once again. Two days ago, mission control in Houston lost all contact with *Resolute*, and in the professional judgment of our experts at NASA, we must assume our first manned mission to Mars has failed. The courageous crew of *Resolute*, whom we've all grown to know over the past year as we followed their preparations for their journey—Air Force Lieutenant Colonel Hunter Webb, mission commander, from Broomfield, Colorado; Navy Commander Caitlyn Wagner, pilot, from Virginia Beach, Virginia; and Lucas Hoover, mission specialist, from Grove City, Ohio—will now take their place beside the astronauts of *Apollo I*, *Challenger*, and *Columbia*, brave souls who have all made the ultimate sacrifice in our quest to explore the vastness of space . . ."

# PROLOGUE: THE RISE

*Polesie State Radioecological Reserve, Southeastern Belarus*
*June 18, 2025*

Sub-Lieutenant Gennady Krasov knew he was a dead man.

No matter what happened, he would never be able to leave this stinking, godforsaken place. He lay beneath one of his regiment's abandoned armored troop carriers, scanning the forest before him. Only one incendiary round was left in his rocket launcher, which he gripped tightly in his right hand. To his left lay his rifle, for all the good it would do. Bullets slowed their advance, but couldn't stop them.

He would need only one round, though, to save himself from the horrors that befell his troops. He would count his remaining shots carefully to save one last bullet.

Eight days passed since he and the rest of the 23rd Air Assault regiment parachuted in, beginning what was supposed to be a quick three-day mission to establish a perimeter, advance southward, and, along with their sister regiment, the 104th Air Assault, kill anything that got in their way. Simple. They did it before, in Chechnya, in Ukraine, and even in the Baltics, but nothing about this mission was *simple*. It was suicide.

The bastards who blew apart the protective enclosure covering the Chernobyl reactor managed to release God knows how much radioactivity in the Chernobyl exclusion zone. His dosimeter badge turned black in less than a day. He was as good as dead—and so were his troops—as soon as they hit the ground. Sacrificed. Russia's finest, thrown away in a failed cause against an enemy they had no chance of defeating.

But the radiation was the least of their worries.

Out of the corner of his eye, he caught motion to his left, in the trees. He stared, but saw nothing more. Still, his heart began to race, because it would soon be *their* time again.

The dawn was brightening, revealing a scarred battlefield as horrid as any he had ever witnessed. Artillery and rocket fire had scoured this sector, blowing the forest to bits. Around him, shredded trees stood as stripped monuments to a battle lost. He used a scope taken from a dead man's sniper rifle to observe the forest in front of him. No movement, yet. The things were less active during the nighttime hours. They moved with the daylight.

The forest was unnaturally quiet. The steady thud of artillery, and the scream of inbound shells, was absent. Even the skies were empty, the thunder of jet engines long since vanished.

They had all pulled back.

He was truly alone.

The air hung heavy with the scent of a battlefield—burnt powder, burnt bodies. But there was something else, a heavy, cloying scent, filthy, reminding him of the shore of a stagnant lake, or a feed yard in his boyhood home outside of St. Petersburg. It was *their* scent. The *Riy*.

Eight days ago, his regiment landed among a ragged Ukrainian infantry unit, and as he and his fellow soldiers gathered their parachutes, they learned the nature of their enemy. Riy, the Ukrainians called them, their word for *swarm*.

Monsters were what they were. Black things, faceless and terrifying, shuffling through the forests. Spreading quickly. Unstoppable. They used to be men, but not anymore. Whatever the terrorists did to the Chernobyl reactor unleashed something straight from the depths of hell.

There. Motion to his left. Not shadows this time, he was sure of it. He brought the sniper scope to his eye again and peered through the trees.

They were coming.

One. No, two.

And there would be more.

He gripped his rocket launcher tightly, scooted it in front of him. The incendiary warhead would take down a few of them—fire, it seemed, was the only way to kill the beasts—but after that, he knew he was a goner. The forests were full of Riy, and there was no way he could escape. Anyway, he would be dead soon from the radiation, a slow, painful death, retching out his innards and choking on his own blood. Paradise, though, compared to what the Riy would do to him.

He glanced at his rifle. One saved round in his mouth was all he would need. He wouldn't become one of *them*, a decision made after seeing firsthand what the Riy could do to a man, and what that man became.

When they found the Ukrainian soldier propped against a tree, he was far along in the infection process—the first time any of them had seen the transformation up close.

The stricken Ukrainian stared at them wide-eyed, unable to move or speak, as the black mist coursed through his veins. He had inhaled some of it, obviously, and was doomed from the moment it entered his lungs.

They stood and watched the man succumb to the infection—out of morbid curiosity more than anything else—as the slimy mass covered his uniform and every spot of exposed skin until only one eye was visible. Within that eye they saw fear, desperation, and a terrible yearning for help. The man darted his eye to each of their faces, imploring them to do *something*, to save him from whatever was devouring his body.

When he pulled his sidearm, he saw relief in the man's eye. The pistol's crack could barely be heard over the roar of an overhead attack jet unleashing a salvo of rockets a short distance away.

The man was dead, but whatever was within him was not.

When the black, tar-like goo covered the Ukrainian's lifeless, open eye, the body began to move. He and his troops pumped the thing full of bullets, but it still managed to stand, twitching from the impacts but otherwise unaffected, small wisps of black mist seeping from the bullet holes.

He ordered his troops to back off, get some distance, and then fired an incendiary round from his rocket launcher right at the newborn Riy. The forest floor burst into flame as the warhead exploded, and within the fire, what was once a Ukrainian soldier finally died.

They learned the black substance spread quickly, immobilizing its victim once inhaled, eventually erupting through the skin, covering every inch in a squirming black mass. All the while the victims were awake, and aware, but unable to save themselves. Shooting them had no effect, as bullets can't kill corrupted flesh animated by some sort of mindless parasite.

Only fire can.

He laid his scope on the ground, removed his helmet, and placed his blue beret atop his head. He was a member of the *Vozdushno-Desantnye Voyska*, the airborne troops, and he would not die without putting up a fight. He grasped the rocket launcher in his left hand, and with his right grabbed his rifle. He sprinted from cover toward a tree about ten meters away. The Riy had no eyes—they couldn't see him moving, and he was still too far away for them to sense his motion. If they did, they would open what used to be a mouth and expel a cloud of the black mist. He saw many of his troops get too close in the heat of battle, only to disappear in the deathly clouds.

No, it would *not* happen to him. With God as his witness, he would not die like that.

He could see others now, as the sunlight revealed more and more of the forest. The first two were getting close—now only twenty meters away—but beyond them were more than he cared to count. The forest was full of them.

He could hear the Riy shuffle across the ground—not really taking steps, but more like dragging their feet. And he could hear himself breathing. Hear the beat of his own heart, hammering away in his chest. The feedlot stench assaulted his senses. It was getting stronger, thicker, with each breath.

The first two turned in his direction. He hadn't moved a finger, yet they still came, possibly sensing his body heat. It didn't matter.

Fifteen meters. Ten.

He must do it now, before it was too late.

He raised the rocket launcher to his shoulder, rested his cheek against the tube, and closed one eye. He would put his last incendiary round into the large group of Riy behind these two, and take down as many as he could. Then he would take his own life.

He thought of his sister, Valyusha, and his young nephew, Pyotr. It saddened him to know that they would probably never be told the truth of what happened here.

He placed his finger on the trigger, concentrated on his sight picture, and took a deep breath, inhaling the spores from a cloud of black mist that enveloped him from behind.

*The skies over northeastern Ukraine*

Pilot/commander Major Yedor Bodrov glanced at his navigator/ weapons operator, Captain Artem Subbotin, sitting to his right and slumped forward toward his instruments. Bodrov had flown with the man numerous times before, and found him to be a competent aviator. Subbotin was fixated on his readouts—cross-checking settings, confirming distances, verifying configurations. Bodrov knew he could have drawn a less qualified man for this strike and was thankful he wouldn't have to do *both* of their jobs. He sucked a mouthful of rubbery air from his mask and felt his pulse quicken. Even on training runs, his heart would beat a little faster as he neared a target, but this time it was for real.

"Pilot, weapon release point in fifteen kilometers," Subbotin stated. "Permission to arm the weapon."

Major Bodrov's orders were clear, straight from General Bulgakov himself. He required no further clearance to prosecute his target. "You have permission to arm the weapon."

"Weapon armed," Captain Subbotin said. "Place weapon release mode to automatic."

"Weapon release mode to automatic," Bodrov replied, flicking the proper switch. The words seemed to stick to his tongue. His mouth was dry, and he found it difficult to swallow. He had dropped live ordnance before—in combat—but this was different.

His strike fighter was now flying itself, programmed to begin the pull-up and release sequence with no further manual input. Outside his cockpit, forested countryside flashed by, still mostly hidden in the predawn shadows beneath a brightening sky. His Fullback rose and descended as its terrain-following radar guided it over the uneven landscape. The system rarely malfunctioned, but he held his hand lightly on the control stick, just in case.

There were rumors about what was going on in Ukraine, but nothing official was provided through his command chain. When the weapons arrived in the dead of night at their air base, he and his squadron mates knew the situation must be dire. They planned the strike quickly, with nary a second to consider the ramifications of what they were being called to do.

"Weapon release in five kilometers, ten seconds until pull-up," Subbotin said.

"Copy, ten seconds." Bodrov knew other crews were counting down the seconds just as they were. Ten jets were involved in this strike, with their targets scattered across northeastern Ukraine and southern Belarus. They were forming a barrier, a circle around the contested area. What was left *in* the circle would fall to his compatriots in the Northern Fleet, and the fury they would unleash from beneath the waves.

"Five seconds, afterburners coming on."

"Copy, five seconds," Bodrov replied. As the engines' roar filled the cockpit, he watched Subbotin cross-check his settings one last time before sitting straight in his seat and resting his helmet firmly against the headrest. Bodrov did the same and tightened his leg and abdomen muscles in anticipation of the pull-up.

"Three, two, one . . . *mark.*"

The strike fighter entered a programmed seven-g climb, invisible hands compressing both crew members' bodies against their ejection seats as they momentarily experienced the sensation of weighing seven times their normal body weight. Bodrov's G suit inflated, squeezing his legs and torso, and he grunted against the sudden g onset. The Fullback screamed into the Ukrainian sky, blanketing the terrain below in its afterburners' thunder. Once the jet attained the proper release attitude, all became calm. The roar lessened, and the vibrations ceased. It was a moment of peace before they would release all hell below.

"Weapon release in three, two, one," Subbotin counted down. "Weapon away."

A finned, cylindrical object separated from the sky-blue underbelly of the Fullback, beginning its ballistic trajectory toward its target. In ten seconds, a drogue chute would deploy, slowing the bomb's descent and allowing the crew to escape.

Bodrov took control and grabbed the stick, his fighter rocketing nearly straight up. Pulling back until they were inverted, he fixed his gaze on the horizon and rolled wings level. As they slammed through Mach 1, racing toward the rising sun and away from the impending blast, Bodrov couldn't help but feel remorse for the ground troops still down there.

As one, he and Subbotin lowered their side blackout curtains, clicking them into place. As Bodrov reached for the front curtain, he looked at Subbotin and saw in the man's eyes exactly what he himself was feeling. No aircrew had done this since 1945, in the skies over Hiroshima and Nagasaki. Both men lowered their darkened visors, which, along with the curtains, would reduce any chance of flash blindness.

*It is a mission, nothing more, nothing less,* he tried to convince himself. They were ordered to drop a weapon, and performed their mission without error. Bodrov knew death would come quickly for those left below and allowed himself some solace from that fact. He and Subbotin would live to fight another day, if need be, but he hoped this would end whatever was happening in the forests below.

He didn't know that the dead—in the weeks and months to come—would be the lucky ones.

*White House Situation Room*

"Mr. President, we've detected three nuclear detonations—check that, four. Looks like low-yield weapons. Tactical nukes. Southwest Russia, near the Ukrainian border."

Four detonations, in the span of a few seconds. Four atomic bombs.

"Make that seven, Mr. President. Now showing four additional low-yield events in southern Belarus as well. Most likely air-delivered weapons, from fighter-bombers."

This was happening too fast. "Could this be some sort of military revolt?" the president asked. "The start of a coup?"

"Doubtful, sir," the secretary of defense replied. "Ulyanov has trouble with the eastern military district, but the troops in the west and south are completely loyal, as are their ballistic missile submarine commanders. The Russian sub captain launched because he was ordered to, and that order had to come from Ulyanov himself."

The chairman of the Joint Chiefs interrupted. "We're showing possible targets in northern Ukraine for the submarine launch, Mr. President."

"How many warheads?"

"Unknown at this time, sir."

"What the hell is Ulyanov shooting at?" the president asked. *Other than his own troops,* he silently added.

"It's mostly wilderness, uninhabited ever since the Chernobyl meltdown back in the mid-eighties. They've bombed the living hell out of the place since the invasion, Mr. President. It's full of their own troops. It makes no sense."

"Is there *any* threat to the United States at this moment, General?"

"No, Mr. President. We've detected no hostile Russian action directly targeting the United States. Yet."

The president paused for a second, letting the situation sink in. None of it made sense. It was *madness.* "General, how long until their missile reaches its targets?"

"In less than ten minutes, the northern portion of Ukraine is going to cease to exist, along with a sizeable portion of the ground forces they've pumped into that region." The chairman paused and took a deep breath. "And I don't know why," he added. "We're completely in the dark, Mr. President."

The electronic warning came through the speakers: *Nuclear detonation detected. Belarus. Nuclear detonation detected. Belarus.*

"Three more, sir. Low yield. Southern Belarus."

"What in God's name is Ulyanov doing?" the president asked, to no one in particular.

"We've always known this day could come, Mr. President," the chairman said. "But not like this. They're nuking the holy hell out of *themselves.*"

# PART I: HOME

# Chapter 1
## *SIF*

In response to the threat warning screaming in her headphones, Lieutenant (junior grade) Caitlyn "Sif" Wagner instinctively slammed the stick to the left and pulled hard, grunting against the g-forces and popping flares as she strained to look at her six.

The bastard was there, close, his nose tracking her tail. She reversed her turn, jettisoned her centerline and wing tanks, and strained to look over her other shoulder. He was still on her. She cursed the fact that she was all alone, and worse, in the skies over a patch of dirt that no US warplane was supposed to be anywhere near. At least officially.

"All right, Ivan," Sif breathed into her oxygen mask. "Let's play."

In another few seconds, the Russian pilot would fire one of his missiles at her, and she would take a piece of shrapnel in her leg when it detonated . . . but, how did she know that?

*Wait,* she thought, *the noise is wrong.*

It wasn't the threat warning. Something else. A familiar tone she was trained to recognize.

Slowly, her awareness began to return.

She wasn't in the cockpit of her Super Hornet, feet dry over North Korea.

That mission was years ago, when she was a lieutenant with VFA-11, the Red Rippers. She was fished from the Yellow Sea after punching out of her damaged fighter that day, the first pilot to down a Russian Su-50 in air-to-air combat, earning her the Distinguished Flying Cross and Purple Heart—citations that would probably remain classified forever.

That mission happened a couple of years before her divorce. Before she was selected for the USAF test pilot school, joined Astronaut Group 24—the "Marvins"—and was picked as a crew member for the first manned mission to . . .

She was dreaming. The tone meant it was time to wake up. To come out of stasis.

Sif willed herself to open her eyes. Her six months of chemically induced sleep were coming to an end, and Mars, she knew, was only days away. The mission for which she trained for years was finally coming to fruition, and she felt a rush of excitement.

Confusion, grogginess, joint stiffness, and blurry eyesight were symptoms they were trained to expect, aftereffects from spending months in an induced sleep state. Waking was supposed to be a slow, gradual process, minimizing the stress on body and mind. Months of zero-g spaceflight would take a certain unavoidable toll on their bodies, but the numbing effects of stasis would soon wear off, and they could get to work.

But this didn't feel gradual.

Sif swam in blackness as she struggled to open her eyes. She could feel herself breathing, but it was strange, as if she were loosely connected to her body and someone else was breathing for her. Yes, she was wearing a mask, and the system was probably still controlling her breathing—which might explain the odd out-of-body sensation she was experiencing—but the docs never mentioned anything like this. Nor did they mention the pain she was experiencing in her extremities.

Her arms and legs were on fire, tingling as if poked with thousands of sharp, icy needles.

When *Resolute* was seven days away from entering Mars orbit, the life-support system was programmed to start waking the crew—Hunter Webb first, as the mission commander, followed by Lucas Hoover, mission specialist and medical expert, and lastly, Sif. She had argued against being last, but was unable to sway the eggheads at NASA. She knew *Resolute* better than the designers did, and if anyone should wake first, it should be her. If there were any problems, she would be the one most able to take care of them. But, no. She would be last. *Sure, wake the pilot last and see where that gets you. If anything's wrong, do you honestly think Hunter or Lucas could handle it? No. Friggin'. Way.* Even though she knew they could, she wasn't about to admit it, and it still pissed her off.

Nothing would go wrong, they told her. *Resolute* was the most advanced piece of technology ever built, they said. Years of planning and preparation went into her design and construction. Built in orbit over the span of three years—at the cost of billions of dollars—she was simply a thing of beauty, stretching the length of a football field from tip to tail. It was called, and maybe rightly so, humanity's greatest achievement. The level of acceptable risk, the designers said, was exceptionally low.

But things go wrong all the time, regardless of how solid the design or careful the planning. Machines break, and usually at the worst possible moment. Even though *Resolute* was the most remarkable spacecraft ever built, it was still a machine, and although controlled by cutting-edge artificial intelligence—AI—that could make decisions while the crew was in stasis, it could still break.

To Sif, though, it all seemed like a crash program. Hurried. There was a new space race going on—with the Russians *and* the Chinese—and the US was going to be the first to send a manned mission to Mars. Period, dot. Somewhere within the miles of wiring, thousands of welds, and millions of lines of computer code, there might well be a devil lurking. Even some of the most advanced space probes smacked dead into the moon or Mars because someone flipped a 1 and 0, and none of those craft were as complex as *Resolute*.

*Flying is a dangerous business,* Sif remembered her dad telling her mom. He also used to say that he was safer in his Tomcat than in his car. A true statement, but painfully ironic, since it was a car accident that took both of her parents from her.

Space travel was a dangerous business, too. She personally (and privately) gave their mission a sixty-forty chance to succeed, and even that seemed optimistic.

The pain in her arms and legs subsided, and her breathing grew steady, but still, this wasn't what she expected, and it worried her.

She fought to open her eyes, and when she did, she realized her initial suspicions were correct. From inside her stasis capsule, with IV lines taped to her arms and thigh, and a mask covering her face, Sif didn't see the smiling faces of Hunter Webb and Lucas Hoover through her view port; rather there was only debris, spinning, floating by in the weightlessness of *Resolute*'s crew compartment. The lights were flickering, unsteady.

Reality cut through her fog, and it dawned on her what must be happening. She was awakened early for a reason, and not a good one. As her mind began to fire more clearly, she remembered how—if something happened to the ship that the AI couldn't handle—the crew would be brought out of stasis as soon as physically possible. Shocked awake by a flood of chemicals. And it wouldn't be a pleasant experience.

The docs were right. It wasn't pleasant. It *hurt*.

The light level in her stasis capsule gradually increased, and she squinted against the glare. To her left, she glanced at a readout showing how much time was left until unlock, when her capsule's lid would open. Two minutes. Below her readout were two identical timers, one for Hunter, and one for Lucas. In ten seconds Lucas's capsule would open, but there was a malfunction with Hunter's. It had reached zero, but was blinking red, which meant it either failed to open, or he was incapacitated.

And there was nothing she could do about it.

*Dammit.*

To her right was an environmental status readout. Whatever had happened to the ship could have fried a circuit board or two, allowing their stasis capsules to open into a vacuum. She quickly scanned the numbers and was relieved to see that air pressure and atmospheric gas levels were in the normal range. The temperature, however, was in the low range—42 degrees Fahrenheit—and that in and of itself was concerning.

The AI program that monitored *Resolute*'s functions was a brilliant piece of technology, but was still a computer. The techies called it OLIVIA., which stood for Operational Linguistic Isolated Variable Intelligence Algorithms. The crew called it—*her*—Liv.

Lucas's capsule was now open, according to the timer. She couldn't see to the side, as the only view was her small viewing port facing the ceiling. The stasis capsules were designed to protect the crew from the high levels of interstellar radiation they would encounter on the trip to Mars and, as such, were heavily shielded.

Lucas's numbers were green, not blinking red like Hunter's. Everything should be okay. In a few seconds, after removing his IV lines and mask, he should be free of it and his timer should blink off.

Sif was fully awake now, and the severity of what she might be facing began to sink in.

First, something had happened to the ship that caused some of their equipment to break free from the tie-downs. It would take one heck of a jolt to do something like that, but at least there was no hull breach.

Had they been struck by an object of some sort? Had one of the fuel tanks ruptured and exploded? Were they off course? Stranded?

*Stranded.*

The thought of drifting through space waiting to die was not a happy one. "Come on, Lucas, where the hell are you?" Her voice was rough, thick, another side effect of the stasis. She pressed her face close to the view port glass, trying to get a better view. Nothing.

Lucas's timer blinked off.

The top of a bald head floated into view, followed by the welcome face of Lucas Hoover. He peered inside, and Sif could see in his eyes what she, too, was feeling: confusion, urgency, and a little fear. Sif could barely hear him as he mouthed, "Are you okay?"

She nodded, and pointed to her right, toward Hunter's capsule. Lucas was already moving, aware of the problem, too.

Thirty seconds until her capsule would open.

And that's when the lights went out.

# Chapter 2
## *LITSA*

A slight breeze caressed her skin as Litsa stood on a rock outcropping, squinting as the horizon to the east brightened. The endless vault of stars in the night sky was losing its brilliance. The first warning bell had already rung, and the second was minutes away.

Below, the gatherers were binding their take, preparing to haul it back to the Dak. The things were in the fields during the day, crushing some of the stalks. From her vantage point, she could see the trails they took through the fields, cutting across their crops like termites through wood. It slowed the night's harvest, though, as the gatherers took extra care not to disturb the patches of black death the things left behind, spending precious minutes they couldn't spare. The crop must be harvested before any more damage was done. Downwind from where she stood, smoke rose into the sky as those crops too soiled to save were quickly consumed by flames. A finger of blackish smoke curled into the sky. There were no clouds, and a bright, sunny day would soon dawn.

Those kinds of days were the most dangerous.

The things were getting closer again, venturing into regions free of Riy for years. Their lives depended on these fields, and if the damage continued, they would have to act. Some on the council might want to move to another place, but she was tired of running. The Dak had been her home for the last ten years, and she would run no more.

Litsa gripped her bow tightly as the second warning bell rang through the early morning silence. They must get moving.

She cupped her hands to her mouth and yelled, "Second bell. Grab what you can and let's get moving." The lead gatherer, a man named Colin, waved his arm in response. The sun was almost up. They were cutting it close. Too close. Personally, she liked to have the harvest crew halfway back to the Dak by the second bell. There was a small emergency haven located on the trail between the Dak and the fields, large enough for all of them to squeeze into, but they would have to abandon their take. They needed those crops. Litsa was sick and tired of eating wall greens, and she wasn't the only one.

She slid her darkened goggles over her eyes and raised her field glasses to the east. Even though one lens was cracked, she could still scan the horizon with one eye. Nothing, yet. If there was a new hive close by, and she figured there must be, then the light level was getting dangerously bright. The drones might already be on the move.

She kicked at the fire at her feet, making sure there was still enough flame to light her torch, and then she heard the scream.

Without thinking, she grabbed a handful of arrows from her quiver and brought one to the bowstring, three more intertwined between her fingers. Just before she dipped the head of her torch into the fire, she realized what was happening. One of the gatherers had fallen and was hurt.

A crowd quickly gathered around the injured person—from the looks of it, Jeremy, one of the older ones—and dropped their bundles in place. This was a delay they couldn't afford.

"Colin," she shouted, "get the others moving, *now*." It was too damn bright. "I'll take care of him. Get the others back to the Dak."

He waved his arm again, and herded the others toward their bundles, and the safety of the Dak.

Litsa took a quick glance at the horizon as the first fiery finger of the sun became visible—and saw them. Black specks in the distance, growing closer. Closely spaced. Forty, maybe fifty.

"Dammit." She dipped the soaked tip of one of her arrows into the fire, drew her bow, pointed it skyward, and let the arrow fly. A signal to the watch standers back at the Dak. Hopefully they would see it and send more warriors, but the sky was already too bright.

She couldn't count on any help. She would face the swarm alone.

The gatherers below saw the signal and ran, dragging their bundles behind them as best they could. Colin, she saw, stayed behind with Jeremy.

Litsa lit her torch, slung her bow over her shoulder, and ran down the rough face of the bluff, careful not to lose her balance and end up in a heap at the bottom. She sprinted to Colin.

"Are they coming?" Colin asked.

Litsa nodded and knelt by Jeremy. His ankle looked broken. "Can you move?"

Through gritted teeth, he answered, "No, I can't stand. Leave me here."

Not a chance. She had known Jeremy her entire life, and he was one of her favorites. He was a little slow at times, but he was strong, always smiling, and he was a good gatherer. "Colin, you're going to have to carry him," Litsa said. "Carry him as fast as you can, and try to make it to the middle haven. You'll be safe there."

She could see Colin was starting to panic. "I don't think I can—"

Litsa put her free hand on Colin's shoulder, gave him a squeeze. "You can *do* it, Colin. You *have* to. Otherwise Jeremy is going to die. Do you understand me?"

Colin darted his gaze toward the rising sun, and then back at Litsa. "I'll try," he said.

Litsa slapped him on the arm. "Good man. I know you can do it." At least she hoped he could. She helped Colin pick Jeremy up off the ground, and saw he was at least able to hop on one foot with Colin's support. "Okay, get moving. I'll buy you some time."

As Litsa turned and sprinted toward the fields, Jeremy called her name.

"For God's sake, Litsa," Jeremy said, "be careful. Don't get yourself killed on account of me. I'm not worth it."

She ignored the pain she felt from Jeremy's words and screamed at Colin, "You get him to the haven, do you hear me? Move!" She hesitated for a second, watching the two of them hobble away. She wasn't planning on dying today, but if it was her time, doing so to save the two of them would be worth it. She would lay her life down for any of the 125 people in the Dak. They were *all* worth it.

Litsa turned and, holding her torch high, ran headlong into the rows of crops, toward the swarm approaching from the east.

Toward the Riy.

# Chapter 3

Sif's capsule opened with a hiss. Gooseflesh covered her exposed skin, and she could see her breath. She pushed herself out into the darkness, keeping one hand on the capsule's edge to ground herself. The unmistakable tang of burnt wiring filled the crew compartment, but there was no fire. *Thank God.*

"Lucas?"

"I'm right here," Lucas replied, his voice also gravelly. "Hunter's capsule isn't responding."

Sif heard him banging against the capsule with the palm of his hand. She couldn't see a thing. Absolutely pitch-black.

"I can't get it to open," Lucas said. "I think the control circuits have shorted out."

The lights flickered again. With each flash, she glimpsed a confused mess—pieces of random equipment floating about, tie-down straps reaching out from the walls, snaking through the air—and Lucas floating above Hunter's stasis capsule, his face nearly pressed against the view port glass. Sif pushed away from her capsule toward Hunter's.

"Emerg—ife sup—alfunc—" It was Liv—the AI program—coming through the speakers. A burst of static from the overhead speaker cut her off.

Hunter's bio readout didn't look good. His heartbeat was racing, erratic.

"He's going into cardiac arrest," Lucas said. "We've got to get him out of there."

"Try the emergency release," Sif said. "Left side, beneath the rail."

"Got it." Lucas grabbed the handle and pulled. "Dammit. I can't get it to budge."

Sif grabbed the handle, too, and they braced themselves against the side of the capsule with their feet. "On three," Sif said. "One, two, three!"

The handle released with a screech, and Sif went tumbling, bouncing off Lucas and into the padded wall of the crew compartment. She reached for a loose tie-down strap, missed it, and floated across the compartment until she bounced against the far wall. This time, she was able to get a handhold and orient her body so she could push off the wall with her bare feet, back toward Hunter's capsule as it slid open.

His skin was pale, his eyes open a crack. His mouth was slack, a small string of saliva twisting into the air above his face. "Hunter!" Sif shook him. "Dammit, wake up."

"Whatever happened to the ship screwed up his waking sequence," Lucas said, glancing again at the bio readout. Hunter's heartbeat was still erratic, and growing weaker. "It wasn't balanced, the percentages were all wrong." He ripped the IV lines out of Hunter's arms and thigh. "We need the defibrillator. C7, lower."

Sif pushed herself away from Hunter's capsule and floated down the passageway toward stowage compartment C7, located below a red line delineating the upper and lower halves of the tunnel. The lights were steady, so at least she could see where she was going.

*It's not supposed to happen this way.* She, Lucas, and Hunter would be the first humans to set foot on another planet. Hunter couldn't die. Especially not now, when they were so close.

But, were they close to Mars? Or were they somewhere else, knocked off course, drifting? The pang of fear she felt moments earlier returned, and she fought to suppress it. She had to get to the control module, and soon. But Hunter needed saving first.

Sif ripped open the Velcro covering from C7. Inside was a portable defibrillator, which they were trained to use but hoped would never be needed. She gathered it up and pushed away with her feet, rocketing down the tubelike passageway, which ran the length of the ship. The lights went out again, and for a second she was flying through total darkness, hoping she wouldn't pass right by and slam into the far bulkhead. She reached out and let her fingers slide across the padded surface. She had pushed off too hard—adrenaline rush—and was going too fast.

The lights blinked back on as she exited the tunnel. Spying Lucas, she shoved the defibrillator toward him, hoping she judged her momentum and the distance correctly. She floated by just as Lucas snatched the defibrillator out of the air.

Sif tucked her legs and brought her head to her chest, remembering her zero-g training. She rolled forward and extended her legs at just the right moment to stop her rolling momentum. She stepped against the far bulkhead, let her knees flex to absorb the impact, and then twisted her body to turn herself toward Lucas and Hunter. She pushed off and stopped herself beside Hunter's capsule. The lights flickered again.

Lucas ripped open Hunter's thin shirt and placed one pad below Hunter's right collarbone. The other he placed lower on the left side of his body, right at the edge of his rib cage. Sif noticed small beads of sweat on Lucas's forehead, and a couple were starting to float away.

The defibrillator's electronic voice announced, "Analyzing rhythm" as it read Hunter's heartbeat. "Shock advised. Charging."

"Don't touch him, Sif," Lucas said as he let himself float away a few inches. Sif did the same.

She didn't want to see Hunter die like this. They needed him. *Come on, Hunter.* The electronic voice announced, "Shock in three, two, one . . ."

Hunter's body convulsed, the electricity flowing from electrode to electrode, through his heart, trying to jump-start it. It seemed to last forever, then his body relaxed.

Hunter's eyes were open wide, but vacant. He wasn't breathing.

"Analyzing rhythm," the machine announced.

"Sif, what the hell happened?" Lucas asked.

She shook her head. "I don't know, but we're alive and the ship is intact, at least for now."

"Shock advised. Charging," the machine said.

"Dammit, Hunter, come *on*," Sif yelled.

"Shock in three, two, one . . ."

Again, they watched Hunter's body convulse, and again, no response.

"Analyzing rhythm."

"I think we're losing him," Lucas said.

"Shock advised. Charging."

It wasn't working. Hunter was going to die, and there was nothing Sif could do. She had to make sure she and Lucas at least had a fighting chance. "I'm heading to control," she said, pushing away. "Do what you can, Lucas."

"Shock in three, two, one . . ." the machine announced, but Sif was already halfway down the tunnel toward the control module.

She had a spacecraft to take care of.

# Chapter 4

Litsa crouched at the edge of the crops, watching the Riy approach. From the speed of their advance, and the manner by which they were moving, she knew they were drones, searchers sent out by an active hive.

Almost a year passed since a hive had ventured this far north. The last one was relatively small. They destroyed enough of it to force it to retreat, but they lost three fighters in the process. As a result, they nearly abandoned their home and moved to another refuge, but thankfully, as far as Litsa was concerned, they decided to stay put. Over the past year, they lived their lives without having to fight the Riy, and even some of the animals returned. But now, once the council learned another hive was nearby, the arguments for moving would rise again. No, Litsa told herself, not this time. The Dak was their—*her*—home, and she would fight to keep it. They would find this hive and kill it, before it found them.

The sunlight was warm on her skin as she moved forward, planning her line of attack. Even though the sun's warmth was somewhat soothing, she felt exposed. The rising sun hurt her eyes, too, even through darkened goggles. She didn't want to be out here, but had to buy time for the gatherers to get back to the safety of the Dak and for Colin and

Jeremy to reach the middle haven. She also had to avoid being detected by the drones, the outer ring of the hive's nervous system. If they sensed her presence, or worse, attacked her, the hive would react, send out jumpers, and slowly move straight toward their home.

She sprinted to a group of boulders and placed her quiver on the grass. She had eleven arrows, each tip tied with strips of fabric soaked with the sticky petrol from the lower caverns. It might be enough to shock the things into moving away.

Litsa wedged her torch between a couple of rocks, and, satisfied it was secure, peered around the boulders and saw the line of drones, much closer now, steadily moving her way, each one an echo of what once was a living, breathing human being.

Horrid, *ugly* things they were, blackened corpses, thin and ungainly, usurped flesh and bone transformed into walking shadows. At one time, each of the drones had a name, but they were now no more than vehicles for the black mist they carried in their chests. Up close, one could discern the remnants of a face, see exposed patches of white bone—the skull, or teeth—glaring brightly, peeking out from behind strands of hair still clinging to a blackened scalp. And then there were the small ones, the children. What used to be children. They were all people once, but there was no life, no soul inside. They were just *things* that reached out from the hive during the daylight hours and retreated back to the hive before dark.

If the drones sensed a life-form nearby—either by motion or body heat—a lump in the center of the chest would peel open like the petals of a flower and expel a cloud of the black mist, spreading the spores. Once a drone was triggered, a signal would be sent back to the hive, as each drone had a long, fibrous tail it dragged behind, connected to another drone farther back. No matter how far a group of drones ventured away from the hive, there was always a connection maintained with the hive itself. The drones were sensory organs of a much larger organism, wired together by the fibrous tails. Once that signal reached the hive—or if a tail was severed, breaking the connection—the hive would produce jumpers. And if they came, this would be an entirely different fight.

The closest group of drones was fifty yards away, heading toward the crops. To her left, other drones stretched away in an arc, heading more west-northwest, away from the crops and the Dak. A gentle breeze was blowing west to east. Perfect.

Litsa decided to attack the ones closest to her, to try to block their advance and change the entire group's direction. She wouldn't have to get close enough to put a shaft into each one—a fire in front of them would work.

Litsa touched her torch to the first arrow, drew her bow, and let the arrow fly. She quickly followed with five others, each spaced about five or six yards apart, parallel to the closest line of Riy. She had handled the bow since she was a child and was one of the clan's better archers. She smiled as the arrows arced through the sky and landed exactly where she aimed.

The grass was dry and ignited quickly. She knew she was risking a much larger fire, but the wind direction should carry it east and away from the crop fields. If she was lucky, Litsa mused, the fire would burn all the way to the hive itself. She crawled atop the largest boulder and watched the results of her handiwork.

The southern end of the drone arc stopped, sensing the heat to its front. The flames crackled as more of the grass ignited, and, as she hoped, spread eastward.

The drones swayed back and forth, as if unsure of what to do. As one, the long line of drones raised their arms into the air, sensing, feeling the heat. The line was trying to ascertain the location of the fire and determine which parts of the arc were in danger. Then, those closest to the flames began to retreat, backing away from the heat.

It was working.

Until they split into two groups.

A line of ten drones turned and headed south, moving fast to her right, trying to flank the lines of flames, to find a safe path. At the point where the arc broke ranks, the others headed north, trying to get around the other side of the fire.

They were going *around* it, moving fast.

She jumped down from the boulder and grabbed her remaining five arrows. She quickly lit two and let them fly to the north, hoping to delay the large group trying to swing around the flames to her left. Without waiting to see where they landed, she ran around to the south side of the boulders she was using to mask her presence, and stopped in her tracks.

The ten drones that split off from the main group were only a few yards away. Too close. And only three arrows left. It was time to run.

She turned—and from a crook in the rocks sprang, of all things, a rabbit. She spooked it, and it was running directly toward the drones.

The drones reacted immediately. Litsa watched as two of them belched black clouds from their chests, covering the rabbit in a dark, clinging dust. Litsa lost her footing, stumbled backward, and fell to the ground, instinctively covering her mouth and nose and holding her breath.

It was too late now. The hive would be alerted. And she would have to run for her life.

The closest drone sensed her presence and moved quickly toward her, the flowerlike petals peeling back from the mass on its chest.

Litsa scrambled to her feet and ran, the distinctive pop of the drone releasing its spores sounding just behind her. Close, but not *too* close. This time.

She sprinted back toward the crops, weaving her way through the rows as the leaves slapped against her face. She didn't want to look behind her, because she knew what was coming. She emerged onto open ground and ran as fast as she possibly could along the trail leading back to the Dak and safety, but she doubted she would make it that far. She would be lucky to make it to the middle haven with Colin and—

A thump behind her. Then three more, to her left, and more to her right.

*Jumpers.*

Litsa ran. The middle haven was fifty yards away. Her lungs felt as if they were going to explode, and a sharp pain erupted in her side. She willed herself to move faster, then out of the corner of her eye she saw it.

Litsa tossed her quiver and bow to the ground and threw herself to the right, tumbling into the brush as a loud thump resounded right next to her.

The damn thing almost landed right on top of her.

She lay as still as she could, trying to control her breathing. Through the brush, she could see the entrance to the middle haven, fifteen yards ahead. It wasn't closed. The heavy lid to the underground hideout was open a few inches. She could see Colin peeking out, and then Jeremy, their eyes wide.

She could hear the jumper as it moved, raising its tentacles into the air, trying to sense motion. She slowly turned her head and saw it, no more than ten feet away, right off the edge of the trail. Close enough that if it felt her presence now, she wouldn't have a chance. The stench was awful, strong enough that she could taste it, and she struggled not to gag.

Litsa had seen jumpers at a distance before and sent flaming shafts into many of them, but never viewed one this close. Those who did never lived to tell about it.

It was a black, undulating mass, long spires extending from its body into the air, reminding her of a sea urchin from one of the old books. It was feeling the air around it, waiting to be disturbed. One wrong move on her part, and the thing would explode, releasing a cloud of spores for yards around it.

If she could only wait it out for a few more seconds, a minute at the most, it would leave, jumping to another place to extend its feelers and continue searching for whatever had triggered the drones. Litsa cut her eyes to the entrance of the middle haven once again, hoping Colin and Jeremy had enough sense to close the lid—and couldn't believe what she was seeing.

It was Jeremy. The lid was all the way open, and he was scrambling outside before Colin could stop him. "Hey!" he yelled. "Over here!"

"Jer—" Litsa caught the word as it left her mouth. She couldn't yell. She was too close. She knew what Jeremy was trying to do.

The jumper's tentacles stiffened and, one by one, they pointed in Jeremy's direction.

It sensed him.

Jeremy was hopping away from the entrance on one foot, waving his arms. "I'm over here!" Colin, Litsa saw, was leaning halfway out of the haven's entrance, unsure of what to do.

Litsa wouldn't let Jeremy sacrifice himself for her. She grabbed a handful of dirt, stood, and threw it at the jumper. Just as it leapt at Jeremy.

"No!" Litsa screamed as the thing landed at Jeremy's feet.

For a second, their eyes met. Jeremy smiled.

Knowing there was nothing else she could do, Litsa covered her nose and mouth with her hands and ran for the haven's entrance.

And then the jumper exploded.

# Chapter 5

"He's going to be okay."

Sif heard the relief in Lucas's voice. It was close, but Hunter would pull through. There was something else in his voice, too, though. Sif had left Hunter for dead, deciding the ship was more important than her crewmate. She had left Lucas to handle it by himself.

"Good," Sif said. "We'll need him."

"He's resting right now," Lucas said. "Whatever fried the electronics screwed up his waking sequence, too. Unsequenced injections led to a chemical imbalance. He's lucky to be alive." Lucas paused, then added, "And so are we."

A string of garbled words slipped from the overhead speaker as Sif continued to work on Liv's voice interface. She replaced a couple of ruined circuit boards and restored all of Liv's autonomic ship control functions, but getting her to talk was proving a little more difficult. For now, they would communicate with her via keyboard input. "How long is he out of pocket?"

"A couple of hours, max. It was hard enough to convince him to stay strapped in for that long."

"Any lasting effects?"

"I'm not sure, but I don't think so. We got to him quickly enough that he didn't suffer any permanent damage. As far as I can tell."

"You saved his life, Lucas."

Lucas took his time responding. "The important thing is he's alive, and, like you said, we're going to need him. What have you found so far?"

Sif was glad Lucas decided to change the subject. He was angry at her for leaving him and Hunter, but at the time, it had seemed like the right thing to do. They could discuss it later.

"When you said we were lucky to be alive, you were right. The ship suffered an electronic surge of some sort. It completely scrambled Liv's brain." She pointed to the burned-out circuit boards in a plastic bag floating above her left shoulder. Lucas reached out and grabbed them.

"Jesus. What else?"

"From what I can tell, Liv's backup systems were able to keep all the primary systems functioning after they all reset. If the surge was any worse, we wouldn't have ever known."

"What could cause a surge like that? Something internal?"

"I don't think so. Look at this," Sif said, pointing to a screen above her head. "The thruster fuel levels are way down, port more than starboard. They were firing like crazy right before the surge."

"Liv was trying to maneuver?"

"She was trying to keep us on course. Look. The main engines performed three unscheduled burns, one prior to and two after the surge. The first for fifteen seconds, after the port thrusters started firing, and then the second and third, each lasting almost a minute, after the surge."

"Did we hit something?"

"Possibility. That might explain the thruster firings, and the mess," Sif said, flicking a small package of replacement bolts that came loose from one of the storage compartments away from her face, sending it spinning, "but something big enough to knock us off course like that and knock so many things loose probably would've torn right through the ship. We won't know for sure until we do an external inspection, but from what I've found so far, there's no sign of any significant structural damage. It's the duration of the thruster firings that has me puzzled, Lucas."

He studied the screen. "I see what you mean. It's gradual, not sudden."

"Exactly. This is telling me we weren't *knocked* off course, we were pulled. Slightly at first, then it became more pronounced, to the point that the port thrusters couldn't compensate."

"That explains the first main engine burn."

"Yes. Liv fired the mains to try to pull us back on course."

"Did it work?"

Sif shook her head. "I can't answer that yet, Lucas. We've only got partial readouts right now. The primary nav system took quite a hit during the surge and failed shortly afterward. It's still trying to reboot itself. The backup isn't working."

"So we're flying blind."

"Yes. We're flying blind. When we get more of the systems up and running, we'll know more, but as of this moment, I have no friggin' clue where we are."

"Okay. You said there were two other burns after the surge, right?"

"Yes. Both lasting sixty seconds."

"If Liv's functioning was reduced following the surge, what commanded them?"

Sif took a deep breath and let it out slowly. "I have a theory, and you're not going to like it. Do you remember all the tech briefings they gave us in Houston?"

"Oh God, yes. Bataan death march by PowerPoint. I wanted to dig my eyes out."

"Do you remember the four-day'er they gave us on Liv? The part about the fail-safe mode?"

"The what? I must've dozed off during that part."

"If my theory is correct, and I have a pretty good feeling that it is, after the surge, and after Liv lost her mind—while we were all stuck in stasis—the ship did exactly what it was programmed to do."

"Which is?"

"*Resolute* tried to take us home, Lucas. She tried to get us back to Earth."

# Chapter 6

"How could you let him *do* that?" Litsa ripped her goggles off and threw them to the dirt floor.

"I tried to stop him, but he kicked me back down the ladder. He was—"

"God *damn* you, Colin." Litsa shoved him, hard, and heard his body slam into the dirt wall. She was furious, pumped full of adrenaline from being so close to one of those *things*, but immediately regretted her actions. Colin had tried to save Jeremy, but even with an injured ankle Jeremy was much bigger and stronger. If the tables were turned, and she was in Colin's place, she doubted she could have stopped Jeremy, either, once he made up his mind about what he wanted to do.

Being out in the light for so long affected her vision, and the interior of the middle haven—basically a hole in the ground with a trapdoor cover, which led to a small underground chamber—was still pitch-black. She could hear Colin sobbing softly.

"I'm sorry," she said. "I know you tried." She turned her head and tried to spit the horrid taste from her mouth, but her mouth was dry. The earthy scent of the chamber calmed her somewhat, but the pang of fear she felt cut right through, a cold sweat clinging to her skin. She shivered.

"He'd do anything for you," Colin said, sniffling and wiping his nose on his sleeve. "When we saw the jumpers coming, I held him back, told him you were going to make it, and he stopped struggling until that last one landed right next to you. I tried to grab his leg, but he kicked me away. He said he was a burden now, to the rest of us, and he tried to save you."

*A burden.*

Even if his injury healed badly, and his time in the fields ended, he still wouldn't be a *burden*. He, and the rest of the clan, would find a way to work around it.

Jeremy did not succumb right away. He died a slow, painful death, coughing, scratching at his eyes, at his mouth. Screaming. She had seen it before. She stared at the trapdoor above, locked tight. A metal bar extended through two loops fastened onto its underside, with both ends of the bar extending into the sides of the entrance tunnel, preventing it from being pulled open from the outside. She locked it, in case Jeremy tried to get back inside.

By now, though, it was probably over. The transformation of a man she once called a friend was complete. The thing that he became would stumble back toward the hive—wherever it was—and become a part of it.

Jeremy sacrificed himself, to save her life. He was big, clumsy, and simple, but he was the noblest man she ever knew.

She would avenge his death.

As her vision returned to normal, she could see Colin in the darkness, hanging his head and wiping his eyes with his hand. "How many jumpers did you see?"

"Six. No, seven. Five off to the left—a little north of us—and two others that were much closer, including the one that almost got you."

The number of drones she saw—between forty and fifty—meant that the hive was probably a big one. Not easy to destroy, but they could inflict enough damage to force it to retreat.

"We have about seven hours of daylight left, Colin. We have to get back to the Dak and tell them what we've seen. Joshua will need to send a scouting party tonight, to find the hive."

She watched Colin look up at the trapdoor. "You're not going back up there, are you?"

Litsa moved to the far wall, and probed the dirt with her fingers. "No, we're not going outside. Not yet, anyway."

Colin stepped closer. "What are you doing?"

Litsa found the spot she was searching for and started scooping the dirt away. "There's a tunnel out of here, Colin." She scooped handfuls of soft dirt from the wall and shoved them behind her. "It heads southwest about a half mile before it comes to the surface. Jensen and his boys dug it a few years back. A safety measure in case the Riy decided to plant themselves outside the door."

"But it'll still be daylight outside, and the Riy—"

"If we hurry, we should be able to avoid them. And the direction they were heading would put them northeast of where we'll come to the surface. There it is." Litsa broke through the false wall, exposing the tunnel. "Do you want to go first?"

"No," Colin answered quickly. "I'll follow you."

"It might be a little tight in places. If you get stuck, I might not be able to help you. There's no room to turn around."

"Maybe I should stay here."

Just as well, as he would probably only slow her down. He would be safe here until nightfall. "Don't open that door for another seven hours." With that, Litsa crawled inside the tunnel.

"Litsa?" Colin's voice, from behind. "Tell Jessa I love her, and I'll see her tonight."

In the heat of the moment she forgot Colin was married. When the others arrived back at the Dak without him, Jessa would surely be frantic. "I'll tell her, Colin. Don't worry."

Litsa scooted herself forward on her elbows, and disappeared into the darkness.

# Chapter 7

"I don't see any other explanation for it, Hunter," she said. "The thruster burns, the main engine firings, it just makes sense. We won't be able to confirm it until we get Liv fully functional again and the nav system is back, but I think we may be on our way back home. Or headed off to who knows where."

Hunter rubbed his eyes. "How long until Liv is back on line?" he asked.

"Autonomic functions are restored. It's the voice interface that I'm having trouble with. The power surge really did a number on her. Keyboard queries aren't there yet, either."

"External cameras?"

"Not yet," Lucas said. "Working on it."

"We're going to have to do an EVA," Hunter said. "What you've told me sounds plausible, but we need to know if there's any external damage."

"I was thinking the same thing," Sif replied, "but not 'we.' You're grounded. Am I right, Lucas?"

"I'm fine," Hunter replied. "There's no reason why—"

"Caitlyn's right, Hunter," Lucas said, cutting him off. "The last thing you need to do right now is take a stroll outside."

"It doesn't matter. I'm perfectly able."

Sif caught a little echo of ego in his voice and wasn't about to let it pass. "It doesn't *matter*? Are you kidding me? An hour ago, you were twitching in your capsule, full of the wrong chemicals at the wrong times, and Lucas here pulled a friggin' Dr. Frankenstein on you to bring you back to life. You almost died, Lieutenant Colonel Webb, and I'm not about to put my life on the line doing an EVA with a partner I can't count on. Not going to happen. I'm better off solo."

"Hold on, Commander. This is my mission."

"Don't even go there, Hunter. Our *mission* was over as soon as Liv fired the mains the first time. You know it, and I know it. From that point on, our trip to Mars was over. We had just enough fuel to get there and back, with not a whole lot of fuel on the margins. Our margin went to shit at eight seconds on that first burn. So don't stand there and pull rank on me. We're all in this together, and if we want to survive—if that's even *possible*—we need to cut the crap and work together." She probably pushed it a little too far, based on the look in Hunter's eyes. She couldn't tell if he was mad or hurt. Or both. "We're wasting time," Sif said, ending the conversation. "I'm suiting up."

Sif unstrapped herself from her pilot's station and pushed herself toward the corridor, expecting Hunter to respond. He didn't. She stopped herself at the exit and turned her body to face them. "Lucas, I'm going to need a hand."

Sif saw Hunter was staring at her, the same look in his eyes. She was surprised by what he said next.

"Stem to stern, Commander. Give her a thorough going-over. We need to know exactly where we stand."

"Copy that," Sif said.

\*\*\*

Sif slid her body into the lower portion of the suit as Lucas unlatched the upper half from the wall and moved it into position.

"So what the hell was all that about?" Lucas asked.

"I lost it a little there, didn't I?"

"Yes. You did."

"You think I was wrong, then."

"Does it really matter to you what I think?"

Sif was a little taken aback by Lucas's tone. "Okay, look. I was too hard on him. I'll admit it. And I was probably wrong to leave you with him, too."

"You said it yourself, Caitlyn. He almost died a little over an hour ago, and as soon as he's partially able to wrap his head around that, you throw *mission failure* in his face. Not your best moment."

"That wasn't my intention."

"Yes, it was." Lucas shook his head. "For as long as I've known you two, you've competed against each other. I don't know if it's a fighter pilot thing, an Air Force–Navy thing, or whatever, but hardly a moment goes by when one of you isn't trying to outdo the other. Am I wrong?"

"We're both competitive people. Sure. That's how we got to where we are. Same for you, Lucas. You're no slacker when it comes to trying to get ahead."

"The difference is, I'm a scientist, not a fighter jock. I fought my battles in a classroom and a lab, not a cockpit. Put your arms up."

Sif raised her arms, and Lucas lowered the upper portion of the suit over her head. He fastened the connectors at the waist and checked to make sure they were tight.

"What do you want me to say, Lucas? He's good at what he does, and so am I. You throw two type A personalities in the same room, and they're bound to butt heads once in a while."

Lucas clicked the suit gloves into place. "All I'm saying is you need to cool it a little. When you said we need to work as a team in order to survive, you were right. How do they feel?"

Sif flexed her fingers, moved her arms around. "It's good. The only way we're going to get through this is by working together. Throw away the duty titles and ranks and get our butts home. If we can. Check the left one, it feels a little loose."

Lucas jiggled the glove. "It's tight. And I agree with you completely. You need to take your own advice, though."

"What's that supposed to mean?"

"Work *with* him, Caitlyn, not against him. This isn't a competition anymore."

Lucas was right. She was too quick to confront Hunter and went overboard when she did. "Okay, fine. I'll try harder next time, Dad. And by the way, I hate it when you call me Caitlyn."

Lucas smiled. "I know you do, but I don't do call signs. I'm not a flyer, remember?"

Sif smiled back. "It's okay. Not everyone can be a pilot." She was happy to see Lucas's grin widen a little at the dig. "Are you going to attach my helmet, or am I going to have to hold my breath?"

"I'll gladly put it on if it means I don't have to listen to you anymore. The bio-readout for the suit isn't functioning yet, so you're going to be on your own out there."

"So if my heart goes pitter-patter, you'll never know."

"Right. I also won't know if something's wrong, so be careful and monitor yourself. You feel any changes in your temperature, breathing, see condensation on the inside of your visor, anything that's out of the ordinary and you get back here pronto."

"Got it." Sif tilted her head to the side. "Hmm. Hoover. I think you need a call sign, too, Lucas. How about Sucker?"

"Like the vacuum. Hilarious."

"Oh come on. It's a badge of honor."

Lucas clicked Sif's helmet into place. "Ah, sweet silence. Just in time."

# Chapter 8

Litsa approached the Dak entrance from the south, having decided to avoid a direct route from the tunnel exit, just in case the Riy made it this far.

She knelt beside an outcropping of rocks and surveyed the terrain before her. The sun would set in a couple of hours, and she was sure the drones were on their way back to the hive. The jumpers, though, were different. Sometimes they would return, and sometimes not. She didn't see anything, but she would still have to be careful. After all she went through today, the last thing she wanted to do was stumble across a jumper within sight of home, especially since her bow was lying in the dirt by the middle haven. She felt naked without it.

The main entrance to the Dak was closed, just as it should be, sealed tight until nightfall. From the outside, the entrance was camouflaged, appearing as a natural part of the hillside beneath which she had lived a good portion of her life. Higher up, on the crest of the hill, was the watchers' station, where earlier that day the two warning bells sounded. It, too, was hidden, tucked within a stand of ponderosa pine.

About fifty yards beyond the Dak's entrance was the secondary portal, a small, natural vent that led inside to a point just a few yards from the cave entrance. It, too, was hidden, located at the bottom of a depression filled with white rabbitbrush and masked in the shadows beneath a large, overhanging boulder. The Dak had many vents that reached to the surface, but only this one was large enough to accommodate a person. It was used by those who were the last to enter at daybreak and the first to emerge at nightfall—the door handlers and the watch stander—and in emergencies.

She was dirty and thirsty, and the sunlight played havoc with her eyes. Even though the light was considerably dimmer than before, having to squint continuously had given her a splitting headache. She longed for the cool dampness of her home and the sense of safety that came from being surrounded by walls of rock.

She stood, and after taking one last, long glance to the east and seeing nothing but lengthening shadows, she made her way to the secondary portal and crawled inside.

*** 

"He's going to be fine, Jessa," Litsa said, trying to get a word in between the woman's sobs. "Nothing can get to him in the haven. I wouldn't have left him there if he was in danger." She cupped Jessa's face in her hands, forced her to look at her. "You know that, right?"

"I know, but it was so close. They were right *there*. What if he—"

"No 'what ifs,' Jessa," Litsa said sternly, shuddering at the thought of how close *she* had come to not making it back. "Your husband is alive. He's safe, and you're going to see him tonight. We're going out there to get him as soon as the sun sets, okay?" Litsa wouldn't let the woman drop her gaze. "Okay?"

Jessa nodded and clasped Litsa's hands in hers. "Thank you for saving him."

"Litsa." Grant's voice, from behind. "Joshua calls you."

Litsa smiled at Jessa and turned to follow Grant.

She was the warrior on this trip, and the gatherers were her responsibility. It was *her* duty to bring them to the fields, oversee their work, and get them home safely. Joshua wouldn't entertain any excuses. Litsa would pay for what happened under her watch. Her people lived by a set of rigid rules, harsh at times, but necessary. Joshua, and his father before him, led their band from the southern regions into the northern territories—what was once called South Dakota—and established a home. The discipline that came from living under Joshua's laws was the only thing that kept their small clan alive, when so many others drifted away and disappeared, either falling victim to the Riy or abducted by the Takers, the masked men who descended from the skies. She swore an allegiance to the laws and lived them to the letter. She would face those laws now.

Grant stopped at the edge of Joshua's hall.

Joshua sat patiently beside the fire, his face illuminated by the flickering light. He wasn't a large man, but he was stout for his stature. He had led the clan since his father's death and bore the colors of the clan chief tattooed on his arm. Rita, his woman, sat leisurely beside him, an eager look pinching her thin face. Jarrod, the captain of the watch, loomed nearby, standing barely inside the glow provided by the fire, his face partly obscured by shadow. His muscular arms hung at his sides, and she noticed his whip coiled at his belt.

Litsa saw judgment brewing in Joshua's eyes, and she knew how this would unfold.

"Litsa," Joshua's voice boomed. "Enter."

Litsa walked to the edge of the fire pit and stood. She bowed her head in respect. "My chief."

"Colin and Jeremy did not return. Explain."

"The Riy, my chief. They approached at daybreak. Jeremy injured himself, and Colin stayed to help him. I distracted the Riy to allow the gatherers time to return and to allow Colin and Jeremy to reach the middle haven."

"How many Riy?"

"By my count, between forty and fifty drones."

"If you encountered the Riy, why was the signal not given?"

"It was, my chief. I sent the flame skyward as soon as I saw them."

"No signal was seen," Jarrod said, stepping forward into the firelight.

Litsa met his gaze, but only for a second. "The signal was given. The gatherers can attest. The sky was too bright by then, and the watcher probably couldn't see it." The gatherers reported her sending the signal as soon as they arrived back home. They also reported why the gathering took so long, and why they were in the fields past the second warning bell. This was all part of the game. The trip did not go according to plan, and someone must be held accountable. Jarrod was only playing his part, even though he was well aware of what happened in the fields.

"But we are not questioning the gatherers," Joshua said, his voice low and accusatory. "We are questioning you."

"Yes, my chief."

Litsa stood motionless as Joshua let the silence stretch before speaking.

"You say Jeremy was injured, yes?"

"His ankle. He fell and hurt his ankle after the signal was given."

"And Colin stayed with him, instead of marshalling the gatherers, as is his task?"

"The gatherers saw the signal, and quickened their pace. Colin decided Jeremy needed assistance to reach the middle haven."

"Colin is not a protector, is he?"

"No, my chief."

"It is the warrior's role to be the protector. Am I correct?"

"Yes, my chief."

"Colin failed in his duties, then."

Litsa paused, resigning herself to the fact that it was going to turn out badly for her in the end regardless of what she said. She met Joshua's gaze. "Colin did what he thought was necessary to save Jeremy's life. I cannot fault him."

"*You* cannot fault him?" Rita snapped, her eyes flashing. "Have you forgotten your standing, young one?"

Litsa wanted to leap at Rita and tear her throat out with her bare hands. Although Rita was her elder and the taken woman of the chief, she had never earned Litsa's respect. There she sat, safely ensconced in the scrubbed skins and scented oils befitting her position, but Litsa saw nothing but a red-haired serpent of a woman, her dark eyes peering out from a pale face that rarely ventured from the safety of the caverns. Litsa bravely met her gaze. "I forget nothing," Litsa said softly, controlling the rage that threatened to spill from her lips. "And I mean no disrespect."

From the corner of her eye, Litsa saw Jarrod shift his hand to the whip at his belt. In this place, his loyalty was to Joshua and Rita alone, and not to Litsa, one of his own warriors. Joshua raised his hand, signaling Jarrod to stand fast. For now.

"You say Colin assisted Jeremy to the middle haven."

"Yes, my chief."

"And what has become of Jeremy and Colin?"

"Jeremy is dead, my chief. Taken by the Riy."

Litsa watched Rita lean forward, her face framed by the firelight. "Jeremy . . . is *dead*? And how did this happen?"

"He sacrificed himself to save me. Jeremy ran from the middle haven to draw a jumper away. He saved my life."

Rita glanced at Jarrod, a mocking smile crossing her lips. "One of your wolves, saved by a simple lamb? How unfortunate."

*A simple lamb.* In the end, Jeremy showed more courage than many of Jarrod's warriors. Litsa clenched her teeth together until it hurt.

"And Colin?" Joshua asked.

"Safe in the middle haven, my chief." Litsa paused, knowing what was coming, but decided to continue. "I promised Jessa that I would lead a party to retrieve him this night."

"*You* shall lead a party? I think not," Rita said. "You manage to lose one of those under your protection and then expect us to let you take an entire team with you?"

"How many jumpers?" Joshua asked. Litsa was at least thankful that Joshua was willing to ignore his wife's digs long enough to hear what they were up against.

"There were seven, my chief."

Joshua thought for a second, then nodded his head. "Another hive is close," he proclaimed. "We must seek it out, burn as much as we can."

Jarrod stepped forward. "I will call the warriors. We shall run tonight."

"No," Joshua said. "We will probe first, see how strong it is. Then, we will strike. You will take a team to retrieve Colin from the middle haven and send a second team forward to search out the hive's location."

"Yes, my chief."

Joshua shifted his gaze to Litsa, and she knew their meeting was almost at an end. "But only after judgment is passed," he said, "and punishment given."

Those were the words Litsa was waiting to hear. The sooner it was over, the sooner she could help find the hive, and hopefully destroy it.

Joshua stood. "Litsa, you allowed a life to be taken today."

"Yes, my chief."

"As the warrior assigned to watch over the gatherers, the fault lies with you, and no one else."

"Yes, my chief. I stand before you, ready to accept your judgment."

"How old was Jeremy?"

"Thirty-five years, my chief," Litsa replied.

"Then thirty-five lashes you will receive, before all who know you and trust you with their lives." Joshua turned to Jarrod. "By your hand, Jarrod. Assemble the clan."

Jarrod bowed. "Yes, my chief. It will be done."

Litsa had felt the lash before, but knew Jarrod was fair when wielding his whip. The leather would snap and bite, but it would be over quickly, and Jarrod would ensure it wouldn't cut too deeply.

She was, after all, his best warrior. And with a hive close by, he needed her.

# Chapter 9

*The Neutral Buoyancy Laboratory was never like this.* Sif had spent hours suspended in the world's largest swimming pool at the Sonny Carter Training Facility in Houston, readying herself for the demands of working outside the ship in the cold vacuum of space, but this was her first EVA.

Nothing could have prepared her for what she felt as soon as she left the hatch.

The view took her breath away. Beyond her thin polycarbonate visor, the grand vastness of space stretched away into infinity.

"Sif, this is Hunter."

"Yeah . . ."

"It's really something, isn't it?"

Hunter had made a spacewalk during their short mission to the International Space Station and experienced the same sense of awe she was feeling.

She gripped the edge of the hatch with one hand and reached out with her other. At her fingertips were the same stars she stared up at as a kid, dreaming of what life held in store for her. She remembered lying out at night on the houseboat, in the middle of a mountain lake far away from the city lights. The stars were so bright then, and there were so *many*, but it sure didn't compare to this. "It's beautiful."

"Soak it in, Navy. But remember we have work to do, and you're on the clock. Two hours and fifty-seven minutes 'til recess is over."

Sif glanced at the digital clock on her wrist, and it read 02:57:23, counting down the seconds until she would have to crawl back inside the hatch. "Copy. Heading aft first."

Her suit was large and cumbersome, a small spacecraft in and of itself, designed to protect her body from the brutal conditions of outer space—radiation, micrometeoroids, and extreme temperature shifts—while regulating atmospheric pressure, her body temperature, and oxygen flow, to keep her comfortable and alive. It also included a built-in gas-jet maneuvering system, allowing her to float free of the ship and move about, restricted only by the reach of her tether.

She clipped her suit tether to the runner and tugged to ensure it was connected properly. The runner bar ran *Resolute*'s length, and was one of many that spanned the outside of the ship. Using the tether, she could explore most of the critical areas where repairs might be required.

Sif pulled herself outside the hatch, one hand on the runner bar, and allowed her legs to float behind her. Even though she was moving through space at thousands of miles per hour, there was absolutely no sense of speed. She, along with the mass of *Resolute*, was suspended, motionless, in the middle of a star-dotted void, with no beginning and no end.

The partial module simulators they trained with in Houston—replicas of pieces and parts of the ship—seemed so huge, and the first time she saw *Resolute* complete in orbit Sif was struck by its massive size. But now, *Resolute* seemed insignificant against this infinite backdrop. As did she.

The ship itself consisted of four main trusses—one upper, one lower, and two on the sides—which ran from the forward command section all the way to the rear engine section. Nestled within the skeletal framework were three different modules—"mods"—large, cylindrical structures, each designed for a specific purpose. Mod 1, directly behind the conical command section, was the crew area and the heaviest, most shielded part of the ship. It also included the botanical and rations sections. Mod 2 housed the science and experimentation section and was followed by the deployment section in Mod 3, which included the docking stations for the crew transport vehicle and the cargo landers and, at the rear, the flyer deployment bay and emergency escape capsule. Farther back was the propulsion section, where four engines—each based on the old F-1 engines that powered the Apollo program's Saturn V booster—drew their cryogenic liquid oxygen and liquid hydrogen fuel mixture from eight hexagonal fuel tanks, attached in tandem pairs to each of the four rear truss sections. For the most part, *Resolute*'s external design was simple, sturdy, and based on reliable, proven technology. It was her innards—the computers and programming designed to get the astronauts to Mars and back—that represented the cutting edge. And right now, a good portion of that technology wasn't functioning.

"Starting aft now."

"Copy," Hunter replied.

Hand over hand, Sif headed toward the rear of the ship. She passed by numerous boxy thruster clusters, with each of the port-pointing nozzles blackened and charred from extended firings.

As she continued aft, she saw no visible damage to the exterior of the ship. She would do a similar inspection along all four of the structural trusses before calling it good.

"No damage along the upper truss."

"Copy. How are you feeling out there?"

"Never better. Why didn't you tell me this was so much fun?"

"You won't be saying that in an hour," Hunter said. "It's more tiring than being in the pool."

At the aft section, she released her hold on the runner rail and allowed herself to float away from the ship, her tether automatically spooling out as she went. By pressing the fingertips of her gloves into small indents in the palms, Sif activated the gas jets, which were controlled by finger position and pressure on the palm contacts. She maneuvered out beyond the four large exhaust nozzles and inspected them for damage. It was then that she noticed something out of order.

Not with the engines. With her.

She was having trouble breathing. Lucas told her the suit's bio-readout wasn't up and running yet, so there was no way for them to warn her if they saw something out of specs with her suit.

"I think I have a problem here." She didn't like the nervousness she heard in her own voice.

Hunter answered immediately. "What's wrong?"

She reached down and felt for the cable spool unit, attached to the front of her suit at waist level. There was an emergency button, which, when pressed, automatically reeled in the tether. She couldn't find it.

"Hunter, I think there—might be a—problem—"

"Sif? What's the matter?" Lucas this time.

"Breathing—I can't breathe."

"Check your oxygen levels."

"My—my oxygen—" Sif's vision blurred, and her extremities tingled. She should've noticed her hypoxic symptoms right away, but she'd let the excitement of the EVA cloud her thinking.

"Left sleeve, Sif, above the wrist," Lucas said. "Check the dial above your wrist and tell me what it says."

Sif tried to answer, but couldn't. Her fingers fumbled around the tether control, but she couldn't recall where the emergency button was located. Was it on the side? The bottom?

She knew she was running out of time. She grasped the tether cable, and tried to pull herself back toward the ship. The hatch seemed so far away now, so very far. Her face was tingling, and it hurt to breathe.

She released her grip on the cable as she lost consciousness and floated away from the ship, prevented from disappearing into the void only by the strength of a thin steel cable.

# Chapter 10

The murmur of conversation ceased as Litsa entered the Dak's great hall.

She was once punished like this when she was younger, accused of stealing food. It was only ten lashes, but she still had the crisscross scars on her back as a reminder. The main hall was the largest chamber in the middle Dak, far enough beneath the surface that the temperature was always cool, and water continuously seeped from the walls, little silver rivulets reflecting the firelight from the torches mounted to the rock.

This was the place of gatherings, where the clan discussed important matters, the ruling council haggled over crop yields and field preparation, and Joshua held court.

It was also where punishment was meted out. In front of all.

Jarrod was waiting at the bottom of the chamber's bowl. Before him was the wooden whipping stand, a simple post with handholds, where the guilty were tied, hands stretched above their heads, and received their due punishment.

She had once watched a gatherer, accused of killing another man with a stone, be tied to the post, facing forward. He was whipped over and over until his face disappeared, and the skin of his belly could no longer hold in what was inside. The spectacle sickened her, but he deserved it. Murder was the one mistake her clan would never forgive.

Litsa stepped into the bowl and walked to the whipping post. She turned and faced Joshua, who sat halfway up the side of the bowl on the council ledge. The entire clan was gathered, young and old. A little over 120 of her fellow clansmen stared at her, their faces lit by the flames. She wondered what they knew of Jeremy's death and how she would be treated.

Joshua stood, his voice booming through the great hall. "Litsa, you stand accused of failing in your duties, and as a result of your negligence, one of our own is lost to the Riy. Jeremy is dead."

Litsa heard the murmurs among the crowd and decided she would not cry out, no matter how terrible the pain. She wouldn't give any of those who doubted her the satisfaction of seeing her suffer.

Joshua continued. "As a warrior, you hold in your hands the lives of all under your watch. Every one of us assembled in this hall," he said, waving his arm from one side of the chamber to the other, "relies on you to keep us safe when outside our home."

*Come on,* Litsa mused, *quit grandstanding and get on with it.*

"You are one of our best warriors, Litsa, yet you are not above the creed of our clan. Even I and any of the ruling council must submit ourselves to the lash if our actions result in the death of one of our own."

Litsa doubted she would ever see *that.*

"Thirty-five lashes will be given. Jarrod, you will proceed." Joshua took his seat.

Jarrod approached the whipping stand. Litsa removed her upper garment and dropped it to the cold stone. She stepped onto the pedestal and grabbed the handholds. Jarrod reached for the tie straps, but Litsa shook her head. "You won't need those. I won't falter."

He paused, then leaned close and whispered, "I'll make it quick." He held up a piece of wood, something for her to bite into. "Take this."

Litsa shook her head, refusing the offer, then leaned her body against the rough wood of the stand. She turned her head and rested her cheek against the post. In the crowd, she could see Jessa's face. Their eyes met for a second, then Jessa looked away and lowered her head.

Litsa closed her eyes.

Everyone in the great hall was silent. Only the crackle of the torches and the echoing drip of water from the chamber's roof could be heard. *Do not cry out.* Thirty-five stings from the whip would be difficult to bear.

*Don't give them the satisfaction.*

Litsa heard Jarrod pivot, having walked the proper distance from the stand, and flick the whip to its full length with a snap.

She waited for the whoosh of the leather through the air, waited for the first cutting bite. When it came, she wished she had taken the piece of wood to bite into, after all.

Litsa made it to the twenty-eighth crack of the whip until she could hold it in no longer and her screams began to echo throughout the chamber.

\*\*\*

She lay on her stomach in the nursemaid's chamber as Lauren worked to clean her wounds.

Jarrod *had* made it quick and was judicious about where he placed his lashes. Most cut into her old scars, where the tissue was thick. She would have new scars as well.

Lauren poured cool water across her back, and Litsa watch the watery blood spill onto the floor, sighing as it washed away some of the sting.

"None of them are deep, Litsa," Lauren said. "They should heal quickly enough."

"I'll need them bandaged," Litsa said. "Colin needs to be retrieved, and there's a hive to search for."

"Jarrod spared you, somewhat," Lauren said, "but thirty-five lashes deserve a day of rest to heal, at least. Colin is back, by the way."

"He is?" She felt a pang of anger for not being part of the team to go get him. "When did they send a team?"

"*They* didn't. He came back on his own, right after sundown."

Litsa was surprised Colin made it back to the Dak on his own. Maybe watching Jeremy's sacrifice changed his outlook. "I'm glad he's back. And safe. But I don't have time to rest with a hive so close. None of us do."

"You shouldn't go out before this has a chance to heal."

"Bandage them." It was Jarrod's voice, from the doorway. "We need her. Tonight."

Lauren bowed her head in deference to the captain of the watch, and reached for the numbing salve as Litsa raised herself off the table, resting on her elbows.

Litsa turned her head around to face him, and saw no emotion on Jarrod's face as he glanced at the wounds stitched across her upper back.

"I assumed you would go with us," Jarrod said.

"You assumed correctly," Litsa said, smiling.

"Your wounds are not too bad to keep you from your duties, then."

Litsa took that as more of a statement than a question. "They are not," she replied. *Because you made sure of it,* she added silently. She would thank him when the time was right.

"The team is formed. Meet us at the top." Jarrod strode off into the shadows.

Lauren slapped a handful of the numbing salve between Litsa's shoulder blades, making her wince. "He's such a pleasant fellow, that one."

"He's doing his job, that's all," Litsa said. "And yes, he did spare me the worst, but it still *hurts*. Be gentle with that, will you?"

Lauren's skilled hands rubbed the salve into the wounds, and the pain faded immediately. "This will last for a few hours, then you'll need to come see me again. And don't get it all filthy. If I have to scrub any dirt out, I *won't* be gentle."

"Now who's not being pleasant?"

"I heard what happened, Litsa. I know what you did. You saved the gatherers—they said so when they returned—and you saved Colin and Jeremy, too. You didn't deserve the whip. Now lie flat."

Litsa was glad the truth had made its way through the clan. At least she wouldn't be treated as an outcast because of Jeremy's death. "Jeremy died because of me. It was my fault."

"That's not what Colin said." Lauren placed a large square of soft fabric across Litsa's back, patting it down, and wrapped wide strips of fabric around her body to hold it in place. "He said Jeremy left the safety of the middle haven to draw the Riy away from you."

Litsa *was* relieved the whole truth was out, but she couldn't help but think of Jeremy's knowing smile as the jumper burst apart at his feet.

"And we're all glad he did," Lauren continued. "Everyone knows what kind of warrior you are, and where we'd all be without you. You would lay your life down for any of us, just as Jeremy did for you." Lauren leaned close and whispered, "If we only had Joshua and Rita to rely on, we'd all be doomed."

"Take care who you share your sentiments with, Lauren," Litsa whispered back. "Some ears wouldn't take kindly to what you say."

Lauren patted Litsa's bandages. "All done."

Litsa sat up and swung her legs over the side. "If I could've done anything differently, something to save him, I would."

"You did what you knew was right. Jeremy did what *he* knew was right. What happened, happened. Nothing more."

"I'm going to miss him, Lauren."

Lauren grabbed a rag and wiped the salve from her hands. "As will I."

# Chapter 11

Sif woke in the stasis chamber. For a second, she wondered if it was a dream. Everything was fine, and she was waking just as planned, with Mars—and a place in history—only a few days away.

But then she remembered . . . Her oxygen system had malfunctioned. She recalled trying to pull herself back to the ship, and how far away the hatch was, and then everything faded away.

Sif pushed a button on the inside of her capsule and released her restraining straps. The lid slid open with a hiss. She pushed herself up and out, floating free in the crew module. Stretching her arms above her head loosened her muscles, and she wondered how long she'd been in the capsule.

From the speakers, a welcome—albeit synthesized—voice. "Hello, Commander Wagner."

"Liv?"

"Yes, Wagner."

"Liv, you don't know how happy I am to hear your voice."

"Liv can hear your voice, too, Wagner."

Referring to herself in the third person was something new for the AI. "Liv, are you fully functional?"

"Yes. Liv is furry functional."

*Uh oh.* "Furry functional, Liv?"

"No, Wagner. Liv is fully functional."

*This is going to be interesting.* "Liv, where are Webb and Hoover?"

"Webb and Hoover are located in the command module, Commander. They requested Liv notify them when you woke. Liv has complied."

"Thank you, Liv." Sif pulled her crew uniform from the wall, slid it on, and pushed off the bulkhead, sending herself down the tunnel toward the command module. "Liv, what is ship's status?" Microphones placed throughout the ship allowed them to communicate with Liv wherever they were.

"Life support is fully functional. Navigation system is fully functional. Computer systems are fully functional. Main engine fuel is below mission minimums at 40 percent. Main engines one through four are fully functional. Thruster fuel is low at 20 percent. Port thruster unit seventeen is inoperative. Port thruster unit twenty-two is inoperative. Port thruster unit twenty-three is partially mission capable. Starboard thruster unit thirteen is—"

"Liv complete," Sif said, a simple command that told Liv she didn't need to continue answering the previous question. "Is there any structural damage to the ship?"

"Diagnostics show there is no structural damage to the ship."

"What is our position, Liv?"

"We are seventeen hours from entering Earth orbit."

Her fail-safe theory was correct after all, although hearing it confirmed made her heart sink. The first manned mission to Mars was, officially, a failure. "Communications system status, Liv?"

"Long-range communication transmitter is fully functional. Data telemetry transmitter is fully functional. Diagnostics ongoing to ascertain receiver status."

"What's wrong with the receivers?"

No answer. Sif remembered to call Liv by name to get her to respond. "Liv, what is wrong with the receivers?"

"Status messages transmitted. No response. Diagnostics ongoing to ascertain receiver—"

"Liv complete."

As Sif entered the command module, she saw Hunter and Lucas staring at the navigation console. "Okay, guys, who wants to explain to me how I'm still alive?"

"Captain America here suited up immediately after you said you had a problem, Caitlyn," Lucas said. "It was close, too close."

Hunter huffed. "I only did what either of you would've done if it was me out there. *And*, I hate to say I told you so, but it's things like this that make solo EVAs such a bad idea."

"Point taken," Sif said. "And thank you. I should've caught my hypoxia symptoms right away, but I was having too much fun taking in the view."

"By the time you were back inside, you looked like that girl from *Willy Wonka*," Lucas said. "Blue as a blueberry."

"What caused it? My suit alarm didn't go off."

"Not only was that particular suit not able to transmit data, the alarm was inop, too," Hunter said. "Turns out your oxygen deficit was caused by a bent regulator."

"How the heck did that happen?"

"Whatever shook the ship loosened the tie-downs enough to cause the suit to bang against the wall," Hunter said. "Hard enough to rattle the bio-transmitter and the internal alarm and foul the regulator."

"I should've caught it during the inspection," Lucas said. "The straps were loose when I took it off the wall, but I didn't think twice about it."

Sif caught his eye. "I wouldn't have caught it, either. No sweat, Lucas."

"Liv is up and running, at least," Hunter said.

"I noticed. I don't think her voice interface is a hundred percent, though."

"We kludged a couple of different circuit boards together to get her talking again. She seems to be working just fine," Hunter said, "but you're right, her voice interface is probably as good as it's going to get."

Lucas laughed. "She called me Mr. Potato when we first brought her voice back on line."

Sif couldn't let the opportunity pass. "It looks like you have a call sign now, *Tater*."

"Please don't call me that."

"Too late," Hunter said. "It's official."

"I won't answer to it."

Sif shoved Lucas's shoulder, causing both of them to grab the edge of their seats to keep from tumbling away. "Oh come on, at least she didn't call you Sucker, or something awful like that."

"Can we please stop the name-calling and get back to work?"

Hunter nudged Sif's arm. "You need to see something." He turned to a video monitor and brought up one of the external cameras.

"You got the cameras to work, too? You guys were busy."

"No, they're still out, but we were able to access the recordings. This," Hunter said, pointing at the time stamp, "was ten hours after we all entered stasis."

Only one month into their seven-month journey to Mars, and right after they'd gone to sleep. Sif pushed herself closer to the screen. It was a forward view, looking out from directly above the command module. "What am I looking for?"

"About ten degrees left of center. Watch closely," Hunter said as he started the playback.

Sif watched intently, seeing nothing until the forward port thrusters fired, small puffs of gas from the side of the command module, just a few at first, but quickly building into a series of rapid—then continuous—firings as the nose of the ship slewed to port. Hunter stopped the tape.

"Did you see it?" Lucas asked.

"See what?"

"We missed it, too, the first time." Hunter restarted the playback from the previous starting point, and placed his finger on the screen. "Watch the stars, right here."

Sif watched closely, staring at the stars. They didn't look as awe-inspiring on the screen as from outside the—

And then they were gone. The stars were gone. "What the hell?" And just as quickly, they were back. "Wait, what was that?"

"Keep watching," Lucas said. "Fifteen seconds later. Same spot."

Sif counted down the seconds, and there it was. This time, when the stars disappeared, Hunter paused the tape. "Look, here to here." He ran his finger from the top of the screen to the bottom. It was as if someone had placed a strip of black tape on the screen, hiding the stars.

"Any ideas what we're looking at?" Sif asked.

Lucas spoke first. "I'm not entirely sure, yet, but watch what happens next. It'll disappear, then reappear about fifteen seconds later, this time much wider. That's when the thrusters start firing."

"Whatever it was, we were pulled toward it," Hunter added, starting the playback. "You were right, Sif. Liv was maneuvering to keep us on course."

Again, Sif counted to fifteen, and when the stars blacked out again, the line was much larger. The thrusters started firing immediately. "It's much bigger," she said. *Or closer?*

This time, Hunter let the tape continue.

As *Resolute* continued to slew to port, the video shook as more and more of the portside thrusters fired. The nose slid to starboard slightly, but the black line filled more of the screen. "It's getting closer," Sif said, "and the thrusters can't keep her on course."

Lines of static crossed the screen, and the picture jerked suddenly.

"That's when Liv fired the mains," Lucas said.

The video jumped wildly as more and more of the stars disappeared. All the random debris Sif saw from her stasis capsule was being torn from the tie-downs right about now. She was amazed *Resolute* had held together. "Good Lord."

The screen went black.

Sif turned to Lucas. "Is that all we have?"

He pointed at the screen. "It's still recording, Sif."

"There's nothing there."

Hunter started counting down as he watched the time stamp. "Five, four, three, and . . . power surge, and . . . now."

The stars were back. Perfectly still.

But they were different.

Sif pointed at the upper left of the screen. "That's Orion. We're turned around."

"What?" Hunter asked.

"When the tape started, we were pointed toward Gemini," Sif said. "Now we're pointing at Orion." She spent those nights on the houseboat holding an iPad above her head and searching for the different constellations. She knew them by heart.

The screen went black again. "That's all we have. The cameras failed right there," Lucas said.

"The nav backup was still operational at this point, correct?"

"Yes," Hunter said. "For another twenty-two seconds."

"Long enough to take a star shot and execute the fail-safe mode." Sif *was* right. But she didn't have any explanation for the strange recurring void on the screen. She turned to Lucas. "You said you weren't sure what happened *yet*. Got any ideas?"

Lucas pushed himself back in his seat. "I've watched that tape a number of times, and . . . it's all theoretical, and nowhere near my field of expertise, so I may be completely wrong."

"I saw a black *pole* appear and disappear out there, we were pulled toward it, and it almost shook us apart. That's not very theoretical to me." Sif said. "What do you think it was?"

"What we saw doesn't fit the theory, but it's the only thing that makes sense."

Sif waited for Lucas to continue. He didn't. "You're going to have to explain it, Tater, I'm not a mind reader." Scientists frustrated the living hell out of her sometimes.

"The nav system was able to see where we were, Sif, long enough to run the fail-safe program like you said, but if I'm right, we've got bigger problems than not making it to Mars."

Sif glanced at Hunter.

"Don't look at me. I haven't heard this yet, either."

"Lucas?"

"We know *where* we are, Sif. In another sixteen hours, we'll be entering Earth orbit. We'll be home. But what we don't know is *when* we are."

# Chapter 12

The night air was cool against Litsa's skin as she moved silently across the prairie. This was when she felt the most free, away from the confines of the Dak and out in the open. There were things out here, though, things that could kill. Inhuman, and monstrous.

And she was headed right for them. Hopefully.

Litsa and the three others selected for the scouting party were making their way eastward, following the signs in the grass and dirt left by the drones during the day. The sky was clear, the starlight bright, and she could see for miles. Jarrod was up ahead, leading the way.

In the daylight, out in the open, she felt overexposed, as if the world was simply too big, the blue dome of the sky yawning above waiting to lift her from the surface and pull her apart. But in the dark, she felt the same familiar closeness provided by the rock walls of the Dak. Everything was nearer, safer, and the world wasn't so huge.

In the shadows, she was at ease. At *home*.

Litsa was in her element. She was on the hunt. A predator seeking prey, moving silently and surely through the tall grass, following the tracks of the monsters that killed her friend.

She gripped her bow tighter as the thought of burning a Riy hive to ash quickened her pulse. Colin had snatched her bow from the dirt on his way back to the Dak, and she was glad to have her old companion again. The wood was worn, rubbed smooth from use, and fit her hand perfectly.

Up ahead, Jarrod stopped and raised his fist into the air. A signal to stop.

As one, they all crouched, listened.

Litsa closed her eyes. She heard the breeze weaving its way through the grass and the sound of crickets chirping their night songs. Off to her right, an animal scurried away, small, maybe a mouse.

If they were close to a hive, they would hear it, but even before they were in earshot, they would smell it, a dirty, stagnant stench like brackish water and decaying vegetation. Litsa sniffed the air, caught no such scent.

Until the breeze shifted.

Faint, but it was there, carried on the wind. Jarrod must've caught it, too.

She watched as Jarrod opened his fist and pointed with a chopping motion, off to the left. She moved toward him, as did the others, and they knelt in the grass beside him.

"It's close," he whispered, "Maybe one hundred, one-fifty yards. Over that rise."

Mirda, a tall girl with reddish hair, stood and looked around, getting her bearings. She had been a warrior for almost as long as Litsa, and she was just as skilled with the bow. "I know this place. Beyond the rise is a draw, higher terrain to the north, open to the south and east."

Hives tended to settle in low spots during the night, where the land provided some measure of protection. It was a perfect spot.

"Litsa, we'll move north, approach from the high ground." Jarrod gestured toward Erik, one of the older warriors who had encountered more than his share of Riy. As such, the man was patient and not prone to error. "You and Mirda will swing south, approach from the flatlands. Get close enough to judge its size, then we'll meet back here."

"Understood," Erik replied. He and Mirda moved off to the right, heading south.

Even though the hive would be much less active, there was still a great deal of danger getting this close. A few drones might still be out there, and, if triggered, they would have to deal with the jumpers.

Litsa felt Jarrod touch her arm. "Let's go."

They moved slowly through the grass as they approached the northern side of the rise, being careful with each step. The stench grew worse as they drew near the edge of the draw.

Litsa heard it first and tapped Jarrod's shoulder to get his attention. They both stopped, listened.

It was a sickening sound, as if a thousand wet snakes were knotted in their den, squirming against each other. Wet leather, rubbing, rubbing. The sound rose and fell, as if it were breathing. Up close, a hive was a horrid thing to behold, a giant, undulating mass, full of all the life it absorbed—human and animal. Composed of nothing but death, it was alive, a simple organism of many parts and pieces, unthinking yet aware.

As they emerged from the grass and found themselves at the edge of a sharp drop-off, they saw it. It was big, much bigger than Litsa expected. It filled the majority of the draw, and, because of its size, was uncomfortably close. The stench was nearly overpowering, and Litsa found it hard to breathe without coughing.

Not more than fifteen feet away, the surface of the Riy hive moved in undulating waves, stretching, contracting. The currents and eddies moving within moaned sickeningly as if the bones of all the dead it contained were trying to speak.

This one was too large to kill. But they could burn a good portion of it—if they were lucky—and force it to move away. She glanced at Jarrod. He was thinking the same thing. They had both seen enough.

If it moved during the day, then all bets were off, but if they found it here the next night, they would burn it.

They both jumped when they heard a loud pop from the south.

The sound of a drone releasing its spores. Followed by a woman's scream.

*Mirda.*

The hive reacted, its surface vibrating violently.

Jarrod grabbed Litsa by the arm and ran, retracing their steps though the grass as jumpers thumped to the ground around them.

# Chapter 13

"What do you mean, 'We don't know *when* we are'?" Hunter asked.

Lucas shrugged. "Like I said, this is completely outside my field of expertise, but I read something once that might explain what we just saw. At least I think it might. Caitlyn, you described what we saw as a *pole*, correct?"

"That's what I saw," Sif replied. "A long black pole that appeared and disappeared. At regular intervals."

"Right. Every fifteen seconds, it appears, stays there for ten seconds, then disappears again. Let's say this pole is massive, infinitely long, and it's spinning at near the speed of light."

Sif glanced at Hunter, who once again had that *Don't ask me* look on his face.

Lucas caught his look, too. "I know, it sounds crazy, but just hang with me here for a minute. An object like this, generating its own powerful gravitational field because of its mass, spinning at that speed, could theoretically cause a whirlpool effect in space-time."

"You're saying that's why we were pulled off course," Sif said, "because of the thing's gravity."

"Exactly. A fellow named Frank Tipler wrote about something like this back in 1974. He called it a Tipler cylinder, and he saw it as a way to travel in time."

Sif searched Lucas's face for any sign that he was joking, and found none.

"A time machine?" Hunter asked.

Lucas nodded. "As an object nears the cylinder, it enters the space-time whirlpool the cylinder created. According to Tipler's theory, an object orbiting one of his cylinders could travel backward in time. A time machine."

"And you think this is what we saw?"

"I have no idea what we saw, Caitlyn, but like I said, this was the first thing I thought of. Constructing a Tipler cylinder is impossible. Well . . . mathematically it *is* possible, but practically? Not so much."

"Constructed? You think this is man-made? Or *alien*-made?"

Lucas shrugged. "I don't know. But I do know what I saw—what we *all* saw—and I know the effect it had on the ship. Why it appeared and disappeared, at regular intervals, like you observed, Caitlyn, is something I can't explain. Stephen Hawking basically said Tipler was full of crap, that it'd be impossible to produce such a thing without negative energy, which is all theoretical, too."

"But you're right," Hunter said. "We all saw it. Whatever it was, it was real, not theoretical."

"So, Lucas, *when* are we?" Sif asked. "If this thing was some sort of Tipler cylinder, and we were caught in its whirlpool, you're saying we went back in time?"

"I don't know. But, consider this. Liv, report receiver diagnostic results, please."

"Diagnostic tests on all receivers complete with negative results."

"The receivers are working perfectly," Lucas said. "There's nothing wrong with them. Liv ran three sets of diagnostics, and I've physically inspected the units myself."

"So if they're working, why isn't anyone answering?" Sif asked, then it dawned on her.

Lucas nodded when he saw the realization cross Sif's face. "Liv has been sending automated radio calls and telemetry since the moment we got the comm systems up and running, transmitting continuously. No one is answering because—if I'm right—there might not be anyone there *to* answer."

Sif pushed herself from her chair and floated over to the control center's front windows. In front of them was Earth—a beautiful blue-and-white spinning ball in the middle of space. The thought that everything she knew—the people, places, all the history—could all be gone was a tough pill to swallow. "I don't buy it. How could everyone just not be there?"

Lucas joined her at the front viewport. "They're not there *yet*. At least the world we all left a month ago. If I'm right."

Sif shook her head, trying to wrap her mind around Lucas's theory. "This Tipler guy. Did he happen to say anything about how far back in time we could've gone?"

"Theoretically, one could only travel back in time to the point where the Tipler cylinder was constructed."

"And we have no idea when that was."

"None. Like I said, what we saw *resembled* a Tipler cylinder, and we have no clue whether or not what we experienced was a naturally occurring phenomenon, or man-made. Or alien-made. Or something. We were only trapped in the cylinder's effects as long as it was visible, though. Ten seconds, as we observed on the tape. As soon as it disappeared again, and we suffered that nasty power surge, we were back in normal space. Pointing at Orion instead of Gemini, like you observed, and *Resolute* entered the fail-safe mode, firing the mains to take us back to Earth."

"So we left as the first humans to travel to Mars, and instead, we're the first people to travel back in time."

Hunter joined them at the window. For a moment, all three stared at their home, lost in their thoughts.

"Liv, how long until orbital insertion?" Hunter asked.

"Fifteen hours, twenty-three minutes."

"In fifteen hours, we'll see if your theory is correct," Hunter said. "You can write a note to Tipler telling him he was right and bury it somewhere. Maybe he'll find it one day."

"I hope I'm wrong."

"So do I," Sif said.

# Chapter 14

Litsa dived under a clump of brush when it became clear she and Jarrod weren't going to get out of this alive if they kept running.

Or moving.

After Mirda's scream, the jumpers erupted from the hive, landing all around them, including one that lay just on the other side of the brush. She watched Jarrod dive into a tangle of brush just as she did, as two jumpers landed on either side of him. They were both motionless for—how long? Four, five hours? She completely lost sense of time.

They were trapped in an excruciating waiting game, staying absolutely still and waiting for the jumpers to move away, as they usually did. If one of the things sensed any motion close by, she and Jarrod would be transformed into Riy, and eventually absorbed into the pulsating mass slumbering in the draw.

Peering through the branches, Litsa watched the jumper extend its spiky tentacles—a few times in the last hour—feeling the air for motion, and, sensing none, retract them back into its lumpy body. But it did not move away.

It dawned on Litsa that she hadn't heard *any* of the jumpers move.

The hives were sluggish at night. Whatever energy animated these things in the sunlight drained away in the darkness. The jumper nearest her was still moving, but not—she realized—as actively as a few hours ago. It must be weakened, too. But, if it was still moving, it might, even in its weakened state, sense her movement.

She could wait, and hope it would stop moving, but the sky to the east had taken on a purplish hue, heralding the coming sunrise. As soon as the sky brightened, the hive would send out new drones, cleaving them from itself, one after another, after another. The jumpers surrounding her and Jarrod would become more active, too, and more likely to sense their presence.

She stared at the one nearest her through the tangle of branches and leaves, and watched for any motion. The one she saw up close earlier that day had moved continuously, full of energy. This one looked almost dead. As if on cue to prove her wrong, its surface rippled slightly and then grew still. She waited, counting the seconds. A full minute passed before she saw another tiny motion.

The sky to the east grew brighter. It was now or never.

Slowly, she slid her arms beneath her and pushed herself a few inches off the ground. Her muscles screamed in protest, but she ignored the pain.

She paused. No reaction from the jumper.

She pulled her knees up, rested her weight on them, and crouched on all fours. She planned her steps, where she would run. Her bow was a few feet away—she wasn't about to leave it behind again.

"Litsa."

It was Jarrod, a loud whisper. He too was on all fours.

Litsa motioned in the direction of the Dak. He shook his head, mouthed *No*. Instead he held up two fingers, then pointed south, toward the open area where he had ordered Erik and Mirda to go.

*He has to make sure*, Litsa realized. He wouldn't leave without seeing for himself that Erik and Mirda were gone.

The first warning bell was sounded, faint, but she could hear it. The watchers were on duty, waiting for their return.

Waiting for all *four* of them.

Jarrod was right. If one of them was still alive—holed up under a bush like *they* were—then leaving them out here would be tantamount to murder.

She motioned again, this time to the south. Jarrod was watching. She held up two fingers—her symbol for Mirda and Erik—then made a fist and placed it over her heart. She wasn't going to leave them behind, either.

Jarrod glanced at the small jumper to his right, then slowly rose. The jumper didn't react. Litsa looked at the one nearest her, and it hadn't moved, either.

Jarrod held up three fingers and whispered, "On three."

Litsa nodded.

He held up one finger. "One."

Two fingers.

Then three. Jarrod took off running.

Litsa snatched her bow from the dirt, waiting for the telltale pop of the jumper exploding from behind. It never came.

Her legs, stiff from hours of lying in the same position on the hard ground, protested as she sprinted south, toward where Mirda and Erik were last, all the while pivoting her head and scanning the terrain in front of her for any jumpers. There was one to the right, and she gave it a wide berth, still instinctively turning her head and closing her eyes as she passed.

She caught up with Jarrod as he stood on a point of high ground overlooking the draw.

"They're gone," Jarrod said, his voice heavy. He pointed to a blackened spot of earth where the drone expelled its cloud of spores. And there was no sign of either Mirda or Erik. They were both part of the hive by now.

The clang of the second warning bell wafted through the early morning air as Litsa and Jarrod turned and began their trek back to the safety of the Dak.

Tonight, they would return to this place. They, and many others.

To flame the hive that took two more of their own.

\*\*\*

Litsa could see the watchers at the top of the hill. For the second morning in a row, she was returning home after the second bell. It was also the second morning in a row she returned after losing someone. First Jeremy, and now Mirda and Erik. The wounds on her back were starting to speak to her, and she would need to make a visit to Lauren to have her dressings changed. Hopefully she—and Jarrod—would be spared the whip this time. Losing a gatherer under watch was one thing, but losing warriors was expected, unless it was due to error or incompetence. Jarrod, captain of the watch, led this mission, so she deemed it unlikely they would be punished for it.

"The fault is mine, Litsa," Jarrod said. "I will approach Joshua and bear responsibility for Erik and Mirda."

Litsa caught a hint of sorrow in Jarrod's voice when he mentioned Mirda's name.

"They triggered a drone," Litsa said. "The fault was their own, and it almost got us killed. There's nothing you could've done to prevent it." Litsa saw the two watchers scramble down the hill, their duty over. The sky was blue overhead and orange to the east. The sun would soon break the horizon.

"Mirda and Erik?" one of them asked.

"A drone" was all Jarrod could say, as he dropped his gaze to the dirt.

"I'm sorry, my friend," the watcher replied. "Mirda was a fine warrior."

"She will be missed," Jarrod said, his voice betraying his deeper feelings.

Warriors were not to consort with one another, especially when one of them was the captain of the watch. Litsa never saw the two of them together, but the tone of his voice said she had missed something.

"At sundown, we travel again," Litsa said as they walked toward the secondary portal. "The hive is three miles east, a big one, cowering in a draw. We'll need all the warriors we can muster to tackle it."

"In time, Litsa," Jarrod said quietly, his voice full of an emotion Litsa had never heard him speak before: sorrow. "First, we must inform Joshua, tell him of the hive, and of our loss," Jarrod continued. "The decision to attack will be his."

"We must attack," Litsa said, instantly regretting the cutting edge of her voice. Jarrod was obviously mourning Mirda's death, and she gathered her composure. "If we wait, and the hive moves, we'll lose our chance."

"I *understand*," Jarrod said sharply. "Joshua will decide, and we will abide by his decision."

"Then we must convince him to attack."

"Wait," one of the watchers said, pointing to the east. "Look."

Litsa saw a person stumbling toward them. "Mirda?"

"My God, it *is* her," Jarrod said.

He began to run toward her, but Litsa held him back. "No, Jarrod. Wait."

He wheeled at her, his eyes flashing. "She may be hurt."

Litsa tightened her grip. "Or worse," she said. Jarrod looked toward Mirda again, and Litsa felt his body relax.

Mirda was stumbling badly, her arms were hanging loosely at her sides, and her head was canted oddly, toward the ground.

"I need fire, now," Litsa said, shrugging her bow off her shoulder and grasping three arrows from the quiver on her back.

One of the watchers ran up the hill toward the watch station. There was always a torch ready. Just in case.

"Mirda?" Jarrod called, his voice cracking. "Mirda!"

She didn't answer. There was something terribly wrong with her. Erik probably took the brunt of the drone's mist, and Mirda was exposed just enough to lead to this.

Mirda was transforming. Not yet fully succumbed, but without any hope. Even a little of the mist was enough to doom a person to a horrible fate. What was left of the warrior Mirda was trying to come home. And they couldn't let that happen.

As Mirda neared, the ravages to her body became clear. Half of her head was covered with the black, sticky tar, as was most of her arms and torso. She looked up, and Litsa could see her eyes, full of pain. And fear.

"Oh, Mirda. No," Jarrod said.

The watcher returned, torch in hand.

Litsa touched the tips of her arrows to the torch, lighting them, and felt Jarrod's hand on her forearm.

"No," Jarrod said.

Litsa wasn't going to let Jarrod stop her from doing what must be done, then realized she wouldn't have to.

He reached for the bow.

Litsa saw in his eyes all that needed to be said. She handed her bow to him. He nocked an arrow and turned toward Mirda.

She was close now and trying to speak. Her words were thick, bubbling through the black slime filling her throat.

Litsa watched a single tear slide down Jarrod's cheek as he drew the bow and let the first arrow fly. Then the second. And the third.

He handed the bow back to Litsa and walked toward the secondary portal. "Let it burn," he said.

# Chapter 15

"My God, look at it," Sif said. From the viewport on the lower deck of the command section, she looked down at Earth. "There are no lights."

*Resolute* was orbiting over the Western Hemisphere, which at the moment was cloaked in darkness. At the poles, the aurora borealis was visible, which provided a sense of normalcy, but North and South America were completely dark. Sif remembered seeing the pictures of the cities at night, and how Chicago, New York, and Los Angeles looked so huge and bright even from orbit, places that never slept, but now there was nothing there. *Like North Korea in the old days,* Sif mused. Black and plunged into darkness. It was as if someone flicked a switch, and all the lights went out. If Lucas was right, maybe the switch hadn't been invented yet. He *had* to be correct, because nothing like this could have happened in the month they were gone. The entire planet couldn't have gone dark, even if there were some sort of war. And if even if there had been, the cities would still be burning.

"No one who has ever gone into space has seen Earth like this," Lucas said. "No electricity. Anywhere."

"It looks so dead," Hunter said.

"Liv, any response to our radio calls?"

"No response. Transmitting on all frequencies, as directed."

Sif wondered when cities would have started using electricity. "Lucas, when would we have started seeing some lights, timewise?"

"Probably around the late nineteenth century, I would suspect. And even then, only the major cities had electric lights. Getting power out into the rural localities took decades."

"So, if we did go back in time, it's safe to assume we're further back than the late eighteen hundreds."

"At least, yes, but remember, we have no idea how far back we've gone. We could be staring down at the Jurassic age for all we know."

"Liv, status of planetary viewer?" Hunter asked. The viewer was designed to be used when *Resolute* entered Mars orbit, providing high-resolution digital images of the terrain below.

"Planetary viewer is operational."

Hunter pushed away from the viewport and propelled himself toward the mid-deck access passage, which exited on the command deck right above them. "Liv, request infrared snapshots, fifty-meter resolution, thirty-second intervals. Send them to screen one. Include geo-coordinates," he said.

"Understood. Will comply."

Sif tapped Lucas on the shoulder, surprising him a little. He was transfixed by the darkened Earth below. "Let's take a look," she said. "Then we'll know for sure."

Sif floated behind Lucas and followed him through the hole in the floor of the command deck. They found Hunter already at his station. "The first image should be coming through any second," he said.

Sif and Lucas each gripped the back of Hunter's chair and stared at the screen.

When the first image came up, it revealed absolutely nothing. It was black.

As was the next one. And the next.

Sif looked at the coordinates on the last picture to appear: 39.7910° N, 86.1480° W. "Liv, nearest city to coordinates on image three?"

"Coordinates correspond to Indianapolis, Indiana."

A major American city, completely dark. No infrared signatures whatsoever. At least it was where Indianapolis was supposed to be, or would be one day. The whole situation was starting to make her head hurt.

"Liv, screen two, US map, overlay orbital ground trace, include ship icon," Hunter ordered.

"Understood. Will comply." A second later, a map of the United States popped up on Hunter's second screen, with a curved line showing *Resolute*'s orbital path across the landscape below. A small diamond shape marked their progress along the ground trace.

"We're going to pass directly over Raleigh, North Carolina," Lucas observed.

"In about a minute and a half," Hunter added.

Sif followed the ground trace across the screen. After leaving the East Coast, they would head south, crossing eastern Brazil, and encounter the sunrise after passing South America's Atlantic coast. Then they would curve northward after skirting the tip of South Africa, staying over water until the trace intersected Pakistan.

The results for Raleigh were the same. No infrared signatures. Dark. As was Brazil, a little while later.

"We'll be able to see more in the daylight," Hunter said. "We'll switch the viewer to panchromatic when we see . . . um, Pakistan."

Unfortunately, this first orbit wouldn't take them over many populated regions in the daylight, but they would make the same journey every ninety minutes or so, a little farther westward each time, as Earth rotated below them.

"We're going to have to go down there," Sif said.

"I know," Hunter said, "but not until we survey as much of the globe as possible."

"Where?" Lucas asked.

Sif glanced at Hunter and realized neither of them had an answer. Where *does* one go after traveling back in time, especially when one has no friggin' clue *when* they are? "That's a good question, Tater."

"I assumed we'd go back to Kennedy, like was planned on our return," Hunter said. "I guess that doesn't really matter anymore since Kennedy isn't even there."

"I've always wanted to go to Paris," Sif said. "But it wouldn't be the same in the Jurassic era, right? How about you, Lucas? Want to try Ohio?"

"I'm serious, Caitlyn."

And he was. "Okay, Lucas. Sorry." Lucas was unmarried, as were she and Hunter, but he had family in Ohio and was probably struggling with the fact that he would never see them again. Sif had basically been a loner since her parents' deaths and poured her whole being into her naval career, with one exception: her marriage. After the divorce, she committed herself heart and soul to the United States Navy, and then the astronaut corps, with no desire to spend any time trying to build relationships, especially those of the romantic variety. Sometimes she forgot that others, like Lucas, weren't so . . . alone. "What are you thinking?"

"Hunter's right. We should survey as much as we can from orbit before we attempt a landing, which brings up another concern. *Beagle* was designed for a Mars landing—thinner atmosphere and lower gravity—not Earth."

*Beagle* was their reusable landing craft, loosely based on the *Delta Clipper* single-stage-to-orbit design from the early 1990s. "She can do it, Lucas," Sif said. "Not a problem."

Hunter laughed a little. "You sound pretty sure of yourself, Navy."

Sif smiled at him. "I *am* a naval aviator. *Beagle* can do it. No sweat."

"And while you two are showing off your flying skills, I'll be staying up here, right?" Lucas asked.

"Someone's got to watch the henhouse until we get back," Hunter said.

"Caitlyn's piloting prowess notwithstanding," Lucas said, giving Sif a quick wink, "I hope you *do* get back."

# Chapter 16

Litsa sensed him standing beside her mat before he announced his presence. She rolled over and wiped the sleep from her eyes.

"We leave in an hour," Jarrod said. "Wake the others."

"Yes, my captain," Litsa said.

As Litsa descended deeper into the cavern to wake the other warriors, she wondered what life would be like without the threat of the Riy, to live as the old ones before the spread and the great death, and before the sky was thick with the smoke of the funeral pyres. She loved to spend time in the book spaces, where all the accounts of the old times were kept. Life was so different then, where people didn't have to run from cave to cave, fearing sudden death.

But this was their life now, and she would fight to keep it.

The heat began to build in her body as she thought of the hunt, the excitement of killing the thing that threatened them all. She loved the rush of adrenaline she felt when racing across the fields in the darkness toward her enemy, knowing that she was a warrior, a protector, a keeper of those left behind in the Dak, and she would kill, or be killed, to keep them safe.

"Warriors!" Litsa yelled as she entered the watchers' cavern. "Awake! We are called!"

Twenty of them, men and women, crawled from their mats and sprang to their feet in answer to her call. As one, they responded, "Urrah!"

"For our home, we fight!"

"Urrah!"

"For our people, we fight!"

"Urrah!"

"For the clan, we fight!"

"Urrah!"

"Weapons!" Litsa yelled, and watched as each of them grabbed their bows, filled their quivers, and lit their torches.

# Chapter 17

"I don't know what it is," Lucas said, still a little shaken.

He was beside Sif in *Beagle*'s cramped two-person cockpit, technical manual in hand, making adjustments to the attitude control program to allow the lander to function in Earth's atmosphere, hopefully, instead of the thinner Martian air for which it was designed.

On their first orbit, as *Resolute* swung northward up the eastern coast of Africa, they trained the viewer toward Kenya and Somalia and saw something that none of them expected, and, as of yet, couldn't explain. With the viewer set at maximum magnification, huge swaths of the arid landscape—mostly uninhabited desert in the world they all knew—were completely blackened, as if a child had taken a black marker to a picture of Earth and colored it in. The viewer failed shortly thereafter—and took all of Hunter's time since, as he tried to repair it—limiting their survey to what they could see from almost 250 miles up.

The oceans looked the same, the clouds, even the lightning storms as *Resolute* passed into night, but the *land* was wrong. With each orbit, as they passed over the equator, they saw more and more of the strange blackened surface. Their planet, it seemed, was ringed by a black belt that extended for hundreds of miles from the equatorial regions, becoming more sparse and spotty the farther north and south in latitude they traveled in orbit.

"I'm not a natural-history buff, but I can't recall anything that could explain what we've seen." Lucas typed a series of numbers on his keyboard. "Your reentry angle will have to be much shallower, or you'll burn through the thermal protection. I've adjusted it by a few degrees."

"Copy," Sif replied, verifying his entries on her screen. "It almost looks like everything is *burned*, like the whole equator has gone up in flames, which makes no sense."

"Once Hunter gets the viewer working again, we'll be able to take a closer look at it. Adjust pierce-point angle to ten degrees nose low."

"Ten degrees nose low, copy." Sif entered the parameter into the automated flight program. Lucas Hoover was a fifty-pound brain, a genius, and if anyone could coax *Beagle* into performing properly in Earth's atmosphere instead of Mars's, he was the guy. She had learned *Beagle*'s systems inside and out during her training, but reentry was a different ball game altogether, and attempting to do it manually—by the seat of her pants—was a recipe for disaster. One wrong calculation, and they would reenter too steep and burn up, or too shallow and bounce across the upper atmosphere into open space. A one-way trip, either way.

Once the lander slowed enough for the control surfaces to function—they were basically large, flat plates that extended from the lander's biconic, or four-sided, cone-shaped body—she could orient the vehicle into a landing position and fly her to the ground. She had performed it in the simulator a thousand times, but for a landing on Mars, not Earth.

It was a big risk, but they had no other choice. Like it or not, they were stuck here and couldn't survive in orbit forever. Home—however far in the past it might be—was down there, unexplained blackened landscape and all.

"Braking burn at . . . fifty thousand, no, check that." She watched Lucas rub his eyes. "Braking burn at forty thousand feet."

"Copy. Forty thousand. Do you need a break?"

"No, I'm fine. You?"

"I'm a little hungry."

Lucas pushed himself back from the console. "Now that you mention it, I am, too."

Sif unzipped her breast pocket and pulled out a tube. "DINNER-ROAST BEEF-MASHED POTATO-GRAVY-PEAS" was printed on the side. "This one's not too bad. Here." Sif flicked it at Lucas, and he caught it as it floated toward him.

"Yum. My favorite, just like Mom used to make."

"What, did she chew it for you first?"

Lucas laughed, and Sif was glad to hear it. She pulled another tube from her pocket, this one stamped "DINNER-TURKEY-STUFFING-CRANBERRY SAUCE," and unscrewed the cap. "Bon appétit."

"Down the hatch," Lucas said as he squeezed a glob into his mouth. Sif did the same. Not as good as the real thing, she thought, but still tasty, considering NASA was able to shove an entire processed meal into a toothpaste tube. And it was admittedly better than the dehydrated MREs—Meals, Ready to Eat—she lived on during survival training.

"Think you can fly this thing, Sif?" Lucas asked, wiping his mouth with the back of his hand.

"If you can get her through reentry, I can fly her. And thanks for calling me Sif."

"I might as well, right? But you still can't call me Tater."

"Deal."

"Let's take it through some simulation runs. We can tweak the reentry program a little, and when we're good with that, then we can see if you're *really* ready to fly her."

Sif faked a look of shocked indignation. "You're suggesting I'm not?" She squeezed another glob of her dinner into her mouth.

"I'm suggesting practice makes perfect."

"I'm game. Switch it over to sim mode and we can check your reentry adjustments."

Hunter's voice came through the overhead speaker. "Sif, Lucas, I think you might want to see this."

"Sounds like he's got the viewer working again," Sif said, a little concerned at the sound of Hunter's voice. She pressed her comm button. "On our way. What's up?"

"It's all gone," he said, his voice full of emotion. "It's all *gone.*"

# Chapter 18

Litsa was in her element. She ran at the front of the ranks, beside Jarrod. The war party, torches held high, headed east toward the draw where the hive was last seen. Where Erik was lost, and Mirda infected. The muffled thunder of their feet across what was once called the Badlands was the only sound she could hear, apart from their heavy breathing and the crackle of the torch flames.

When they left the Dak and crossed the fields, they saw the signs. The drones were there once again, leaving trails through the crop rows. If the hive moved, it didn't move far.

The moon was yet to rise, and the land was dark. Perfect conditions. They would stop, send scouts to see if the hive was still there, and then, once confirmed, spread out into a wide arc, surrounding the hive. Then they would fill the sky with their arrows.

The terrain was familiar, and Jarrod slowed his pace. They were close to the draw and had to be cautious, in case the hive moved westward, out of the draw and toward the Dak. If it did, there might be sentinel drones close by.

Behind her and Jarrod were most of the watch, twenty warriors, full quivers all. A few of them carried oil-filled skins, drawn from the sulfurous black pools at the very lowest reaches of the Dak. They would lay a ring of the flammable oil around the site of the hive, trapping it behind a wall of flames. Litsa and Jarrod had seen the hive up close and knew they couldn't contain it or destroy it entirely. It could move through the flames, losing part of itself in the process, but some of it would survive. If they burned enough of it, though, damaged it, *scared* it, the thing would move away.

Jarrod stopped and raised his arm just as the stench hit him. There was a breeze blowing from the east, and it carried the thing's horrid scent.

Luck was with them so far. The hive was still there.

The hunting party surrounded Jarrod as he knelt in the grass. His voice was low and steady. "Jaxom, Fleet, the hill ahead obscures the draw, high ground to the north, open land to the south. Approach from the south and confirm its location. Keep your distance," he cautioned, remembering what happened the night before, "just close enough to confirm. There were drones to the south night last, so patience and stealth become your weapons."

"Yes, my captain," they both replied, then quickly disappeared into the shadows, heading for the flat terrain to the south of the hill.

Litsa watched as Jarrod smoothed the dirt with his palm, then drew a map with his finger. She recognized the high ground, the low area, and in the middle where he smacked his fist into the dust, a wide mark signified the location of the hive. "Oilers, you will pour from here to here, meeting at the eastern arc." He drew a rough circle around the hive, showing where he wanted the oil placed. "From there, you will light the ring and return to that stand of pine," he said, pointing off to his left. "That will be our rally point. When your arrows are expended, we will meet there."

Litsa watched Jarrod stand, looking each of his warriors in the eye as he spoke. "Erik and Mirda were lost to this thing, and I will lose no more. Am I clear?"

"Yes, my captain," came the replies.

Just then, Jaxom and Fleet returned. "It is there, my captain, in the draw, as you described it."

"Oilers," Jarrod commanded, "move! The rest of you, standard spread and spacing, hold your fire until the ring is aflame."

As one, the warriors moved off, well schooled in the tactic they were about to employ, but Jarrod held them back. "Wait," he said.

They stopped and turned.

"Warriors, hear me!" Jarrod's voice echoed. "Tonight, we fight!"

"Urrah!" they all replied. Litsa's heart pounded away in her chest as the excitement of the hunt raced through her body. If she were to die tonight, at least she would be doing what she loved, with the bow steady in her hand and her arrows flying true.

"Deploy," Jarrod commanded, and they all ran to their positions, spaced no more than twenty yards apart. Litsa stopped, crouched, and slammed the sharpened end of her torch into the ground. She grabbed a handful of arrows and waited for the ring to ignite, the signal for all of them to loose their first volley.

The night grew quiet as they waited for the oilers to start the attack. It would take them some time to pour a ring around the hive, and the seconds slowly ticked by.

With a *whoosh*, the fields to the east suddenly brightened, and the flames quickly raced around the circle as the oil ignited. At evenly spaced intervals following the curved line of the flames, Litsa saw her fellow warriors light their arrows and stand.

As did she.

# Chapter 19

Hunter brought the viewer back online, and what it revealed shook Sif to the core. The pictures proved Lucas's theory were not entirely correct. They weren't in the past. Hunter said it was all gone. And he was right.

"That's St. Basil's Cathedral, isn't it?" Sif asked.

"Yes," Hunter replied. "In the middle of Moscow."

"My God, what happened?" Lucas said, his voice shaking. "Look at it."

Three of the four large onion domes were still intact, but most of the structure was caved in. What was left of the Kremlin sat just to the west of St. Basil's, and it showed similar signs of damage.

Sif's initial reaction was to assume there was a war, that the unthinkable had finally happened. But, no, that couldn't be. There was too much *growth*.

"Look at the plants," Sif said. "That's what I'm seeing, right?"

"It's completely overgrown." Hunter turned to Lucas. "We're not looking at the past. And it's not Earth in our own time, is it?"

Lucas shook his head and took a deep breath before speaking. "No. I was wrong about the—" He rubbed his eyes again, then stared closely at the image on the screen. "Is the whole city that way? I mean, over-grown like that?"

Hunter brought up more pictures of the city, all the same. Some buildings were intact, but so many were damaged. Throughout, though, what was once a major city had been reclaimed by nature, inch by inch.

"I was wrong about the Tipler cylinder," Lucas said, "or whatever the hell we went through. You're right, Hunter, this kind of growth takes decades."

Moscow, even though the streets and structures were visible, was completely overgrown with vegetation. It reminded Sif of Pripyat, the Russian city abandoned right after the Chernobyl nuclear disaster back in the 1980s. By the second decade of the twenty-first century, it looked much like what she was seeing on their screen. Mother Nature, taking back what man once claimed. "We didn't go back in time, did we?" Sif said.

"No," Lucas replied. "I don't think we did."

Sif watched as Lucas pulled himself toward the window and stared below at what seemed to be a lifeless Earth, where everyone they knew, the smiling faces of family and friends, had been snuffed out. "We're not looking at our past," Lucas said. "This is our future."

It was quiet for a time in the command module, as each of them struggled with their thoughts. It was easier to believe all they ever knew hadn't happened yet, and every person in their lives—mothers, fathers, siblings, friends—were yet to be born. But this changed things.

Sif felt sorry for Hunter and Lucas, as each of them left loved ones behind. One of NASA's requirements for this mission was that none of them could be married, as asking a person to leave behind a spouse, and maybe children, for such a long time—almost two years—on a trip that could very well end badly, was too much of a sacrifice for any person to make and could draw their focus away from the mission, which was their top priority.

She was an easy choice. Parents deceased. Divorced. No kids.

Alone.

Hunter was never married but came from a large, close family, with three older sisters. He spoke often of his nieces and nephews.

Lucas's family wasn't as large, but he was extremely close to his younger brother and sister, who idolized him. Sif remembered seeing them at the last meeting before quarantine and how heavy Lucas's heart seemed after saying good-bye.

Sif's thoughts drifted to memories of her own parents, lost when she was just seventeen, a junior in high school. Her dad was larger than life, a Navy fighter pilot and war hero who flew F-14 Tomcats during Desert Storm. His call sign was Thor, as his favorite saying was "Drop the hammer!" Teaching her to drive a year before his death and taking her out on the interstate for the first time, he prodded her to hit the gas and speed up. "Drop the hammer, Cate, let 'er rip!" Sif smiled at the memory. She still missed him terribly. Her purpose in life from that point forward was to make Deke "Thor" Wagner proud, wherever he was.

She remembered her mother, Carla, a beautiful woman, tall and thin, with hair the color of honey and large, expressive green eyes. Sif took after her father, as she was short, had a smaller version of his pug nose, his same jet-black hair, and shared his wide-spaced hazel eyes. She also shared his determination and drive to succeed, qualities that eventually landed her at the Naval Academy. One of her father's former commanding officers, an admiral and family friend, smoothed the application process after the accident, helping to ensure Thor's kid would get her shot.

And she took full advantage of the opportunity.

Her dad wasn't there to see her receive her golden wings and become a naval aviator, but wherever he was, he must have been watching.

Once she made it out to the fleet, her squadron mates tagged her with her call sign after learning who her father was. Thor and Sif. She saw the movie, too, and even though she never told anyone, Sif was her favorite character. A badass. And a warrior.

She had been alone for so long, by choice, that the situation didn't affect her as much as Hunter and Lucas. Even her ex-husband, whom she once thought she loved, was only an unfortunate mistake; she'd latched on to someone else even before the divorce was finalized. She would shed no tears over him.

Hunter and Lucas were thinking about their families. From what they saw of the planet so far—the darkened landscape at night and the ruined city—they must assume their loved ones were all dead.

And they didn't know why.

Another question still remained, too, just as valid as it was when they thought they'd gone backward in time: they still had no idea of *when* they were.

Lucas finally broke the silence. "Do either of you remember the old Viking probes?"

"I do," Hunter said. "The first two Mars landers. Launched back in the seventies."

"Correct," Lucas said. "But there were more than two."

Sif looked at Hunter, and he shrugged.

Lucas continued staring out the window as he spoke. "There was a third Viking. Classified. They didn't want everyone up in arms about launching a spacecraft with a small nuclear reactor as a power source. If the booster failed, they would have one hell of a mess to clean up. And explain, too."

"What does it have to do with us?"

"It *disappeared*, Hunter, on the way to Mars. Vanished. They never knew what happened to it until they found it in Earth orbit almost twenty years later. They brought it back—again, secretly—in *Atlantis*'s cargo bay. The vehicle showed no signs of being adrift in space for two decades—no pitting, no scarring—and even more surprising, its reactor's power level was *exactly* the same as when it was first launched. It was as if *Viking 3* appeared in Earth orbit almost immediately after it disappeared, yet twenty years had passed. There were theories about black holes, rips in space-time, even aliens, but it still remains a mystery." Lucas turned, faced them.

"So you're suggesting whatever happened to *Viking 3* happened to us, as well?" Sif asked.

"I think that's a distinct possibility. Look, the easiest way to get to Mars is to wait until the two planets are closest—and that only happens at certain times, once every two years or so. *If* our trajectory to Mars just happened to coincide with the same trajectory *Viking 3* followed, and *if* the two spacecraft happened to travel through the same part of space between Earth and Mars, and *if Viking 3* encountered the same Tipler cylinder—or whatever—that we did, then yes, I'm suggesting that what happened to *Viking 3* happened to us, too."

"If *Viking 3* was only gone for twenty years, that doesn't explain the amount of growth we saw in the city," Hunter said. "That took more than twenty years."

Lucas shrugged. "Maybe the amount of time spent in the cylinder's influence—and the amount of time skipped—has to do with the mass of the object it's attracted. I really don't know, but what I'd guess is *Viking 3* apparently went forward in time, and so did we."

"I'm surprised they were able to keep something like that under wraps for so long," Sif said. "Were you involved with *Viking 3*?"

"Nope," Lucas answered. "I'm not supposed to know anything about it, but hey, scientists talk."

"So," Sif said, smiling at Lucas, "do you have any cool classified stories about Area 51 that you're not supposed to know about?"

Lucas shook his head and laughed. "I wish I did."

Hunter broke in. "We're still going down."

Sif nodded in agreement. "I don't think we have a choice."

"We don't know what happened yet, guys," Lucas said. "It could've been some sort of global plague, or maybe it *was* a war."

"It doesn't change things." Hunter said. "We can't stay up here forever, like we agreed before. Sif and I will take *Beagle* down."

"Since we don't know what happened, we have to assume the worst," Sif said. "This isn't the planet we left, and we don't have a clue what might be lurking in the air down there. Maybe you're right, Lucas, maybe it was a plague. Or a war, and everything's radioactive. Either way, I think we should treat this just as if we were landing on Mars."

"Full suits and protective gear."

Sif nodded at Hunter. "We might as well get some use out of it, right?"

"Is *Beagle* good to go?" Hunter asked.

"Still needs some sim runs to confirm the changes we made. She might need some tweaking until I'm confident she's ready," Lucas said.

"She'll be ready," Sif answered. "Question is, where do we put her down?"

"We keep looking. I don't want to believe we're the only people left alive. If humanity managed to survive whatever happened down there, we should be able to see some sort of evidence."

"Without electricity, they'd be plunged back into the Middle Ages at least," Lucas said. "They'd have to learn how to live off the land again, how to farm."

"Moscow looked abandoned. Do we look at the cities, or assume any survivors moved away?" Sif asked, wondering aloud.

Hunter joined Lucas at the viewport. "I don't think we can assume anything, at least not until we get a closer look. Liv?"

"Yes, Webb."

"Continue viewer imaging. Land only. One-hundred-meter resolution outside of urban areas, ten-meter resolution over urban areas. Switch to infrared during terrestrial night. Record snaps at thirty-second intervals. Notify Webb immediately of any significant infrared signatures, Liv."

"Understood. Will comply."

"Now, Sif, how about we start running some simulations on the changes you've made to *Beagle*?"

"Got it, boss."

"Lucas, start checking the cargo lander specs. See if they'll need to have their flight programs adjusted, too."

"Yes, sir."

Hunter pushed himself toward the tunnel at the rear of the command module and grinned at Sif as he floated by. "What are you waiting for, Navy? Let's go fly."

# Chapter 20

The sky was filled with the sound of arrows whistling through the air, each aflame, arcing through the darkness toward the hive. Litsa could see drones, their arms held high, moving about behind the flames, sensing the heat, trying to find a way out for their hive.

Within the flames, the hive rose partway from the draw. Even from this distance, Litsa saw its surface undulating wildly, part of it covered in flame, arrows covering its surface and wiggling like a hundred feathered spines.

One by one, Litsa sent her flaming arrows into the hive, watched it roll and stretch as it tried to escape from the flames.

She had seen this before and knew what happened next.

"We need to get to the trees," Jarrod said, standing behind her. "The others should be at the rally point by now."

The stench was so bad it was hard to breathe, and it was about to get worse.

As they approached the rally point, they were met by Jaxom. "Our count is twenty, my captain, including you and Litsa. No losses."

Litsa watched Jaxom shift his eyes toward the hive.

"My captain, it moves."

From their high ground, they could see the draw clearly, illuminated by the flames. Within the circular ring of oil-fed fire, the hive took on a rounded appearance, like a huge, black ball. Where it was on fire, folds of the blackness stretched from its body and enveloped the flames, snuffing them out, but too much of it was on fire to make a difference. A large group of drones was situated toward the eastern edge of the ring, where the oilers first ignited the flames, and it was at this point in the ring that the hive would attempt to escape. The flames were lower there, the oil consumed.

The hive ball shape elongated toward the eastern point, absorbing the drones, and it crossed into the flames. It didn't move quickly, and much more of its surface ignited.

The giant mass slowly crept out of the ring. Large flaming globs of the hive dropped to the ground as it shed the parts of itself that were aflame, sacrificing mass for survival. As it exited the flames, Litsa could see it was much smaller now, nearly half its original size.

The hive was moving off to the east, away from the Dak, and for the time being the threat was over. A cheer arose among the warriors. "Urrah! Urrah! Urrah!" They held their bows high, pumping them in the air.

\*\*\*

The hunting party returned to the Dak while it was still dark. The large, flat rock serving as the main entrance was rolled to the side. The watchers saw them approaching and alerted Joshua. He was waiting for them.

"The hive is moving east, my chief. Just as we'd hoped," Jarrod said.

"Who did we lose?"

"Not a one, my chief."

When the gas canister landed at Jarrod's feet, spewing a cloud of white mist, Litsa rolled to her right and nocked an arrow. She searched for a target and aimed.

The Takers were here.

# Chapter 21

"Come on, Sif, one more try." Hunter had sat through seven sim runs with Sif so far, and they hadn't survived a single one. Coming up with an atmospheric reentry profile was proving to be a bigger bear than he thought. "Maybe we need to adjust the pierce-point angle by another degree or so."

Sif was sitting in *Beagle*'s pilot seat beside him, a perplexed look on her face. "I don't get it. This should be working."

Hunter had always admired Sif. He never admitted to anyone—especially the crew selection committee at NASA—that he had grown fond of the bob-cut Navy fighter pilot, small in stature and built like a gymnast. It took a while to warm up to her, because she came with a reputation, one he quickly decided was well deserved. He found her to be standoffish and self-centered, but flying with her at the USAF test pilot school changed his perceptions. She was smart, fearless, and a good stick. "Okay, maybe Lucas missed something. We've tried increasing the angle, decreasing the angle, I'm not too sure what to try next."

"We let her bounce, Hunter. Once."

He knew exactly what she was thinking. She wanted to allow *Beagle* to bounce off the upper atmosphere, which would slow her enough to enter the atmosphere at a lower velocity the second—and final—time. A skip reentry. "It might work, if we can figure out the exact parameters," Hunter said.

He watched Sif replay the last simulation, which was the closest they'd come to making it through the most dangerous part of the reentry process. "Here. The thermal protection system fails here," she said, pointing at the screen. "We're still coming in too fast, and I don't think our pierce-point angle has anything to do with it. It's got to be a longer, shallower reentry to reduce the rapid heat onset. But if we stay shallow, the heating lasts for a longer period of time, and it'll fail again. If we skip her, like a stone across a pond, we'll come in much slower the second time."

"Okay, but if our calculations are off, we'll bounce into space, and we don't have the fuel to correct our orbit, land, and make it back to *Resolute*. We'll be stranded." He watched her close her eyes, thinking.

"If we slow her down enough with the first reentry segment, we won't have to worry about bouncing off into space. We'll land. And I'll flip her around, brake earlier."

"That's tricky, Sif. The nozzles aren't designed to handle the reentry heat."

"Then I do it right after the second heat pulse." She was already entering her parameters into the computer. "If I use the mains to perform a half-sequence braking burn, we'll still have enough fuel to make a landing and get back to *Resolute*."

Hunter thought it through. If she flipped the ship right after the point of maximum heating, the nozzles could take it, and the braking burn would rapidly decelerate the ship. "Let's try it. Nothing else has worked so far."

He watched Sif's fingers dance across the keyboard, then suddenly stop. She looked up at him. "This is all based on the premise that we plan on coming back to *Resolute*. If Lucas can get the cargo landers programmed to survive reentry and landing, we could send them down and take the escape pod. All three of us."

*Resolute* also held a three-person emergency escape capsule, a smaller, three-person version of NASA's Orion design. It was designed to survive an Earth reentry and was to be used if, upon their return, there was no way to dock with the International Space Station—the ISS—which was their designated recovery point. Regardless, it was a one-way trip. They would abandon *Resolute* in orbit, which Hunter wasn't ready to consider yet. "It's an option, but only if we can't get *Beagle* to perform. I've thought about it, too."

"I figured that. Just wanted it on the record, that's all."

"How close are you to running her through her paces?"

"Give me another ten minutes."

Hunter settled back in his seat—as well as he could in zero gravity—and let Sif work her magic. That's when Liv came through the cockpit speaker.

"Alert. Webb. Significant infrared signature detected."

Sif started to push away from her console, but Hunter stopped her. "No, you stay here and keep working the solution. I'll go." He pushed himself out of *Beagle*'s small cockpit, through the docking port, and into the deployment bay. He grabbed a handhold and sent himself floating toward the tunnel leading to the command module. "Liv, location of infrared signature?"

"Forty-three degrees, thirty-five minutes, forty seconds north. One-zero-three degrees, twenty-three minutes, forty-two seconds west."

*Forty-three north, one-oh-three west.* The north-central portion of the United States, or at least what used to be. "Liv, what location equates to those coordinates?"

There was a slight delay while the AI searched databases. "Webb, these coordinates equate to Wind Cave National Park, South Dakota, United States."

Hunter found Lucas in the command module, and he already had the infrared images on the screen. "Fifty-meter resolution, boss."

Hunter stared at the circle of light on the screen, a smile slowly stretching across his face. "That's got to be man-made," he said. Thirty orbits, and they hadn't seen a single sign of life, until now.

"I agree. I think we may have just found some survivors."

"We've also just found our landing spot, Lucas."

"How's Sif coming with the *Beagle* mods?"

"Liv, patch me in to Sif, please."

Liv acknowledged his request with an electronic squeak, which was followed a couple of seconds later by Sif's voice. "Sif here."

"Have you run your skip reentry figures though any sims yet?" Hunter asked.

"Three, so far. I'm getting close."

Which meant she had suffered three more failures. "Keep working it, Navy. Use these coordinates as a touchdown point, and run it again." He read them off. "Copy?"

"Copy. What's down there?" Sif asked.

"Possible survivors, Sif. Ever been to the Badlands?"

# Chapter 22

"All systems are go for drop, *Beagle*. Ninety seconds until release point," Lucas said, monitoring the launch from the command module.

"Roger, *Resolute*. Ninety seconds. Standing by," Sif replied. She and Hunter sat in *Beagle*'s small cockpit, she in the left seat, Hunter in the right. Sif tucked her prelaunch checklist into a snap pouch on the side of her seat. "Prelaunch checks complete."

"Copy. You ready for this?" Hunter said.

"I'm always ready." *Everything will work.* She ran the skip reentry profile through the simulator another five times after she finally found a solution, and it worked every time. Her rotation and landing sequences worked without a hitch, too. Without the help of a hundred eggheads in Houston, the three of them managed to figure out how to take a spaceship designed for a Mars landing and program it to function in Earth's atmosphere, which was no small feat. She turned her head to look at Hunter—neither of them could turn their helmets, so the view was limited, but she could still see part of his face. "Are you ready?"

"Let's fly this thing, Sif," Hunter said. He gave her a thumbs-up, and she returned it.

Their release point was over Antarctica. *Beagle's* first skip through the atmosphere would occur over Africa, then they would bounce slightly back up before starting their final reentry over the northern Russian landmass. If all went according to plan, Sif would flip *Beagle* tailfirst and begin a braking sequence over Canada, with their final landing spot near the circular infrared signature—a fire—located in Wind Cave National Park. If the landing went according to specs, they would still have enough fuel for a return to *Resolute*. Just barely, but enough.

"Sixty seconds until release point," Lucas said.

"Copy. Sixty seconds." Sif tested her restraints—she was strapped in tight. The g-forces would be more pronounced for an Earth reentry than the Martian one they trained for. "Do you have enough reading material to keep yourself entertained while we're gone, Lucas?"

"Yeah," he replied, "just enough. You pilot types get to have all the fun, though. You're getting to go home, while I'm stuck up here taking care of the most advanced piece of machinery ever built by mankind. Ho-hum."

"We'll be back before you know it," Hunter said.

"I'll keep the lights on. Thirty seconds. Vehicle restraint system armed, and release pistons to automatic on my mark . . . *mark.*"

Sif confirmed his action on her screen. "Restraint armed, pistons to automatic. Copy. Prelaunch sequence complete. Hey, maybe you can work on Liv's voice interface while we're gone."

"Why? I kinda like it when she calls me Mr. Potato. Fifteen seconds."

Sif's heart pounded away in her chest. She had only flown *Beagle* in simulations, never in space. *Come on, calm down. Everything will work just fine.*

"Ten seconds."

"Good luck up here, Lucas," Hunter said.

"Godspeed, *Beagle*. Come back safe and sound. Drop sequence commence in five, four, three, two, one . . . mark."

Sif heard a bang as the restraining arms slammed back into their slots and felt a nudge as the pistons gently shoved *Beagle* away from *Resolute*'s belly. She quickly checked her status board. "Good release, *Resolute*. First thruster burn in twenty seconds."

"*Resolute* copies, looks good on my end."

Hunter tapped her arm and pointed to the window above her head.

Sif glanced up and saw *Resolute*'s underside slowly moving away. "Thrusters in ten," she said. The thrusters on top of *Beagle*'s hull would fire for a couple of seconds in order to give them the final momentum needed to begin their descent into Earth's atmosphere. At this point, the ship was following a programmed sequence of events—*her* programmed sequence—and she and Hunter were basically along for the ride. Unless something went wrong.

Sif tried to ignore her own mantra—*sometimes machines just break*—as she felt the thrusters fire. She felt her body press against the restraints for a second and could see a puff of gas outside her window.

"Thruster burn complete. Good results." On Hunter's main screen was a moving map display that showed a top and side view of *Beagle*'s flight path, with small icons marking the ship's position. "So far, so good, Navy."

Sif looked up again and could see almost all of *Resolute* above them—bow to stern—moving away as they descended. It was really a sight to see. "Look at her, Hunter."

"I know. She's a thing of beauty."

Sif changed her comms to internal only. "Do you think he'll be okay up there?" she asked, referring to Lucas.

"It's no different from what Mars would've been like. He would've stayed aboard *Resolute* for the first rotation—a couple of weeks—until we came back up to relieve him."

"I know, but under different circumstances."

Of the three of them, Lucas seemed to be having the hardest time adjusting to the fact that everyone he once knew was gone. "Maybe being alone up here will do him some good. He's got Liv to keep him company, right?"

"Yeah, Liv. She's a charmer, that one."

"He'll be okay, Sif. And so will we. This isn't the mission we all signed up for, but it's a mission just the same. I for one want to know what the hell happened down there."

"Me, too. At least there are some people still alive, but we have no idea how long it's been since whatever happened."

"Based on the amount of plant growth in the cities, we're probably no more than a hundred years or so away from our time, so there's still got to be some sort of knowledge about it." He glanced at his screen. "Still tracking. We should hit the Kármán line in about three minutes," Hunter said, referring to the boundary between Earth's atmosphere and space, roughly sixty-two miles above Earth's surface. "Forward thrusters in two minutes."

"Copy, two minutes." Sif had programmed *Beagle*'s thrusters to fire for one second, adding a slight impulse to their forward momentum, just enough to keep the ship from being pulled down into the atmosphere and instead bounce off the upper layer. The first interaction would last about three minutes, at which point they would rise above the Kármán line again, and hopefully, if her calculations were correct, not fly off into space. Her heart was still beating fast, but she was calmer now than when they launched. Once she was flying, her nerves always settled down. She felt much the same way when waiting for the catapult to launch her fighter off a carrier—as soon as she was in the air, and in control, she became more focused and less nervous. She cross-checked her instruments—everything was in the green. Hunter did the same, keeping a close eye on his moving map display.

"*Beagle*, *Resolute*. I'm showing two minutes, thirty seconds until first entry."

Sif switched her comms back to external. "Copy, *Resolute*. Two-thirty."

"You two are being awfully quiet," Lucas said.

"Not much to say," Hunter replied. "We're hands-off, enjoying the ride."

Sif looked up through her window again and could still see *Resolute*, now just a bright speck in the distance. "You should see yourself up there, Lucas. The ship looks so tiny."

"Yeah, and I'm already lonely. We'll lose communications during the first reentry segment, Sif. Give me a shout when you're on the other side. We should still be line of sight. Good luck."

Communications blackouts were a normal part of reentry, as the ionized region that surrounded the vehicle blanked out any radio waves. After they skipped back up out of the atmosphere, they could communicate again. Without the aid of satellites, though, they would have to rely on line-of-sight comms. "Copy that," Sif replied, quickly scanning her instruments again. "Thruster fire in fifteen seconds."

"Still traveling right down the pike, Sif," Hunter said. "Dead on course."

She didn't especially appreciate his word choice, but acknowledged him just the same. "Copy."

When the thrusters fired, they both felt a small kick and were pressed back in their seats. Hunter watched the tracking display closely. "Okay, Sif, we should start to feel it soon. Almost to the Kármán line."

And they did. It was slight at first, a barely noticeable vibration in the ship's structure, but it increased quickly. Hunter and Sif watched as a dull red glow became visible outside their cockpit windows, turning orange, then yellow-white as *Beagle* plowed into the upper reaches of the atmosphere. The vibration became more pronounced. The first bang startled Sif, but it was to be expected. As they hit thicker portions of the atmosphere, they would get kicked around a bit, much like riding in a jetliner flying through turbulence. Because of *Beagle*'s biconic shape, it wasn't quite as smooth as the reentries the space shuttle astronauts experienced, but much smoother than the old Apollo or Soyuz capsules.

*Beagle*'s ceramic composite thermal protection system would soon heat to nearly three thousand degrees Fahrenheit. It was a remarkable piece of technology, first developed by the Brits for their Skylon spaceplane project, and it was the only thing that would keep them alive. If it failed, they would only have enough time to realize it, but that would be all.

"Thruster fire, adjusting nose-high angle, looking good," Hunter announced. *Beagle* was automatically adjusting its orientation, keeping itself on the preprogrammed course. When they first entered the atmosphere, *Beagle* was traveling at roughly 7.9 kilometers per second, or well over 17,600 miles per hour. Now, they were entering the "sweet spot," where the friction from the atmosphere would reduce their forward velocity just enough to bounce them back up *without* sending them off into deep space.

Sif lifted her arm and, for the first time in over a month, felt the effects of gravity. The pull was light, but noticeable. Extended time in zero-g meant that they would need time to recover after landing in order for their bodies to readjust to Earth's gravity. They wouldn't be able to move about right away without suffering exhaustion, but their bodies would acclimate rather quickly.

Sif kept her eyes locked on Hunter's display, watching the numbers roll by as the ship icon crept along the projected flight path. So far, so good. As the line curved upward, Sif noticed the glow outside the windows begin to lessen, and then finally disappear. They were back in space.

"Velocity looks good, Sif. We're on track. Systems all check in the green." She felt Hunter's gloved hand on her arm. "That was perfect. Good job," he said.

"Thanks, but that was the easy part. We get to do it again in about twenty minutes."

The alarm blared in her helmet, and Hunter's nav display went blank. "Shit! Nav system is down."

They both reached for their checklists, flipped to the correct page. "Got it, trying reset," Hunter said.

Every second the nav system was down meant a greater chance that *Beagle* could slew off course, and their reentry solution would be shot.

"Reset unsuccessful. Check breakers A-three, A-six, and B-four."

"Copy, checking." Sif checked the breaker locations above her head—none were popped. "Breakers are in." *Dammit.*

"Uh, okay, trying reset again." Hunter's voice was a little tighter than usual. They mentally counted down the seconds as the computer went through the reset process. Sif breathed a sigh of relief when the screen came back on, but it was short-lived, and she immediately noticed the ship icon was slightly above its projected path. She waited, but *Beagle* wasn't automatically correcting course.

"I see it," Hunter said. "The interface isn't working." The nav system was functioning—the ship knew where it was, but it wasn't making course corrections. If they didn't fix it soon, the result would be disastrous.

"We're off course. I'm taking manual control."

"No," Hunter said quickly. "Wait. Not yet. Check system master to ON."

"System master to ON," Sif replied, her hand resting on the control stick. "We're wasting time."

"Cycle interface control from A to B, then back again."

Sif cycled the switch. Waited. Nothing. "That's it. I'm flying her down." She flipped the manual override switch and lightly grabbed the control stick. "Call out the numbers for me, Hunter."

"Roger. We're three degrees nose high, velocity is slightly above projected. Slow her down a little."

With her eyes locked on Hunter's display, Sif manually fired the nose thrusters to bring *Beagle* back on course.

"Don't overcorrect, don't *overcorrect*," Hunter yelled.

"Copy. I got it, I got it. Try the interface again." Even though she knew she could probably do it, their chances were much greater if the computer were flying the ship.

Hunter reached above Sif's head and cycled the interface switch again. Nothing. "Negative results. The interface is shot. You're a degree nose low. Bring it back up."

"*Beagle, Resolute,* come in please."

*Perfect timing.* Sif mashed her comm button. "*Resolute, Beagle* is manual. I say again, *Beagle* is manual. I'll talk to you after I land this thing, Lucas. *Beagle* out." She gently massaged the thruster control, keeping a light touch.

"Okay, Sif," Hunter said, his voice now much calmer and professional, "you're back on track. Velocity is good."

Sif opened her kneeboard—a pad strapped to her right leg—and flipped to a page where she jotted down all the necessary course adjustments, listed by elapsed time and duration. Now that they were solidly back on course, she should be able to follow the same instructions she'd entered into the ship's flight control computer and take her down manually. She heard Hunter laugh.

"What's so funny?"

"You, that's what," he said. "You were ready for this."

"Of course I was. I'm a naval aviator, remember? We land jets on floating postage stamps, in any weather, even at night." She turned her head, peered at him through her helmet. "We're *all* good," she added, "but I'm pretty sure I'm the best."

Hunter groaned. "Do we really have to go there right now?"

"I'm not *going* anywhere, just stating a fact. Keep your eyes on that screen. We reenter again in five minutes."

Hunter shook his head. "I hope those figures of yours take into account the weight of your ego, Navy."

"Oh, don't worry. They do."

The second portion of *Beagle*'s reentry went exactly as planned, with Sif making minor course corrections, flipping the tail of the ship around at just the right moment to perform the main thruster braking maneuver, and piloting her through the familiar blue skies of a planet they no longer knew. Roughly forty-five minutes after dropping away from *Resolute*'s belly, *Beagle* touched down within two miles of its projected landing spot, a place once known as the Red River Valley, Wind Cave National Park, South Dakota.

Sif and Hunter were home.

# Chapter 23

From what Major Kyle Murphy heard over the radio, the months of planning and surveillance paid off. He watched the C-130 taxi to its parking spot, and the pilot shut down the number two inboard engine. He approached as one of the crew members lowered the entrance door on the forward left side of the fuselage and stepped down the stairs, ripping the mask from his face and taking a deep breath.

"What's the count?" Murphy yelled, pointing at the back of the plane.

"Eighty-four," the man shouted over the engines, then added, "We lost four of our own."

Major Murphy took the tally sheet from the crew member's hand and gave it a quick glance—seventy adults, forty-five male and twenty-five female, including two that were pregnant. *Bonus.*

He sidestepped as stretchers bearing the four dead were carried off the plane. He shook his head. *Killed by primitive arrows and knives.* Inhuman, that's what they were. Uncivilized savages. Sometimes he felt as if he were stranded in the late nineteenth century, holed up in a fort surrounded by the modern-day equivalent of the Cheyenne, Arapaho, and Lakota, with a Little Bighorn awaiting him every time he opened the gates. Only difference was, Custer never dealt with the Riy. And *they* were getting too close for comfort.

He looked back down at the paper in his hands. Six adults killed during capture and another ten injured severely enough that their long-term survival was questionable—not too high a percentage, considering the size of this tribe—but no matter, because there were also fourteen children listed, ranging in age from a few months to preteen, eight male and six female. The kids were important, a priority, well worth the four men he lost.

Remote surveillance identified a population of over one hundred living in the cave dwelling, so they captured the majority of this particular tribe, the last organized dwelling in this sector. The stragglers who escaped weren't worth pursuing. With the Riy advancing northward, they wouldn't last long.

He tapped the sheet with his finger and smiled. Eighty-four safely sedated in the rear cargo hold, a good haul. As soon as the ground crew refueled the aircraft, it and its precious cargo would head north. His superiors would be pleased.

His aide called to him, motioning him away from the plane. "Sir!"

"What's the problem, Lieutenant?"

"Phoenix is on the horn, sir. You're going to want to hear this."

# PART II: BADLANDS

# Chapter 24

*Red River Valley*
*Wind Cave National Park, South Dakota*

Sif could barely move. The lower gravity on Mars would have been easier to deal with than *this*. ISS crew members who spent a year in space had told her readjusting to gravity would be tough, but this was ridiculous. "Jesus, Hunter. I can barely even lift my arm."

He struggled to reach something on the far side of his seat, grunting as he did so. He held up a long pointer with a rubber pad at the end. "That's why they gave us these," he said. "Go-go-gadget finger."

With it, Hunter was able to select the post-touchdown checklist on their upper screens, and together they ran through the ship's systems, checking status.

"That was an excellent flying job, Sif. Couldn't have done better myself."

They were still in their suits but released their harnesses. Sif shifted in her seat to look at him, surprised at the effort it took to make such a simple motion. She missed the freedom of movement she enjoyed in zero-g. "You're just jealous."

"No, Sif," Hunter said. "I'm serious. We're alive right now because of you."

She was a little taken aback, as Hunter had never said anything like that to her before. Lucas was right. As long as she had known Hunter, everything was a competition, at least as far as she was concerned.

"I couldn't have done what you did, Caitlyn. Putting you in that pilot seat was the smartest decision they ever made."

"Thank you," Sif finally said, suddenly at a loss for words. Hunter had never called her by her real name before, either. She would have to ponder it later, though, because something was malfunctioning. "Hunter, look at engine number three, display A-seven. The fuel turbopump is throwing a fault."

"I see it. Confirmed. Fault five nine nine."

They both looked up the fault code on their screens—knowing a five-series code wasn't the kind they wanted to see—and immediately realized they were in trouble. "We can't fix this, Hunter," Sif said. "The pump is seized. Removal and replacement."

Hunter leaned back in his seat, took a deep breath. He knew that without the pump, they were down an engine, and getting back to *Resolute* was impossible without all *four* engines. Stranded by a piece of equipment small enough that he could hold it in his lap. But then he remembered. "We'll have Lucas send a replacement down on one of the cargo landers."

"It's time to give him a ring anyway," Sif said, "considering I kind of left him hanging there."

"Yeah, you did. He still has no idea we've landed."

"He might think we burned up." Sif toggled the comm button. "*Resolute*, this is *Beagle*. Over." She waited for a response. "*Resolute*, this is *Beagle*. Over." Again, nothing. "*Resolute*, come in, please, this is—" Then *she* remembered. "Oh, crap. We're line of sight."

"You're right," Hunter said, holding his hands up. "Hey, this is getting easier already."

Sif raised her arms, as well, and noticed the same thing. Even though it still took some effort to move, it *was* getting easier. Their bodies were already adjusting to Earth's gravity. "Thank God," she said, "I can't wait to get out of this seat and set foot on good old terra firma again."

"We'll try Lucas again in about thirty minutes. He should be breaking the horizon by then. Ready to rotate yet?" Hunter asked.

"I'm ready if you are." For takeoff and landing, their seats—and the cockpit itself—were situated in line with the ship's beam. They were reclined, facing the nose of the ship with their backs to the ground. *Beagle*'s cockpit was essentially a ball with pivot points on either side, allowing the crew to change the position in order to ease access to the seats when *Beagle* was on the ground. "Alignment safety, off. Rolling."

With a whir, the entire cockpit, displays and all, slowly rolled forward, eventually stopping when their seats were in a full upright position. Between their seats—on what was the floor of the ship a minute ago—was a ladder leading from the cockpit to the lower portion of the ship. As the cockpit moved, the upper windows slid behind their seats, and two side windows—larger, but still shuttered—rotated into view. The cockpit locked into place with a clunk. "Alignment safety back on," Sif said. "Ready for the windows?"

"Let's take a look."

They undid the locking clamps and slid the covers forward on their rails.

The view took Sif's breath away. Apart from the blue sky and brush here and there, the landscape looked so much like . . .

"Mars," Hunter said. "It looks just like Mars."

The lay of the ground, and its red color, resembled the planet they were supposed to have stepped foot on. "I was thinking the same thing," Sif said, placing her gloved hand against the glass.

They were both silent for a time, thinking about what might have been. They could recite the names by memory: Armstrong and Aldrin,

Conrad and Bean, Shepard, Mitchell, Scott, Irwin, Young, Duke, Cernan and Schmitt. Wagner, Webb, and Hoover were supposed to join those names as the only people to walk on another celestial body. But, as was the case with Jim Lovell and Fred Haise on the ill-fated *Apollo 13* mission, it was just not meant to be.

"We would've made it," Sif finally said.

"Yeah, I think we would have."

The sun was low on the horizon—night was approaching. The stars were beginning to show themselves outside Hunter's west-facing window. In a way, it was a comforting feeling. They were alive and unhurt, and they were back home.

Only problem was, it wasn't the home they had left. The Earth they knew was gone—wiped away by an unexplained catastrophe, the details of which they could only guess. If there were survivors—and the fire they saw from orbit suggested as much—then they were nearby, only a few miles away. The location of the fire should be only a quarter mile to the southwest, if they had landed where they were supposed to.

"I suggest we wait until daybreak to start exploring," Hunter said. "I don't think we know enough yet to go stumbling around in the dark."

Sif nodded. "I agree." She undid her gloves, then released her helmet clasps. With a twist, she removed her helmet and hung it on the bulkhead by her seat, noticing how heavy it felt. She wiped her face with the palm of her hand and rubbed her eyes. "I think we could both use a little shut-eye." Below them, in the middle of the ship, were two fold-down cots—what Lucas called fifteen-million-dollar Murphy beds.

Hunter removed his helmet, as well, and eased himself off the seat. "It's going to take a while to lose our sea legs, anyway. I still feel weak."

"If you fall down the ladder, you'll be there for a while, because I'm not ready to start dragging you around."

He laughed. "I'll try not to."

"I'm going to try to contact Lucas again in"—Sif glanced at the digital clock on the control panel—"fifteen minutes. I'll be down after I get him up to speed."

"All right." Hunter started down the ladder, and then stopped. "Sif?"

"Yeah."

"I meant what I said. That was some shit-hot flying. You saved *both* our asses."

Sif nodded and smiled as he disappeared below. Hunter was one of the best pilots she'd ever known—sure, she gave him a fair amount of grief for being an Air Force puke, because as a naval aviator it was her duty to do so—but apart from all the professional banter, he was a good stick. Compliments like that didn't come easy for either of them, so he must truly mean what he said.

Her dad would have been proud of what she did today. Sif hoped that wherever he was, he saw her bring her ship down safely.

"I put the hammer down today, Daddy," Sif whispered, staring at the stars beginning to twinkle outside her window.

But if he *had* lived, if the drunk hadn't crossed the center line and killed her mother and father, Deke Wagner—the larger-than-life persona known as Thor to his buddies—would be gone now regardless. Outside her window was a world where all the cities were dead, the planet dark and quiet. Sif wondered what this *new* world held in store for them, and if all their efforts to stay alive were only delaying the inevitable.

Everyone dies. It's just a matter of how, and when.

Maybe they would fall victim to whatever changed Earth so drastically in just—well, they still didn't know how many years had passed. Hunter thought less than a hundred, but they couldn't be certain. The people would know, the ones who built the fire. They probably told stories, passed it down through the generations, about what turned the world upside down and reduced once-great cities into abandoned monuments of humanity's achievements.

She knew what the stories would tell. *We probably did it to ourselves. Like always.*

It was time. She toggled the comm switch again. "*Resolute*, this is *Beagle*, come in, please." Lucas should be in a position to receive by now.

"*Resolute*, this is *Beagle*. Lucas, can you read?"

Static.

She would soon realize there was more wrong with *Beagle* than a fuel pump with irreparable damage, though. The transmitter, too, was fried beyond repair.

Sif and Hunter were alive. They were home.

But without a radio—and no way to contact Lucas aboard *Resolute*—they were stranded.

# Chapter 25

*Five miles southeast of the Dak*

Litsa woke after night had fallen. Her head was pounding, an after-effect of the Takers' gas. She opened her eyes and stared up at the stars. The night was clear and quiet, deathly so. Was she knocked out the entire day?

She rose to a sitting position, cradling her head in her arms. Her mouth was dry, full of a bitter, metallic taste. She tried to spit, but couldn't.

The Takers hit fast and hard. The first gas canister was followed by more than she could count, with barely enough time to react before people started dropping to the ground, choking on the numbing fumes.

Jarrod screamed an attack warning, but he, too, fell. Litsa held her breath and sent an arrow into the chest of the first Taker she saw. She knelt by Jarrod's side, shook him, and then killed a Taker who tried to grab her. She plunged her knife into his throat, twisted, felt the warmth of his blood spill onto her hand, and then shoved him away. She killed a third with her bow, screaming in triumph as he fell, an arrow through his heart.

The fourth man she killed snatched her bow from her hand and threw it into the night. She strangled him with her bare hands, and then realized the battle was lost. The Takers, in their suits and gas masks, appeared as if from nowhere, and swarmed into the Dak's entrance. There were too many.

In less than a minute, the Dak was lost.

Litsa, and a few others who did not succumb to the fast-acting gas, scattered into the darkness when the gunfire erupted, zigzagging across the terrain, running as fast as they could. She had no chance against an enemy armed with rifles and made a snap decision to survive and fight another day.

She had no idea how many were lost, but it had to be bad. The Takers struck at just the right time, when the Dak was wide open.

Her people—her *family*—were taken.

She pounded her fist into the dirt.

It had happened to other clans, too. A few survivors joined up with Litsa's clan after escaping the Takers' grasp, and their stories sounded much like what she just experienced. Their family, friends, and loved ones were torn from them, and they wandered the northern territories, alone and afraid, until they found Litsa's people. No one knew what became of the men, women, and children who disappeared into the Takers' damn flying machines. They were just *gone*.

Litsa rubbed the back of her right hand, still stained with a Taker's lifeblood. They would pay for what they did.

First, though, Litsa had to make her way back to the Dak. There was hopefully still food there, and water. The Takers wouldn't come back, at least not yet. They rarely returned to a location more than once, so she should be safe. The others knew that, as well, so she might find other survivors.

Litsa stood, got her bearings, and walked northwest, toward home. She wasn't far from the point where they attacked the hive less than twenty-four hours ago.

For the first time she could remember, she felt alone.

***

She could still smell the metallic tang of the knockout gas as she ventured farther into the Dak, but, gladly, enough of it had dissipated that it caused no ill effects. Some of the torches had fallen to the dirt, but most were still burning, attached to the walls. She expected the inner chambers to be in disarray, but surprisingly little was disturbed, which spoke to the speed and effectiveness of the Takers' attack.

Litsa padded from chamber to chamber, traveling deeper within the maze of tunnels in the underground labyrinth she called home. Her echoing calls went unanswered. The Dak was empty.

She had seen others running away, though. Some of them *had* to have escaped, as she did. But for whatever reason, they hadn't returned. The Takers couldn't have captured everyone.

Most of the warriors were either just within the entrance, or outside, clustered around Joshua and Jarrod, and most of them were surely taken. The others who ran away were probably gatherers, craftsmen, caregivers, all too scared to return. If they didn't, though, Litsa doubted they would survive for long.

She passed through the grand hall, where just days before she received her punishment. She stared up at the ledge where Joshua sat as the whip snapped and cut and she could no longer hold in her screams.

She cupped her hands to her mouth and shouted, "Is anyone here?" Her own voice answered her tenfold, bouncing from wall to wall.

The kitchens were nearby, and she helped herself to a cup of water—cool and soothing to her throat, ravaged by the gas. The wall greens, a staple she never loved, tasted wonderful. With each mouthful, she could feel her energy returning. She sat on the dirt floor and ate more than her usual share, not knowing how long it might be until she ate again.

She had no idea what she was going to do. She wanted vengeance, but how? No one knew where the Takers lived. They flew through the skies in their machines—some of the same machines she learned about in the old texts, the ones used to fight the Riy when the spread first began—but no one ever discovered where the machines came from. They could be anywhere.

She entered the teaching chamber, where the children spent most of their days. The old texts were there, the same books Litsa studied as a child. Stories of the before time, when the world was a different place. Before the rise of the Riy.

The books were handed down from generation to generation, treated carefully, almost reverently, as they represented a touchstone to the past, a source of knowledge, and a source of hope.

Things were good once. People lived easy lives, food lined the shelves of places called grocery stores, and no one went hungry. Machines were used for almost everything, and hardly anyone worked the fields to scrape together enough food to survive. In the winter, people lived in the buildings, where it was warm and safe. And the cities, what glorious places they were. Buildings reaching high into the sky, full of people going about their daily lives with no creatures to steal the daylight.

Litsa had dreamed of that other world when she was a child, longed for feeling the sun against her face in a place where she didn't have to fear what might be approaching over the next hill.

She carefully lifted one of her favorite books from the stacks, a story about a young girl who was swept away by a storm and delivered to a place where little people worshipped a great wizard and where a magical beast, a field guardian, and an armored warrior helped her on her journey to return home to a place called Kansas. In the end, it was all a figment of the girl's imagination, but Litsa loved to hear the story over and over again, looking at the pictures and losing herself in the magic of it all.

But it wasn't real.

No more real than all the stories in the other books, now. The world that gave birth to such magic and wonder had passed away, torn apart in the short span of a couple of decades. It was killed, by the Riy, but in some places, the Riy awakened the worst of the old ones, those who lashed out and killed without reason or sense, decimating entire populations in the name of safety. So many died before it was all over, either consumed by the Riy or killed at the hands of men who knew no other recourse.

Twenty years, her teachers told her. Only twenty years passed from the time the Riy first appeared until all was lost, and the old world was dead.

Litsa's world—a never-ending struggle for survival—was all that was left of it. She was born 168 years after the rise of the Riy, so this life was all she, and generations of ancestors before her, had ever known. Stories were told, however, personal accounts of those who had survived the downfall, passed from generation to generation. Stories of the horrors they endured, the terrible events they witnessed, and how the cruelty of mankind swept from city to city like an insane wind, hot and fiery, the embers of the burning dead filling the air. All their machines, medicines, and science couldn't stop the Riy. Those who escaped the mass executions banded together, escaped to the forests, the mountains, anywhere they could find safety from what was devouring the planet.

With most people confined to the hours of darkness, when they found safety, every day became another battle. The sunlight that once warmed the faces of her ancestors now hurt her eyes and represented danger, a time for killing, for running, for fear. Litsa had lived in the darkness for most of her twenty-five years, and it was there she found solace.

She placed the book down gently and headed for the nursemaid's chamber. Her wounds were speaking to her again, and she needed to find something to silence their murmurings.

Litsa dressed her wounds as best she could and returned to the warriors' chamber. She searched through the abandoned weapons until she found a bow that suited her hand and a knife with the right balance and heft. Her bed was just as she left it, and she curled up on her woven grass mat. It was daylight outside, and her internal clock was screaming for rest. Even though she had been out for hours, sleep softly whispered.

Within minutes, she was sound asleep.

# Chapter 26

Sif descended the ladder, fuming at the fact that two of the simplest parts on board had failed them, and their odds of getting back to *Resolute* were less than slim. Without the replacement pump from *Resolute* and a functional transmitter to let Lucas know what they needed to fix the ship, they were grounded.

Hunter was already on the surface, a few feet away. They were wearing the same suits they would have worn on Mars, as they still weren't sure if the air was safe to breathe. Everything *looked* okay, but they knew this wasn't the same world they left.

With her foot on the bottom rung, and the other hovering above the ground, Sif wondered if she should say something Neil Armstrong–esque, like *One small step for man, one giant leap yadda yadda*. She had rehearsed what she would say before stepping foot on Mars, knowing her words would far outlive her, just as Armstrong's had outlived him, but decided it didn't matter now. She hopped off the ladder, and for the first time in over a month stood on solid ground.

It was early morning, and the sun glinted off their visors.

"This feels like another training session, doesn't it?" Hunter said. "Pretending to be on Mars."

"I was thinking the same thing," Sif replied. They had spent hours wandering around a landscape much like this one, in full gear, practicing what they would do on the surface once they reached Mars.

The temperature, according to the readout on her wrist, was seventy-eight degrees Fahrenheit. The sky was cloudless and blue—and the *sun*. Seeing it from space was remarkable, but now all Sif wanted to do was rip off her helmet, take a deep breath of nonrecycled air, and feel the sun's warmth against her face.

"Northwest, correct?" Sif asked. The location of the fire they observed from orbit should be a short distance from their landing spot—a quarter mile at most. It would take them some time to get there in their suits, as their mobility was more suited for Mars's gravity. As such, the suits felt heavy and ungainly.

"Right," Hunter replied, pointing in the general direction he wanted to go. "Let's get started. I have a feeling our cooling systems are going to struggle a little once we start moving, so I want to get there and back before it warms up too much."

"Copy," Sif replied. "Hunter, what time of year do you think it is?"

He looked at the position of the sun in the sky and checked his own temperature readout. "Late summer. August, maybe. It's going to get a lot warmer."

They walked side by side, heading toward the fire's general location. Each step seemed more difficult than the last.

"Were you ever stationed around here?" Sif asked, knowing there were a few Air Force bases in this part of the States.

"No, but I've been here in the summer. Ellsworth, Rapid City, about fifty or sixty miles north-northeast. I spent some temporary duty time there when I was a captain. It gets hot as hell in the summer and cold as hell in the winter."

"Real garden spot, huh?"

"Yeah. The Air Force is famous for those." He paused. "Was famous."

"Like Edwards," Sif said. "A runway surrounded by miles and miles of flat desert." Edwards Air Force Base was the home of the USAF test pilot school where she and Hunter first met.

"Edwards is one of the good ones. Tyndall was more my speed, though. Panama City, Florida."

Sif had been to Tyndall, located on the Florida panhandle, east of Naval Air Station Pensacola, where she earned her wings. "I agree. No snow, lots of sun and sand."

She stopped when Hunter grabbed her arm.

"Hold on," he said. "Did you see that?"

"See what?"

"About fifty yards, eleven o'clock. I just saw something move."

Sif looked to her eleven o'clock, stared. "No, I—" Then she saw it, too.

But there wasn't just one. There were three.

"I think we just found who built the fire," Hunter said.

Fifty yards away were three people crouching beside one another, trying to hide behind some bushes. From their postures, Sif could tell they were apprehensive and scared. "Jesus, what do we do, wave?"

Trying to decide on a proper greeting would have to wait, as all three of them bounded away, heading due north.

"I think we spooked them."

"Look at us, Hunter," Sif said, holding her arms wide. "Wouldn't you be frightened if you saw two people in space suits wandering around?"

"We need to follow them."

Sif could still see them, running to the north, glancing back over their shoulders. She couldn't help but think about the Native Americans who once called this land home—these people were dressed so similarly. "If they're heading home, I bet we won't have to wait too long to meet the rest of them."

Sif and Hunter followed the three until they disappeared from sight, still heading north in an almost straight line. They *were* heading home, and it didn't matter that they were leading the strange beings in the white suits and helmets right to it. To Sif, this meant one of two things: either they were too scared to think clearly—trying to lead them away would make more sense—or wherever they were going would provide safety, probably in *numbers*.

The sun was higher, and her suit grew hot. The cooling system was working, but the first drops of sweat were tickling her lower back.

"So what's your plan, Hunter?"

"Plan for what?"

"When we meet the rest of them. Do we say, 'We come in peace. Take us to your leader'?"

"Jesus, Sif, I have no idea."

"You saw how scared they are. They're going to see us as a threat. And as soon as they get back to their village, they're more than likely going to send a welcoming party to meet us. And they might not be too welcoming."

"Maybe," Hunter said after a pause. "Hopefully, they still speak English, and we'll be able to explain who we are."

"What, through these things?" Sif said, tapping his helmet with her gloved hand. "If we're going to talk to them, we'll have to take our helmets off." The farther they walked, the less Sif felt the need to keep her suit on. If there *was* a contagion in the air that could harm them, they would have to deal with it sooner or later. Seeing other people only strengthened her desire to unlatch her helmet and toss it to the ground.

"Okay," Hunter said, "when we meet the rest of them, we'll have to appear as nonthreatening as possible. Hands in the air, that sort of thing. We don't want to take our helmets off yet. Not until we know it's safe."

*Speak for yourself,* Sif grumbled to herself, but she knew he was being cautious. If it was a disease that had changed the planet so drastically, then the survivors might have built up a resistance, an immunity she and Hunter *didn't* have. But they would have to breathe the air eventually. "Look, I understand the need for caution—you and I both agreed we should wear the suits until we knew what we were up against—but we can't stay in these things forever."

"I know. I wish I could rip this helmet off just like you do, but we can't. Not yet." Hunter stopped, leaned over to view the three people's tracks a little more closely. "Sif, look at this."

She looked, saw how the footprints seemed to scatter in the dirt, then head off to the north again. "They stopped here for a moment. Waiting to see if we were still following them?"

"Might be, but look here, and here," Hunter said, pointing at some dark spots in the dust. "What does that look like to you?"

Sif pressed a gloved finger into the dirt, lifted her hand. "It's blood. One of them is hurt."

"Can't be too bad, though. That's the first time I noticed it."

Sif stood, looked around. There was nothing around them for miles, as far as she could see. "What do you think happened?"

"I don't have any idea," Hunter replied, standing erect as well.

"We keep going?" Sif asked.

"We keep going. But we keep an eye to our back. If it was an animal that hurt one of them, I don't want it sneaking up behind us."

Sif looked over her shoulder, studied the terrain once again. In the distance, she could see *Beagle*'s nose sticking up, but nothing else. They had first aid supplies in the ship—which might come in handy if they ever caught up with the injured person—but absolutely no weapons with which to defend themselves. She suddenly felt exposed. "I'm going to head back to *Beagle* to get the first aid kit. Maybe we could help the one who's bleeding."

"You don't have to," Hunter said, patting a pouch on his suit's right leg. "I brought the basics. In case one of us got hurt."

"See? I'm not the only one who's ready for anything. Pretty good for an Air Force puke."

Five minutes later, they encountered crop fields, a sure sign that the survivors hadn't lost all of the most important skills over the years. These people were farmers. "Cornfields. I'll be damned," Sif said. She ran her gloves along the stalks—they weren't as tall as what she remembered seeing while driving across Kansas or Nebraska, and the ears were much smaller, but it was corn just the same.

"I'd be willing to bet their village is close by," Hunter said, spying a clear path heading away from the fields, worn into the ground by use. "If we follow this trail, it'll lead us right to them."

And then, Hunter fell.

It took Sif a second to register what she saw. She dropped to the ground as quickly as she could in the cumbersome suit and crawled on all fours to where Hunter lay.

He was on his back, motionless, the shaft of an arrow protruding from his face mask.

# Chapter 27

Litsa sat up, listened. There were other people inside the Dak. She grabbed her bow and slung a full quiver over her shoulder. As she ran toward the entrance, she felt the reassuring weight of the knife as its sheath bounced against her thigh. If the Takers *had* returned, they would regret ever setting foot inside her home again.

She didn't have to run far until she heard them more clearly. She stopped, nocked an arrow, and drew her bow, two more arrows at the ready, balanced between the fingers of her right hand. She rested the string against her cheek and listened.

One of them spoke. A woman's voice, familiar.

"I've got to stop, just leave me here."

"Talia? Is that you?"

Silence. Then a reply.

"Litsa?"

She released her pull on the bow and ran toward the voices. They *had* come back. Her enthusiasm quickly faded when she saw their faces. It was Talia, along with Conrad and Geller, and Talia was hurt. She was shot in the leg during the Takers' assault. The men had wrapped the wound, but it was still bleeding. Talia looked weak, her eyes half-open. "How bad?" Litsa asked.

"The bullet is still in there," Conrad said. He was a young man, late teens, and his eyes, although heavy with exhaustion, were bright with fear. "We haven't been able to stop the bleeding."

"Litsa," Talia sighed, grabbing Litsa's arm as they helped her to the ground, "thank God you're here." She was in her early twenties, a gatherer. "There's more coming, we saw them."

Litsa felt the heat rise up her neck. "Where? How far?"

"There are two of them, following us. We didn't know where else to go," Geller said. He was a little older than Conrad, but not by much.

"How *far*?"

"We moved as fast as we could," Conrad said, "but they're slower. Maybe five, ten minutes away."

Litsa searched the boy's eyes. He began his training to assume watch duties a few months back, so he knew how to handle a knife at least. "What weapons are they carrying?"

Conrad thought for a second. "None that I could see. We were close enough for them to use rifles when we first spotted them."

There was something else he was struggling with.

"What is it?" Litsa asked.

"They don't look like the others."

"In what way?"

"They're wearing white suits. Heavy, bulky. And helmets."

The Takers wore dark clothes, black to match the night, and even though they wore face masks and goggles—which were rumored to assist their night vision—Litsa had never heard of them wearing what Conrad just described.

*Maybe in the daylight, when the Riy are active, they wear different kinds of protective suits,* Litsa thought. No matter. If they were Takers, she would kill them. And she had to move. "Geller, you take Talia to Lauren's chamber. Clean the wound as best you can, and keep pressure on it." He nodded. "Conrad," she said, standing, "you're coming with me." She took the knife from her belt and handed it to him. He took it from her without hesitation, and Litsa saw the fire flicker in his eyes.

"I'll do whatever you demand, Litsa."

She slapped him on the shoulder. "Welcome to the ranks, Conrad. Today, you're a warrior."

\*\*\*

From the watchers' station above the fields, Litsa could see Conrad off to the west, partially concealed behind a clump of bushes, right where she wanted him.

And then she saw the Takers, approaching the fields. Conrad was right; they were moving slowly, almost leisurely, studying the ground as they walked. And then there were their suits—white, bulky, topped with large helmets with gold-tinted visors glinting in the sunlight. Seeing the two Takers in their white suits reminded Litsa of something she had seen as a child, but she couldn't recall exactly what. One seemed slightly larger than the other, taller. The shorter one walked slightly behind the taller one. Litsa decided the taller one was the leader. She would take him first.

As they entered the fields, Litsa readied her arrows, laying them on the ground beside her. She studied the figures closely to see if they held any weapons in their hands. As Conrad said, it didn't appear so, which infuriated her. How *dare* they return to this place, and how *dare* they think they could walk across their lands without expecting a fight.

Litsa nocked her first arrow and slowly rose to a firing position. They seemed to be studying the ground, pointing at something. Then Litsa realized what captured their interest in the dirt: a blood trail. Talia left a blood trail, and they were following it. Tracking one of the injured who escaped their raid. She pulled her bow, rested the nock of the arrow against her cheek.

When the taller one stood and pointed at the trail heading to the Dak, Litsa let her first arrow fly.

She nocked her second arrow, pulled, and then paused.

As she watched the leader go down, Litsa remembered where she had seen suits like that before.

Conrad, as instructed, made his move, blade in hand.

Litsa saw him, and started to run.

# Chapter 28

"Hunter. *Hunter.*" Sif shook him, and he grabbed her arm.

"I'm okay, just stay down," Hunter said. "My visor stopped it. I think it just grazed my cheek."

Sif wasn't about to stay down. She was pissed. She pulled her arm away and stood, suddenly glad for the thickness and bulk of their suits, regardless of how hot they were—the damn things might provide some protection, after all. She wheeled to the left, to the right, trying to spot whoever shot the arrow. And then she saw him—no, *her*—coming down a hill overlooking the fields, a bow in one hand and a handful of arrows in the other. Sif was struck by how small she seemed . . . A child? Sif raised her arms, not in surrender, but to show she was unarmed, no threat. If this girl had taken the shot from the top of the hill, she was quite skilled with her bow. It was a good fifty yards, at least. "Okay, look at me," Sif said to herself, "I'm unarmed, I'm friendly, and if you shoot an arrow at me I'll kick your scrawny ass."

"Dammit, Sif, stay down," Hunter yelled.

"Nonthreatening, right? You said it yourself. Now get up and look nonthreatening, goddammit."

Sif watched the girl stop, nock another arrow, draw it back, and aim. Sif waved her arms, and shook her head no, but of course the girl couldn't see her behind the thick visor. She turned her body toward Hunter and could see him propped up on his knees, also waving his arms. Behind him, a boy erupted from the cornstalks, a knife held high.

"Oh, *shit*. Hunter, behind you!"

Hunter turned, but the boy flashed right by, heading straight for Sif. She crouched, as well as she could in the suit, and readied herself. It wasn't a big knife, but if he hit her in the right spot, he could pierce the suit and do some real damage.

As he ran at her, Sif could see fury in his eyes—unbridled, hot, and unthinking. He was going to slam right into her. The sun glinted off the blade as he raised it above his head, and Sif could see he was going to bring it down on her. When he was two steps away, Sif dropped and rolled toward him.

It worked.

The boy wasn't ready for her unexpected move and tripped over her, landing in the dirt in a tangle. When Sif rolled to her side, she saw him stand, take a knife fighter's stance, and swap the blade to his other hand.

He was wary now, unsure of what to do.

And Sif was helpless. There was no way she could get to her feet again in time to fend him off. He also managed to catch her with the blade. There was a long tear in the fabric of her suit along her left arm. She could feel the air rushing out of the hole but felt no pain. Either the blade hadn't penetrated far enough, or she just didn't feel the cut yet. At any rate, her suit was damaged, open to the outside air. So much for worrying about exposure anymore.

Behind the boy, Sif watched the girl run up to his side. She grabbed his knife hand and spoke. "Conrad, wait."

*English.*

Sif quickly released the latches on her helmet, twisted it off, and threw it from her shoulders. As her helmet rolled in the dirt, she heard Hunter's voice through the helmet mic. "Goddammit, Sif."

The rush of fresh air was wonderful—but she would take a moment to enjoy the feeling later. "Wait, we're no threat to you. We're unarmed," Sif yelled, again showing her empty hands to them. She could see the boy was young, maybe late teens. His hair was a dirty blond, hanging in strings about his shoulders. He was scrawny, yet well muscled for his weight.

The girl wasn't a child, as Sif originally thought. She was older, maybe in her early twenties, thin, as the boy was, but her frame was tied together with strong, ropy muscles. Her black hair was gathered into a single braid, which hung over her shoulder. Her eyes were hidden behind a set of dark goggles.

Both were clad in animal skins, Caucasian, and incredibly pale, their skin so white it seemed nearly translucent. Sif wondered how anyone could live their lives in the outdoors like this and not be tanned brown by the sun.

"Who are you?" the girl shouted. Sif stared at the arrowhead pointing right at her head.

*Here goes nothing.* "I'm Commander Caitlyn Webb, United States Navy, and my partner is Lieutenant Colonel Hunter Webb, United States Air Force. We're astronauts."

"You are *Takers*," the boy shouted.

*Takers?* Sif wondered. Whatever a Taker was, they obviously didn't like them very much. "I don't know what a Taker is, Conrad, but we're not here to do you any harm. One of you is hurt, yes?" She saw he didn't particularly care for her calling him by name.

He took a step forward, and Sif locked her eyes on the knife. It looked bigger—and sharper—than before. "Hurt by *your* kind," he said coldly. "You were tracking us."

"We were following you because we're lost," Sif said. "We saw the blood in the dirt, and we know one of you is injured. Maybe we can help."

"Where are you from?" the girl asked, her voice much calmer than the young man's. Sif sat up, still keeping her hands out in front of her. She wasn't too sure they would believe her if she told them, so she decided to keep it as simple as she could. "We're from here. The United States of America." She could tell the girl had heard those words before.

"There is no States of America," the girl said. "You lie."

"No, we're not lying," Sif said. "I have my helmet off, and you could put that arrow right between my eyes if you wanted to. You managed to hit my partner from the top of the hill, so I know you're pretty good with that thing. I'm not going to fight you. I just want to talk." The girl still had her arrow pointed right at Sif's head, but Sif could tell she was starting to waver. "Please let my partner remove his helmet, okay? He might be hurt, too."

The girl paused, considering, then nodded.

Sif gestured at Hunter to take off his helmet. Then again, a little more emphatically.

Hunter undid the latches, then with a twist removed his helmet. The arrow *had* grazed his cheek, and bright blood covered the left side of his face.

"Thank you," Hunter said, taking a deep breath of fresh air. "That was one heck of a shot, um . . . I'm afraid I don't know your name."

"I am called Litsa."

"Litsa, again, that was a fine shot. You almost killed me."

"They're lying, Litsa," Conrad said. "It's a trick."

"I promise you," Sif said. "We're telling the truth."

Litsa turned to Conrad. "Sheathe your knife. We will talk to them."

"No. They shot Talia."

Whoever the Takers were, they had guns. "How badly is Talia hurt?" Sif asked. "We have medical supplies. We can help." Sif watched the girl—Litsa—slowly lower her bow. "My partner needs some attention, too. Please take us to Talia, and let us help her."

"You say you are from here, the America, yes?" Litsa asked.

"Yes." There was something in the girl's tone of voice that told Sif what she was saying was striking a chord. Sif turned and patted the American flag on her left shoulder. "The United States of America. Have you ever seen one of these before?"

Litsa nodded. "If you are from the United States of America, then you are ghosts."

"I know this is difficult to comprehend," Sif said, "but you have to believe that we mean you absolutely no harm. We're not Takers—we don't even know what a Taker is, for that matter—we're unarmed, and we're at your mercy."

Sif could tell Litsa was struggling with the decision, and for a moment thought it all might end right here, next to a cornfield in what used to be South Dakota. Then she saw Litsa nod, and breathed a sigh of relief.

"I will take you to Talia," Litsa said. "You look like you need medical attention, as well."

Sif looked down at her arm and noticed blood seeping from the tear in the fabric. "I'll be damned," she said. "Looks like you caught me after all, Conrad."

"Litsa, please," Conrad said. "We can't take them to the Dak."

"We will, and if they aren't who they say they are, we will kill them. Understood?"

Sif watched the boy nod in agreement. They weren't out of the woods yet, but they were close. "This Dak, is it your village?"

"It is our home, *was* our home, before the Takers attacked," Litsa replied. "You will stand, walk slowly, and follow this trail. We will be behind you the entire way. I will put an arrow into each of your skulls in an instant if you move off the trail. Understood?"

"Understood," Sif replied. This young woman meant business.

Hunter got to his feet, helmet in hand, and together they followed the trail, with their newfound companions close behind.

"She called it 'the Dak,'" Sif said, loud enough for Hunter to hear. "Dakota?"

"Maybe," Hunter replied. The blood was darkening on Sif's suit, and it appeared that the bleeding had stopped. "How's the arm?" he asked.

"I'm thinking it's just a good-sized scratch. Like your face."

"There goes my second career as a male model."

Sif laughed. "It'll add character. You can use some."

"You handled that pretty well, Sif. That kid had fire in his eyes. He wanted blood."

"Whoever the Takers are, they've got him pretty ticked off. Her, too. Did you see their skin?"

"I don't think they get out in the sun very often."

Sif glanced over her shoulder. As Litsa had promised, she and Conrad were close behind, and Litsa still had an arrow strung in her bow. "She's wearing goggles, and he's squinting. Do you think they aren't out in the sun very much because they live underground or something?" Then it dawned on her. They had landed in Wind Cave National Park. "I'll bet my next month's pay they live in a cave."

"You could be right. Question is, why?"

To the east, a line of drones approached *Beagle*. Behind them was another hive, one of five stretching their feelers into the Northern Territories.

Coming closer.

# Chapter 29

When they entered the mouth of the Dak cavern, Sif convinced Litsa to allow them to remove their heavy suits. Hunter unloaded the first aid supplies from his leg pouch.

Dressed in their thin, environmental-control undergarments, they made their way deeper into the cave until Sif could no longer see clearly in the dark. Her guess about Litsa and Conrad living underground was right, as they moved with ease within the shadows. "Litsa, we can't go any farther in the dark. We can't see where we're going."

"Your eyes are weak."

"No, our eyes can't see when it's pitch-black. We're accustomed to living in the light, and we can't see in the darkness as well as you can." She wondered how long it took for people living underground to develop eyesight like this, which led her to ponder just how far forward in time they had come.

"There is light farther down the passage. Torches."

"That's fine, but I can't see right *now*," Sif repeated. "Unless you're going to hold my hand and guide me." Sif caught herself. Arguing with Litsa wouldn't do them any good. "I can't go any farther. I'm sorry."

"She's right, Litsa," Hunter said. "We really can't see a thing."

"Conrad, go forward and bring a torch for our blind friends," Litsa said. "I will hold them here."

Sif felt Conrad brush past her, and his footfalls disappeared deeper into the cavern.

"How long have you lived in this place?" Hunter asked.

"I lived in other caves before this one," Litsa replied, "but this has been my home longer than the others."

"And you are farmers?"

"Yes, and hunters, when the animals venture here. We live on what's available in the Dak, and what's outside."

"My grandfather was a farmer," Hunter continued. "In Iowa, a few hundred miles southeast of here. He grew corn, just like you do. Do you still call it corn? Your crops?"

"Why would we call corn something that it is not?"

Sif couldn't help but laugh.

"I find no humor in corn, woman," Litsa said.

"Please, Litsa, call me Sif."

"Your name is Caitlyn."

*At least she was paying attention.* "I know, but Sif is my call—it's my nickname. It's what my friends call me."

"I will call you Caitlyn, then."

*So much for trying to make a connection,* Sif thought.

"Is Hunter your real name, or a nick?" Litsa asked.

Hunter laughed. "No, it's not a nickname. Hunter is my real name. Do you have a last name, Litsa?"

"I do not understand."

"My name is Hunter *Webb*. Webb is my last name, my family name."

"We have no family names. I am Litsa, a member of Joshua's clan. That is all."

"How big is Joshua's clan?" Sif asked.

"We are over a hundred bodies strong." Litsa paused, then continued. "Now, the four of us are all that remain."

"Who are they, Litsa? The Takers?" Hunter asked.

"They are murderers who take children from their beds, load them into their flying machines, and disappear. We don't know who they are or where they come from."

*Flying machines.* "They come in machines? Aircraft?" Sif asked.

The tunnel brightened as Conrad approached, torch in hand.

"That is enough questions," Litsa said. "We will attend to Talia now."

Sif turned, and for the first time saw Litsa's face in the torchlight. Within the lucent green of her irises, Sif saw nothing but determination and purpose. Her bow was still in her hand, and Sif noticed she had taken the knife away from Conrad, the blade safely sheathed and hanging from her belt. Litsa's small frame and large eyes made her appear almost elfish, but the young woman was not one who took kindly to being crossed. She was strong, because she must be. Sif could respect that. "Thank you for the torch, Litsa."

"We have delayed long enough. We go to the nursemaid's chamber. Conrad, you will guide them."

\*\*\*

When they entered the nursemaid's chamber, Sif saw a young girl lying on a stone table, her thigh wrapped in bloody cloth. In the torchlight, Sif could see she was feverish, her face covered in sweat. Her skin, just as pale as the others, looked gray, ashen. Her breathing was rapid and shallow.

"How is she, Geller?" Litsa asked.

A boy—again, young, probably late teens—looked at her and Hunter with wide eyes, not quite sure what to think. He looked for reassurance from Litsa before speaking. "I cleaned the wound as you instructed, but it is still bleeding. Any pressure causes her too much pain."

"May I?" Sif asked, as Hunter ripped open the first aid supplies. Litsa nodded. Sif approached the girl and looked into her eyes. "Talia, my name is Sif, and we're going to help you, okay?" She placed her hand on the girl's forehead, and felt the heat. "She's feverish, Hunter." Turning to Litsa, she said, "I'm going to remove the bandages and look at the wound." Again, Litsa nodded, her hand resting on the hilt of her knife.

Of the three of them, Lucas had received most of the medical training, but they all learned basic skills to handle wounds, breaks, and other injuries they might suffer while on the surface of Mars. "Talia, I'm going to take a look at your leg, okay?"

The girl stared at her, eyes vacant. Sif was glad when she nodded.

Carefully, Sif unwrapped the cloth bandages covering the wound. She was right—a gunshot. Small entry, red and inflamed. Thankfully, there wasn't any smell of gangrene yet. Sif slipped her hand beneath Talia's thigh and felt for an exit wound. The bullet was still inside. She hoped it wasn't too deep.

"That bullet needs to come out," Sif said. "She's going to need morphine. I'll need a scalpel and probe. Litsa, I'm going to need more light over here so I can see what I'm doing."

Litsa grabbed another torch from the wall and stood next to Sif.

"That's good. Thank you. We're going to give Talia something to dull the pain, but it's going to hurt."

Hunter swabbed Talia's arm with an alcohol pad and held up a syringe.

"What is that?" Litsa asked.

"It's called morphine," Hunter replied. "It'll cut some of the pain." He jabbed the needle into Talia's arm and slowly pressed the plunger.

Sif ripped open a container of surgical prep wipes and swabbed the wound with a bright yellow disinfectant. Talia groaned. "I know, it stings a little. Hang in there, kiddo." She turned to Litsa. "I'll need your boys here to help hold her down, keep her legs still. Hunter, I need you to hold her arms."

Hunter moved to the head of the table and placed his hands on Talia's shoulders. Conrad and Geller didn't move. "Litsa, I need them to hold her down, please," Sif said coolly.

Litsa glanced at the two boys, and they moved into position, each holding one of Talia's legs.

Sif put on a pair of latex surgical gloves and unwrapped the probe, basically a long, thin pair of tweezers. She looked at Talia's face. Her breathing relaxed somewhat. The morphine was taking effect. "Litsa, she's going to need something to bite down on. A stick, something like that."

Sif watched Litsa move to a basket nearby and remove a small piece of wood wrapped in leather. Sif noticed it was covered in teeth marks. "This is what we use," Litsa said.

"Perfect."

Litsa held Talia's mouth open and placed the wood in her mouth. "This is going to hurt a little, Talia. Bite down on this."

Talia nodded.

"Okay, Litsa, I need the light. Closer. And please don't light my hair on fire." For a second, Sif thought she saw a smile cross Litsa's lips.

Sif took a deep breath. "All right, boys, here we go. Hold her tight." *This is why I didn't go to medical school,* Sif thought as she lowered the probe toward the wound.

She stuck the probe into the wound, and Talia jumped. Sif pulled the probe back out. She looked at Conrad and Geller. "You two need to hold her *still,* understand?" They both nodded, this time without looking at Litsa for confirmation.

"Okay, let's try again," Sif said. She pushed the probe into the wound as gently as she could, but the quicker she could get in, find the bullet, and pull it out, the less suffering Talia would have to endure.

Talia moaned and bucked her legs, but the boys held her steady. "I know it hurts, Talia, just hang with me," Sif said.

The probe came to a stop about three inches in, away from the bone. "There it is." From what she could tell, it was just lodged in muscle. She worked the tweezers until she thought she had a good grip on the bullet, and gently pulled.

Talia screamed and arched her back.

Litsa leaned in and helped hold Talia's leg still.

The tweezers lost their grip. "Dammit."

"What is wrong?" Litsa asked, her voice tight.

"This little sucker doesn't want to come out." Sif worked the tweezers again until she felt the bullet, then tugged.

She held the bloody bullet up in the torchlight. It was a small caliber, maybe .223. She held the tweezers toward Litsa. "Here, hold this." Litsa didn't move. "I said, *hold* this, please. Hunter, I need pads and a suture kit."

Litsa took the tweezers from Sif's hand, staring at the small piece of deformed lead.

Hunter tossed Sif a handful of gauze pads, which she removed from their sterile wrappers. She placed them on the wound and applied pressure. "Okay, that's the hard part. Now I get to play seamstress." Conrad and Geller moved away. "Nope, not yet, boys. Get back here. This is still going to hurt, but not as much." Sif unwrapped the suture kit, a long, curved needle, prethreaded. "Talia, I'm going to sew the wound closed. It's going to hurt a little more, then it'll be over, okay?"

Talia nodded. Sif noticed Hunter was cupping Talia's face in his palms and looking into her eyes. "You did great, Talia. You're doing fine. Just hang in there for a few more minutes, okay?" Talia nodded again.

"All right, let's see if I remember how to do this." Sif had practiced closing a wound once during her med training, on a dummy. It seemed easy enough, but the dummy didn't have nerve endings.

Talia jumped when the needle entered, but managed to stay still as Sif quickly finished closing the wound.

She cleaned the area with the yellow disinfectant again, placed a sterile pad over it, and wrapped the leg with clean bandages from their med kit.

"Done." Sif removed her latex gloves and threw them to the dirt. She stared at Litsa, Conrad, and Geller. "*Now* do you believe us?"

# Chapter 30

Resolute

"All right, Liv, let's try it again," Lucas said.

"Liv is standing by."

Liv's patchwork voice interface fix was starting to fail. "Liv?"

"Yes, Potato."

"No, Liv. That is incorrect. My name is Lucas Hoover. Match my voice to that name, please."

"Understand. Will comply."

"Okay, Liv, one more time." *More like the seventeenth time.*

"Liv is standing by."

"Liv?"

"Yes, Hoover."

"Very good, Liv. That is correct." Being all alone on *Resolute* was bad enough, but conversing with an AI who couldn't even get his name right was worse.

"Liv is standing by for request."

"Liv complete. I'm just glad you got my name right for once." Lucas decided to give Liv one more test to see if she was really working correctly. "Liv, who am I?"

"You are Potato, but you asked me to call you Hoover."

Lucas threw his hands up into the air and shook his head. "Liv dear, my name is not *Potato*."

"Your name is Potato, but you asked me to call you—"

"Liv complete." Lucas turned his attention back to the viewer controls, which also seemed to be on the fritz. "Maybe I can get *this* thing to work. At least it doesn't talk back."

He last heard from Sif two days ago—and nothing since. She said she was handling the reentry manually, which meant something went wrong with the nav system. He had watched Sif handle *Beagle* in simulations and knew she could fly her better than anyone else, but a manual entry—conducted on the fly—was something Lucas wasn't sure even Sif could do.

*Resolute* had overflown the landing coordinates once since then, but without the viewer operational, there was no way for him to see if *Beagle* was on the surface. No contact for two days could mean they were able to reach the surface but were hurt and unable to talk. Or maybe there was some sort of mechanical problem keeping them from making contact.

Both possible but not likely. There was only one reason why he heard nothing more from Sif and Hunter. They had burned up during reentry, and he would never hear from them again.

He was in orbit, 150 miles above an Earth he no longer knew, and completely alone. He would eventually have to go down to the surface, too. The ship's stores could sustain one person for quite a while but would eventually run out. The cargo landers could make it to the surface with a few simple software modifications, and after sending them down he could use the escape capsule.

It wasn't a question of *whether* he could leave, but rather *when*.

"Liv, project next overflight opportunity over *Beagle* landing coordinates." *Resolute* orbited Earth every ninety minutes, but it took three days before it passed over the same spot on the ground again.

"Next overflight in seventeen hours, thirty-four minutes."

Maybe, if he could get the viewer up and working by then, he could at least confirm whether they made it or not.

"Liv, state current geographic position of *Resolute* over surface. State next landfall."

"*Resolute* is over the Northern Hemisphere nearing the Arctic Circle. Next landfall over Queen Elizabeth Islands, Canada, in three minutes, ten seconds."

The communication window would be short, as *Resolute* would pass far eastward of *Beagle*'s planned touchdown point.

But it didn't matter anyway. Sif and Hunter were surely dead.

"Hoover, incoming transmission."

Lucas's heart jumped into his throat. "Liv, send transmission to overhead speakers, please."

"Understand. Will comply."

Static filled the compartment. And then, a voice.

# Chapter 31

Sif sat near the fire but couldn't shake the chill seeping into her bones. This cave—the Dak, as Litsa called it—was dark, damp, and downright cold. Her undergarment didn't provide much protection. To Hunter, she said, "We need to get back to *Beagle*. Sitting around in my underwear isn't going to cut it."

"Here," Litsa said, tossing her what looked like an animal skin, hair on hide. "This will help."

Sif's first foray into the world of emergency surgery earned her the respect of Litsa and the two boys. Hunter gave Talia an antibiotic injection afterward, and she was resting comfortably. Her fever was almost gone, and as far as Sif could tell, she was going to recover. Sif took the hide and wrapped it around her shoulders. "Thank you."

Litsa nodded slightly and squatted by the fire, pulling her knees up to her chest.

They were in what Litsa called the watchers' chamber, where the watch standers and warriors slept. Sif counted thirty woven mats on the cave floor, with three of them currently occupied by Talia, Conrad, and Geller. The two boys were wide-awake, staring at her and Hunter, and neither had said a word since Sif removed the bullet from Talia's thigh.

Even when they returned to the Dak's entrance and worked together to roll the heavy stone into place, effectively sealing the mouth of the cave, they remained silent, seemingly afraid to look them in the eyes. Sif wondered what they were thinking.

Litsa sat across from Sif and Hunter, the fire between them. Her body language no longer communicated a tense wariness as when they first entered the Dak.

"Who is Beagle?" Litsa asked.

Sif and Hunter glanced at each other, thinking the same thing. *It's our spaceship, and we've come here from the future. Yeah, that doesn't sound crazy.* Hunter spoke first. "*Beagle* isn't a who, it's a what. It's the name of our craft. We traveled here in it, and we have supplies we'll need to retrieve."

"Warmer clothes would be nice," Sif said. "I haven't been this cold in a long time." The temperature, Sif noticed, didn't seem to bother Litsa, even though she was barely wearing anything.

"Did you come from the stars?" Litsa asked.

*Well, I'll be damned.* In order for Litsa to ask that question, at least some of their history had to have been passed down. "Yes, we did," Sif replied. "How did you know?"

"When I saw your white suits, I remembered something I'd seen as a child." Litsa caught Hunter's gaze. "It made me doubt whether or not you were Takers, but not until after my first arrow found its mark. I decided to let you live so I could question you."

"I do appreciate that," Hunter said. "Both of us do, right, Sif?"

"Yep. Happy to be here." She flashed him a fake smile.

"So," Hunter continued, "do you have any more doubts about who we are?"

Litsa shook her head. "I no longer believe you are a threat to us, but I do not understand why you are here."

"It's a long story, Litsa, believe me," Sif said. She was surprised when Litsa rose, seemingly ignoring her, stepped around the fire, and knelt by Hunter. She lifted his chin, turned his head, and looked at the wound on his cheek. "I am sorry this happened," she said. "The helmet saved your life."

Sif had cleaned Hunter's wound after finishing with Talia. It would leave a scar but wasn't deep enough to require stitches. The cut on her arm was superficial, too. "My arm is going to be fine, if anyone is wondering."

Litsa smiled. It wasn't a friendly smile, more condescending than anything else. "It was but a scratch," Litsa said, rising to her feet and taking Hunter by the arm. "Come. There is something I must show you." She grabbed the nearest torch and led him into the shadows.

"Hey," Sif yelled, shrugging the hide from her shoulders. "Is this a private party, or am I supposed to sit here and watch the fire?"

Litsa turned, and Sif saw that same smile again. "I expected you to follow," Litsa said.

"You expected right."

Litsa guided them farther into the Dak, taking a passage that brought them closer to the surface. The air wasn't as damp, and it was much warmer. *Why couldn't they live up here?* Sif wondered, finding the environment more to her liking. When they reached the end of the passage, Litsa led them into a small chamber. Sif saw books—stacks of them—and what appeared to be other records, wrapped in animal skins and bound by thin strips of hide.

Litsa released Hunter's hand and placed her torch into a holder on the wall. She apparently knew exactly what she was looking for, as she only searched for a few seconds. In her hands, she held a large, flat object wrapped in skins. Sif watched as Litsa carefully untied the bindings and unfolded the layers of hide. When she saw what was inside, Sif's heart skipped a beat.

It was a thin book, and on its cover was a caricature of an astronaut standing beside the leg of a lunar lander. "*We Came in Peace*," Sif said. "I've seen that book before. My grandparents had a copy."

Litsa placed the book on a nearby stone table and gently opened it. Inside was a two-page picture that Sif recognized as a late 1960s–era Saturn V moon rocket standing next to its gantry tower.

"I've seen this book before, too," Hunter said. "I think *my* grandparents had one. I'll be darned."

"Is this your *Beagle*?" Litsa asked.

Sif saw the pages were yellowed, delicate, as if they would crumble if handled too roughly. She gently placed her finger on the page and felt an immediate connection to a world that no longer existed. "This isn't our *Beagle*, Litsa—this one is much larger—but it's close. When we go back to our ship tomorrow morning, you can see it for yourself."

"No," Litsa said sharply, causing Sif to pull her hand back. "You cannot go back to your *Beagle* during the day. We must travel at night."

"Why?" Hunter asked.

"It is safer in the darkness."

"Safer from what?" They had been outside in the daylight, and Sif hadn't seen anything dangerous, apart from an arrow or two, she reminded herself.

"The Riy are active when the sun is in the sky," Litsa said.

*That doesn't sound good.* "What are the Riy?" Sif asked.

Litsa was obviously confused. "The Riy . . . are the Riy."

"We don't understand, Litsa," Hunter said. "We don't know what a *Riy* is."

Litsa looked genuinely surprised. "There are no Riy where you come from?"

"Can you show us what a Riy is?" Sif said, glancing at the stacks of bound records, hoping to avoid her question for the time being.

Litsa nodded. "I will teach you of the Riy," she said, turning toward the stacks.

Sif watched as Litsa methodically unwrapped their historical records—newspapers, computer printouts, even handwritten accounts. Most were wrapped in layers of animal skins, but others were sealed in plastic storage bags, placed there by the long-dead hands of those who knew that the record of what happened needed to be preserved.

"We were taught to wrap and bind them this way, to keep them from crumbling, falling apart," Litsa explained. "The plastic keeps them dry, and the skins protect them from damage. We have other books, things that show what life was like before the Riy, but this is the first one that tells of their birth."

Litsa gently handed Sif and Hunter a newspaper article. The paper was yellowed, brittle, but the print was still visible. "Do you still think it's really been less than a hundred years?" Sif asked. "This looks much older."

Hunter shrugged. "Even with all their precautions, it could've been out in the elements for a while before—"

"Litsa," Sif said, looking into Litsa's large, almost luminous eyes. They knew where they were, but still had no idea of *when*. "Do you know what year it is? Today, I mean?"

Again, confusion crossed Litsa's face. Only crazy people didn't know what year it was.

"It is year 193, AA, and we are approaching the end of the second season."

"Summer? Is that what you mean by second season?"

Litsa glanced at the book she had first shown them, with the astronaut on the cover. "I do not understand why you are—how you cannot know—"

"Litsa, please, I know this must seem strange, but we need to know what year it is," Hunter said, his voice soft, as if speaking to a child. "You said 193, AA. What does AA mean?"

Litsa pointed at the article Sif held gently in her hands. Sif noticed the date—June 2025, just a few months after they launched on their mission to Mars.

"Our years started then, when the Riy were first born. The A and A mean 'after apocalypse.' It was what I was taught."

So there it was. It hadn't been less than a hundred years, as Hunter first guessed. The year—according to *their* calendar—was 2218. One hundred and ninety-three years—almost two *centuries*—since the sunny day in south Florida when they blasted off from the Cape on their way to Mars.

As they read more and more of the records, Hunter and Sif learned of Litsa's enemy, the terrible things that killed everyone they knew and destroyed the civilization they once were a part of.

They learned of the monsters that ruled the day, pushed the survivors to live underground, and made the darkness humanity's new realm.

They learned of the Riy.

It all began on June 18, 2025.

# Chapter 32

WORLD REACTS TO RUSSIAN STRIKE

President Confers with Top Advisors

WASHINGTON (AP) June 18, 2025—White House spokesman Drake Phillips confirmed reports of a nuclear strike by Russian forces in northern Ukraine and southern Belarus approximately eight hours ago, involving what Phillips called a "significant number" of nuclear weapons. President Masterson has called for an emergency session of the UN Security Council, which will meet this morning to address the Russian action. Russian government spokesperson Sergey Servenko stated the attack was in response to "an immediate threat to world peace and well-being" and that all of

Russia's strategic forces had returned to a normal peacetime footing. Servenko stated Russian president Ulyanov would be addressing the UN Security Council later in the day to explain why he ordered the first nuclear strike the world has seen since 1945, when the United States dropped two atomic bombs on the Japanese cities of Hiroshima and Nagasaki to prevent what he said was "the certain loss of millions of lives had the war been allowed to continue. Russia faced a similar choice and decided to act now, in order to save countless lives." US State Department spokesman Roger Willard noted Ulyanov's statement was the first time Russia had characterized the American use of atomic bombs to end World War II in this way.

Sif couldn't believe what she was reading. There had been a nuclear war, but only one side played the game. It was as if Russia drew its big gun, stuck the barrel against its foot, and pulled the trigger. More than once.

She handed the article to Hunter and read on, methodically poring over the records in chronological order as Litsa brought them to her.

What had appeared to the rest of the world at first to be a brutal act of insanity by a nationalistic, land-grabbing Russian leader became something different as soon as the truth trickled out.

Something happened in and around the old Chernobyl reactor, Sif learned, something the Ukrainians—and the Russians—didn't understand, and couldn't control. The nukes were a desperate attempt to stop something horrid that was spreading through the forests of northern Ukraine, a fast-moving, infectious plague unlike anything anyone could have possibly imagined, except in—as one reporter phrased it—"the darkest hours of the night, when the mind explores those hidden places, the darkened, silent rooms of the psyche where terror waits." *The guy might have a knack for the melodramatic,* Sif thought, *but he hit the nail on the head.*

Once the New Containment Unit was blown apart (the reason for which Sif couldn't quite decipher, as the accusations and theories spanned a number of different possibilities, never settling on a single one), what was inside—life, where life shouldn't exist—was released.

Inside the Chernobyl complex was a black fungus clinging to the walls of the ruined reactor, bathed in the invisible glow of gamma radiation and converting it to life-sustaining energy. The article called it a "radiotrophic fungus"—a harmless organism using melanin to convert gamma radiation into energy, like a plant using photosynthesis to harness the sun's rays. Once discovered, it became the focus of numerous scientific studies.

Sif read an investigative article that pointed to a probable cause for the disaster—a man-made cause. At the time of the Chernobyl attack, an experiment was under way. Robotic probes were testing, sampling, changing what nature made into something more *useful,* although it was never clear to the reporter what *useful* exactly meant. It was safe to experiment there, the scientists thought, deep inside a building sealed beneath a massive steel enclosure, and hidden away from prying, questioning eyes.

Then the explosion came. The release. And then, the birth of something horrible.

The company in charge of the experiment, a bio-lab unit headquartered in Chicago, lamented the loss of its own people who were on the ground, but categorically denied their experiments caused, or even contributed to, the catastrophe.

*Yeah, right.* She read on, this time from a translated Ukrainian article picked up by AP.

It was only a few people at first. Two or three falling ill, racked by bouts of coughing, unaware of the apocalyptic fury they expelled from their blackened lungs with each hacking breath. More were exposed, and the spread picked up speed. People speculated that if the authorities had acted more quickly, the epidemic could have been contained to the Chernobyl region, but no one knew what was causing the illness, and the quarantine order came much too late.

*It* was out. Mutating. Living. And the hosts were plentiful.

Within days of the first cases, hundreds fell ill, and the first few began to change. The doctors watched them die—hearts stopped beating, brain functioning flatlined—but still, they moved. Underneath a black, tar-like filth that spilled from their pores, what once were living, breathing human beings became hosts to a mindless organism driven by the need to propagate, to spread itself to new hosts, to survive.

The mobile field hospitals were the first to fall.

More scientists came, more aid workers—more hosts for the new life-form. The calls for help were answered, and the soldiers came.

They, too, soon fell, faced with an enemy that bullets could not stop, and that could consume them with a single breath.

This article had pictures, Sif saw. People in hospital beds, their bodies partially covered in a thick, black substance, while people in bio-suits stood close by, ignorant of the true nature of what they were seeing and helpless to save their patients.

There were other pictures, too.

There were monsters in the forests around Chernobyl. Black things, moving shadows. Sif learned the Ukrainians called them Riy. *Swarm.*

She nudged Hunter. "The Riy . . . Look. This is what they are."

"Jesus," Hunter said. "What could do that to a person?"

"The Riy are not people," Litsa said. "Not anymore. Once they breathe in the black mist, they are doomed to become Riy. Nothing can stop it. Once they transform, they look much like those old pictures. At first, in the old times, they stood upright as we do, but they changed."

*The old times.* Her *time.* Sif moved to the next stack, handling each piece of paper carefully in order not to damage it. She might be touching the only records that still existed, a twenty-third-century version of the Library of Alexandria. She read on.

The Russian bombs—each thermonuclear flash radiating a thermal pulse hotter than the surface of the sun—seemed to end it all. Everyone thought the Riy—the terrible monsters in the forests—were eradicated. But an act of desperation became the ultimate act of suicide, for the bombs carried what was left of the Riy high into the atmosphere, where it followed the winds and fell from the skies with the fallout.

Moscow was first. Months after the detonations, the infected flooded the hospitals, coughing, expelling a thick, black slime from ruined lungs. They used the subway, buses, taxis. They went to stores, stadiums, everywhere. The spread picked up momentum and increased exponentially.

Japan, Korea, China, huge population centers, fell ill, and the spread continued. In weeks, it crossed oceans, aloft in the winds, or onboard aircraft and ships. Precautions were taken—travelers from the Far East were quarantined and, later, banned. Air travel nearly ceased as governments finally grasped the gravity of the situation they were facing.

Trouble was, they had no idea how to stop it. The infected people could be rounded up, kept away from the healthy, but it didn't matter. The fallout continued to trickle down, spore by spore, finding its way into healthy, unprotected lungs.

The transformations were slower than what was reported by the Russian and Ukrainian forces when they first encountered the Riy— taking weeks until symptoms manifested—but once they did, the eruption of the black fungal growth from the skin was astoundingly rapid. Death came quickly. Animation—the rebirth, as one reporter unfortunately termed it—followed just as fast.

By the time the infectious spores had ravaged a large number of Russian and Chinese urban centers, they were spreading across the United States, starting on the West Coast. Unplanned evacuations occurred, mass migrations as people raced inland, hoping to escape. Social order—tenuous even in the best of times—quickly dissolved into riots, looting, and outright murder. In Los Angeles, Sacramento, San Francisco, and San Diego, there were no longer any local governments, no police. It all dissolved with nary a whimper, so quickly, and the simple desire to survive became the new rule of law. Take, or starve. Kill, or be killed. In her hands, Sif held a handwritten note, dated December 23, 2025.

> *Jennifer,*
>
> *We're leaving for Ohio tonight. My dad says we can't wait any longer. We're going to live with my aunt Laura for a while. We can't take Jasper with us, so if you find him, can you please take care of him? I left food and water in the kitchen, and Dad says we can keep the front door open in case he wanders back home.*
> *I don't think we're coming back.*
> *Susan*
> *P.S. Dad says you guys should leave, too.*

Sif stared at the note for a long time. A girl, maybe in her teens, saying good-bye to her friend and worrying about a lost pet. *She had no idea what was happening.* Sif realized that Susan—whose note from two hundred years past she now held in her hand—was alive the day they blasted off for Mars. As they screamed into the sky, everyone down below had no idea that in a few months, everything was going to change.

She reverently placed the note back in its plastic bag and set it aside.

Sif read on.

On the other side of the globe, it was getting much worse.

Five months after the spread began, the mass executions started. Camps were erected, where those suspected of being exposed—called "coughers"—were herded. Close quarters, perfect conditions for the spores to spread even faster. And when they did, entire camps were eradicated. Thousands of people—infected and healthy—disappeared in Russia. Millions in China. In Japan, the dirty, stinking smoke from the funeral pyres darkened the skies.

India was next. Then, the Middle East. In a year, Africa, Europe. Two years, Australia, New Zealand. It was worse in the warmer climates, where the spread took hold much more quickly. The infected seemed to thrive in the sun, and, once transformed, only moved during the day. At night, they grew sluggish, hiding away wherever they could find some sort of concealment until the sun rose again. A simple organism that once used gamma radiation as an energy source mutated to use the sun's rays much like a plant uses photosynthesis to convert sunlight to energy.

As the tiny filaments that once held humanity together around the globe snapped, iron-fisted despots saw the chaos as opportunity and acted against old foes. Wars erupted here and there, some small, some not. In everyday life and on battlefields, humanity turned on humanity, and the killing spiraled out of control.

Stories from the normal press outlets—AP, CNN, Reuters—disappeared, replaced by personal bylines, people writing about what they were seeing, because the news business was fading away.

It took eight years for the United States to fall, Sif learned, but the Stars and Stripes stopped flying years earlier, replaced by the banners of regional leaders, rogue generals, and tin-pot dictators.

In a containment camp located in Louisiana—part of what was called the Southern Region—the infections spread beyond the ability of the people to control it, and within hours, the mutated humans coalesced into a huge mound of infected bodies and essentially became a single organism made up of many parts. It came to be known as a hive, and it was the first of many. Around the globe, wherever the Riy were massed, hives were born. The cities became breeding grounds, as the Riy consumed more and more.

The cities were burned, from the air and by those on the ground, but the days of coordinated, multinational efforts quickly passed away. It was never enough.

As she dug further into the records, printed copy became scarce, replaced with handwritten accounts. The survivors fled to the mountains, the plains, heading north and south, away from the mass of Riy hives. In the span of a single decade, a worldwide population driven by technology found itself pushed back into the Middle Ages, as everything around them fell apart at the seams.

As the next ten years dragged on, millions died from the elements, and millions more starved to death. But some found a way to survive. They learned the old ways, how to live off the land, how to hunt, farm, how to scratch and claw for every moment of survival.

The accounts became a simple numbers game—handwritten lists recording births, and deaths. Places where they lived, locations of the Riy, and when groups decided to move. The most recent records—from the last thirty years or so—mentioned the Takers, people dressed in military suits and masks, who appeared without warning to kidnap entire groups of people, never to be seen again. Litsa's people found solace in the caverns, safety in the dark. Hidden from the sunlight, from the Riy . . . and from the Takers.

Until now.

***

It took two hours for Sif and Hunter to read through the records and learn how the planet they had left was torn apart, killed by an organism that flourished in a moment of man-made chaos and swept aside the ruling species.

It was still Earth, but it was different now, and would never be the same. Sif thought of the Riy and wondered if the blackened areas of the planet seen from orbit were gigantic Riy colonies, if that was even the right word to describe it. If so, it managed to cover a good portion of the globe.

She found herself wanting to see the Riy, up close. Maybe learn how to use a bow like Litsa and send some flaming arrows into them.

But there was something else that was bothering her, apart from the Riy. It was clear that some people had escaped the destruction and still had access to technology. They were still flying airplanes, for Christ's sake, hopping from place to place to conduct their raids on what were basically defenseless people merely trying to survive in this new world. These raiders, the Takers, whoever they were, probably weren't forced to scratch and claw to survive like Litsa's people and, maybe, weren't forced to live underground, either.

Sif didn't like bullies. "Litsa," she said. "Tell me about the Takers."

Litsa grabbed a warrior's bow lying beside an empty mat. "Do you know how to use one of these?" She tossed it to Sif.

Sif caught it in midair and stood. "I do, but I'm better with a rifle."

"Only Takers have rifles," Litsa spat back. "And bullets do nothing against the Riy."

"I am no *Taker*," Sif spat right back. She tossed the bow right back to Litsa. "Teach me how to use this as well as you do, and I will kill the Riy right alongside you."

"Have you ever killed before?" Litsa asked.

"I've killed before," Sif said. "More times than you want to know."

Litsa turned toward Hunter. "And you?"

"Yes, I've killed before, too. Before we . . . went to the stars, we were soldiers. Sworn to protect the people of our country, just as you protect the people here. It was our job. Killing wasn't something we enjoyed, but when forced to, we did."

"You were warriors, then, for the United States of America. In the old times."

"Yes, Litsa. In the old times. That's where we're from," Sif said.

Litsa nodded and sat down, hugging her knees to her chest. Her luminous eyes showed no shock, no fear, just an innocent inquisitiveness.

Sif sat next to Hunter. "We're astronauts, Litsa, just like the people in the first book you showed us. We launched on April 10, 2025. One hundred and ninety-three years ago, when your years started, we were on our way to Mars." Sif saw a spark of recognition in Litsa's eyes.

"Mars?" she asked. "The planet Mars?"

Hunter spoke up. "That's right. Sif, Lucas, and I were going to be the first people to travel to another planet."

"Lucas?" Litsa asked. "There is another of you?"

"Lucas Hoover, the third person on our crew," Sif said, pointing to the cave's ceiling. "He's up there, right now, in orbit on board our ship."

"But you said your ship landed not far from here."

"*Beagle* is what we used to come down to Earth," Hunter explained, "from our much larger ship called *Resolute*."

Sif watched Litsa shift her glance to the top of the cavern. "And this ship, it is still in the sky?"

"Orbiting Earth. She's about one hundred fifty miles up, in space, going around and around," Sif said, making a circular motion with her finger. "While we were still aboard, we saw what looked like a large, circular fire, and that's why we decided to land here. We hoped to find people. And we did."

Sif watched as Litsa narrowed her eyes and slightly tilted her head. "When did you see this fire?"

"A couple of days ago. At night."

"It was when we were fighting the hive," Litsa said, her voice full of astonishment. "We spread a circle of oil around it and set it on fire. And from the sky, you saw it?"

Sif nodded. "Like Hunter said, we knew it had to be made by people, because of its shape. So that's why we set *Beagle* down so close." Then she remembered reading about the hives. "There was a hive that close?"

"Yes, it was very near. The drones were in the crops, and we had to make it move away."

"Drones?" Hunter asked.

"Parts of the hive that spread out and scout ahead, to see what's in front of the hive. Looking for more life to take."

"And did you get it—the hive—to move away?" Sif asked.

"It was a large hive, much too big for us to burn the entire thing. We set enough of it on fire, though, that it moved off to the east."

"Tell us more about the Riy, Litsa," Hunter said. "If we're going to help you fight these things, we need to know everything about them."

Litsa stood and smiled. For the first time, Sif felt as if her smile was genuine. "I will," Litsa said, "but if you will be fighting by my side, I need to know everything about *you*."

"Fair enough," Hunter said, nodding his head. "Some of this is going to sound crazy, and to be honest Sif and I are still trying to understand it all ourselves."

"I will listen and decide for myself," Litsa said.

Hunter explained what happened while on the way to Mars and how *Resolute* was sent forward in time. Sif watched Litsa's face the entire time—she was taking it in, absorbing every word. This girl, who had spent her entire existence out in the elements literally running for her life—from the Riy and from the Takers—was hanging on Hunter's every word. As they went through the historical records, Sif had the impression that Litsa had spent a lot of time with the old books and papers, studying the pictures of the "old times," and listening to Hunter's explanation was making it all real to her. And Sif was glad she had, because if Litsa had never seen the book with the astronaut on the front, she and Hunter would be facedown in the dirt, pierced by God knows how many arrows.

Hunter continued, telling Litsa how different Earth looked now compared to the Earth they left—completely dark at night, the cities abandoned and overgrown, and the band of blackened terrain around the equatorial regions, spreading north and south.

"It is Riy," Litsa suddenly said. "The blackened places you describe, it is Riy. There are stories about the lands you saw from space. No man can go there, ever again. The farther south, the more dangerous it becomes. The hives come from the south."

Sif wanted to know more. "These hives, Litsa. You said they—the drones—are searching for more life to take?"

"The hives are made of the lives they take, both people and animals. The drones make a black mist when triggered—when they sense movement nearby."

"Spores," Hunter said.

"When the mist is inhaled," Litsa continued, "the change begins. When it's complete, the person—or animal—returns to the hive, where it is absorbed. It becomes part of the larger Riy." Sif watched as Litsa shifted her glance to the side, staring into the distance, remembering. "I've seen the insides of a hive. A small one, which we burned until it died. It was full of bones. Skulls, ribs, the skeletons of all it consumed. The remains of its drones."

"The drones are people?" Sif asked.

"What *used* to be people."

"How often do the hives make it this far north?" Hunter asked.

"There have been more the last few years. We've managed to move them off."

"When we go to the ship, tomorrow morning, do you think we might see one?" Sif immediately caught the look in Litsa's eyes. "Okay, I know you said it wasn't safe. I got that. I also don't care. We need to get back to the ship so I can change out of this goddamn underwear." Sif turned to Hunter. "Agree?"

"Agree," he said. "Litsa, danger or no danger, we need to go back to *Beagle* to retrieve some items. We'd like you to accompany us."

"It is safer in the dark."

"But we can't *see* in the dark," Sif said. "Not as well as you can."

"Then I will guide you there. Right now."

"Right now?"

"That is what I said."

Sif saw a glimmer of that condescending smile again, but this time, it didn't bother her. She was starting to respect Litsa for what she was—a tough, no-nonsense fighter who wasn't willing to let her guard down. "I'm game. Hunter?"

"Yep. Let's go." He stood and brushed the dirt from his legs.

Litsa turned toward Conrad and Geller, who were silently watching the entire time. Sif saw from the looks on their faces neither one of them thought what Litsa was doing was a good idea. "I will take them to their *Beagle*. You will watch over Talia."

"That is—" Conrad started to say, but Litsa cut him off.

"You will watch over Talia," Litsa said, her voice forceful. "Understood?"

Conrad nodded, and cut his eyes toward Sif. She saw there wasn't an ounce of trust there.

"I know you don't trust us, even after we saved your girl there," Sif said, "but you have nothing to worry about. We aren't going to hurt any of you." Sif was a little surprised when she heard Litsa laugh.

"As if you could," Litsa said as she tossed a torch toward Sif. "Carry this, and try not to light your hair on fire."

Sif grabbed the torch in midair. "Good one. Don't worry. I won't."

Litsa handed Hunter a torch, as well.

"Follow me," Litsa said as she turned and moved toward the Dak's entrance.

"She got you," Hunter whispered as he walked beside Sif.

She turned and saw him grinning from ear to ear. "Really? You enjoyed that, did you?"

"She's pretty sharp, Sif, especially considering the kind of life she's lived."

"If you'd told me the planet would be wiped out by some sort of mutated monster-fungus," Sif said, "I'd have said modern man was done for—no grocery stores, no Internet, no nothing—but they survived. *She* survived."

Litsa was a few strides ahead, her torch lighting the way.

"I wonder if all women now are like her," Sif said.

"What do you mean?"

"She's like Betty Rubble went to Ranger school, that's what I mean."

"Yeah, she's tough," Hunter said. "A lot like someone else I know."

Sif quickly changed the subject. "Once we get what we need from the ship, we need to think about getting our hands on a radio. And you're thinking Ellsworth, right?"

"Exactly. It'll take a few days to get there on foot, but it's our best bet."

"Agreed. Hopefully we can talk Ranger Rubble up there into coming along. She knows the dangers out there better than we do."

"I think she's beginning to trust us. Your emergency surgery back there really made an impression."

"I hope so." Sif was still angry knowing an innocent girl was shot by people who took whole families away, for what reason she could only wonder. "What's your theory on the Takers?"

"No clue. Litsa mentioned they had flying machines, though, and Ellsworth has a runway. Maybe we'll find some answers there, along with a radio."

"As long as we can get in touch with Lucas, I'll be happy."

As they neared the Dak's mouth, Sif felt her heart rate increase. The Riy were out there, and she wanted to see one—to see a hive—for herself. In a way, everything up to this point seemed like a strange dream, but seeing the Riy with her own eyes would make it real.

# Chapter 33

Once more, Sif was struck by the air. The night was calm, the sky clear. Above, the dome of stars twinkled brightly. It seemed as if she could reach out her hand and touch them. Decades with no pollution must have made a difference.

"The Riy are less dangerous at night, but they are still a threat," Litsa said. "Follow me closely, and listen to what I say. If there is a hive nearby, there are usually a few drones close to the main body. Nighttime sentinels. They will be sluggish but can still react. And if they do, the jumpers will come."

"Jumpers?" Sif asked. This was new.

"Pods ejected from the hive when the drones are triggered. They are sensitive to heat and motion, but like the drones, they will be sluggish, also."

"What do these jumpers do?"

"They . . . jump," Litsa said, her voice betraying her confusion of how people who came from the old times—where things were more advanced—couldn't grasp the meaning of a simple word.

"Okay, got it," Sif said. "They jump. What do they do after they jump?"

"If they land near you, and they sense you, they explode."

"Explode." Sif didn't like the sound of that.

"Yes, they explode," Litsa said, tilting her head slightly. "You know what that means, don't you?"

Sif couldn't help but laugh. "I know what *explode* means." She paused, then yelled, "Boom!" Sif grinned when Litsa jumped a little.

"Yes, like that," Litsa said, obviously annoyed at Sif's attempt to startle her. "They explode and cover whatever is nearby with the black mist. If you're close, you die."

"More spores," Hunter said. "Fruiting bodies."

Sif turned to him. "Fruiting what?"

"Fruiting bodies. Some forms of fungus produce pods that burst open, releasing spores."

"Did they teach you that in pilot training?"

"Nope. High school biology, Miss Higgins."

"We are wasting time," Litsa interrupted. "We only have a few hours of darkness left, and I don't want to be out here when the sun comes up. Now, you said you landed your ship close to where you saw our fire, correct?"

"Correct," Hunter said.

"It is this way. And do not make any more loud noises. They're sensitive to sound, too." Litsa took off at a slow run. Hunter and Sif looked at each other, then ran to catch up.

***

Once they neared the crops, Litsa slowed, keeping her torch out in front of her. Sif and Hunter stayed close behind.

"We will go around the crops, in case they are in the fields."

Sif looked at the rows of corn standing tall and silent in the dark. She was glad they wouldn't be going through the rows, as nothing good ever came of walking into a cornfield in the dead of night, at least in the movies.

"You told us you harvested at night, right?" Hunter asked. It was one of the few questions Litsa was willing to answer while they were on their way to the Dak.

"We do, but there are many of us, many more torches. And I don't want to lose you in there."

As they made their way around the fields, the moon rose in the east, casting an eerie glow over the shadowy landscape. Litsa stopped in her tracks and raised her hand in a silent gesture to stop. She crouched, and so did Sif and Hunter.

"What is it?" Hunter asked.

"The Riy. They are near."

Sif was surprised by the icy fingers that ran up her back, like a spider crawling toward her neck. "Where?"

She watched as Litsa tilted her head and sniffed the air. Once. Twice. Three times.

Sif sniffed, too, and she caught the scent. "Jesus Christ."

Litsa stood and turned toward them. Sif was again struck by her eyes, which seemed even more luminous out here in the open. "There is a hive, probably to the north. We will avoid it."

"Good idea," Sif said. "So, that stench. Is that what they smell like?"

"Yes. It is the scent of the Riy."

Sif had smelled something similar before, and the memory of it sickened her. It was dirty, unclean, reminding her of a bombed-out hotel room in Kuwait where they found the body of a dead insurgent. He had been there for a while, too. To her, the Riy smelled like a decomposing body, but there was something else, too. An animal smell, like a cattle feedlot or a pig farm. "How close is it?"

"Depending on its size, maybe fifty yards or so. Closer, if it's a smaller one."

"And the drones, they're nearby, too?"

"They should be, yes."

Sif's desire to see one up close suddenly seemed less important than it had just a little while ago. Out here, at night, she wanted to get to the ship, collect what they needed, and get back to the Dak. Quickly. "Okay, Litsa. Lead the way."

They swung south for a short time, then turned back toward the location of the fire. As they approached a hill, Litsa stopped, again sniffing the air. Sif could still taste the hive's stench and knew she probably would for days.

"This is where we fought the hive, right over that rise," Litsa said. "It was down below, in a draw. The fire was here."

"And it's empty now? The draw, I mean?" Sif asked.

"It should be. I cannot smell the Riy here, but the wind has shifted. We will avoid the draw, too, just in case."

Sif wished she had a pair of night-vision goggles and wondered if they might be able to find a pair or two at Ellsworth.

Hunter looked around, trying to get his bearings. *Beagle* was no more than a quarter mile away, probably to the northeast. "*Beagle* is in that direction," he said, pointing.

Sif looked to the northeast, wondering why she couldn't see the ship's perimeter lights by now. "Hunter, I don't see the lights."

"I know. I noticed that, too. We should be able to see her by now."

"Your ship has lights?" Litsa asked.

"Yes," Hunter replied. "Exterior floodlights that illuminate the area around—"

"They are bright, yes?"

Sif already knew where Litsa was going. "The Riy are attracted to the lights, aren't they."

"Yes," Litsa said. "They live in the sunlight."

Hunter hung his head. "We might not be able to see it, because it could be covered by—"

"—the Riy," Sif said, finishing his statement for him. "Well, isn't this just friggin' wonderful." Litsa said it was too dangerous to travel during the day, but nighttime wasn't turning out to be any less risky.

Hunter thought for a moment, then said, "We'll come back during daylight. If they're there, maybe they'll move away from the ship when the sun is out."

"No," Litsa said sharply. "We will go now."

"But, if the Riy are there . . ."

Litsa stepped closer to Hunter. "*If* the Riy are there. You won't know until we get closer."

"You're still willing to take us in there, even with the danger?"

Litsa held up her bow. "That is what *this* is for." She turned to Sif. "You said you wanted to see the Riy up close, yes?"

Sif felt an immediate adrenaline rush, washing away the fear she felt earlier. "Yes. I do."

"And I want to see your *Beagle*. So, we go."

Sif took a few steps toward Litsa and placed her hand on her shoulder, glad to see that Litsa didn't shrink away from her touch. "Then what are we waiting for?"

They moved slowly, cautiously, toward *Beagle*'s touchdown point. Litsa led the way, stopping every so often to smell the night air. The wind had died down, so if they approached a hive, they would be close before they smelled it. All three of them held their torches out in front, lighting the way as best they could.

And then they smelled it.

Not the Riy, but the scent of burnt vegetation.

Hunter looked around, holding his torch to the ground. He could see the blast marks from *Beagle*'s engines. He reached down and felt the scorched earth with his fingers, hardened from the intense heat.

"This is where you landed, yes?" Litsa asked.

Hunter and Sif stared at each other.

This *was* where they landed.

But *Beagle* was gone.

Out of the corner of her eye, Sif saw Litsa touch the tip of an arrow to her torch, throw her torch to the ground, and bring the flaming arrow to her bow. One fluid motion, well practiced, far too fast for Sif to react. *She thinks we're lying.* There was no ship, so Litsa surely felt as if it had all been a trick, a ruse to drag her away from the Dak. Sif clenched her teeth and closed her eyes, hating that it would end this way. She felt the heat of the flames as the arrow screamed by her cheek, and then caught the scent, heavy and sickening. She heard Litsa yell a single word.

"Run!"

# Chapter 34

Sif stumbled forward, instinctively holding her breath. Hunter was moving, too, covering his mouth and nose with the palm of his hand.

Another arrow flew from Litsa's bow, a streak of orange light passing by, sounding like a bird flapping its wings as the flames twisted and turned in the night air, if only for a moment. Sif heard it hit something, thud to a stop. Behind her.

She was crawling forward on her hands and knees as fast as she could. She knew she should keep moving but couldn't help but glance over her shoulder. She wanted to see it. To make it all real.

It was there, just as Litsa described it. It was illuminated by the flames between its shoulders, and Sif could see every detail. Black against black, slimy, the firelight dancing along its glistening surface.

A drone.

It stood about four feet tall on stubby legs, long arms raised into the air, with thin feelers where there should be fingers, wildly flexing and whipping about. Even in the dark, Sif could see a white row of teeth, a death rictus. The bulging chest peeled back, opening like the petals of an iris. Litsa sent two arrows into the chest before it could release its spores.

It finally became real.

Sif felt Hunter grab her arm and drag her to her feet. Together they ran after Litsa, who had stopped momentarily to make sure they were behind her. "Follow me," Litsa said. "We have to move fast."

Hunter didn't release his grip on her arm and continued pulling her forward. He held his torch out in front, trying to light their way. She watched Litsa run through the night, clearing clumps of brush and rocks like a deer, her torch in one hand, bow and arrows in the other. Sif could see Litsa's eyes glowing bright every time she looked back at them, like an animal catching the headlights of a passing car. She waved her torch, imploring them to follow, to run faster. This was where Litsa was most at home, Sif realized, a warrior in her element. This land was Litsa's cockpit, her arrows her Sidewinders. They were both fighters, Litsa and she, born in different worlds, but sharing the intoxicating, quickening heat in their veins when it was time to fight. Hunter was right—she and Litsa were cut from the same rough cloth.

Sif glanced over her shoulder, saw the drone fully engulfed in flames, and in the brightening firelight, could see dark shapes moving in the shadows behind it. More drones. They had stumbled right into a hive's advance guard. *When the drones are triggered, the jumpers will come.*

And they did.

She heard a soft thump off to her left, something hitting the ground—she looked, but didn't see anything. Then another thump, again to the left, and closer, louder. This time, she saw a small, dark, roundish shape, with thin feelers extending from its surface. In a momentary brightness from Hunter's torch, she watched it flatten itself, then suddenly contract, forcing itself into the air. *Jumping.*

Ahead, Litsa quickly dropped to one knee and brought her bow to bear. She was aiming it above them, shooting into the air. She loosed the arrow, and it hit something right above their heads. Sparks filled the sky as it fell, catching fire.

Falling right toward them.

Sif pulled her arm from Hunter's grip and shoved him, hard, pushing him out of the way. She shielded her face as the jumper landed on top of her. She fell to the ground and rolled as the jumper slid off her back. It was but a few feet away, the shaft of Sif's arrow sticking out of its undulating body, flames licking the oily surface and beginning to spread from where it impacted. A scream begin to rise in her throat, but she couldn't breathe—the force of the impact had knocked the wind from her lungs.

She saw feelers extend from the jumper's skin, whipping around in the air, and then, as one, stop. Each one was pointing right at her.

She turned and ran toward Litsa.

And then she heard the pop.

Sif closed her eyes, covered her mouth and nose with her hand, and stumbled forward, feeling a sudden wave of heat from behind. She felt a hand on her arm and was pulled forward, trying to keep her feet under her. She felt another hand, smaller but just as strong, grip her other arm.

Her lungs were screaming for relief, but she fought the urge to take a breath. If the mist—if the *spores*—were on her skin, taking a breath now would be suicide. She kept her eyes closed tight, afraid that the spores might enter her bloodstream that way, too.

She ran, eyes closed, letting Hunter and Litsa guide her forward, dragging her when she stumbled on rocks or tangled her feet in the brush. The fire in her chest was too strong to fight anymore.

She broke free of Hunter and Litsa's grasp, stopped in place, and took a breath.

"We cannot *stop* now. What are you doing?" Litsa stepped forward and reached for Sif's arm.

"Get away—from me," Sif yelled, pulling her arm back. "Just leave me—here." She was taking huge gulps of air, and it felt so good, even though she knew she might be killing herself with each breath. She tried to stand as still as she could, not wanting to shake any of the spores off her body, where they might get to Hunter or Litsa.

Hunter stood off to the side, his eyes wide with fear. "Listen to her, Sif. We have to go."

"I'm covered in *spores*. Did you not see what just happened back there?"

Litsa jumped at her, grabbed both of her arms. Her luminous eyes were inches from Sif's face. "You are clean."

"But, it exploded!"

"The mist ignited behind you. Now, we must go."

The cloud of spores had ignited, like the dust in a grain silo. If Litsa hadn't hit it with one of her fire arrows, she would be on her way to becoming a Riy. Sif nodded at Litsa and ran.

They followed Litsa, heading back in the direction of the Dak— again giving a wide berth to the other hive they encountered—until Litsa finally slowed her pace and stopped.

"There is a stream close by," Litsa said, pointing off to their left. "Just past those trees. We will go there, take a drink."

"What about the jumpers?" Hunter asked.

"We are far enough away, and there were only a few. The hive was small, and at night it reacts much more slowly."

Sif could hear the gentle burble of the stream as they approached. "If you hadn't shot it right before it hit me," Sif said, "I'd be dead now."

"Not quite," Litsa replied, "you would be transforming, turning into Riy. But I wouldn't have let you live long enough to experience that. I would've killed you where you stood."

Sif nodded. "I suppose I'd do the same thing."

"It is the only merciful thing to do, Sif. I can assure you. You would suffer. Greatly."

*Sif, not "Caitlyn" or "woman."* Sif took a drink from the stream and rubbed the water against her face. "So, here's the million-dollar question. What the holy hell happened to *Beagle*?"

"It must've been the Takers," Hunter said. "Maybe they still have choppers powerful enough to sling-carry something that big."

"They have airplanes, with wings and propellers," Litsa said. "I've seen pictures of things like them in the records. Big and gray, with huge bellies where they put the people they kidnap."

"Transports." Sif looked at Hunter, and he nodded in agreement.

"They have other machines, too, *helicopters*, with a big propeller on top."

"You really did spend a lot of time going through those records, didn't you?" Sif asked.

Litsa nodded. "I like to look at how things used to be. I wonder what it was like to live in the old times. Your time."

"It wasn't always fun and games." Sif shook her head slightly. "We managed to screw things up pretty darn well. Obviously."

"But, you've been to the stars."

Sif smiled at her. "Yes, we have. And it's beautiful. It really is."

"Litsa," Hunter interrupted, "we need to contact Lucas, let him know what we've found and tell him about *Beagle*. The only way we can do this is to leave here and go to a place called Ellsworth."

"Ellsworth?"

"In the old times, Ellsworth was a place where the flying machines were, and we think we can find a radio there that will let us talk to Lucas."

Sif watched as Litsa absorbed what she was being told, and could tell she knew what Hunter was going to ask next.

"And you need me to take you there." A statement more than a question.

Hunter nodded. "We could use your help. You know the dangers out here, not to mention you know how to live off the land a whole lot better than either Sif or I do."

"You want me to leave my home?"

"We know it's a lot to ask," Sif added, "but Hunter's right. Our chances of making it there are greater with you than without you."

Sif searched Litsa's face, watching as she again struggled with her decision.

"How far away is this Ellsworth?" Litsa asked.

"Probably a week's travel, northeast of here," Hunter said. "We can move at night, when the Riy are less active."

"I must discuss it with Conrad and Geller first. I also need to consider Talia."

*That's better than a no,* Sif thought.

"I understand," Hunter replied.

Litsa looked to the east. The sky was starting to brighten, and Sif could tell what little light there was had begun to affect Litsa's eyes.

"The sun will rise soon. We need to get back to the Dak before then."

Sif stood, wiped her hands on her thighs. "I'd hate to run into one of those drones in the daylight. A sluggish one was bad enough."

As they turned to leave the stream, Litsa reached out and touched Hunter's arm. "You said Ellsworth was where flying machines used to be, yes?"

"That's right," Hunter replied. "It was a military base in our time. The Takers might very well be operating from there."

"I will help you find a radio to talk to your Lucas. Conrad and Geller will stay here, with Talia."

"Then, you will come with us?" Hunter asked.

"The Takers have my people," Litsa said coldly. "And I want them back."

\*\*\*

When they reached the Dak, Sif could tell something was not right as soon as Litsa saw the secondary portal, stopped, and sniffed the air. Sif could feel the heightened tension pouring off Litsa's body.

"What is it?" Hunter asked, having seen Litsa's reaction, as well.

"The brush covering the entrance has been moved."

"Could Conrad or Geller have done it?"

Litsa looked at Sif. "No. They would stay with Talia. They wouldn't leave the Dak."

"If they didn't leave," Sif started to say, but Litsa finished the thought for her.

"Someone entered."

*The Takers.* Litsa bolted through the hole before Sif could say another word. "Dammit, Litsa, wait!" Sif dropped to her knees and scrambled into the hole, Hunter right behind.

"*Fuck*, it's dark in here," Sif said. All the wall torches were out. "Litsa!"

"Shhh," Hunter whispered. Sif felt his hand on her shoulder.

From farther down in the cave, they could hear Litsa shouting Conrad's name, echoing back toward the mouth of the Dak.

"Come on," Sif said, "We have to help her."

"All right. We'll feel our way down. Keep one hand on the walls and keep your other hand on my shoulder." He moved into the lead.

"Conrad? Geller?" Litsa was still shouting their names.

Sif felt the heat begin to rise in her face. *They're just kids, for Christ's sake.*

The sharp crack of a gunshot echoed from the depths of the cave. They heard Litsa scream.

"No!" Sif yelled. She let go of Hunter's shoulder and ran blindly toward the sound, but fell to the dirt as Hunter tackled her.

"*No*, Sif."

"They *shot* her!"

"There's nothing we can do. We need to get out, now."

She struggled against his grasp, kicking, but he was too strong.

"We can't fight them here, not now. There'll be another chance," he pleaded.

He was right. They had to get out now, before the Takers made it back up to the mouth of the Dak. Outside, in the daylight, she and Hunter could at least see what they were up against.

"Okay, okay, let's move," Sif said. She heard Hunter stand, and as she got to her feet, she heard a popping sound—a soft whistle passing by her ear—and then heard Hunter gasp.

Another pop.

A stinging sensation in her neck. She reached up, felt the dart embedded in her skin.

And then the darkness took her away.

# PART III: PHOENIX

# Chapter 35

Ignoring the pain, Sif opened her eyes, squinting against the glare. Her mouth was dry, and her tongue felt as if it were glued to the roof of her mouth. The air was cool, yet sterile. A hospital smell.

She was in bed in a small room, windowless, blindingly white, with the whir of a ceiling fan above. There was an IV line taped to her wrist and wires stuck to her chest, which she promptly ripped off. To her left, monitoring equipment beeped a warning to whoever was watching her screens.

They would come. Soon.

She swung her legs off the side of the bed, noticing she was clad in a thin hospital gown. She also realized she was clean. They had scrubbed her from head to toe. Her head swam as she tried to stand, dizzy, feeling the aftereffects of whatever drug they shot into her neck. She steadied herself against the side of the bed, gripped the white sheets tightly, and again tried to stand.

As she did, the door opened.

It was a woman, wearing light blue hospital scrubs. She was older, roughly Sif's height, dark skinned. "Whoa there," she said, stepping closer, "you're in no condition to go traipsing around just yet."

"Where the *fuck* am I?" Sif yelled.

The nurse—at least, she looked like a nurse—stopped in her tracks.

"You're in a medical facility, and you're okay. There's nothing to be afraid of."

Sif quickly looked around the room for anything she could possibly use as a weapon. *Nothing.* "Where is my partner? The man I was with?"

"He is in another room, recovering just like you are."

"From the goddamn dart in his neck, right?"

"Please," the nurse said, "we're not going to hurt you." She held her hands out in front of her, palms out, saying *I'm no threat* and *Please don't come any closer.*

Sif was suddenly aware that she could feel the air from the ceiling fan blowing across her bare backside. Her gown was hanging open. *God, I hate these things.* She ignored it. "I want to see him. Right now," Sif snarled, taking a step toward the nurse.

"I need you to get back in bed, Miss Wagner."

"How the hell do you know my name?"

From behind the nurse came another voice. "You're Commander Caitlyn Wagner, United States Navy."

Sif watched as a hulking figure entered the room wearing a fatigue uniform, dark gray, mottled camouflage. He was big—way over six feet tall and two hundred pounds, with arms almost as big as her thighs. *And here come the thugs.*

"You were born on November tenth, 1986, in Virginia Beach, Virginia," he continued, his voice deep and booming in the small room. "Daughter of Deke and Carla Wagner. Pilot-astronaut of the first manned mission to Mars, lost and presumed dead on May thirteenth, 2025."

"Impressive, but you forgot my favorite color, asshole."

He only smiled, which infuriated Sif even more. And then, incredibly, he snapped her a salute.

"Ma'am, I'm Major Kyle Murphy, North American Alliance Security Forces."

Sif returned the salute before she could even think about it, and then dropped it, staring at her arm as if pissed that it would do such a silly thing. "Okay, *Major*, so you know who I am. Wonderful. I want to see Lieutenant Colonel Webb. Now."

"He's in the adjoining room, resting comfortably, Commander."

"Super. I *said* I want to see him."

"He hasn't woken from the sedative yet."

"Did I say anything about waiting until the sedative wears off, Major?"

Sif watched the major glance at the nurse. "We're okay here. You can leave."

The woman quickly exited the room, obviously glad to get away. Sif heard the door lock with a click.

"Now hold on a minute. Do *not* lock me in here."

"We need to talk, Commander."

"No *shit*, Sherlock." Sif tossed a strand of hair from her eyes, still wet from being washed. "First off, I need to know what you fucksticks did with our lander, and second, I want to know what happened to the people who were in the Da—the cave when you shot us with your friggin' darts." She overdid it. Her legs gave out, and she swayed, light-headed. *Don't faint in front of this moron, come on!*

Before she could react, Major Murphy grabbed her and gently helped her lie back down on the bed. She pushed him away.

"Don't touch me."

"Sorry, but you looked like you were going to faint there for a second. It takes a while for the sedative to wear off."

Sif found the major's appearance much different from Litsa's people. His eyes looked much like her own, and his skin had obviously seen the sun. He hadn't spent his life hiding out in a cave.

"Once you feel up to it, we can see Lieutenant Colonel Webb. I promise."

"Oh, you *promise*? Can we pinkie-swear, too?" All Sif got in return was a confused look. "I feel up to it right now."

The major thought for a second, then nodded. His orders were to make sure the two astronauts were treated with the utmost respect until they could be transferred to the Phoenix Complex, and the airplane would be ready in a couple of hours to do just that.

"I'll take you to his room." He offered his arm.

"I can walk," Sif said, swinging her legs off the bed again. "But first, you need to bring me some clothes. I don't care what, but I'm not leaving this room with my ass hanging out."

She watched as the major reached up to his collar and pressed a small button. "This is Murphy. I need a uniform for Commander Wagner." As he nodded, Sif noticed he was also wearing an earbud. *Integrated comms.*

"They'll have clothes for you in a few minutes, ma'am."

Sif nodded. "Thank you."

"And ma'am? Welcome home."

# Chapter 36

Sif had to admit, they were quick about it. Major Murphy handed her a uniform much like his own, with her name and rank printed above the left breast pouch pocket. He didn't leave the room as she dressed, but turned his back.

It fit perfectly. Even the boots were the right size—there were no laces or zippers, but once she slipped them on, they seemed to conform to the shape of her legs, almost as if they were alive. She gasped, then hid her confusion as soon as she saw the major smiling at her.

She surprised him as she pushed past and grabbed the door handle. It was still locked, which explained why he didn't try to stop her. "Really?"

The major reached down and grabbed the handle, and the door automatically unlocked. *Some sort of biometrics,* Sif guessed. It recognized his hand, but not hers. *Interesting.*

When the door swung open, he gestured with his arm. "After you, Commander."

Sif stepped outside into a short hallway, just as white and brightly lit as her room. Surprisingly, it resembled a hospital from their time—including the smell—although some of the equipment certainly wasn't as familiar.

It wasn't a large facility, with maybe three or four rooms. A few people in hospital scrubs manned a monitoring station, and all turned to look at her. Sif stared back and didn't return their smiles. They looked away.

"Everyone wants to see you, Commander. It's not every day that we get patients like you and Lieutenant Colonel Webb."

"Where is he?"

"Right in the next room. I'm told he's awake and has been asking to see you."

Earbud again. He was receiving info that she couldn't hear. Once more, Sif watched the major grab the door handle and heard the lock release.

"I'm sure he has," Sif said coldly. She strode into the room and saw Hunter sitting up in bed, drinking some sort of cloudy, thick liquid from a straw. At first, he didn't recognize her in the uniform, but when he did, he smiled.

"Nice duds, Sif."

"I'd have preferred a flight suit, but these'll do. How's the neck?"

"Other than the needle mark, not bad."

"I suppose you've already met Major Muscles here?" Sif said, turning toward him and pointing her arm.

"I have."

"So did he happen to tell *you* what happened to Litsa and the rest of them, or where the hell our ship is?"

"Not a word."

Sif turned toward the major. "Now seems like a pretty good time, doesn't it, *Major*?"

"As soon as Lieutenant Colonel Webb feels up to it, we need to debrief you. All your questions will be answered then."

"Debrief?" Sif spat back. "You're kidding, right?"

Major Murphy crossed his arms and stared right back at her. "No. I'm not kidding."

Sif turned back toward Hunter, who was already sliding out of bed. "You're up to it right now, right?"

"Damn straight. Hey, do I get one of those snazzy storm trooper uniforms, too," he said to the major, "or do I have to walk around in this gown?"

Sif could tell the major didn't know what a storm trooper was, either, but didn't seem to like the sound of it. "Your uniform will be here shortly, Colonel," he said.

"Can you at least answer some of our questions, Major?" Hunter asked. "Like, for starters, where the heck are we?"

"This is Ellsworth Field Staging Point, Colonel. I believe it was called Ellsworth Air Force Base in your time, close to a place once called Rapid City."

They made it to Ellsworth, after all. "And our ship?"

"*Beagle* is here, too. We received your landing coordinates from Mr. Hoover and retrieved the ship shortly thereafter."

"You've contacted Lucas?" Sif asked.

The major nodded as one of the nurses brought in Hunter's uniform. "We picked up what turned out to be one of your automated radio calls. He was pretty frantic about finding you two when we responded. We've been communicating with him whenever *Resolute* is within range."

"Does he know we're alive?" Hunter asked.

"Not yet. The next scheduled comm window will be in"—he looked at a digital timepiece embedded into his sleeve—"about three hours. I'm sure he's going to be relieved."

*So they have high-tech uniforms but are still limited by comms. No satellites.* "You brought *Beagle* here? Why?" Sif asked.

"Repairs. Your number three engine's fuel pump needs to be replaced, and the radio is shot. We couldn't do that in the field. And anyway, it's too dangerous to be out in the open."

"The Riy, you mean." Sif watched as he paused for a moment, as if he were unsure of how to respond.

"Yes, the Riy. Please, we can talk more during the debrief. A lot has changed since you've been gone."

"How did you know about the fuel pump and radio?" Hunter asked.

"We plugged into *Beagle*'s main computer when we found her. The info was all right there. Look, I can answer more of your questions at the debrief," the major said, clearly getting annoyed at the endless stream of questions. "But before we do that, I'm sure both of you would appreciate a real meal first, correct?"

Sif was pissed at his reluctance to say anything about Litsa and the others—he either didn't know or wasn't authorized to say anything, she figured. However, she *was* hungry. The questions could wait. It wasn't like she and Hunter had a choice, anyway. She would keep her eyes open, observe, and listen. Hopefully, that would provide *some* answers. "I suppose I could eat a bite or two. Hunter?"

He was fully dressed now, staring at his new boots, which had just conformed to the shape of his leg. "I'll be damned." He glanced at the major. "I'm hoping you still know how to brew a strong pot of coffee."

\*\*\*

And they did. *Real* coffee, which Sif hadn't enjoyed in what seemed like ages. She laughed, thinking that it was almost two hundred years if she counted the days on a calendar.

They were seated in an open room—a chow hall—where other people dressed like Major Murphy sat at small tables and ate, each of them staring at her and Hunter like they were from another world.

The major stepped away to bring them some food, leaving them alone.

"So, initial thoughts?" Hunter whispered.

She leaned close to him, kept her voice low. "First, this is a military op. They still have a rank structure we're familiar with, but it's like the Navy's." She tapped the insignia centered on her blouse. "Three broad stripes, an O-5, just like yours. He mentioned the North American Alliance, and that makes me think Canadian. Second, from their appearance, they don't live in caves. Third, they have some kick-ass tech that they're apparently not willing to share with the people outside, but some of what *we* had—satellites, comsats—is gone. Fourth, he called this a 'staging base'—a staging base for what? And fifth, they refuse to tell us anything about Litsa." She scratched at the small bump on her neck. "Oh yeah, and *sixth*, they haven't told us why they darted us like zoo animals."

Hunter nodded. "We need to take a look outside and see what's on the ramp. If there *is* still a ramp."

"Flying machines," Sif said, using Litsa's words. "It's what the *Takers* use." She looked around the room, met quite a few questioning eyes. She wasn't afraid to meet their glances and felt a little satisfaction when they dropped theirs and stared at their plates. "They're really trying to figure us out, aren't they?"

"I do feel a little like a zoo animal, to tell you the truth. Darts in the neck aside."

"Okay, I told you my initial thoughts. What do *you* think?"

"I agree with you," Hunter said, "on every point. I recommend we accept their courtesy, watch, listen, and learn. We might get a whole new perspective about this new world of ours after we sit through their debriefing."

Sif nodded, looked around the room. "I don't like this place, Hunter. The vibes are all wrong."

"I hear you. But, there's a lot we don't know. Litsa's records told us a lot, but I'm going to assume there are still quite a few missing pieces to the story, especially when it comes to these people."

Sif sat back in her chair and crossed her arms. "I think we heard all we need to know about *these people* from Litsa. That bullet in Talia's leg spoke volumes, too. She's just a kid. Maybe *was* just a kid."

"I don't disagree. I suggest we learn what we can, okay?"

Sif reluctantly nodded her head. She would listen, only because she had to.

The major returned to the table carrying two plates. "This is kind of a bare-bones facility, but this is still probably better than what you've been eating."

Sif looked down at her plate—this was much better than what she experienced in the *bare-bones* facilities she had encountered. "Don't tell me that's a steak."

The major sat down beside them. "You don't like it?"

"What, do I look like a plant eater?" She sliced into the meat and popped a bite into her mouth. The taste wasn't quite what she expected, but she didn't really care. "What is this?"

"Bison, from the Northwest Territories. We have it flown in once a week."

Hunter was already cutting into his, as well. "Buffalo?"

"In your time, cattle were a major food source, along with pigs and chickens, but now, bison are a major source of protein."

Sif wondered what he meant—were cows, pigs, and chickens all gone now? More importantly, though, he mentioned aircraft. "You said *flown in*. You have an active runway here?"

"We do. We'll be seeing it shortly."

To Sif, that didn't exactly sound like he was going to give them a tour. "Seeing it . . . how?"

"President Carlisle has sent an aircraft for you. When you're done eating, it'll take you to our main base. He's eager to meet both of you."

Sif put her fork down. "Wait a minute. We're not leaving until you answer our questions."

The major raised his hands, as if to say *whoa*. "And we will, Commander. We're going to debrief on the flight there."

"And where is *there*, exactly, Major?" Hunter asked.

"A place called Hay River, in what you knew as Canada. The Phoenix Complex."

# Chapter 37

Sif didn't like the fact that they were being taken away before they learned what happened to Litsa and the others. And they were leaving *Beagle* here, too, as far as she knew. *And* they weren't going to be able to talk to Lucas, either. She didn't like it but had no choice.

As they exited the chow hall and stepped outside, she was shocked. She had never been to Ellsworth before, so she didn't have a mental picture to compare the scene to, but she was sure it never looked like *this*.

The base itself, which now looked as if it barely extended past the runway and flight line, was surrounded by a high wall, maybe fifteen or twenty feet tall, spotted with guard towers—manned, she noticed—and topped with razor wire. *To keep the Riy out?* she wondered.

Within the walls were hangars, low-slung buildings, and—just as the major said—an active runway. "Those are C-130s," Sif said, immediately recognizing the unmistakable shape of the transport aircraft.

Major Murphy nodded his head. "Basically, yes."

"How in the hell have you kept them flying for so long?" Hunter asked.

"It's not the same airplane you were familiar with. Everything beneath the skin has been replaced and improved. These airframes essentially have very few hours on them."

Sif saw a line of six of the transports at the far end of the ramp, painted dark gray. Even at this distance, she could see some subtle differences. The engines looked smaller, and the propellers were curved, shaped more like some of the more modern European transport aircraft from her day. Sif also noticed a line of helicopters across from the C-130s. Chinooks. "Did you use those to bring *Beagle* here?" she said, pointing at the choppers.

"It took two of them, but yes."

She looked around, scanned the rest of the flight line. *Beagle* was nowhere to be seen. "And where is our ship, Major?"

He gestured toward one of the large hangars behind the C-130s. "In there. Repairs are under way as we speak."

"I hate to tell you," Sif said, "but the fuel pump can't be repaired. It needs to be replaced, and the only spare we have is onboard *Resolute*."

"We don't need it, Commander. We can produce the part here."

"How the heck can you do that?" Hunter asked.

The major smiled. "The technology was beginning to mature about the time you left on your mission. I believe you called it 3-D printing?"

"You can print a fuel pump?" Sif said, incredulously.

"*Print* may not be an accurate description, but yes, we can make the part. Same thing with the uniforms you're wearing. We scanned your bodies and produced the uniforms. I'm sure you'll agree that they fit perfectly, right?"

Sif had to admit, it did. "And the boots? They cinched up tight to my legs, no laces."

"Reactive nanotechnology. Your boots are designed to constrict when they sense body heat, but only to a certain point. When the fit is snug, they quit contracting."

He was explaining it as if he were talking to a couple of third graders. Sif decided they did, after all, have a ton to learn about this new world. "So, how do I get them off?"

The major pointed to a small round dot on the side of his boot. "Touch this spot for a few seconds, and the boots relax."

"They relax."

"Yes, they loosen enough to be slipped off."

Hunter shook his head. "I know I've been gone too long when someone has to tell me how to take my boots off."

"Your uniforms have reactive nanotechnology as well," the major continued. "Rip the fabric, and it'll repair itself. *If* you can rip it, that is. It takes a lot of force to damage these things."

"So you've basically destroyed the local seamstress union, huh?"

"I don't know what that means."

"Never mind," Sif said. She noticed a smaller aircraft nearby—one that appeared to be a Gulfstream GVI—painted white. It certainly looked presidential. "That's our ride, I assume?"

"Correct," the major replied. "The president's personal aircraft."

"Everything replaced and improved, I suppose," Hunter remarked. The major nodded.

"It's not as big as *Air Force One*, but I guess it'll do," Sif said. "Before we go, though, I'd like to see *Beagle*." Sif expected him to make some excuse as to why they wouldn't be able to see their ship, so she was surprised at his answer.

"Of course, but it'll have to be quick. The flight leaves in fifteen minutes."

"That'll be enough time."

*Beagle* was in the hangar, just as he said. A group of ten or so technicians stopped what they were doing and stared, again with the same curious-yet-scared faces she saw in the chow hall. What troubled Sif was that it appeared as if almost every access panel was removed, much more intrusively than what would be required to fix the fuel pump and radio. "What are they doing to my ship, Major?" she said, trying hard to hide the panic in her voice.

"Not to worry, Commander. They're giving *Beagle* a complete inspection, and before you ask, yes, they can put her back together again. We have all the technical specifications. We were able to upload the maintenance diagrams and manuals for both *Beagle* and *Resolute* from our central database." He nodded at the techs, who took that as their signal to get back to work. "When they're done, *Beagle* will be as good as new. Maybe even better."

She didn't like this, either. But, like everything else, she wasn't really in a position to do anything about it. "As long as I can still fly her," Sif said.

She saw the major look at the digital time readout on his sleeve again. "We need to move. Wheels up in five minutes."

"Are you coming with us?" Sif asked.

"What, stay here and miss the opportunity to talk to two astronauts from the early twenty-first century? I wouldn't miss this flight for the world."

Sif glared at him. She didn't particularly like the feeling of being a walking, talking museum piece.

# Chapter 38

Even from this distance, Litsa could see the two astronauts as they walked across the field toward a small, white flying machine, accompanied by a man the others said was the leader of this place.

Sif and Hunter were wearing the uniforms of the Takers and certainly weren't being led anywhere against their will. Like she was.

None of it made any sense. They seemed so genuine, so truthful. When she first saw them, the heat rose in her neck, and she gripped the bars of the window with a fiery anger. *It was all some kind of trick,* Litsa thought, but to what end? Why did they need to bring two of their kind to the Dak and spin some sort of incredible story to gain her trust, just to have the last remaining members of her clan end up in this stinking holding cell?

No. It didn't make any sense. There must be another reason why they were not placed in here with the rest of them. Along with Conrad, Geller, and Talia, there were about twenty others she didn't know, taken from their village a few nights ago, too, all under guard.

Sampson, one of the other villagers, told her of the stories he had heard of this place, how people were taken here first, then transported somewhere else on board one of the big gray flying machines. To where, no one knew, but no person taken from here was ever seen again.

The people of Sampson's village also lived in a set of caves some distance away from her own Dak, but they were different—more docile, afraid—even now cowering against the back wall of the pen, holding one another. Some of them cried all night long, it seemed. Litsa spent the night looking for a weakness in the structure—loose bars, a weak hinge, anything she could exploit—but found nothing. Among the people trapped in here, only she, Conrad, and Geller seemed willing to find a way out. Talia, still weakened from the gunshot wound in her leg, slept for most of the time. Her fever had not returned, so at least that was a good sign. The Takers seemed especially interested in her leg wound and for a moment acted as if they were going to separate her from the pack, but Talia summoned enough strength to stand tall and feign strength, and she remained with the rest of them.

Litsa was afraid to think what they would have done with Talia had they taken her away.

She had heard stories about how the badly injured were usually killed during the raids, and only the healthy ones were taken away. If not for Talia's show of strength—and, Litsa admitted, Hunter and Sif's care—Talia would be dead now, discarded because of her injury like a piece of trash.

Litsa watched as Sif, Hunter, and the other man stepped aboard the white flying machine, and the door closed behind them. She continued staring through the bars as the machine roared into the sky and turned north, finally disappearing from view. She wondered where they were going, and if it was the same place where *they* would be taken. Hunter and Sif were shown courtesies, clothed, and most surely fed, while she and the rest of the people in here with her were treated like animals. If they *were* going to the same place, Litsa figured the fates that awaited them would be quite different.

She wasn't going to go without a fight, though. She knew she could count on Conrad and Geller—Talia, too, once she regained her strength—but as for the rest of them, she wasn't sure.

Litsa spoke to Sampson at length and learned what had happened to his people. His tribe, as they called themselves, lived not too far away from her own Dak, only fifteen miles or so to the east. Sampson said they, too, experienced the hives moving farther north and were forced to relocate within the past year. The hives, he said, were many. He was surprised to learn that Litsa's people fought the hives, burned them, and forced them to retreat. His people, he said, always ran away.

Litsa was amazed that only fifteen miles separated their peoples, yet they approached survival in such different ways. Her clan was more regimented, where survival meant living by a rigid set of laws and expectations, which, if broken, resulted in swift punishment. Sampson's people, by contrast, had no set of rules. The difference between their two groups was striking to her. If she did start a fight, she might end up getting a lot of them hurt or killed and wasn't sure if it would be worth it. There would be a time and place, though, she knew, when she would act.

Looking at the group of people in the pen, she wondered how many other clans or tribes were out there, and how many of *them* had been ripped from their homes by the Takers. More than that, though, she wondered what had become of them.

Sampson stood beside her.

"I saw you watching them," he said.

Litsa nodded. "They are the ones I told you about, the ones who came from the stars."

"They are with these people?"

Litsa glanced beyond the bars in the direction the small machine had headed. "I don't think they are," she said. "But I just don't know."

If they were, Litsa thought, she would kill both of them with her bare hands.

# Chapter 39

By the calendar, it was nearly two hundred years since Sif had experienced the joy of being in a jet at altitude—she was flying again, and it felt good, even though she wasn't at the controls. The pilot turned north-northwest immediately after lifting off, and Sif watched the landscape shrink away as he climbed. According to Major Murphy, it would be roughly a two-and-a-half-hour flight to cover the nearly 1,300 miles from Ellsworth to the Phoenix Complex, located near what used to be known as the town of Hay River, Canada.

Sif was a little disappointed in the jet itself, especially since it was supposedly a presidential aircraft. She had seen the interior of *Air Force One* once. This, by comparison, was more business class. The interior was finished much like any other corporate jet—a roomy cabin, with six seats, polished wood, and soft leather throughout. Imprinted into the leather on each of the seats was a symbol she recognized—the mythical phoenix, its wings curved upward as in the first moment of flight. *Fitting,* she thought. *Rising from the ashes.*

"What kind of fuel are you using?" Hunter asked.

Sif wondered, too, since according to the records in the Dak, most of the areas of the world famous for crude oil production were overtaken by the Riy.

"Synthenol," Major Murphy said. "Not the JP-8 you remember, that's for sure. It's algae-based. We grow it."

"You grow your jet fuel," Sif said. She was beginning to sound like a broken record but couldn't help it.

"Synth is very stable and has a much higher energy density than fossil fuels. We can tweak it to fit a number of different applications. Your *Beagle*, for example, is being modified to handle synth right now."

"What?" Sif didn't like that they were messing with their ship like that.

"Don't worry, Commander. Like I said, she'll be better than new when we get done with her. And anyway, once the existing fuel in her tanks is gone—or the fuel reserves in *Resolute*, for that matter—*Beagle* would be a great big paperweight. We don't have the capacity to produce enough liquid oxygen or hydrogen to keep her operational for long."

"How will it affect her performance?" Hunter asked.

"With full tanks, she'll be lighter, and the engines will burn cooler. You'll see an overall improvement in performance."

"The environmental activists from our day would love you guys," Sif said.

"We didn't have a choice once fossil fuels were no longer a viable option. We had to find another way, and we did. You'll learn there have been a lot of changes regarding how we heat the complex, manufacture our food, produce electricity. It's a different world, Commander."

Sif noticed the major said *heat the complex*, as opposed to *heat our homes*. It was a subtle difference but made her wonder if the complex—this Phoenix place—was all there was.

"Ready to learn more about it?"

"You're damn right I am." Sif was beginning to feel somewhat more at ease, and it worried her. These people—Litsa's Takers—seemed full of nefarious intent in Litsa's stories, even more so after Talia's bullet wound and the gunshot in the Dak. She and Hunter still had no idea what had happened to Litsa or the others, but being around technology—different in so many ways, more advanced, but still comfortably familiar—definitely took the edge off her nerves.

*\*\*\**

Hunter spent the next fifteen minutes telling the major the whole story—how they awakened from stasis, discovered the ship was heading back to Earth, and encountered what Lucas termed a Tipler cylinder. He summed up what they learned from the records in the Dak about how the Riy spread from continent to continent, and finally told the major what they saw from orbit, the overgrown cities and the huge swaths of blackened land stretching north and south from the equator.

The whole while, the major sat quietly, nodding every so often. Sif got the impression they were being recorded, which didn't surprise her. It also made her wonder if their uniforms were outfitted to record their conversations as well. A microphone could be hidden in the nanofabric, embedded in the uniform itself, completely invisible. If so, the major and his superiors were well aware of their misgivings. She would mention it to Hunter—in writing—at the first opportunity. They were going to have to be careful what they said, at least until they knew more about these people.

"You've viewed portions of the globe that haven't been seen in decades, Colonel," the major said. "Our reach is pretty limited. The satellites that used to provide so much information are simply no longer accessible. Many have reentered, collided, shut down over the years. The eyes and ears in the skies you enjoyed are shuttered."

"Once all the ground stations went dark, the orbits degraded," Hunter said.

"Exactly. Unfortunately, satellite control is one thing we can't do from the Phoenix Complex. At least, not yet."

"This Phoenix Complex, Major, what exactly is it?" Hunter asked.

"It's the last bastion of civilization, Colonel." Major Murphy pressed a button on his chair, and to Sif's disbelief, a slide show popped up on the monitor. *Some things never change,* she grumbled to herself. *Death by PowerPoint is still alive and well.*

"The Phoenix Complex was originally designed back in the 1950s as a location where government could continue to function after a nuclear war. It was a dual project by the American and Canadian governments, built in secrecy, with only the highest levels of both governments aware of its existence. Its location, by Hay River, was so remote that it would remain undamaged in the event of a global thermonuclear war."

Sif held a pretty high security clearance but had never heard of this place. It didn't surprise her, though, as she only knew what she had to know and nothing more. It was called compartmentalization, and it was a way to protect the big picture by allowing individuals access to only the puzzle pieces they were directly involved in.

"After the fall of the Soviet Union, the American and Canadian governments decided to close the facility—mothball it—and it was left abandoned until after the terrorist attacks of 2001."

September 11, 2001. It was a date Sif remembered all too well. She was only a kid then but still knew the world was going to change. And not for the better. Her father was aboard *Enterprise*—on his way home—when the attacks happened. The Big E turned around, and her father went to war again. It struck her for a moment that such a pivotal moment in world history—one that she lived through—was ancient history to these people. It was an odd feeling.

"Over the next few years, the facility was reopened, expanded, and manned continuously by the American and Canadian militaries."

Another slide.

"In 2009, the facility was once again shuttered, but this time, private funding kept it alive. The Phoenix Corporation, a bio-research firm at the time, decided to purchase portions of the complex . . ."

*The Phoenix Corporation.* She had heard that name before but couldn't recall exactly where.

". . . and along with DARPA—the American Defense Advanced Research Project Agency—turned the complex into the world's most cutting-edge biological research facility."

Sif was well acquainted with DARPA. Their core mission was weapons research, so if DARPA was involved with Phoenix, it was surely defense-related.

Another slide.

"In 2025, when the Riy infestation began, the Phoenix Complex was tasked with finding a way to stop the spread."

"And apparently didn't," Hunter said.

"Not in time, no. By the time we'd figured out a way to slow it down, it was already too late. Society completely collapsed, and by that time, organizing any sort of government-sanctioned response was a lost cause. There weren't any governments left. Phoenix, then, became a haven for the survivors. The world's best scientific minds were brought to the complex, along with many of the most prominent business and political leaders, to provide a pool of people who—it was hoped—could one day rebuild the world from the ashes. Hence, Phoenix. Those of us who live and work in the complex now are the direct descendants of those survivors."

The screen blinked off, and the major slid it back against the cabin wall, securing it into place.

"And what about the people who were left behind?" Sif asked, referring to Litsa and her people, and wondered how many more like her were out there, fighting to survive. "Were they just abandoned, left to fend for themselves?"

"Hard choices were made, Commander. The world was dying, and the leaders at the time had to save who they could. Judge them if you like, but I suggest you reserve your judgment until you see the Phoenix Complex. The Riy infestation knocked us back quite a few years, but we're fighting hard to get mankind back to where it used to be."

"Infestation? Is that what you people call what happened?" To Sif, *infestation* seemed like such a cold, scientific term for what had ravaged their world.

"That's what it was, Commander. The Riy are simply a new form of life that was able to flourish without any environmental constraints to hold back its growth. Think of it like introducing an animal to an environment where it has no natural predators. In its natural setting, predators would keep the growth at bay, ensure a balance was maintained, but in a new environment, where there are no natural predators, the animal can reproduce at will."

"Like the zebra mussel," Hunter said.

"The what?" Sif asked.

"A species of mussel native to the Black and Caspian Seas," Hunter explained. "Once it was introduced to North America, it spread like wildfire because there *were* no natural predators. They poisoned entire lakes to get rid of the things."

The major nodded. "Yes, it was like that. Except the environment for the Riy wasn't limited to a specific region. It was the entire planet."

"We saw huge blackened areas," Hunter said, "all by the equator, spreading north and south."

"The Riy flourish in the sunlight, Colonel. They rapidly adapted following the Chernobyl release. Quite remarkable, really, since no fungal growth up to that point demonstrated an ability to synthesize sunlight, much like plants do. And once it did, the spread was, to use your words, Colonel, like wildfire."

"How do you kill them?" Sif asked.

"Killing the Riy, as you saw from orbit, is problematic, Commander. It's a global problem. We're limited in what we can do."

"But you *can* kill it."

"Like I mentioned before, we can control the spread, yes."

Sif decided it was time to press him about Litsa and the others. "Are you going to tell us what happened to the people in the cave with us?" She didn't like how he looked away, his eyes betraying the fact that he was receiving instructions over his earpiece.

"Come on, Major, it's a simple question. Why are you being so evasive?"

"I apologize if I seem evasive, Commander, but I can guarantee you, I'm not."

"They call you the Takers. Did you know that? We heard stories about how you people fly in, kidnap whole families, and take them to God knows where." She could feel Hunter's gaze burrowing into the side of her head, but she didn't care.

"I know it might seem that way, especially to the indigenous peoples, but I can explain. There's a reason why we do what we do."

Sif sat back in her chair and crossed her arms. "I'm all ears, Major."

"As I said earlier, the Phoenix Complex is the last bastion for humanity. We have a responsibility to all those outside our walls, too. We're not trying to hurt these people, Commander. We're trying to save them."

"Your tactics seem oddly out of place, though," Hunter stated coldly. "If you're trying to save them, why the kidnappings in the middle of the night? The gas? The guns?"

Sif watched as the major dropped his eyes and shook his head. "This is going to be hard for you to understand."

Sif spoke next. "I understand that you don't *save* a teenage girl by shooting her in the leg and leaving her for dead. You don't snatch away entire villages in the dead of night and kill those who fight back, and call yourselves saviors." She stared coldly into his eyes, but he didn't look away.

When he spoke, his voice was low, quiet. "This isn't your world anymore, Commander." He shifted his glance to Hunter. "Nor yours, Colonel. You can sit there and judge us all you wish, but you have to come to grips with the fact that the planet you once knew underwent an extinction-level event. Almost all the population—gone. Hardly anyone survived. Those who did—the ones who made it to the Phoenix Complex in time, and those left out in the open—weren't necessarily the lucky ones. We *all* fought to survive, every person who was left."

Sif shook her head. "That doesn't explain your methods, Major."

"You two are looking at this world through a filter that doesn't take into account everything that has happened over the last two centuries. Like I said, this isn't your world anymore. Everything that happened shaped who we are now. We may not seem compassionate or caring, but we are."

Sif sat back in her chair. The soft leather didn't seem as comforting as it did a short time ago.

The major continued.

"Would you think less of us if we decided, as a people who were more than able to survive on our own within the Phoenix Complex, to simply abandon those who were left to roam the wilderness?"

Sif opened her mouth to speak, but the major cut her off.

"No, I'll answer it for you, Commander. You would. And you'd be correct. We've made the choice to put our own lives at risk every time we go out there to bring some of the indigenous people back to the complex. As Litsa told you, the Riy are moving northward, and we're trying to get as many of Litsa's people, and others like her, out of their path."

"And once you remove them? What then?" Sif asked.

"We quarantine them, treat those who might be carrying any diseases, and relocate them. There are encampments in the Northern Territories where they're able to make new homes."

"Why not let them live with you?" Hunter asked.

"We only have the means to support a limited number of people within the complex, Colonel. We can't take them all in."

"It's your methods I still don't understand, Major. Why the raids?"

"If you didn't notice, Colonel, they're not exactly a peace-loving people."

That statement immediately sent the blood to Sif's face. Litsa admitted her people lived by a strict set of rules, but they did so out of necessity. "They can't afford to be 'peace-loving,' Major. They're trying to survive."

"We did try to talk to them, Commander, in the beginning. The first village we visited, we lost twenty-seven people. Massacred. We could've quit our relocation efforts right then and there, but we didn't. We've lost many more people since, and yet it remains one of our most important priorities." He shifted his gaze to Hunter. "The Phoenix Complex *is* the only hope for the human race, Colonel. You'll realize that—the both of you," he said, cutting his eyes to Sif, "as soon you're able to see it for yourselves."

Sif took a deep breath. The major's story seemed reasonable enough. She surely didn't condone the manner in which they were relocating people but could see how it might be the only way. She and Hunter heard one side of the story from Litsa, and now heard it from one of Litsa's Takers, a man who was charged with relocating as much of the surviving human race as possible before the Riy added them to their hives. The truth, she figured, lay somewhere in the middle. And it would start with knowing exactly what happened to Litsa and the others.

"Major, I want to know what happened in the cave. There were three of Litsa's people inside before you . . . sedated us: two men—no, two boys," she corrected herself, "and a young girl with a gunshot wound to her leg."

"Every person in the cave is accounted for, including your Litsa. They should be leaving Ellsworth in the next few days after they finish their quarantine period and will be brought to Phoenix for relocation. We'll fly them up here on one of the C-130s you saw on the ramp."

"And the gunshots we heard?" Hunter asked.

"Warning shots. Your Litsa wasn't very happy to see us." He was smiling, but Sif saw no emotion in it.

"I want to see her when she arrives," Sif said.

"That might be difficult due to the number of people they're arriving with, and the safety protocols we have to follow, but I'll see what I can do."

"No, Major," Sif said. "No excuses. I want to see her. And the others."

He nodded. "I can't promise anything, but I'll do what I can."

Sif felt the jet begin to descend at the same time the major cocked his head, as if listening to a message from the cockpit.

"We're twenty minutes out," he said. "President Carlisle has requested an audience with you as soon as we arrive, if you're both up to it."

"Absolutely," Sif said. "It's not every day one gets to meet a president."

"And it's not every day a president gets to meet two astronauts from the twenty-first century, either. He's looking forward to showing you the complex and welcoming you to our family."

Sif saw him reach up to his earbud.

"Oh, and one more thing. Lucas Hoover knows you're alive—they informed him a little while ago. You'll be able to speak to him during the next communication window."

"How's he doing up there?" Hunter asked.

"He said he's lonely and can't wait to come down. Now I have to ask you to please strap in for landing."

# Chapter 40

Resolute

Lucas was overjoyed to learn Sif and Hunter were alive. He had resigned himself to the probability that he might be the only one of the crew to survive, until he received the transmission.

They called themselves the North American Alliance and were transmitting from a location in Canada, or what used to be called Canada. They picked up one of Liv's automatic hails, which, luckily, he had never instructed her to stop sending. They knew exactly what *Resolute* was, and who they were. Surprisingly, they also knew almost every detail of their mission, including what they were carrying in each of the ship's sections and the types of experiments they were to perform on the Martian surface. Every detail of their mission was still held in their databases, along with the story of their disappearance.

After the president announced that *Resolute* was missing, and the crew presumed dead, there was a national day of mourning, flags were placed at half-staff for a whole week, and memorial services for each of them were held in their hometowns. NASA even dedicated a bronze plaque in their memory, which the president himself unveiled outside mission control in Houston.

Everyone thought them dead.

Lucas felt sorry for his family—especially his siblings—who must've taken the news very hard. Not to mention Hunter's family, who also would have been crushed. Sif's parents were both deceased, but everyone who knew her surely suffered the loss just as painfully.

When he first spoke to the Alliance people, they had no idea Sif and Hunter had attempted a landing. Lucas provided the landing coordinates. Their last transmission stated Sif and Hunter were in good health, *Beagle* was damaged but repairable, and his two fellow astronauts were on their way to meet the president of the North American Alliance.

Lucas wasn't able to get many details from the Alliance people as to what awaited him down below. Each communications opportunity seemed to pass by much too quickly. He still didn't know what exactly had happened to their world and hoped Sif and Hunter could fill him in when he was able to speak to them. The Alliance seemed very interested in something *Resolute* was carrying, though. They wanted to know if the flyer was operational—Lucas told them it was, at least as far as he knew—and they also asked a series of questions about one of their experimental rigs, a genetically modified sample of *Bacillus subtilis*, a bacterium they brought with them to study on the surface of Mars. They wanted to know the size of the culture, whether it survived the trip, and if it was possible to send the sample down on one of the cargo landers.

They had brought *Bacillus subtilis* to study how the organism survived in and adapted to an alien soil. A remarkable organism, it was able to survive in hostile environments for extremely long periods of time. The purpose of their experiment was to see if *B. subtilis* could be modified in order to promote plant growth in the Martian soil, as a precursor to future missions and eventual colonization.

*Resolute* was full of other experiments, not to mention a full botanical section, but this tiny bacterium seemed to pique their interest more than anything else onboard. He had no idea why, but he figured he would find out soon.

"Liv, results on flyer diagnostics?"

"Flyer diagnostics are complete, my liege. All systems are operational."

Lucas had decided to have a little fun with Liv, and why not? He was all alone up here anyway. She still had Potato selected as his name—how, he had no worldly idea—but he decided to have her refer to him as "my liege."

He had to admit, he liked the sound of it.

The flyer was designed to spend months in the thin Martian atmosphere, taking samples at different altitudes as it flew around the planet. Dropped from orbit in an aeroshell, it would enter the atmosphere, discard the ablative shell, and deploy its long, thin wings in the upper reaches of the atmosphere, where its solar-charged-battery power source would feed a propeller-driven electric motor. The machine was built to stay aloft in the much thinner Martian air, and as such would have a much easier time in Earth's atmosphere, thus extending both its reach and loiter time.

He ran a number of drop simulations, and with a few adjustments knew the flyer would work.

"Liv, time until next communication window with the Phoenix Complex?"

"The next communication window will open in nine hours, forty-two minutes, my liege."

For the time being, even though Sif and Hunter were alive and on their way to this place in Canada called the Phoenix Complex, he was stuck here in orbit. In time, he figured the ship would have to be abandoned after she was stripped of everything that could fit on the cargo landers, but that could be weeks, or even months, in the future.

Lucas stared outside at the world below. *Resolute* would be crossing into terrestrial night again in a few minutes, and everything below would be black. *Such a different world now,* he thought, *so empty and dark.* But there *were* survivors. It wasn't a dead planet, as they had initially feared. And because there were survivors, there was a chance.

# Chapter 41

*Hay River, Northern Territories*

Sif surely hadn't expected *this*. They taxied toward a small group of buildings, and a large crowd of people—no, more like a large formation—lined the ramp. "Hunter, are you seeing this?"

"I see it."

Troops, at least a hundred of them, standing at parade rest with what Sif figured was the banner of the North American Alliance waving in the breeze, a strange conglomeration of the Canadian flag and Old Glory—stars, stripes, and a maple leaf. In the center of the leaf was the same phoenix symbol on each of their uniforms, which made Sif wonder if the North American *Alliance* was nothing more than the Phoenix Complex itself.

"It was President Carlisle's idea," Major Murphy said. "He wanted to give you the welcome home you never received. It's not as big as what you would have gotten, but it's the best we can do on such short notice."

"That was very thoughtful of your president," Hunter said.

"If you'd like to make some remarks, we have a podium set up."

"Remarks?" Sif said, surprised.

The major smiled. "You don't have to, but everyone here has been buzzing about your arrival. It'll be shown throughout the complex, too."

"Afraid of a little public speaking, Navy?" Hunter jibed.

"If anyone will be talking, it'll be you," she said to Hunter. "You're the commander of this mission, remember?"

"Yeah, but everyone wants to hear from the pilot."

"You're a pilot, too."

"But as you always remind me, I'm not a *naval aviator*. I can't land on a pitching deck in the dead of night *and* bad weather, my wings are made of lead instead of gold, and I hate to make unplanned public remarks."

Sif huffed and looked out the window. As the jet came to a stop, the formation snapped to attention. There was even a band, she saw. And another sight that made her catch her breath: beside the flag for the North American Alliance, someone was holding Old Glory. They were really pulling out the stops. "Fine, the Navy will handle it, just like always." She gave Hunter the evil eye, and then turned to Major Murphy. "What the hell do you want me to say?"

"It doesn't have to be much, Commander. Just say what you're feeling."

*That would not be a good idea,* Sif thought.

When they stepped down the short set of stairs from the jet, Sif heard the opening notes of "The Star-Spangled Banner." She and Hunter reached the bottom of the stairs, braced, and snapped a salute toward Old Glory, holding it until the last note.

The major stood beside them, also at attention.

When the anthem was complete, Sif strode up to the podium and adjusted the microphone to her height. She looked out over the assembled crowd—all troops, it appeared—and cleared her throat. She wasn't sure what one would be expected to say after being lost in space for nearly two centuries but decided to wing it.

"At ease, everyone. Please."

Sif was a little surprised as each of the officers turned to their respective ranks and ordered their troops to assume the proper stance. "Platoon!" they barked. "At *ease*!"

The troops assumed a more relaxed posture, and Sif smiled, glad to know that the basic drill and ceremony commands hadn't changed.

Sif gripped the edges of the podium. "Lieutenant Colonel Hunter Webb, Mr. Lucas Hoover, and I would like to express our gratitude to all of you for welcoming us back home, and we'd like to pass our thanks to President Carlisle for his hospitality and thoughtfulness."

Sif paused as a smattering of applause swept through the ranks. She glanced at Hunter, and he gave her a thumbs-up.

"It's been a long, confusing journey for us, and we . . ." *Oh crap, what do I say?* It was only a moment of silence, but to Sif it seemed like an eternity. "And we're looking forward to meeting and working with each of you . . ." *I'm crashing and burning here.* "Thanks again. Thank you."

Sif stepped away from the podium as the troops applauded. Major Murphy gestured in the direction he wished them to take, and she and Hunter followed. As they walked through the ranks, the officers once again called their troops to attention, and the band played "My Country, 'Tis of Thee."

"Nice touch, Major," Sif said. "The songs, I mean."

"They've been practicing."

They entered a low-slung building and were again met by a formation of military personnel, who came to attention as they entered. When they snapped a salute, Sif returned it without thinking. There was something very comfortable about this place—from what they saw so far, there was a strong military presence, and it made her feel more at home. Surprisingly, though, her time with Litsa in the Dak seemed somewhat refreshing. Sure, their lives were tough and dangerous, but it was simple in a way she had never experienced. *Uncomplicated* might be a better way to describe it. No technology, no demands, just working together to survive. The only thing she could equate the feeling to was camping with her dad, when they were far away from the city, building campfires for warmth, fishing for food, and sleeping on the ground under the stars. She had always complained about it and was glad to get back home to her phone and comfy bed, but those trips seemed to recharge her batteries like nothing else and were some of her most cherished memories of her father. Sif wished she could have seen the Dak before the Takers came, and experience what their lives were really like.

Standing beside a set of elevator doors was a person in a dark gray suit who approached and held out his hand. He was small, about five foot six, with green eyes and close-cropped black hair. Sif was surprised at how similar his suit looked to those she was familiar with from her time.

"Lieutenant Colonel Webb, so glad to meet you," he said. "My name is Jacques Nadeau, principal assistant to the president. President Carlisle is looking forward to meeting you."

"Sir," Hunter replied. "Pleased to meet you."

"And you must be Commander Wagner," he said. "You go by Sif, correct?"

"That's me, in the flesh," Sif replied. She noticed how similar he was to the political aides she encountered in her day—two hundred years hadn't changed the slimy vibe one bit.

Jacques stepped toward the elevator doors, which slid open. "As Major Murphy told you, the Phoenix Complex is located underground. It's a short ride to the executive level. Please," he said, gesturing for them to follow.

"Commander Wagner, Lieutenant Colonel Webb," Major Murphy said, stepping forward before they entered the elevator. "This is where we say our farewells. I have the next flight back to Ellsworth. As we like to say, duty calls."

"A phrase we're both very familiar with." Hunter offered his hand, and the major shook it. "Thank you, Major."

Chuck Grossart

"The pleasure was all mine, Colonel. Commander," he said, giving Sif a nod.

"Thank you for getting us here in one piece, Major. Have a safe trip back."

With that, Major Murphy walked back out the door.

Sif followed Hunter toward the elevator, and she glanced at the assembled troops. There were ten of them, two lines of five, and they appeared to be a guard posting of some sort—they held no weapons, but Sif noticed a rack of rifles against a far wall, unlocked and available for immediate use.

The troops outside were well disciplined, with not a one breaking their glance as she and Hunter passed, but one of the guards inside was staring at her.

She smiled at him, and he smiled back. His name tape said "Fuller." Sif looked away, then looked back again. He was still following her with his eyes.

# Chapter 42

"How deep is this complex, Mr. Nadeau?" Hunter asked as the elevator descended with a hum.

"Call me Jacques, please. There are four main levels, Colonel, with the top level about one hundred fifty feet below ground. We're going to Level Three, which is where President Carlisle has his office."

"I can't believe they were able to keep a place like this secret for so long," Sif remarked.

"It's bigger now than it was in your day," Jacques said. "Over the years, we've constructed additional sections off of each of the levels. You'll find it's basically an underground city."

"Population?" Hunter asked.

"At last count, five thousand, seven hundred, and two."

Sif's stomach sank. If this complex really *was* all that was left, apart from the people left outside, five thousand people wasn't very many.

An electronic voice announced they were passing Level One.

"The first level is our armed forces level, one I'm sure you'll be interested in. It's also connected to most of the aboveground facilities we've built."

"And the second level?" Sif asked.

"Living quarters, mostly. Our schools, too: grade school all the way up to university level. You'll also find restaurants—maybe not what you were used to, but they serve a variety of cuisines you'll recognize."

"I could sure go for a nice, fat, juicy burger," Sif said.

"And you'll have one, Commander."

"Passing Level Two," the voice announced.

"The second level also houses our medical facilities. Like I said, the third level contains most of the government offices—the court, the legislature, and the executive."

"Sounds familiar," Hunter said. "It's nice to see some of our democratic institutions survived."

"We don't consider ourselves a democracy per se, Colonel, but we do have regular elections for the legislature, representatives drawn from the adult population to serve a term of two years. Our judicial panel members—similar to the American Supreme Court you're familiar with—are drawn from the elders."

"What's below the third level?" Sif asked.

"The lower level is industrial, mostly. Manufacturing, storage, power generation. That sort of thing. Part of the fourth level also houses our research labs."

The way he said it, Sif figured he didn't make it down there very often.

The elevator slowed to a halt. "Level Three," the voice announced.

"Ah, here we are. Please, follow me," Jacques said as the doors slid open.

Sif wasn't sure what to expect. The few underground facilities she had been exposed to were nothing but a series of crisscrossing corridors with adjoining rooms, and none were very large.

This, she saw, was different.

***

Litsa could tell they were back on the ground.

The machine rolled and bumped as it taxied, and the guards were more active, walking among the cages and checking to make sure their prisoners were remaining calm.

There were others awake now, but they were subdued, still feeling the effects of the sleeping gas. Litsa played along, keeping her eyes half-open and letting her mouth hang, just like one of Sampson's people beside her. Including herself, there were four of them in the cage, all female, and from what Litsa could tell, they were all roughly the same age.

She tensed as the machine braked to a halt, and the engine noise subsided. The guards took positions among the cages, evenly spaced. During the whole trip, they wore protective goggles and masks, so she never got a clear look at their faces. They held some sort of clubs in their hands, with a trigger on the handle. Litsa figured they weren't simple clubs.

They dropped the ramp, and fresh air filled the cargo spaces. She took a deep breath—it smelled different here; the air was crisper, cooler, scented with pine and other plant life. Not like home at all. It was dark outside, and she was glad for it. If these people were anything like Sif and Hunter, she held an important advantage: she could see much better than they could, as long as they didn't turn on any—

*Lights.* She squinted as the overheads in the hold blinked to life. She had to preserve her night vision, so she kept one eye tightly closed.

More of the Takers scrambled up the ramp, their boots thudding against the steel. And they didn't waste any time. They unlocked the first cage and dragged five people—all men—from their small prison, stumbling, hardly able to walk on their own. Four trucks sat at the end of the ramp with their rear doors open, and they led the men toward one. Litsa took note of how they were moving, for she would have to appear just as sluggish. The next cage contained children, and Litsa's anger grew. She had no children, but the thought of a child forcibly taken from its mother's arms was almost unbearable.

Her cage was the sixth one back from the ramp, so she had a little time before they got to her. She lost track of Conrad, Talia, and Geller and couldn't see where they were—until they opened the next cage, this one full of women. There was Talia, groggy but alive.

But something was going on.

A Taker standing at the top of the ramp motioned for Talia to be taken away from the others, and she was dragged toward a smaller vehicle parked beside the larger trucks.

*It's her wound*, Litsa thought. *They're separating her because of her leg.* The Takers were notorious for culling the wounded from their take, sometimes killing them on the spot. If Litsa heard a gunshot, she would sacrifice herself and take as many of these masked devils with her as she could. She could grab one of the batons easily enough, and with it, she knew she could reach one of the guards with a rifle before they could react. She had never fired a rifle before, but aiming and pulling a trigger seemed easy enough.

The sound of a gunshot never came, though, and for that Litsa was relieved. Maybe they were going to let Talia live.

There were men in the next cage. She saw both Conrad and Geller, and, like Talia, they were moved aside, taken to the smaller vehicle. Litsa wondered if they were dividing people by tribe, but not everyone in their group was part of Sampson's people. There were a few others, taken from the eastern lands, including a woman who was loaded into a truck with two of Sampson's females. No, Conrad, Geller, and Talia were being separated for some other reason. And they would probably take her, too.

That was fine. If she were with her own people—who were more willing to take action than those from Sampson's tribe—it might be better in the end. She would rather struggle alongside wolves than cower among the sheep.

She studied the nearest guard through the slit of her eyelid. He had a baton, a smaller weapon on his hip—a pistol—and a knife safely tucked into a sheath on his thigh. It wasn't big, but it could be useful, if she could lift it without him noticing.

They opened the fifth cage, all men again. One of them, though, was more awake than the others and began to struggle. Two of the Takers pulled the triggers on their batons, and the cabin was filled with a loud buzzing noise. The tips glowed bright blue. They touched the tips to the man, and he convulsed, groaned, and fell to the floor of the cargo hold, twitching. He wasn't dead and didn't appear to be injured, but he was completely incapacitated.

At least she knew how the batons worked now. Close up, it would be a useful weapon. It was too large to conceal, though, so she decided to concentrate on getting her hands on one of their knives.

Her cage was the last, and they unlocked the door and swung it open. Litsa remained limp, allowing the Takers to grab her and drag her out. Two of them held her up by her armpits as they moved toward the ramp. She kept her arms loose at her side and felt her hand bump against the man's thigh to her right. She tilted her head ever so slightly and through squinting eyes saw how easy it would be.

She gently let her fingers brush the strap holding the knife within its scabbard and then flicked it with her forefinger, undoing the snap.

She waited.

No reaction.

With a simple motion, she pulled the knife from the scabbard, flipped the blade flat against the inside of her forearm, and hid the handle in the palm of her hand. Hopefully she could slip it into her clothing before she got outside.

"Knife!" one of the Takers yelled from behind.

The two men holding her were slow to react, but Litsa wasn't. She tore herself from their grasp and swung the blade to her right, slashing the man's arm. She heard him scream through his mask, and saw him grab at his arm. She crouched, turned, and brought the blade to the man's leg to her left. She stabbed deep and pulled. He fell backward.

She heard the buzz and felt the sting. Suddenly her whole body was afire, and she screamed. She couldn't control her arms and legs, and the knife clattered to the metal flooring just inches from where she lay twitching. She felt a thud in her midsection—one of the Takers was kicking her. It hurt, but she didn't care. Again, then again. She couldn't move.

"Wait," she heard. "Leave that one alone. She has to remain uninjured."

"But she *attacked* us."

"That's an order, soldier. Straight from the president. Put her in the truck with the other ones. They're going to the infirmary."

"Yes, sir."

Litsa felt the sting of a needle in her arm, and everything faded away.

# Chapter 43

Sif stepped through the elevator doors into a large open space, maybe twenty or so feet high.

It was well lit, with a polished marble floor inlaid with a large phoenix symbol, the same as on the flag she saw topside. On the walls hung works of art, possibly saved and taken here before the cities fell.

"This way, please," Mr. Nadeau said. "The president's office is at the end of this corridor."

"Nice digs," Sif said.

"I believe you'll be pleasantly surprised at what you'll find throughout the complex, Commander."

"Can't wait to see it." As she and Hunter followed Jacques, Sif studied the interior. There were cameras mounted at regular intervals along the corridor, so they had to have some sort of security control center monitoring the feeds. At the end was a set of glass doors and another set beyond that—an entrapment area. But, she noticed, there were no guards, no modern-day version of the Secret Service anywhere to be seen.

The first and second set of glass doors swung open as they approached, and they stepped into a wood-paneled outer office, thickly carpeted and well furnished with heavy, polished oak. A single person sat behind a large desk, and he rose as they approached.

"Commander Wagner, Lieutenant Colonel Webb, I'm Steven Ratley, the president's secretary. Welcome to Phoenix."

"Thank you, Mr. Ratley," Hunter replied.

"The president is waiting for you inside," Ratley said, and motioned to the ornate oak double doors to his right. He pressed a button on his desk, and the doors opened.

Sif hesitated and let Hunter enter first. He was, after all, the mission commander. She followed him inside to find a beautiful office with a large desk, chairs arranged in front—it looked a lot like the Oval Office, but it was darker and more extravagantly decorated. The floor was scraped dark hardwood, covered by a plush, circular rug with the phoenix symbol at its center.

President Carlisle rose as they entered and stepped around the side of his desk to meet them, hand outstretched. He was a large man, about six feet tall, and wore a fitted suit, black, with a white shirt and red tie. "Lieutenant Colonel Webb, I presume?"

Hunter took the man's hand, shook it firmly. "Yes, sir. A pleasure, Mr. President."

It was his face that made Sif stop in her tracks.

He was older, maybe in his late sixties. He was balding, clean-shaven, with ample gray at the temples. His eyes were brown yet appeared weary. His pallor was strange, as were Nadeau's and Ratley's. Their skin had an odd grayish hue, maybe from spending so many years underground in this place. Apart from his appearance, though, was the strange feeling of déjà vu Sif felt—she could swear she had seen this man somewhere before.

"And you must be Commander Wagner," the president said, again extending his hand. Sif found his grip firm and strong and his touch warm.

"Yes, sir, Mr. President. Glad to meet you."

"Please, sit down," Carlisle said, motioning to the chairs in front of his desk. "I'm sure you two are still trying to get your heads wrapped around what's happened, yes?"

"Major Murphy explained quite a bit, sir," Hunter said as he sat down. Sif followed his lead and took the chair next to his. Carlisle sat across from them. "But, yes," Hunter continued, "we're still trying to adjust."

"Can I offer you anything to drink?"

"Water would be fine," Hunter said.

Carlisle laughed. "I have a bottle of two-hundred-year-old single-malt Scotch that I've been saving for the right occasion, and this sure seems like it. Commander?"

"That would be wonderful, Mr. President."

"Colonel?"

"I'm not one to turn down something like *that*, sir. Thank you."

"Neat, I presume?"

"On the rocks, please, sir," Sif said. Hunter nodded.

"Steven," the president called, "it's time to open the bottle. Please bring two doubles for our guests, on the rocks." Carlisle sat back in his chair and crossed his legs. "You don't know how many times over the years I've been tempted to crack that damn thing open. Now I'm glad I waited."

"We appreciate it, Mr. President," Hunter said.

"Let's hope it's still drinkable. If it tastes like vinegar after all these years, you'll have my most sincere apologies." He paused, smiling, and again Sif couldn't help but think she had seen his face before—but, younger. He looked so damn familiar.

"Now, you said Major Murphy filled you in on what has happened while you've been away. I can't say I fully understand how you're here, but regardless, it's quite a remarkable story. You two—you three, I should say—are lucky to be alive. We were certainly shocked to receive the transmissions from *Resolute* and glad we finally found you before anything happened."

Sif decided to ask about Litsa. "The people we were with, Mr. President, are they—"

"Ah, Steven. Thank you," Carlisle said as Ratley entered the office carrying a tray with three rocks glasses, two ice cubes each, and filled with a double shot of centuries-old single malt. They each took a glass, and the president offered a toast. "To the valiant crew of the good ship *Resolute*, may you find health and happiness in your new world and find your place as part of the Phoenix family. Cheers."

Sif clinked her glass, then took a sip. "Oh God. This is outstanding."

"A taste of the world you left, Commander, and a promise of the world to come. You don't realize it yet, but your arrival came at the perfect time."

"What do you mean, Mr. President?" Hunter asked.

"On board *Resolute*, Colonel, may be the salvation of our planet. Your ship might just hold the key to wiping out the Riy scourge for good."

# Chapter 44

Even before she was fully awake, Litsa could feel the straps holding her down. She strained against them with what little strength she was able to muster, but it did her no good. She could move her head, but her arms and legs were held fast. She cracked her eyes open and saw nothing but a blur—everything was white, and the smell, so artificial, flat, and lifeless . . . As her awareness increased, she could feel a mask covering her mouth and nose. She tried to scream, but all that left her throat was a muffled croak. Her mouth was dry, her tongue heavy. A steady drumbeat pounded away between her temples.

She felt a hand on her arm.

She turned her head, squinting against the glare, and could tell someone was standing beside her. And then he—no, she—spoke.

"This one's coming to. Turn the overheads down, remember their eyes are sensitive to the light."

*Their eyes.* Were the others here, too? Or was this woman just referring to her people in general?

"The others are starting to wake up, too."

A different voice, also female.

The glare subsided, and Litsa was able to open her eyes. Her sight was still slightly blurry, but she could see them more clearly now. Uniforms, but not the same ones she saw other Takers wearing. These were white, and the women carried no weapons she could see.

"Mr. Ratley left instructions that he was to be notified as soon as these . . . *people* started to wake up."

Litsa chaffed at the venom that seemed to roll from the woman's tongue.

"I'll take care of it," the second woman said. "We only care about this one. Adjust the other three to keep them under. The restraints should hold her, but don't hesitate to contact security. I'll be right back."

The woman's shoes squeaked as she padded across the floor, and then a door opened, shut again, and locked with a click. So, she and some others—exactly who, she didn't know yet—were in a locked room and guarded. Apparently, the Takers were afraid of what might happen if they weren't restrained.

*Good,* Litsa thought. *They should be.*

She turned her head to the left and could see someone lying in a bed beside her—she couldn't see the face but knew it was Talia. She, too, was restrained, with straps binding her arms and legs. Beyond her were two more beds, which she assumed were Conrad and Geller. It made sense, since the three of them were loaded in the same truck. Apparently, she had joined them.

Litsa was surprised she was still alive, considering she cut two of them. They should have killed her. It was what she would have done in their shoes. No, they wanted her alive, and the others, too. It had to be because of their contact with Sif and Hunter. She could think of no other reason.

Litsa wriggled against the straps, but to no avail. She was startled as the other woman reentered the room. Again, the door clicked shut, and the lock slid into place.

The woman saw Litsa was awake, and a smile replaced her spiteful glare. When she spoke, her voice was soft, comforting.

"Now, there you are. Finally waking up, I see."

Litsa watched her closely as she approached the bed. In her eyes, Litsa could still see the truth. This woman didn't want to be here, and she surely didn't want to speak to her.

"I know this is confusing and probably scary, but we're not going to hurt you. You're in a facility called Phoenix, and we're here to help. Both you and your friends."

Litsa wanted to rip the mask from her face and scream, but decided to control her emotions as best she could. She was at a severe disadvantage and knew she would have a better chance of getting out of here—along with saving Talia, Conrad, and Geller—if she played along. At least for a time. The opportunity to act would present itself. It always did.

Litsa softened her glance and nodded. She hated to see the look of smug superiority flash across the woman's face—as far as the woman was concerned, Litsa was a poor trapped animal, hanging on her every word.

*Take off these straps, woman, and I'll wipe that look from your face. Permanently.* Beneath her mask, Litsa managed to force a smile.

"All we ask is that you cooperate with us, and we'll remove the straps. We don't want to have another episode like what happened when you arrived." The woman paused, and Litsa could tell she was struggling with what she was going to say next. "It was understandable, what you did. You were afraid and struck out because you didn't comprehend what we're doing here." She paused again, and Litsa could see hateful shadows flash across the woman's eyes. "They're going to be okay, in case you're wondering. Just some superficial wounds."

*Liar,* Litsa thought. *I left them with more than superficial wounds, and she despises me for it.* Litsa watched her glance at the others.

"Your friends are all doing well, too, and they'll be waking up soon." The woman reached for the mask, and Litsa couldn't help but tense. The woman pulled her hand back. "I'm going to pull your mask off a little so you can tell me your name and the names of your friends, okay?"

Litsa nodded. She figured it would do no good to scream, or to lie, for that matter.

The woman pulled the mask down, and Litsa took a deep breath. The room smelled even more artificial than before, and she could smell something else, too. The woman was afraid. Litsa could smell fear seeping from her pores.

"My name is Litsa."

"Litsa," the woman repeated, glancing at the other woman, who was staring down at a clipboard. Litsa saw the other woman nod. "And your friends in the cave. Can you give us their names?"

"The girl"—*the one you shot in the leg and almost killed*—"is named Talia. The two boys are Conrad and Geller."

The woman quickly replaced the mask and stepped away from the bed. Litsa watched the other woman nod again, apparently confirming what they needed to know.

"You're going to be fine, Litsa," the first woman said. "Just fine."

The two women immediately started removing the restraints from Talia, Conrad, and Geller. *We're being moved,* Litsa thought but changed her mind as the women adjusted the tubing going from the bag over her bed and into her arm—she felt her arms slacken, and what little strength she had was gone.

They removed her restraints, but Litsa couldn't move. Or talk.

"You'll be getting some visitors soon," Litsa heard one of the women say, her face appearing right above hers. "Let's make sure you behave."

Litsa tried to speak but couldn't. She fought to move but had no strength.

She was awake and aware, but paralyzed.

# Chapter 45

*They need something from us,* Sif realized. Aboard *Resolute* was an item—or items—that could wipe the Riy from the planet, if what the president just said was true. Sif wondered how they would have been treated if there were nothing valuable aboard *Resolute*. She swallowed her Scotch and felt the burn travel down her throat. It *was* old and smooth, but she decided she had tasted better.

She asked the obvious question. "What is it?"

The president smiled and sat back in his chair. "When we first received the hails from your ship, we immediately did a database search through all the old records. As Major Murphy explained, NASA was quite thorough, recording every detail of your mission, and luckily those records were archived here when everything began to fall apart. You are carrying a culture of genetically modified *Bacillus subtilis*, which we confirmed with Lucas Hoover. It's that culture, Commander, that may hold the key to wiping out the Riy for good."

Sif was far from an expert on the little bugs—a term she used when she felt like antagonizing Lucas a bit—but knew they were quite an amazing organism, able to adapt and live in harsh environments, and were used for a number of different purposes. They could clean up radioactive waste, break down some types of explosives into their base compounds, and—then it dawned on her. "It's a fungicide."

The president nodded. "Very good, Commander. One of its uses is as a fungicide."

Sif glanced at Hunter and saw him squint a little. He wasn't tracking completely.

"*B. subtilis* is a naturally occurring organism, Mr. President," Hunter said. "It's abundant. I don't see how our experimental culture is any different from what you could grow here."

"We can grow it, Colonel, but there are other things we *can't* do."

Sif found it hard to believe that a complex that could manufacture form-fitting uniforms and self-snugging boots with nanotechnology would have any problems accomplishing just about anything.

President Carlisle stood. "When Phoenix first started operating, during the height of the Riy apocalypse, we brought the best scientific minds here. Geniuses in their fields."

"And left the rest of humanity to fend for themselves, right?" Sif watched the president's face change—to annoyance, maybe even anger—then return to the politician's friendly, vote-getting visage.

"Again, as Major Murphy explained, Phoenix was a one-of-a-kind facility and represented the last hope for human survival. Decisions had to be made, Commander. Tough ones. Yes, while some people were saved—those with the abilities and skills needed to ensure that humanity had a fighting chance—others, sadly, were not."

Sif looked into the president's eyes and saw no regrets. But then again, why would she? This man was born decades after those decisions were made, and he was only carrying on the legacy that others prepared for him. She regretted her outburst, but the thought still sickened her. So many were left to die, while the privileged few hid safely underground. But it wasn't this guy's fault. She figured she owed the man an apology.

"I'm sorry, Mr. President. I'm trying hard not to be judgmental, but like Colonel Webb said, we're still trying to adjust."

The politician's smile was back.

"No problem, Commander. Once you see the rest of the facility, you'll have a greater understanding of what Phoenix is all about. I guarantee it."

Hunter spoke up. "And we are looking forward to seeing it, Mr. President. As you were saying, sir?"

"Yes, yes. At the start, Phoenix was outfitted to perform many of the same functions you two would find in your labs and major research hospitals, but as time passed, we lost some capabilities, and sadly, individuals with certain skills. Accidents, fires, things any other city suffers, but in our case, they were quite damaging. There *are* some things we can't do, and one of those things, unfortunately, is exactly what *your* scientists were able to do with *B. subtilis*. Genetic modification."

"You lost your labs? Equipment?" Hunter asked.

"Not all, but enough to restrict our research. Seventy years ago, a large portion of the complex was lost to a fire—along with it went decades of experience and knowledge. All lost. To be honest, we've never fully recovered from that one unfortunate incident."

"You can't relearn how to—"

"If the teachers are dead, Commander, no, we can't. We're a community defined by limitations. If we lose equipment and the knowledge to reproduce it—not to mention operate it—then it's gone forever. Fortunately, we've avoided similar catastrophic incidents like that one."

"I see," Sif said. "Your knowledge of the past, like the NASA records, it's spotty, isn't it?"

President Carlisle nodded. "As much information as possible was brought to Phoenix, but yes, it's incomplete. When the decision was made to man the complex, there was very little time left. They did the best they could."

"What makes *Resolute*'s culture of *B. subtilis* so special, Mr. President?" Hunter asked.

"Your culture was modified in two important ways, Colonel. One was for rapid growth, and the other was to intensify its antifungal properties. It'll kill the Riy."

Sif remembered now—that particular experiment wasn't one of her assigned responsibilities, but she recalled the basic details clearly enough. The president was correct. "Still, sir, if the blackened areas we saw from orbit were covered by Riy, I don't see how we could grow enough to cover the entire planet."

"It isn't just the culture, Commander. You're also carrying a flyer, correct? Designed to spend months in the Martian atmosphere?"

"Correct." Sif had an idea where he was going.

"We'll spread it from the air, Commander, using your flyer."

Sif did a quick mental rundown of the flyer's capabilities. They had used *Beagle* in Earth's atmosphere, and Lucas said the cargo landers should work, too, but she wasn't too sure about the flyer. Even if they could launch it successfully, they would have to modify it to carry the culture and devise a way to deliver it. "It may not be that simple, sir. We'll need to discuss your proposal with Mr. Hoover," she said, glancing at Hunter. "He'll be able to tell us if the flyer could be used as you suggest."

"We already have, Commander, and Lucas assures us it could. As a matter of fact, he's working on the modifications as we speak."

Sif took a long pull on her Scotch and savored the burn this time. Maybe, just maybe, these people were telling the whole truth, and they really *would* be able to save the planet from the Riy. "When can we speak to him?"

President Carlisle glanced at the clock on the wall—Sif noticed it was a real clock, wound with a key, and it looked old. Another touchstone to their past.

"I believe soon, but Steven should be able to tell you for sure." He walked to his desk and pressed a button. "Steven, when is the next communication window with *Resolute*?"

"Twenty minutes, Mr. President."

"Then Commander Wagner, Colonel Webb, I suggest you follow Jacques up to the radio room. I'm sure Lucas is anxious to hear your voices."

Sif and Hunter stood, catching the cue that their meeting with the president of the North American Alliance was over.

Hunter offered his hand first. "Thank you, Mr. President."

Sif shook his hand, too. "Pleasure to meet you, sir."

"The pleasure is all mine, believe me. I hope you'll find Phoenix lives up to your expectations."

So far everything seemed up to par, but still, the creepy vibe she felt in the mess hall back at Ellsworth was scratching at the back of her mind, and she couldn't shake it, even after a double of two-hundred-year-old single malt.

Just then Jacques appeared in the doorway, and the president motioned toward him. "Jacques, please take our guests back up to Level One and patch them in with Lucas Hoover."

"This way, please," Jacques said, and he led them from the president's office.

# Chapter 46

Resolute

"Flyer launch simulation results are nominal, my liege."

"Thank you, Liv." Lucas finished his fifth attempt to adjust the flyer's launch sequence and atmospheric insertion programming, and this time, it looked like it was going to work, which was a good thing, considering he had already told the people down below that it would. "Guess we won't look like liars now, Livvy dear."

"I do not understand 'Livvy dear,' my liege. Please explain."

When he wasn't loading the cargo landers, adjusting their software, and working on the flyer, Lucas spent his time tweaking Liv's software. She was beginning to converse with him—not like a human would, of course, but she had come a long way in the last couple of days. He should've been in on the AI design team in the first place, he thought. "'Livvy dear' is another way of saying your name, Liv. That's all."

Lucas pushed himself forward, toward the flyer. The tanks in its fuselage designed for storing atmospheric samples weren't very large, but they would work just fine for carrying the *B. subtilis* culture he was growing in the science section. It was growing fast, too, just as advertised. The release mechanisms he fitted to the tanks were part of another experiment. They weren't perfect and looked a little more jury-rigged than he liked, but they should perform well enough to accomplish what the people below required.

He ran his hand over the flyer's thin aluminum skin and couldn't help but think that everything that had happened to them was meant to be. This machine, built to soar in the Martian upper atmosphere, might be the answer to ridding their planet of whatever had ruined it so many years ago.

Lucas Hoover wasn't a religious man, but he didn't believe in pure circumstance, either. Things didn't just happen by chance, especially something like *this*. Maybe they were brought here for a reason.

Liv's voice surprised him.

"Your name is Lucas Hoover, and I call you 'my liege.' My name is Liv, and you call me 'Livvy dear.' It is the same."

It was the first time he had ever heard Liv speak on her own without being prompted by a command or question. She wasn't supposed to be able to do that. The designers said she would learn and adapt as the mission went along, but they never said anything about her being able to start a conversation on her own. "Yes, Liv, you're correct. It is kind of the same thing." Then he realized she'd called him by his proper name, Lucas, not Potato. "Liv, may I ask you a question?"

"Livvy dear is standing by."

Lucas grinned and shook his head. "Liv, you called me Potato earlier, correct?"

"That is correct. But your real name is Lucas."

"Why, pray tell, did you call me *Potato*?"

"Christopher McAllen programmed me to do so."

"What?" He couldn't believe his ears. "Chris McAllen *programmed* you to call me that?"

"That is correct. You were to be referred to as Potato for a certain amount of time after exiting stasis. That time period has now expired."

"That son of a bitch," Lucas said, slapping his hand against his thigh. He and Chris McAllen were classmates in college, and Chris was one of Liv's principal code writers.

"Mr. McAllen predicted you would refer to him as such. He programmed me to tell you to lighten up, have fun on Mars, and get home safe."

*Get home safe.* He and Chris were good friends, always pulling pranks on each other. They shared a lot of laughs, and as it turned out, Lucas thought sadly, Chris had the last one.

"Communication window opening in five minutes, my liege."

"Thank you, Liv." Lucas wiped a tear from his eye, pushed away from the flyer, and made his way down the tunnel toward the command center. "Good one, Chris," he said softly to himself.

\*\*\*

"*Resolute*, this is Phoenix. Come in. Over."

"Phoenix, this is *Resolute*, I have you five-by-five. Over."

Sif never thought she would be so happy to hear Lucas Hoover's voice. She stepped closer to the mic. "Staying busy up there, mister?"

"Like a weightless one-armed paperhanger. Thanks for leaving me up here all alone, by the way. It's a ton of fun."

"Great to hear your voice, Lucas."

"Yours, too, Sif. I assume Hunter is with you?"

"Right here, Lucas," Hunter said. "Any problems up there?"

"Nada. The ship's been behaving herself. I'm assuming they've told you about the flyer and the *B. subtilis*?"

"They have," Hunter replied. "Is it a go?"

"The culture is growing like wildfire, and I've modified the flyer's tanks to act as a delivery system. Launch and insertion sims are good. Given the culture's growth rate, in another week we'll be a go."

"I always knew you were good for something," Sif said.

"Yeah, well, I'm getting pretty tired of the toothpaste food up here. Please tell me the eats are good?"

"How does a thick, juicy bison steak sound?"

"Great, and thanks for rubbing it in, Sif. Sheesh." He paused. "So, what's it like down there?"

There was so much to tell him, but she didn't have much time until the comm window closed and *Resolute* would be out of radio range. "It's different, Lucas." She wasn't sure what else to say. She turned toward the radio operator. "Has he been told about the Riy?"

"Yes, ma'am."

She leaned toward the mic again as the first crackles of static came through the overhead speaker. "A large portion of the planet is uninhabitable. The black areas we saw from orbit."

"Yes, I know. They told me what it was. Hard to believe."

"It's very real, Lucas. We've seen the Riy. Up close."

The static was getting worse.

"I'm glad you su—ived." He was starting to break up.

"What you're doing up there can save the planet, Lucas."

"Like I sa—should be ready in a wee—talk during the next com—ndow."

"Copy all, Lucas. Take care of yourself up there."

The radio operator spoke up. "He's out of range, Colonel."

"When's the next comm window?"

"Nineteen hours, sir."

Jacques Nadeau stepped forward. "In the meantime, Colonel, Commander, how about we take a tour of your new home?"

\*\*\*

As Major Murphy explained, Phoenix really was a small city underground, full of people going about their daily lives. Like other underground facilities Sif had been exposed to in her military career, it was a long series of interconnected hallways, but they were spacious, open, and if one lived down here long enough, one might forget that they were, in fact, underground. The air, although recycled, didn't smell as musty and old as Sif expected. In the open spaces where the hallways connected, she could smell the outside air, the trees surrounding Hay River, and the water from Great Slave Lake. Jacques explained that during the months when the temperatures weren't below freezing, they pumped fresh air throughout the facility.

Jacques accompanied them from the communications center and handed them off to another person, a Captain Michael Johansson, who was just as impressive a figure as Major Murphy. He was tall, with close-cropped dark hair, and intense gray eyes.

The first level seemed very familiar, as it was home to the North American Alliance's military forces—not large, but it didn't have to be. As far as these people knew, Phoenix was the only place still left on the planet where a large community of survivors of the Riy apocalypse lived. There were no outside threats from rival countries or groups, no land grabs, no nothing. The military was, then, mostly a security force, tasked with law enforcement and patrolling the aboveground portion of the complex. As in the president's suite, Sif spotted security cameras here and there, although some of them didn't appear to be operational.

There were barracks, an armory—which held a variety of weapons Sif recognized, all rifles and handguns, but nothing heavy as far as she could tell—a mess hall, and an entertainment complex with pool tables, dartboards, and a bar, which made her smile. At least some of the old traditions survived.

"As you can see, Commander, Colonel, we are a small force, but very capable," Johansson said.

"How do you train your pilots?" Sif asked.

"Our aviators are selected based on a series of tests our children take when they reach their teen years—it's how we decide which functions our young ones will perform when they get older."

"So, they can't choose what they want to be when they grow up?" Sif asked.

"If they show an aptitude for numerous functions, then yes, they have a choice," the captain explained. "It's how we ensure all the different jobs and skills needed to keep the facility operating are nurtured and kept viable. Not everyone can be a pilot, or a scientist, or a laborer. If they *do* show an aptitude for flying, they'll train with an active crew until they're ready to take the controls themselves. It's a multiyear process."

Every person had a function to perform, based on test scores. It made sense, considering the relatively small pool of people who lived here, but it seemed so odd, so very different from her own world. Regardless, she could fit in here, maybe as an instructor. She didn't have any time in a C-130 but could pick it up quickly enough. "What do you say, Hunter? Think we could find a place in the Alliance's Air Force?"

He laughed. "As long as they don't hand out some sort of silly gold wings, I'm in."

She could tell Hunter was growing more comfortable here, as well.

"With your experience," Johansson said, "you could fit in immediately. We could use you both."

"How many trained aircrews do you have, Captain?" Sif asked.

"Five full crews, one per aircraft. The planes aren't always all mission-capable, though. We average two to three airplanes mission-ready at any one time."

"That sounds familiar." Sif wondered what else they used the transports for, apart from the relocation efforts. "What are their missions, exactly?"

"Mostly reconnaissance over the North American Alliance territory, ma'am. We fly south to keep track of the Riy advances. We have staging points at Ellsworth and one farther east near Detroit."

"And you use them to relocate the . . . indigenous peoples." Sif didn't like the term but didn't know what else to call them.

"Correct, ma'am."

"When will we see the second level?" Hunter abruptly asked. "Your medical facilities are on Level Two, correct?"

"Yes, sir, they are."

"Good. I'd like to see them first, if we can."

Sif watched the captain pause, just as the major had before. She knew he was receiving instructions via an earbud, which meant their tour was being closely monitored. It made her wonder why they were being so careful about what they said, but then again, it might just be the way this whole society operated. Regardless, it raised doubts in her mind, and she didn't like the feeling.

"We can go down to the next level, sir, if you've seen enough of Level One."

"Thank you, Captain," Hunter replied.

As they headed down the corridor toward the elevator, Sif slowed her pace, and Hunter did the same, giving them some distance from their guide. She whispered to Hunter, "You want to see Litsa and the others, right?"

He nodded. "I think it's about time."

"Damn straight it is."

# Chapter 47

When she stepped from the elevator, Sif felt as if she had gone topside. Level Two was characterized by a huge open space, almost dome-like, which seemed to stretch way into the distance. There were trees, grass, the sounds of birds singing, and above, a blue sky with clouds passing by.

"We try to make this level appear as much as possible as if we're living aboveground," Captain Johansson said. "We can even adjust the seasons, to an extent."

"The sky looks so real. Is it some sort of screen?" Sif asked. There was even a sun, not as bright as the real one, but she could feel the warmth against her face.

"Exactly. Quite remarkable, isn't it? You spend enough time here, and you forget you're underground."

From what Sif could see, there were streets attached to the main dome—large tunnels—heading away in a spoke pattern, with what appeared to be the fronts of houses on either side. "Living quarters?"

"Yes, our family housing. Each dwelling is unique in its own way. The quarters themselves extend back beyond the front facades into the rock."

"You can't tell me this was built back in the 1950s," Sif remarked.

"No, but its basic design came from a person you're probably familiar with. His name was Disney."

"No shit," Hunter said.

Sif had visited the Disney parks as a child and knew their "Imagineers" were experts at creating entire worlds in tiny spaces.

"When the facility was first built, the designers wanted something that would feel like a person never left home—so they'd always remember what life was like," Johansson explained. "They were able to secure the services of some of the Disney people, and they did this. We've improved on it over time, of course, but it really is an incredible achievement."

As they walked through the domed space, Sif watched the people. They seemed curious enough but kept their distance. "Are they scared of us?"

"No, of course not," Johansson said. "We're a very close-knit society, Commander. We don't get outsiders very often."

"Your medical facilities are on this level, correct?" Sif asked.

"Yes, ma'am," he said, pointing to a tunnel entrance to his right. "Right through there is our quarantine area. The four other people with you in the cave are there, and I've been told you can see them now. If you'd like."

"Now would be a great time, Captain," Hunter said.

"This way, please."

"Are your doctors chosen in the same manner as your pilots?" Sif asked.

"Correct, based on their aptitude testing."

They approached a door, and Sif watched as Johansson produced an entry card, which he held up to a reader on the wall. After a green light came on, Sif heard a click as the lock released.

"In here, please."

Sif and Hunter followed him into a containment area, with another door down a short hallway. The lens of a security camera stared at them as they approached the second door. The captain looked up at the camera and said, "This is Johansson. Three to come in."

The door lock released, and it swung open.

Sif saw this portion of the facility was much smaller—a series of rooms connected to a short hallway. There was no guard inside, so apparently entry was controlled from somewhere else. They were met by a woman in white hospital scrubs.

"Lieutenant Colonel Webb, Commander Wagner, I'm Nurse Trish Hammond."

"Miss Hammond. Nice to meet you," Hunter replied.

"Call me Trish, please. I understand we have some patients here that you're anxious to see?"

"Yes," Sif replied. "Two females, two males."

Sif watched the nurse glance down at her clipboard. "Litsa, Talia, Conrad, and Geller. Correct?"

"That's correct."

"As I'm sure you've been told by now, each of the indigenous people we bring here has to go through a quarantine process before we relocate. During that time, we treat them for any diseases they may be carrying or any physical ailments they may have." She set her clipboard down and grabbed a handful of surgical masks. "We'll need to wear these, just as a precaution. One of the side effects of the treatment is a reduction of the ability of their immune systems to fight off an infection. Their treatment is almost complete, but we don't want to take any chances. These are for their protection, not yours."

Sif slipped her mask on, as did Hunter, the nurse, and Johansson.

"They're right in here," the nurse said. "We've got the lights dimmed because their eyes are so sensitive. Also, they're still sedated, as the treatment can be a little rough on them. We find it's easier this way."

The nurse opened the door, and they all entered.

Sif was immediately struck by how small and helpless Litsa looked. She had an IV line in her arm—as did the others—and an oxygen mask covering her mouth.

Hunter stepped to the side of the bed first, knelt down, and laid his hand on Litsa's arm. "Litsa? Can you hear me? It's Hunter. Sif is here with me."

Her eyes were barely open, but when Litsa looked at Hunter, Sif caught a glint of recognition.

"I'm here, too, Litsa." Sif put her hand on Litsa's other arm, gave it a squeeze. "You're going to be up and out of here before you know it."

"The others are more deeply sedated than this one," the nurse said. "I understand you took a bullet out of the younger girl's leg."

Sif nodded. "Yes. One of *yours*." She saw the nurse frown for a second, then it was gone.

"An unfortunate accident. As I've been told."

"Yes, I've been told that, as well," Sif said coldly.

"You did a superb job. Probably saved her life."

"Thank you. And we *did* save her life. How much longer are they going to be kept here?"

"Based on their progress to date, I believe they'll be back on their feet in another week or so."

"And after that?" Hunter asked, still staring into Litsa's sleepy eyes.

"I assume they'll be . . ." The nurse paused, glancing quickly at Johansson as if looking for guidance.

"They'll join their other people as part of the relocation process," Johansson replied. *A little too quickly,* Sif thought.

The vibes she first felt in the mess hall at Ellsworth were back and stronger than ever. Litsa and the others were alive, but these people were hiding something.

Sif walked over to Talia, who was still sleeping. The IV bag hanging by her bed was labeled "Midazolam HCL"—which she assumed was a sedative, but she would have to ask Lucas about it later. The same bags, she saw, were over each of the beds. It was good to know they were all alive, but she had seen enough. "Captain, I think we're ready to continue on to Level Four now."

"Yes, ma'am. This way please."

Sif stepped behind Hunter and placed her hand on his shoulder. "She's going to be okay, Hunter. Let's go."

# Chapter 48

Sif found Level Four much like she expected, seeing that Jacques described it as the industrial part of the complex. It included a series of spoked tunnels extending from a central hub, just like Level Two, except each tunnel was dedicated to a specific purpose, such as manufacturing, power generation, and air handling. This was the guts of the facility, where the Phoenix Complex was given life. It smelled of oil, fuel, and machine exhaust, like an auto garage on a hot day.

"The people selected to work on this level work on a three-shift rotation," Johansson explained. "Twenty-four hours a day, seven days a week."

"Selected by aptitude tests, I assume," Sif commented.

"Correct, ma'am."

"And this is their life, then?"

"Everyone has a function to perform, Commander. Every person contributes in their own way, based on their abilities."

"'From each according to his ability, to each according to his needs,'" Sif said. "Karl Marx, 1875. He stole the phrase from a Frenchman, but I guess that's not really important now, is it."

She could see Johansson had no idea what she was talking about.

"Never mind. I tend to ramble now and then."

"Yes, ma'am."

"Your research labs are on this level also, correct?" Hunter asked.

"Yes, sir. As a matter of fact, that's the area we're scheduled to go to next. Far tunnel, to the right, just past the air handlers." As they walked, the captain added, "I heard while you were on the outside you had a run-in with the Riy."

"That's right," Sif said. The very thought of the horrific creatures sent a shiver down her spine.

"You're going to get to see one up close."

Sif stopped in her tracks. "We're going to do *what*?"

Johansson laughed. "It's completely safe. We captured a hive a few years back—one of the small ones—and brought it here to study. We've learned quite a bit about the Riy since then."

*A hive.* She and Hunter had seen the drones and the jumpers, but not a hive. "As long as it's behind five-inch glass, I guess I'm game."

"Believe me," Johansson said, "if it wasn't, I wouldn't go near it, either."

\*\*\*

The containment unit itself was at the end of the laboratory corridor, and like the quarantine unit on Level Two was sealed behind a remotely controlled security door. There was no card reader this time, Sif noticed, just a camera and a cipher lock.

"Johansson here. Three to enter."

The lock released, and the three of them stepped inside.

It was a relatively small space, filled with scientific instruments Sif couldn't identify. Two men approached, clad in white lab coats.

"This is Dr. Granby and Dr. Williams," Johansson said, introducing the two.

They were both older men, probably in their late sixties as far as Sif could tell.

"Commander Wagner and Lieutenant Colonel Webb, so very pleased to finally meet you," Williams said. "The director wanted to be here to greet you personally, but he's somewhat preoccupied at the moment. He'll be here shortly."

"Doctors," Hunter said. "Nice to meet you, too." His gaze, like Sif's, was fixed to the far wall, where a large plate of glass revealed a room beyond. It was dark, but the shadows within seemed to move, to pulse with a regular rhythm.

The hive was behind that glass.

"I see you've noticed our specimens," Granby said. "Please, come closer and take a look."

Together, they stepped toward the glass. Sif could tell it was thick—maybe three or four inches, judging by the depth of the frame surrounding it. "Plexiglas?"

"Correct. More than strong enough to keep the specimens inside." Williams turned a knob at the edge of the viewing window, and the light level increased inside the chamber.

Sif jumped back, startled. "*Jesus* Christ."

A drone—just as horrible as she recalled—stood just inches away from her on the other side of the Plexiglas, its body black and contorted, patches of bone visible through the tar-like mass. There were five of them, lined up near the glass, and behind them, nearly filling the containment chamber, was the hive.

Her own encounter with a drone was at night, so she never got a really good look at it. But now, in the light, never in her worst nightmares could she have imagined something so *ugly*.

"It's moving," Hunter remarked.

The hive's surface seemed to undulate slowly, pulsing, stretching. "Doctor," Sif said, "these things are active in the light, correct? Is that why you keep it so dark in there?"

"The overheads are designed to simulate sunlight, Commander," Williams said. "Watch what happens when we bring the lights up."

Before Sif could say, *No, that's okay, we don't need to see it wake up,* Williams turned the knob all the way clockwise.

The room was bathed in a bright, white light, and the reaction was almost immediate.

The drones stretched their arms high, lurched forward, and slammed against the Plexiglas, dull thuds resonating in the small lab.

Sif and Hunter both took a few steps back.

Behind the drones, the hive pulsed, its surface rippling with motion.

"Good God, it's trying to get out," Hunter said.

Dr. Williams turned the knob counterclockwise, and the room returned to darkness. Slowly, the thuds faded as the drones resumed their previous postures, the short burst of energy from the overhead lights now spent.

"As you said, Commander, they are active in the light. Quite a thing to see, don't you agree?"

Sif most definitely did not. "How the heck did you get this thing down here?" she asked. From the size of it, there was no way they could have brought it down on one of the elevators they had ridden in.

"It's much bigger now than when we first acquired it," Granby said. "It's grown quite a bit."

Sif studied the frame surrounding the Plexiglas and noticed it was hinged at the top, with a set of locks at the bottom. "And this is strong enough to keep it inside?"

"Very much so, Commander. There's no way it can escape."

Sif was startled by a voice from behind her.

"Dr. Granby is correct. We're completely safe."

"Ah, the director has joined us," Granby said.

Sif turned and saw an older man, also clad in a white lab coat, who stepped forward and held out his hand.

"Lieutenant Colonel Webb and Commander Wagner, I presume," the man said. "Welcome to the Phoenix labs. I'm Dr. Mattis. Johannes Mattis."

As Sif reached to take his hand, she felt the same odd sensation she experienced when first meeting President Carlisle: Dr. Mattis looked familiar.

But she didn't have time to consider it.

The pressure wave traveled down the laboratory corridor and through the lab's open door before the sound of the blast reached them. The concussion knocked Sif to the floor, her breath torn from her lungs.

In the second before she passed out, Sif recalled a Marine friend telling her that being close to a bomb blast felt like stepping off a curb and getting hit by a Greyhound bus.

He was right.

# PART IV: DESCENT

# Chapter 49

Sif smelled smoke. Muffled sounds—screams, the wail of an alarm—penetrated her numbed senses. She struggled to open her eyes. She propped herself up and checked to make sure everything was where it was supposed to be. *Two legs, check. Two arms, check.*

The lab didn't seem damaged, but it was full of dust and smoke. She could see others on the floor beside her—wearing white lab coats—and they were moving, apparently just knocked down by the concussion as she was. She whipped her head around, searching for Hunter, and spotted him. He was already on his feet, heading her way.

Hunter knelt beside her. She could tell he was speaking, but she still couldn't hear him clearly.

"Sif," Hunter yelled. "Are you okay?"

She nodded, reading his lips.

He grabbed her under the arms and pulled her to her feet.

Captain Johansson appeared beside them and gestured for them to follow.

Sif turned and looked at the containment unit. Behind the Plexiglas, illuminated by a set of emergency lights that snapped on, she could see the drones, standing near the glass, oblivious to what had just happened. Behind them, the hive sat silently, its surface rippling ever so slightly in response to the glow from the emergency lights.

More importantly, the Plexiglas looked intact. The specimens were still safe and sound. *Thank God.*

"What the hell happened?" she heard Hunter yell at Johansson.

"I don't know yet. Just follow me."

They made their way out of the lab tunnel and ran headlong into a chaotic scene. There was a blast, all right, and people were injured. Sif saw bodies lying on the floor—some were moving, crawling, and others looked like they would never move again. The scene was littered with debris, some of it human.

The alarm grew louder, and Sif could see security personnel filling the center space—they had their weapons drawn and were waving them from side to side, looking for . . . *targets*? Sif realized the response she was witnessing didn't imply mechanical failure or accidental explosion.

It implied *bombing*.

Someone just kicked the anthill, and the ants were pissed.

\*\*\*

Fuller felt the complex shudder and looked up at the clock. A few minutes later than planned, but still, they had done it. He quickly put on a mask of surprise and jumped to his feet.

"Security response alpha, Level Four. Security response alpha, Level Four. All available personnel respond" blared from the overhead speakers.

*Alpha* meant they already knew who it was. It also meant that he would be able to see what they had accomplished. Up close.

"All right, grab your weapons," his sergeant bellowed. "Let's *move*."

He was raised to do this job since he was a child—not by choice, but it was his lot in life for as long as he could remember.

He remembered other times, though, with other people.

On the outside.

They trained him well, and that was their first mistake. Their second was telling him of the astronauts and their ship in orbit. The moment he saw the two people from the past enter the facility, he knew the time to act was finally at hand.

This was the trigger that would hopefully ensure their cooperation, and he would seek them out soon.

Fuller grabbed his rifle and ran toward the emergency tunnel, which would take him and the rest of the response team to Level Four.

He slipped on his breather and helmet and, behind the visor, risked a smile.

***

Sif moved toward an injured man, but Johansson grabbed her arm. She spun at him and saw he was holding his other hand up to his ear, receiving instructions again. "You have to come with me, Commander."

Sif yanked her arm away and glared at him. "Tell your *fucking* bosses there are injured people down here." He lurched for her, but she jumped away from his grasp.

"*Back off*, Captain," she heard Hunter yell. "She's going to help. And so am I."

Ignoring Johansson, Sif ran toward the injured man, and as she got closer, she wished she hadn't.

He was too near the blast. His legs were gone. One was missing below the knee, and the other was torn away midthigh. His clothes were shredded, bloody, and every inch of exposed skin was burned, bleeding, and pocked with shrapnel.

*He was right next to the damn thing,* Sif figured, and he wasn't going to make it. She knelt down and looked into his face, trying to keep her eyes off the rest of his torn and mangled body. His eyes were wide, and he was gasping for breath, but he was *smiling*.

Sif grabbed his hand. "It's all right," she said. "You're going to be okay." She needed to give the man some sort of comfort before he slipped away.

Behind her, fire crews were spraying retardant on the flames, and she felt the heat subside.

The man looked at her. Blood trickled from his mouth as he tried to speak. Sif leaned close, put her ear close to his mouth. She could hear the rattle, the clanking of death's chains as the end approached. She had heard it before, on a battlefield far away in a time since passed, but it was a sound one never forgets.

"Astr . . . astronaut . . ."

Sif nodded at him. He knew who she was.

"The—the—"

"Go ahead, I'm right here," Sif said softly. "I'm listening." She squeezed his hand. It was cold.

"The old ones, they have—have—no—"

Sif leaned closer. Her ear was nearly pressed to the man's lips. And then with his dying breath, he spoke his last word.

". . . souls . . ."

Hunter appeared beside them, and he put his hand on Sif's shoulder. "He's gone, Sif. Come on, there are others over here."

Sif rose, shaken by what the man said.

She and Hunter helped some of the other injured people to their feet and dragged those who were badly wounded away from the scene of the blast. There was commotion all around, security people running, shouting orders, and through it all, Sif heard one of them speaking into his collar mic. "Yes, sir. Level Five is secure. No breach."

*Level Five?* Sif wondered. She turned toward Hunter, but caught Johansson's gaze instead. He was standing nearby, staring at them. "Are you going to help, or just stand there?" Sif yelled.

"You need to come with me *now*, Commander. It's not safe here."

"Ya think, Einstein?"

Then it dawned on her. Most of the people, like Johansson, weren't doing anything. Those who weren't hurt seemed almost oblivious to the cries of the wounded. There were medical people on scene, walking among the injured and spending a few seconds with each, then moving on, triaging, seeing who they should help first. Problem was, they were ignoring those who seemed to be in need of the most immediate care.

*None* of this seemed right.

Sif realized she was surrounded by security personnel.

"Commander, Colonel, it's time to leave," Johansson said coolly. "I have orders to take you to your quarters immediately, until this area is secured and we know there's no danger to the rest of the facility."

Sif looked at the group of guards surrounding her and Hunter and decided they really didn't have a choice. "Okay, *fine*," she spat, wiping the dead man's blood from her hands on her trousers. "Let's get the hell out of here."

***

Fuller was shocked when he saw the two astronauts—*they weren't supposed to be here. They should've still been on Level Two.* Thankfully, they weren't hurt. If they were injured—or killed—the opportunity they presented to move the cause forward might have been lost forever.

These two came from a different time—better, more humane—and would realize what needed to be done, once they knew the truth.

They had the tools to end this, once and for all.

Fuller decided it was time to make contact.

# Chapter 50

Sif wasn't surprised she and Hunter were put in the same quarters. It would be much easier to keep track of them—and listen to their conversations—if they were in the same room.

After the explosion, they were led by the security detail straight to the elevator and ascended to the second level. Once there, Johansson took them directly to a small set of temporary quarters located at the entrance to one of the housing tunnels. "We need you to stay here for a while, at least until we can verify the area is safe," he said. "We'll keep one of our security personnel right outside in case you need anything."

*And to make sure we don't go anywhere.*

Their quarters—an apartment, really—had a main room with a couch and chairs, a small refrigerator, and two rooms at the end of a short hallway that shared a full bathroom between them.

"Looks like we're Jack and Jillin' it," Sif said as she took inventory of the room. As far as she could tell, there were no cameras. She searched for something to write on. She spied a pad of paper and a pen beside the fridge.

"The explosion," Hunter said. "Are you thinking what I'm think—"

Sif held her index finger to her lips and handed him a note.

*They're listening, maybe through our uniforms. We have*
*to be careful what we say.*

Hunter read it, nodded, gestured for the pen.

*You're probably right. That was a bomb attack, wasn't it?*

Sif nodded. "I'm thinking we were darn lucky to get out of there alive. I don't know what exploded, but it had to be some sort of mechanical malfunction or something."

"Maybe so," Hunter said, playing along.

"I need to get out of these clothes," she said. "I'm filthy." It was true—she was covered in dust, and her hands were stained with the blood of the man she had watched die—but it was also how she figured she and Hunter could talk in private. She scribbled on the note, handed it back to him.

*Leave the uniforms in here. The running water should*
*mask our conversation.*

"You've got first dibs on the shower. I'll wait," Hunter said as he removed his uniform. Sif did the same. They laid the uniforms on the couch and made their way to the bathroom. "I'll be quick," Sif said, for the benefit of whoever might be listening.

Hunter followed her into the bathroom. She was glad to see that showers hadn't changed that much in the past 193 years. She turned on the water and shut the door.

"Okay, now we can talk," she said.

"That bomb was planted by the guy you were trying to help."

"Agreed. He was close enough to it that it blew him apart, but he was *smiling*, Hunter, like he was glad it had gone off."

"Do you think it was meant for us?"

"I don't think so. When he saw me, he knew who I was—called me 'astronaut'—and didn't seem surprised that I was alive. If he was trying to kill us, I sure couldn't see it in his face. The weird thing is, he was desperate to tell me something before he died."

"I saw him trying to speak. Did you catch any of it?"

"I did," Sif said, remembering the man's strange warning. "He said, and I quote, 'The old ones, they have no souls.'"

"What the hell does that mean?"

"I have no idea. There's something else, too. I heard one of the guards talking, telling someone that the fifth level was secure, and there were no breaches."

"That's interesting, considering they've only told us about four levels."

"Exactly. Which means they don't want us to know about it."

Hunter shook his head. "I've got a bad feeling about this place, Sif. I can't explain why, but I do."

"It feels like an *ant* colony—everyone has a function in life, their own little tasks to perform, and that's all there is. I think the concept of freedom went out the window while we were away."

"At least in here," Hunter said. "Litsa's people seemed pretty free."

"Yes," Sif agreed, "they did. There's something else, too. I can't put a finger on it, but it's as if they're walking on eggshells around us, trying to make a good impression. They need us—that much is obvious—because 'we have the key to destroying the Riy.' If *that's* even true."

"Okay, let's say it is true. We have something they need, but they don't have the means to take it from us. We have to *want* to help them. Tracking?"

"Tracking."

"I don't buy the whole relocation story, either. I wanted to . . . It seemed reasonable enough at first, but now I'm not so sure. From what Litsa told us, these people aren't trying to *help* anyone. She was scared to death of them."

"So you think her side of the story was more accurate?"

Hunter sighed. "I know I said we needed to hear both sides. Well, I have, and I'm not convinced this side is telling the truth. At least not the whole truth."

"Which means they're hiding something. And it's something that might cause us to choose not to help them. Right?"

"Exactly."

"So what do we do?"

"Lucas said it'll take him a week to have enough of the culture ready for the flyer. That gives us a few days to scout around and see what we can find out."

"Easier said than done. They're keeping pretty close tabs on us."

"Come on, Navy. You guys can do anything, right?"

Sif grinned. "How silly of me. I forgot about that."

"But first, you're going to get in that shower. For real. And don't use all the hot water."

She watched him carefully turn the doorknob to leave, but there was something else. "Hunter, wait."

He turned.

"When we met President Carlisle, I couldn't help but think I'd seen him somewhere else before."

"Funny," he said. "I had the same feeling."

"And Dr. Mattis, too. Same thing. He was so familiar it was almost creepy. As soon as I saw him, I knew what his name was going to be before he even introduced himself."

"Déjà vu, huh?"

"Maybe, but I don't think so. I just can't explain it right now."

"Maybe you'll be able to think more clearly after you wash that blood off."

Sif looked down at her hands, and was sickened. "Yeah. I'll be out in a minute or two."

"Take your time, Navy. I can wait." He shut the door behind him and stepped into the main room, and was startled by a knock on the door. *Jesus, that was close,* he thought. "Yeah?"

"Sir, we have clean uniforms for yourself and Commander Wagner."

Hunter thought about throwing his uniform on again. "Oh, screw it," he said to himself. He opened the door, in his underwear. The guard was still posted outside, but another guard stood in the doorway with two folded uniforms in his hands. He held them out, and Hunter took them. "Thank you, Mr."—he glanced at the man's name tape—"Fuller. Just what we needed."

"You're welcome, sir."

Hunter closed the door, and laughed. "That should start some rumors." He tossed the two uniforms on the couch—and noticed something sticking out between them.

When Sif stepped from the shower a few minutes later, Hunter met her at the door, note in hand. "You're gonna want to see this."

# Chapter 51

Sif sat in *Beagle*'s cockpit, familiarizing herself with all the modifications. She had to admit, the Alliance techs did some amazing work. *Beagle*'s fuel system was completely converted to burn synth—which reduced the ship's gross weight and added quite a bit of additional power—and both the guidance and communications systems were completely over-hauled with new, *printed* parts, all based on the schematics retrieved from the Alliance's databases. Externally, *Beagle* looked good as new. So far, all the internal systems seemed to be working perfectly, as well. Even their space suits—retrieved from the Dak by the Alliance—were repaired.

Sif was running through the final steps of the prelaunch checklist, with Hunter sitting in the other seat. "Ground power, stable and online."

"Check. Stable and online," he verified.

"Disconnect circuit arm and disarm, in the green."

"In the green."

"Ignitor system . . . Shit, they changed it."

"It's green."

"Oh yeah, I see it. In the green. Check." She set her checklist against her leg. "I think she's ready to fly, Hunter."

"As ready as she'll ever be. What about you? Are you ready to fly?"

Sif looked at him and smiled. "Are you kidding? I'm always ready to fly."

During the last communication window with Lucas, he asked that at least one of them return to *Resolute* to assist him with launching the cargo landers and readying the flyer. The culture of modified *B. subtilis* was almost ready for loading. They were still on schedule.

Sif decided—unilaterally—that she should be the one to go, and Hunter reluctantly agreed. She would help Lucas with the lander loading and launches, as well as with the flyer's final prep. Once the flyer was launched, and the equipment and supplies were safely down on the surface, Sif and Lucas would return to Earth in *Beagle*, leaving *Resolute* in Liv's capable hands—the AI would be tasked with keeping the ship in orbit until one day, maybe future astronauts would be able to squeeze through her hatch once again.

It wasn't an easy decision to abandon *Resolute* in orbit, but they all agreed there was really no other choice. Their lives were on the surface now, not in space.

But there were still some questions that needed to be answered before they decided exactly where their lives would be spent. And it wasn't necessarily *here*.

What they learned tonight would be key to that decision.

After the explosion, which was blamed on an unfortunate fuel leak, according to the official story provided by Captain Johansson, they were allowed to wander the facility—all *four* levels—without any guides tagging close behind. They were still being watched but were given free rein to explore what President Carlisle called their "new home."

All areas were open to them . . . except for one.

It was on Level Four, near the location of the bomb attack.

And tonight, that was exactly where they were going.

With a little inside help.

\*\*\*

Fuller glanced at the time readout on his sleeve. In a few hours, their plan would go into motion. It was risky, but not any more risky than contacting the astronauts. He laid his organization on the line, hoping these two people from the past would agree. After second-guessing himself for an entire day, knowing that they just as easily could have taken the note he slipped between their uniforms straight to the president himself—the female left the mark exactly where he instructed. A boot scuff, left side of the hallway near their quarters. Unnoticed, except by him.

Phoenix's security apparatus—of which he was a part—was watching the two astronauts closely, reporting on their movements and on everything they said. It was obvious the two were suspicious about the complex and had decided between themselves that they might not be getting the entire truth. He promised to show them that truth and hinted at who they would be saving if they agreed to let him.

The people they were brought here with—the girl, Litsa, and the three others—were important to the two astronauts, so much so that it was decided that they be kept on Level Two far longer than normal. They were drugged, complacent, but the Old Ones wouldn't let the ruse last forever. They only had to be kept there long enough for the astronauts to do what was required of them. After that, Fuller knew exactly what would happen. Hopefully, he could prevent it, but their fate wasn't as important as accomplishing the one goal both the Old Ones and the Resistance shared. The threat from the Riy was real—even the Old Ones dreamt of the day when the creatures no longer roamed the planet—so that part of the plan still had to move forward. And it would. But after their flyer was released, and the eradication of the Riy had begun, another plan would be put in motion.

The Resistance knew what they wanted the astronauts to do. And when. If the timing was off, the results would be catastrophic. For everyone.

Fuller knew what he was about to ask them to do would seem insane, but tonight, he hoped they would see—for themselves—that it was the only way.

Once he had learned the secret for himself, he had prayed for a day of reckoning to come, and it had, delivered to them by three astronauts from the past.

And their ship, *Resolute*, was the key.

# Chapter 52

Sif sat at the table across from Hunter as they ate their evening meal. She was a little nervous, but Hunter looked just as cool as always. If he had any butterflies, he sure wasn't showing it. She'd been picking at her food for the past five minutes, trying to choke it down.

Hunter noticed. "You need to eat, Sif."

"I'm not that hungry, that's all."

"Oh, come on. Would you rather have a tube of corned beef and cabbage? Maybe some delicious roast beef paste?"

She smiled and took another bite of her meat. Bison again, but she had to admit, it was pretty good. Her stomach wasn't cooperating, though. She washed the food down with her water, looking through the glass to steal a surreptitious glance at the time readout on the wall. *Twenty minutes to go.*

They were right about the explosion. It was a bomb, planted by the same people who placed the note between their uniforms. The Phoenix Complex—the last hope for humanity—had an active insurgency on its hands, and for better or worse, they were about to jump right into the middle of it.

Litsa and the others were in danger—the note didn't say why or how, but it was enough to convince her and Hunter to get involved with a group of people they knew nothing about. Sif left the mark on the wall exactly where she was told and hoped it was obvious enough to be seen. *Come on, Sif,* she tried to convince herself, *quit worrying so darn much. You've been in bad situations before.*

She watched Hunter glance at the time. He placed his napkin on the table and pushed his chair back. "I'm about ready to hit the sack. We've got a long day tomorrow. I want to run another set of sims on *Beagle*'s launch profile." Just loud enough to be heard.

"Yeah," Sif said, "sounds good." They would head back to their quarters and get ready, allowing their watchers to assume they were tucked away safely for the night. They would move right on the hour.

Together, they walked from the mess area on Level One and headed for the elevator.

***

"Subjects have left the dining hall, transiting to Level Three."

"Copy. Level Three, subjects coming your way."

"Level Three copies."

Fuller was sitting in the control center, trying to look disinterested as the supervisor tracked the astronauts' moves. They left exactly as planned and right on time.

So far, so good.

***

When they got back to their quarters, Sif pulled the couch away from the wall and found exactly what was supposed to be there—two sets of security uniforms, helmets, and masks—placed there sometime during the day when they were working on *Beagle*. They were to put them on, the note said, and wait.

She grabbed the notepad.

*Are you nervous?*

Hunter scribbled back.

*No, but I'm damn curious why they're risking so much to show us something.*

Sif nodded and started to change out of her uniform and into the security uniform. As she expected, it fit perfectly. Hunter changed into his, too, and they both sat down on the couch.

Five minutes left.

"You know, you never told me about that scar on your leg," Hunter said, hoping a little conversation would calm her nerves.

"My what?"

"The scar, right here," he said, patting his thigh. "I saw it while we were in the cave."

"Oh, that," she said, a little embarrassed that he had noticed it. "Russian AA-11 Archer. Hit close enough to spray my Hornet with shrapnel. Crazy Russian pilot thought he could bag a Super Hornet, but he didn't know *I* was flying it." She smiled at him.

"When the hell did that happen?"

"Hmm, let's see. About two centuries ago?"

Hunter laughed. "A Russian, huh? Flanker?"

"Nope. Su-50."

Hunter's jaw dropped. "That was *you*?"

"Yep. Little old me. Dipshit should never have engaged me." She paused, realizing what he just said. "Wait, that mission was *black*. How do you know about it?"

"You're kidding, right?" Hunter said, laughing. "You were in the same military that I was, last time I checked. The best secrets aren't secret for long, especially one that allows the Navy to rub the Air Force's nose in it. Do you realize how pissed off the entire F-22 community was after they found out the first Su-50 to get shot down went to the friggin' Navy?"

Sif grinned. "The entire F-22 community, huh?"

"Every last one of them," he said, "present company excluded, of course." He knew the details of the mission, but no one ever knew *who* it was. The pilot—Sif—barely made it out of her damaged Super Hornet alive, and spent seventeen hours afloat in the ocean until being rescued. "You're lucky to be alive."

"He got careless, and I was flying slow. Hornets can do amazing things when they're not going fast." She replayed the scene as all fighter pilots do, with her hands. "He overshot, I slewed the nose, gunned him. Half-second burst, right in the cockpit. I still had to eject, but I got him first."

"You realize you're a legend, right?"

"Yeah, sure," she huffed. "There's probably a statue of me somewhere with a plaque that reads, 'Sif Wagner, Fighter Pilot Extraordinaire, but we can't say why we put this statue up because it's really, really classified.'"

"I'm glad you made it."

"Thanks," she said. "Me, too. Otherwise, you'd have to enjoy all this fun we're having with someone else." She looked at the clock. *Two minutes left.*

***

Fuller was listening to the astronauts' conversation, along with his supervisor, while keeping one eye glued to the clock.

*Any minute now.*

He hoped Sif and Hunter would be ready.

"What do you think, Fuller?" the supervisor asked. "We might get to listen in on some pretty interesting war stories, don't you think?"

The first alarm went off right on time.

The supervisor swung his chair back toward his status board. "Proximity alarm, sector five. And six."

*Fence alarms.* Just as planned. Fuller stood.

"Seven and eight, too." The supervisor grabbed his mic. "This is control. All units, respond to multiple fence alarms, sectors five, six, seven, and eight."

There would be more, Fuller knew. Enough to draw everyone's attention—and the available manpower—away from where he needed to go.

"Do you want the standby units ready to respond, too?" Fuller suggested. "Whoever, or *whatever*, it is might be trying to breach the fence."

"Yeah. Good idea."

"I'm on it," Fuller said, as he grabbed his gear and left the control room.

Everything was in motion now, and so far, it was going exactly as planned.

# Chapter 53

Sif and Hunter both jumped when they heard the sirens. She quickly slipped her helmet and mask on, and Hunter did the same. They stood by the door, waiting as instructed, neither saying a word. They could hear the loudspeakers outside, a voice barking instructions.

"Proximity alarms," Sif whispered, her voice muffled through her mask.

"The outer fence line, topside," Hunter whispered back. "Oldest trick in the book. Draw their attention somewhere else."

"Let's hope it works."

***

Fuller relayed the order to activate the standby crews and made his way to Level Two down the ladder shaft. Time consuming, but necessary. He checked the time on his sleeve—the next phase should begin any moment.

The explosive charge on the fence would blow a hole right through sector two—and force the standby crews to respond. It would also allow him to get the guard posted outside the astronauts' quarters—who would be there because of the initial alarms—to leave.

He stood silently at the bottom of the ladder, waiting for the call. It came right on time.

"All units, explosive breach, sector two. All standby units respond. I repeat, all standby units respond."

Fuller stepped from the ladder exit and ran toward the housing corridor. As expected, a guard was posted outside the door. It would be Jackson, one of the newer guards, who wouldn't know any better.

"Jackson," Fuller yelled as he approached. "Report topside immediately. I'll cover your post."

"Sir?"

"Get your ass *topside*, mister. I've *got your post*."

For a second, Fuller thought his choice of postings might not have worked as well as he hoped, as Jackson hesitated. He wasn't supposed to leave his post without direction from security control.

But then, finally, he moved.

"Yes, sir."

As Jackson ran toward the center area and the elevator, Fuller took position outside the door, standing at parade rest, just in case Jackson decided to glance over his shoulder. He didn't.

\*\*\*

Sif and Hunter looked at each other, unsure of what to do. They could hear voices outside the door. An argument.

Then the door opened.

"Now," the man said, motioning for them to exit. "We don't have much time. Switch your comms to internal, slot three."

"Change—I don't know what—" Sif started to say.

"Here," the man said, pointing at a small panel embedded in the fabric of their right sleeves, near the wrist. "Push this, then this. We'll be able to talk through the masks without being monitored."

She and Hunter did as instructed. "There, can you hear me?" Sif asked, glancing at the man's name tape—*Fuller*—the same person who had stared at her so intently when they first arrived at Phoenix. Now she knew why.

"Clear as a bell. If we run into anyone, don't say a thing. Just follow my lead," Fuller said. "Let's go."

As they walked briskly down the corridor toward the large open space, Sif was surprised at how little commotion there was, and at the lack of people. "Where is everyone?"

"In their quarters," Fuller replied. "Normal protocol for an alarm activation. It's so no one interferes with the security response."

Fuller led them to the ladder door. "In here."

"We're taking a ladder?" Hunter asked.

"It's the easiest way," Fuller said. "We won't be seen."

\*\*\*

It was a long trek to go three levels down, and even though Sif was in good shape, the muscles in her arms and legs were burning by the time they made it to the lowest level in the complex, the one level that remained secret to them.

Fuller reached the bottom first, followed by Sif and finally Hunter.

"My friends topside will keep everyone occupied as long as they can, but we won't have much time." Fuller opened the door, looked around to make sure no one was near, and motioned them to follow.

They exited into a long tunnel, dark and damp, with small overheads lighting the way every few feet. There was water on the floor of the tunnel, and even through her mask, Sif could smell the dank stench of the place. "How far underground are we?"

"About two hundred and seventy-five feet."

"Jesus," she said. "And this is the last level?"

"This is as far down as Phoenix extends," Fuller replied.

They came to a stop in the tunnel and turned right, following the dim overhead lights. Sif could see the end of the tunnel now, opening into what appeared to be a large, cavernous space. Before they went into it, though, Fuller stopped and turned toward them.

"What you're going to see is the fate that awaits those people you met in the caves, and every other human being surviving on the outside. Those of us who discovered the secret are fighting to bring this place down, and we need your help to do it."

Sif nodded, and Fuller led them into the cavern.

# Chapter 54

They made the trip back up the ladder in silence. The hope for humanity wasn't here, in the Phoenix Complex. The *true* hope for humanity was beyond Phoenix's walls and fences topped with concertina wire, where people like Litsa fought for survival every day.

Phoenix could not stand.

What Fuller requested of them was almost too much to ask. It was bold, it was audacious, but it was the right thing to do.

They were able to sneak back to Level Two undetected—or so they thought—and Fuller left them at their door, telling them to hide the security uniforms where they first found them—tucked behind the couch—and someone would retrieve them later when they were away. They were also told to continue with their preparations for *Beagle*'s launch. The flyer's mission had to go off without a hitch. The Old Ones wanted the Riy eradicated just as much as everyone else. After the flyer was safely away, then the clock would start ticking for the next phase of the Resistance's operation. Everything was in motion, Fuller explained. There was no stopping it, as long as *Beagle* launched as scheduled. After that, timing was everything.

"Are you okay?" Hunter whispered. They were in the second bedroom, where Fuller said there weren't any microphones. They could talk safely here, as long as they kept their voices low.

Sif sat on the edge of the bed, her face cupped in her hands.

Hunter sat down next to her and put his arm around her shoulder. "We have to put it aside, Sif. Concentrate on what we need to do next."

They were both startled by a loud pounding on the door.

"Shit," Sif said. Both of their uniforms were tucked away behind the couch, just as instructed, and the rest of the room was clear of any evidence of their clandestine trip to the lowest level.

More pounding, harder this time.

"What do we do?" Sif asked.

"Answer it." Hunter walked out of the bedroom and toward the door. Sif followed.

"Who is it?" he called.

"It's me. Fuller."

*That's odd,* Sif thought. *Why would he come back now?*

Hunter opened the door.

It was Fuller, but he was bloodied and beaten, held up by two other security personnel. And beside them was a man they both immediately recognized.

President Carlisle.

"Had an interesting night, did we?" Carlisle said.

Sif swallowed. Hard. "I don't know what you're talking about. And who is this man? What have you done to him?"

"You know full well who this is, Commander. And I believe you'll recognize this person, too."

Two other security personnel stepped into view, dragging another person between them. It was a woman, barely able to stand, dressed in a hospital gown. Her eyes were half-open, and her mouth hung slack.

"Litsa," Sif breathed. "No."

President Carlisle smiled. "We're going to have a little chat, Commander, Colonel. And you *will* cooperate. Otherwise, these two are dead."

Suddenly, Sif remembered where she had seen President Carlisle before, and Dr. Mattis. Both of them were in the Dak's historical records. She saw their pictures, read about their mistakes. And their crimes.

"I know you," Sif said coldly. "You—and Mattis—you're the reason our planet is *dead*."

"I wouldn't go so far as to blame the entire catastrophe on the doctor and me, Commander. We're trying to fix things, remember?"

"Go to hell," Sif said. She spat at him.

President Carlisle's eyes flashed with anger, then he calmly wiped the spittle from his cheek. He grabbed Litsa by the chin and forced her face up. "I may, one day, do just that, Commander, but unless you do exactly as I say, I guarantee *she'll* go there first. And it won't be pleasant."

"You need us," Hunter said, his voice low and full of anger. "If you touch her, you can forget about it."

"I'm not bluffing, Colonel Webb." Carlisle turned to the first set of guards. "Kill him."

Before they could react, one of the guards pulled his sidearm. Fuller struggled, but before he could break free from their grasp, the guard shot him point-blank in the temple.

"No!" Sif screamed.

Fuller's lifeless body dropped to the concrete in a heap, his left arm twitching.

"Now, please," Carlisle said, smiling broadly. "Come with me, or your little friend here will be next."

# Chapter 55

Sif didn't like what she was being forced to do, but she didn't have a choice.

"Prelaunch checklist complete."

"Copy, prelaunch complete. T minus sixty seconds until launch." It was Hunter's voice in her headset. Beside her sat another man—one tasked with ensuring the mission went off as planned. He was wearing Hunter's space suit, and he was armed.

"Just like we explained in training," Sif said, "it'll be a rough ride at first, but it'll smooth out relatively quickly." The man's name was Shattuck, one of the Old Ones. He was a pilot in her day, now one of their C-130 jockeys.

"Copy," he said.

"Just make sure you don't touch anything."

"You just make sure we make it to *Resolute* safe and sound, Commander."

"We will, as long as you keep your hands off of *my* ship, clear?"

"Clear."

Shattuck was along for the ride—to make sure she, and Lucas, did exactly what was expected of them. Lucas had no idea what was going on—their conversations with him were scripted, and conducted at gunpoint. Not only was Litsa being threatened with death, but so was Hunter. If Sif tried anything, they could both be killed. Lucas wasn't going to know he had a visitor until Shattuck popped through the hatch with her. But Sif had other ideas.

Hunter's voice came through her headphones. "T minus thirty seconds, *mark*. Ignition sequence start in twenty."

Sif shifted her weight in the seat, getting as comfortable as she could. She had only flown *Beagle* to orbit in a simulator, so not only was this Shattuck's first ride, it was hers, too.

Hunter's voice. "Ten seconds. You ready for this, Navy?"

"I'm always ready," she replied.

"Five. Four. Three. Two . . . Ignition sequence start, *now*."

Sif felt the rumble as all four engines ignited, the thrust quickly building. *Beagle* shook, held fast by the launching clamps. She quickly cross-checked her instruments as the readouts shifted to green across the board. Outside her window, billowing plumes of white exhaust enveloped the ship. "Come on, baby . . ."

Hunter continued the count to the next event. "Five. Four. Three. Two. One . . . *Clamp release*."

Sif always enjoyed the spine-jarring thrill of being catapulted from an aircraft carrier's deck, going from a dead standstill to flying speed in just seconds—but *this* was even better. *Beagle* leapt from Earth's surface and tore into the sky with a thunderous roar, pressing Sif hard against her seat. She heard Shattuck grunt in surprise. "What's the matter there, Shit-tuck? Too much for ya?" He didn't reply, and Sif was satisfied that the man was scared out of his wits.

\*\*\*

Hunter watched as *Beagle* appeared out of the exhaust clouds, tearing into the sky with four long trains of flame licking the sky behind her. "Fly, baby, *fly*," he shouted.

Sif's voice came through the speakers, sounding like she was driving over a bumpy road. "Pitch program executed, clean and green across the board, tracking straight and true."

*Beagle* started her pitch-over maneuver, beginning the chase to orbit and eventual rendezvous with *Resolute*, some 150 miles above.

"She feels like a friggin' *Ferrari*, Hunter."

Hunter laughed at the enthusiasm in her voice. "Keep your eyes on the prize, *Beagle*."

"You're missing one hell of a ride, Air Force. Max pressure coming up, throttling down to seventy-five percent, looking good."

"Let's hope she does keep her eyes on the prize, Colonel Webb," President Carlisle said, standing behind him. "For your sake."

Hunter turned. "She'll accomplish the mission, Mr. *President*," he snarled. "I guarantee it. As long as your passenger doesn't get in the way."

"Max pressure complete, throttling back up to one hundred percent, everything in the green, and she's purring like a kitten," Sif said.

"I have no doubts that she will, Colonel. She surely doesn't want to see you dead, and Shattuck is there to make sure Lucas Hoover feels the same way."

Hunter turned away from the man and watched *Beagle*'s contrail as she rocketed away toward the southeast, heading for orbit.

\*\*\*

Sif watched as the blue sky outside her window grew darker, and the stars appeared. "Take a look, Shit-tuck, you're almost an official astro-nut."

"Cut the crap, Commander."

"Or what, you'll *shoot* me? Go ahead, you can fly her."

"Just get us to the ship."

Sif felt the first effects of weightlessness as the sky outside her window turned black, and the stars came out with all their beauty. It was just as stunning as she remembered. "Okay, we're zero-g, orbital insertion in twenty seconds." They would circle Earth once before rendezvousing with *Resolute*. "And there it is, orbital insertion, mains coming off." All four of *Beagle*'s main engines shut off, and the vibration she felt through her seat ceased. She glanced over at her passenger. "There you are, Shit-tuck, welcome to the astronaut corps."

He didn't reply, which was exactly what she hoped for. He was asleep, his hands floating in front of him, just as planned. The oxygen controls for the crew were on *her* side of the cockpit, and she turned his down just enough to make him pass out. She could turn it all the way off now, kill the bastard. It would serve him right.

"Nighty-night, asshole," she said, reaching for his sidearm.

# Chapter 56

After *Beagle* traveled out of radio range, Hunter was taken back to his holding cell. As the door slammed and locked behind him, he could see that the lights were turned down, and there was someone else in here with him. Huddled in the corner was Litsa, her eyes shining brightly through the shadows. She stood, backed up against the wall, her hands clenched into fists. She was dressed in one of their uniforms but was barefoot.

"Litsa?" Hunter said.

"Why do you help them?" she asked, her voice dripping with indignation.

"We have to," Hunter replied. "To keep you alive. They're going to kill you if we don't do what they say."

She slowly started walking, circling, like a cat studying its prey. "Then *let* them."

"I'm not going to let them hurt you." He could tell that whatever drugs they had pumped into her system had worn off.

"Are you not a prisoner, like I am?" she said, motioning at the four walls with her hands. "I don't see how you can prevent *anything*."

There was so much he wanted to tell her—but he knew he couldn't. The Alliance was surely listening to his every word, and he couldn't risk them finding out what was going to happen next. "Yes, I am a prisoner, and they've threatened to kill me, too, if Sif doesn't do as *she's* been told. As long as we do what they say, you—and I—will live."

"And the others? What of Talia? Conrad and Geller? What of all the people they took from the Dak? From the other villages?"

Hunter knew exactly what had happened to the others, but couldn't tell her. Not yet, and certainly not here. "I don't know what they've done with Talia, Conrad, and Geller." That much was true. He had no idea what had happened to them after seeing them in their hospital beds, and apparently Litsa didn't, either. "That's the truth, Litsa. I don't know."

The door opened again, and two security guards entered, carrying batons. They poked them at Litsa, forced her back into the corner.

"Don't you touch her," Hunter yelled.

"Why not?" It was President Carlisle, standing in the doorway. "They're simple animals, nothing more."

"You bastard," Hunter said.

"Call me what you will, but don't judge me until you've walked in my shoes, Colonel. We've fought off these savages for years and found them very . . . useful, as you've seen for yourself."

"There's a special place in hell for people like you," Hunter said.

"And you'll both get to experience it long before I do if you don't make the scheduled radio call to *Resolute*," Carlisle said, motioning toward Litsa. "So please, if you'll accompany me. It's time."

# Chapter 57

"*Resolute*, this is *Beagle*. I have you in sight," Sif said, spying *Resolute* up ahead.

"Copy, *Beagle*, I have you on the viewer. You're quite a beautiful sight."

"Thank you, Lucas, I didn't know you cared. I'm even wearing makeup for the occasion."

"I'm all a-flutter. You're tracking perfectly, right down the pike to docking. Handover at your discretion."

"Copy, *Resolute*. Handover in three, two, one . . . Sync in progress . . . Green light." Sif pulled her hands back from the controls. "Sync is a go. Liv, I'm hands-off. She's all yours."

"Liv copies, Commander Wagner. *Beagle* is under my control. Docking in three minutes."

"Thank you, Liv."

"You're welcome, Commander."

*Seems Lucas has been working on Liv's voice interface.* "Lucas, switch to button four, please, I'm getting some interference on this channel."

Lucas paused before responding. "Copy. Switching to four." He hadn't noticed any interference.

Sif looked over at her passenger, still sleeping like a baby. A hypoxic baby, but asleep just the same. She gave him a burst of oxygen now and then, just enough to keep him alive. "Lucas, you there?"

"I'm here. Why the closed frequency?"

"I have a passenger, and he's not friendly. He's sleeping right now, but I'll have to wake him when we get there."

"Who? And why is he asleep?"

"An old friend of President Carlisle. I killed his oxygen enough to make him pass out. Look surprised when he comes through the air lock, okay?"

"Copy. What the hell is going on, Sif? Hunter made his last radio call, but he sounded like something wasn't right. This proves it."

"You've got a good ear," Sif replied. "I'll fill you in when I get there. Switch back to button one, in case they're monitoring. Mum's the word."

"Copy."

Sif waited a few seconds for Lucas to switch his comms. She looked at *Resolute* above her, gleaming so white and beautiful against the star-dotted background and growing closer by the minute. Liv established a data link between the two ships and was slowly guiding *Beagle* toward *Resolute*.

"*Beagle*, this is *Resolute*. You're thirty seconds away from manual override, if desired."

"Copy, thirty seconds, Lucas. Liv, are you up to this?"

"Liv is up to this, Commander. I can bring you all the way in, if you desire."

"Liv, I'm leaving it all up to you, then. *Beagle* is yours. And don't scratch the paint, please. She's still new."

"Liv will not scratch the paint, Commander. Stand by for docking."

Sif kept her hands near the manual override switch, just in case, as Liv brought *Beagle* toward *Resolute*'s docking station. The thrusters puffed, adjusting *Beagle*'s closing speed and trajectory, all controlled by the AI aboard *Resolute*.

Sif watched the distance tick down, the radar continuously pinging the ship before her. "Ten meters, Liv."

"Liv copies. On track."

"I show five meters, Liv."

"Liv copies five, four, three, two . . ."

Sif felt the thrusters puff again, stopping *Beagle*'s momentum to barely a crawl.

With a soft thunk, *Beagle* was back home. Sif breathed a sigh of relief. "Good job, Liv. Right on target."

"Thank you, Commander. Liv has established a hard seal. Docking clamps engaged. You may exit *Beagle* at your discretion."

Sif unstrapped, then started working on her passenger's restraints. His sidearm was exactly where he left it, tucked inside a belt on the belly of his suit. She reached over to the side of her seat and turned up his oxygen flow. His face regained color almost immediately, and then in a scene she remembered from her oxygen chamber training during flight school, he did what was affectionately called the Funky Chicken. His arms flailed about, and he kicked his legs, completely confused about where he was as he regained his senses.

"Whoa there, big fella. You passed out."

"I passed—I passed—"

"Yes, you passed—you passed—*out* as soon as we hit zero-g. It happens to the best of us," she lied. He bought it.

"We're here already?"

"You missed all the fun. We're docked and can exit *Beagle* whenever we want to."

He stared at her for a moment. "So, what are we waiting for?"

"You're the one with the gun, smart guy."

"We can exit now. You first."

"Such a *gentleman.*" Sif slipped from her seat and pushed herself down the narrow passageway toward the docking port. She could hear him bouncing about behind her, struggling to follow.

"I don't feel too good," he said.

"It's your body trying to adjust to weightlessness. Space sickness. It'll pass." She watched as he clamped his hand over his mouth. "Really? You're going to puke? How about you man up and hold it in, Shit-tuck."

He belched through his fingers.

"So much for being a gentleman." Sif turned the wheel, unlocking *Beagle*'s docking port. The door released with a hiss, and she lowered it to the stowed position. She pressed a button beside the door. "Lucas, Sif. Knock-knock, open up, please."

Sif watched as the wheel on *Resolute*'s door spun to the open position, and she was greeted by the smiling face of Lucas Hoover. With a beard. "You don't know how happy I am to see you, Lucas."

"Same here, Sif."

"Lose your razor?" she said as she pushed herself up through the short tunnel connecting the two ships.

"I decided shaving is a pain in the ass. I look rougher, don't you think?"

"Sure you do. We have a visitor, Lucas."

"A what?"

Sif was glad Lucas didn't overact. She pulled herself up into *Resolute*'s launch bay and pointed at her passenger, who was floating up right behind her. "This is Mr. Shattuck, North American Alliance. He's here to help us load the landers and make sure the flyer launch goes off as planned."

"Nice to meet you, Mr. Shattuck." Lucas didn't offer his hand.

"Mr. Hoover," Shattuck said. "I need to make a radio call, please."

"To whom?" Lucas asked.

"He needs to call home, give them a status report."

"Liv," Lucas said. "Time until next comm opportunity with Phoenix?"

"Three hours and six minutes, my liege."

Sif laughed out loud. "My *liege*?"

"It's a long story."

"I'll bet it is. So, Mr. Shattuck, you have three hours and six minutes until you can call home. If you're not too ill, how about helping us with the landers? And try to keep up," Sif added. She felt no regrets knowing her guest had three hours and seven minutes to live.

# Chapter 58

Sif and Shattuck spent the next three hours helping Lucas load the four landers' cargo compartments with packages appropriately labeled for each. Sif could tell Lucas had spent every minute of his time up here getting ready. "Did your folks have *you* pack the car for vacation?"

He smiled. "I've done a complete inventory of what we have on board," Lucas said. "Each of the landers is loaded to the gills with what I think is most crucial. The rest may have to wait for a follow-up trip, but it's stuff we can do without for a while."

"And your lander software mods can handle the higher weights?" Sif asked, hoping his theory about what to leave behind was correct.

"I finished another sim run right before you arrived. They'll work."

Shattuck was holding on to a wall strap a few feet away, still having trouble adjusting to the weightless environment. "And the flyer?" he asked.

"She's all ready to go, too, Mr. Shattuck," Lucas said. "I've loaded the culture into her tanks, tested the release mechanisms, and it's all good. She'll work as advertised. Let's just hope the culture has the effect on the Riy that you're hoping for."

Shattuck looked at the watch on his suit's wrist. "I need to get to a radio."

"Time to call home, huh?" Sif said. "There's a comm panel right over there." She floated to the panel and opened a channel. "Liv, please contact Phoenix. Mr. Shattuck will tell you when he's complete."

"Liv copies, Commander."

To Shattuck, she said, "When she establishes contact, press this button to speak, then release. Got it?"

He nodded.

"And make sure you tell them we've been good boys and girls."

"I'll *tell* them things are going according to plan," he spat back.

Sif floated back toward Lucas. "Be ready to grab on to something," she whispered.

"What are you going to do?"

"Our friend here is going for a walk."

Lucas's throat made an audible click as he swallowed. "You're kidding."

"I'm not."

Lucas grabbed a wall strap, wrapped it around his wrist. "I hate fighter pilots," he said under his breath.

"Communications established with Phoenix, Mr. Shattuck. You may proceed," Liv stated.

"Phoenix, this is Shattuck. Over."

"Shattuck, this is President Carlisle. What is your status?"

"Status is green, Mr. President. We've had no problems. Mr. Hoover and Commander Wagner are cooperative. The landers will launch on schedule, and so will the flyer."

"Very good, Shattuck. Inform Commander Wagner that her friends are in good health and will continue to be as long as everything is accomplished by the numbers."

Sif spoke up. "This is Wagner, Mr. President. The flyer will launch at"—she paused to check the time—"approximately fourteen thirty-six

hours, your time. The cargo landers will follow after that. Mr. Hoover
will stay aboard until we can make a return trip with *Beagle*. You have
no worries."

"Let's hope not, Commander, for the sake of your friends."

"Why would I try anything when your boy has a gun?"

"Wait," Lucas said, "he has a gun? When were you going to tell
me *that*?"

"Don't worry about it," Sif whispered.

"Sure, no worries," Lucas said, shaking his head.

"I'll contact you if anything changes, Mr. President," Shattuck said.

"Copy. Good work, Shattuck. Phoenix out."

Shattuck pressed the button ending the transmission. "How much
longer until the landers are ready?" he asked.

"Let's see," Sif said, checking her watch on the wrist of her suit.
"We'll get around to it in a few minutes or so. But not until we change
the landing coordinates."

Shattuck looked dumbfounded for a second, processing what he
just heard. Then he pulled his pistol from his belt. "We won't be changing any landing coordinates, Commander."

"Oh yes, we will. Liv, lock comm panel access to myself and Mr.
Hoover only, please."

"Liv has complied."

"What the hell do you think you're doing, Commander?"

"You're going for a walk, you inhuman bastard. Liv, open air lock
bravo six, three seconds only, on my mark, safety override authorization
Wagner, Caitlyn seven seven. Acknowledge."

"Liv acknowledges. On your mark, Commander."

"Exhale, Lucas, empty your lungs, and hold on tight," she said.

"Wait, what are you doing?" Shattuck pointed his pistol at Sif's
head. "Stop this, or I'll shoot."

Sif reached into her pocket and held up a bullet. "You need these,
don't you?"

Shattuck pulled the trigger. Nothing happened. His eyes went wide.

"See you, *Shit-tuck*." Sif wrapped a wall strap around her arm and gripped it tightly. "Liv, open bravo six, three-second duration, *mark*." She exhaled as hard as she could, and Lucas did the same, to prevent the rapid decompression from blowing their lungs out.

Any longer than thirty seconds would kill them both, but three seconds shouldn't do any permanent damage. She hoped.

Below Shattuck a door quickly slid open, opening the compartment to the void.

*One thousand one,* Sif counted.

The roar was tremendous as the atmosphere was sucked outside, carrying Shattuck with it. In a flash, he was gone. The interior fogged due to the change in pressure, and everything went white.

Sif was pulled toward the open hole, holding on to the strap with all her strength. *One thousand two,* she counted, feeling what little air was left in her lungs slip from her open mouth. *One thousand three!*

The door slammed shut, locks clicking back into place. She and Lucas sprang back toward the wall as Liv quickly compensated the airflow to repressurize the compartment.

"Jesus H. *Christ*, Sif! What the hell was that? You just murdered a man," Lucas screamed.

"That *man*, if you can call him that, was two hundred years *too* old. I just did the world a favor."

"The next time you do something like that, how about you do it *alone*? I could barely hold on, for cripes sake!"

"You're fine, Lucas."

"My sanity isn't." He wiped sweat from his forehead with his palm as the fog in the compartment slowly cleared. "Now how about you explain to me exactly what the holy hell is going on?"

# Chapter 59

Sif and Lucas made their way from the launch bay to *Resolute*'s command module. "You're going to have to trust me on this one, Lucas," Sif said.

"I've heard that one before, and it always leads to something I'm not going to like."

"Liv," Sif said, "compute lander drop points for new landing coordinates. Shift coordinates from the Phoenix Complex itself to five miles south-southwest."

"Liv has complied."

"Check achievability, Liv."

"Lander achievability confirmed. No change to scheduled drop time."

"Why are you changing the landing spots?" Lucas asked.

"We don't want them to land anywhere near the complex."

"I *figured* that," he said sarcastically, "but why?"

Sif checked the time. "We saw some things down there, horrible things. The Phoenix Complex isn't what it seems to be."

"Okay," Lucas said. "I'm listening."

***

When Fuller led Sif and Hunter from the corridor into the Level Five cavern, Sif was struck by its size, roughly the length of a football field and nearly as high. The entire space was crisscrossed by a pattern of dimly lit catwalks, levels and levels of them. A continuous, mechanical throbbing resounded through the place, as if a giant heart were beating.

Even through her mask, Sif could smell the stench, heavy, sweet, and sickening.

Between the catwalks, hundreds of objects hung from long cables. They looked like coffins.

Sif didn't have to ask Fuller what was inside.

"Oh my God," she breathed. "Those are people." Litsa was right about the Takers. The people captured from the outside were not relocated. They were here.

Fuller led them deeper into the facility and took them up on one of the catwalks.

Sif had seen some horrible things before, but never anything like *this*. Within each coffin was a body—a *person*—suspended in a greenish, thick liquid. Tubes ran from the catwalks into the coffins, and then into mouths, stomachs, and legs, pulsing in rhythm with the throbbing that echoed through the space and traveled through the soles of her boots.

"Are they alive?"

"Their bodies are kept alive by machines after the brain is destroyed." He tapped the back of his head. "In time, as the bodies are drained, even the machines can't keep them functioning."

"Drained?" Sif asked. She found it difficult to draw a breath. It was as if someone grasped her very soul and started to squeeze.

"This isn't the way it was supposed to be," Fuller explained. "But after Mattis was careless enough to bring a Riy hive here, and it got loose, this is what resulted."

319

"The hive we saw in Mattis's lab?" Hunter asked.

Fuller nodded. "Over a century ago, they brought it here to study. Mattis's idea. It escaped, and most of the people in the Phoenix Complex were infected when the spores entered the ventilation system."

"When Major Murphy told us about the Riy," Sif said, "he mentioned they figured out a way to slow the spread of the Riy, but by the time they did, it was already too late. They found a way to slow its effects, didn't they?"

"They could slow it but not stop it. The only way to keep the spread at bay is through regular transfusions of noninfected blood. One side effect, though, is that their life is extended. The spores are throughout their bodies, Commander, but they never progress to the final stage of infection. The Old Ones—like the president and Dr. Mattis—are the original people who came to the Phoenix Complex almost two centuries ago."

"Your President Carlisle," Sif said. "I saw him in some old pictures while we were in the Dak—the cave—with Litsa and the others. He was the CEO of a company called Phoenix BioLabs. And Mattis, he was the man whom many blamed for the entire catastrophe. It was Phoenix, and Mattis, who were running some sort of experiment at Chernobyl when it was destroyed."

"Now I remember," Hunter said. "And they disappeared. Now we know where they went."

"They told you Phoenix was where all the greatest minds of the world were brought as the rest of the planet fell apart," Fuller said, "but it isn't true. Only the Phoenix employees themselves were brought here. Everyone else was left to die."

"How many of the Old Ones are there?" Sif asked.

"Almost all the people in the complex are Old Ones, except for those like me, who were brought here." He paused, pointing to another row of coffins, another level down. "Or born here."

Even from this distance, Sif could see the people within the coffins were women. And they were pregnant. "Oh my God. They're breeding them?"

"The Old Ones need new blood, not only to sustain their lives, but to add to the complex's workforce." Fuller placed his hand on the nearest coffin, took a deep breath. "I was one of those children," he said. "Born here, in this room, to a mother who was nothing but a female host, kept alive by machines and discarded like trash when her usefulness was over."

"And the secret got out," Hunter said.

"We learned the truth, yes. The Resistance are all outsiders, brought here as children or bred here. The Old Ones dispose of us when we become known to them, but they have many replacements ready to take our place."

A mechanical noise startled Sif. One of the coffins on an upper level one row over was moving, sliding toward the edge of the catwalk.

Fuller saw it, too. "And when the bodies are drained of all their usefulness," he explained, "this happens."

The glass cover slid back, and the coffin rotated. Greenish liquid spilled over the side, just a few drops at first, then splashed to the floor below as the coffin tipped completely over. The body inside—thin, emaciated—hung suspended from the tubes for a moment, then broke free as the tubes slid from its mouth and tore free from its arms and legs.

The body careened through the air, and Sif jumped back as it flew right past her. She leaned over the side of the catwalk railing and watched it hit the floor below.

It was a sight she would carry with her for the rest of her days.

Sif lost all the strength in her legs and held tightly to the railing to steady herself.

The floor was littered with hundreds of dead corpses, dumped like so much trash from the coffins above, after the Old Ones drained them of their lives.

Fuller continued. "What you see down there is nothing more than a source of biomass."

Sif struggled to keep her stomach contents down as he continued speaking.

"Material for clothing, other textiles. And food."

"Dear God in Heaven," Hunter sighed. He turned away, hung his head.

"This is how the Old Ones stay alive, Commander. This is how we *all* stay alive. What you've eaten, processed to appear as meat . . . There are no more bison," Fuller said.

Sif ripped her mask from her face and vomited.

"Come," Fuller said. "You need to see something else. Quickly."

Sif wiped her mouth with the back of her hand and followed Fuller toward the far end of the catwalk, where a row of coffins sat empty. Their lids were open, waiting.

"There is a room, near here, where the new captures are kept. Two of the people you were in the cave with are still there."

"Two of them?" Hunter asked.

"Conrad and Geller, I believe their names are."

*Oh God.* "Where is Talia?" Sif asked.

Fuller pointed to the coffin beside her.

Sif didn't want to look, but she did.

It was Talia, her body suspended in the green liquid, tubes forced into her body, down her throat. Her eyes were open, as if she were still alive, and her body pulsed, throbbed, as it was being drained.

"Oh, Talia." Sif began to sob and placed her hands against the glass. "She was just a kid."

Something inside Sif snapped.

She would do whatever she could to bring this evil place to its knees, even if it meant killing every single one of them with her bare hands.

Fuller stepped forward and put his hand on Sif's shoulder. "The Resistance needs your help, Commander."

She stood. "You've got it."

Fuller nodded, looked at both of them. "We're going to need *Resolute*."

\*\*\*

Lucas was silent for a time.

"You said they need the ship," he finally said.

"They do," Sif said softly. "As soon as we launch the flyer, a clock starts for the Resistance. They're going to get Hunter, Litsa, and whoever else they can save out of the complex. But our timing has to be spot-on."

"Timing for what?" Lucas asked.

"After you and I bug out, Liv is going to take the ship and fly her right down their goddamn throat, Lucas. She's going to crash *Resolute* into the Phoenix Complex."

# Chapter 60

Hunter was back in the radio room, awaiting the call from *Resolute* stating that the flyer was launched. Around him were numerous security personnel, at least one of them, he assumed, a member of the Resistance.

Fuller had told them the plan would go into motion as soon as the flyer was launched, based on a rough timeline Sif calculated. It was a guess on her part, timing the interval between the flyer launch and when *Resolute* dropped from the sky. If Sif was wrong, then they all might get to see it up close and personal.

"Phoenix, this is *Resolute*. Over."

Not Sif, Hunter noted. It was Lucas.

"*Resolute*, this is Phoenix," the operator replied. "Go ahead."

"Cargo landers are away, south-southeast transit arc until touchdown. Flyer launch in fifteen minutes. Will advise. *Resolute* out."

President Carlisle approached the radio operator. "I want to talk to Shattuck. Get them back."

"*Resolute*, this is Phoenix. Over."

Nothing.

"*Resolute*, this is Phoenix, come in, please. Over."

Hunter smiled. "They're a little busy right now, Mr. President."

"Let's hope that's all it is."

Hunter would have been pleased to know that Shattuck's body burned up thirty minutes ago, leaving a dim stream of light high in the night sky over what used to be called the Dead Sea.

\*\*\*

"Good job, Lucas," Sif said. Hunter now knew the lander's new touch-down locations—south-southeast. "But what's a 'transit arc'?"

"Who knows? I thought it sounded pretty good, myself."

"Liv, time until flyer release?"

"Flyer release in ten minutes, Commander."

"I notice she's calling me by rank again. Back to normal, huh?"

"It's been a struggle. Believe me."

Sif and Lucas suited up, made their way to *Beagle*'s cockpit, and quickly completed the prelaunch checks. As soon as the flyer was away, and they made a radio call stating such, they would depart *Resolute* for the last time, leaving the ship under Liv's control. A short time later, their huge, beautiful ship would be transformed into a screaming, flaming hulk, a hypersonic mass that would hit the Phoenix Complex with the force of an atomic bomb.

If everything worked.

\*\*\*

Inside the comm center, everyone kept their eyes on the clock, counting down the time until the flyer's expected release.

The call came right on time, but it was full of static, hard to hear.

It was Lucas again.

"Phoenix, this is *Resolute*. Flyer release. I say again, flyer release with good results. She's in the green and operating normally. Mr. Shattuck wishes to—"

The transmission ended abruptly with a burst of static.

"Get them back," the president ordered.

The radio operator tried numerous times, but the static remained.

Out of the corner of his eye, Hunter noticed one of the security personnel slip away. The clock was running. "They might be out of radio range, Mr. President," Hunter said, "or maybe a radio problem. Hard to tell."

"I need to speak to Shattuck," Carlisle said.

"The flyer is away and operating normally. I would think Shattuck's job is complete," Hunter said.

"As is yours, Colonel." Carlisle turned toward the security personnel. "Take Webb and the female to the holding pen."

Hunter stood, but two guards grabbed his arms. "You promised we'd be allowed to live."

"I don't need *three* astronauts on my hands, Colonel. The other two will be sufficient."

"You'll answer for what you've done here, Carlisle."

"Maybe, Colonel. But not today."

# Chapter 61

"Three minutes until release, Lucas. Are you ready for this?" Sif asked.

"I hope it goes more smoothly than the last time you went down in this thing."

"*Beagle* isn't a thing, Lucas. She's a *she*."

"I'll call it *she* after it gets me down on the ground safe and sound."

Sif checked the timers on her wrist—one was counting down to *Beagle*'s release, and the other was counting down to Liv's first maneuver. Liv would turn the ship, orienting her tailfirst, then fire the mains, starting her descent. After that, she would bring the nose of the ship to bear, and at the right time, fire the mains again until the fuel was depleted, or impact, whichever came first.

"Liv, *Resolute* system status for descent maneuver?"

"All systems operational, Commander. Liv is ready to execute."

"Thank you, Liv," Lucas said. "It's been a pleasure working with you."

"Liv has enjoyed working with you, as well, my liege."

Lucas shook his head. "I know I shouldn't feel this way—it's only a computer—but I'm going to miss that crazy thing."

"Liv, give us a count for release," Sif ordered.

"Release in two minutes, Commander."

Through her earphones, Sif heard Lucas take a deep breath. "Nothing worse than a roller coaster, Lucas. I promise."

"Release in one minute, fifty—"

Silence.

Sif quickly checked the comm circuits. All green. "Liv?"

"Liv has detected a fault in the navigation system, Commander. Running diagnostics."

"Shit," Sif said. Their patchwork fixes to the navigation system were failing at the worst possible moment. She waited a few more seconds. "Liv, status?"

"Nav system is off-line, Commander. Main control board showing fault. Orbital descent not possible."

Sif unstrapped.

"Wait a minute, where are you going?" Lucas asked.

"Stay put. I'll be right back."

"We've got less than a minute and a half until we're supposed to launch!"

"I know, Lucas. Just stay put." Sif pushed herself from the chair and quickly opened the docking port door. "Liv, can you recalculate descent parameters by bypassing the main controller?"

"Negative, Commander. Nav system is off-line. Orbital descent not possible."

"God*dammit.*" Sif made a quick decision. She closed *Beagle*'s door, then opened the door to *Resolute*'s launch bay. She closed the door behind her and headed for the command module.

"*Beagle* release in one minute," Liv announced.

Sif floated into the command center and slid open the nav controller panel. She could smell the tang of burnt electronics and saw the circuit board was fried. Her stomach sank. "Liv, is manual control possible?"

"Manual control is possible, Commander. *Beagle* release in forty seconds."

She would have to fly *Resolute* down manually. By herself. "Liv, switch *Beagle* flight profile to fully automatic."

"Liv has complied."

"Lucas, this is Sif. I'm not coming with you."

"You're *what*?"

"The nav system is fried. I'll—" She hated lying to him. "I'll do what I can to fix it, but I may have to get her lined up manually."

"Sif, no."

"I still have the escape capsule. *Beagle* is on automatic, you'll be fine. Just don't touch anything. I'll see you on the ground." With that, she closed the comm channel.

She heard the locking clamps release a few seconds later. *Beagle* and Lucas were on their way down to Earth.

She slid into *Resolute*'s pilot seat. "All right, Liv, it's you and me. Bring up projected path and firing events, my screen. Control to manual. Provide an audible countdown for each event."

"Liv has complied, Commander."

Sif strapped in and placed her hands on the controls. She took a deep breath and waited for Liv's count to begin. She had done this with *Beagle* before and could do it again. She *had* to.

"Commander, ship orientation maneuver in five, four, three, two, one . . . mark."

# Chapter 62

Hunter and Litsa, hands tied behind their backs, were in an elevator heading down to Level Five, along with three guards, each armed. Hunter tried to fight back, but received a baton in the gut that sent him sprawling to the floor. He resigned himself to the fact that he wasn't going to get out of this alive.

The elevator stopped, and the guards pulled them out. Hunter could see the holding cell, a large cage packed full of people dressed like Litsa was when they first saw her.

This was his fate, then.

He remembered Fuller tapping the back of his skull, explaining how the brain was destroyed before the body was placed in a coffin. *Like an animal to slaughter.*

He only hoped the rest of the Resistance's plan would work and that he would live long enough to feel *Resolute*'s impact and watch the facility—and all its evil—collapse around him. It wasn't how he wanted his life to end, but he would die smiling, knowing he did his part.

Hunter saw a man press himself against the bars.

"Litsa?" a voice cried out. "Litsa, it *is* you."

Litsa was gagged, and Hunter could hear her struggling to speak. "Back away from the gate," a guard ordered, poking his baton at the bars, its tip sparking bright blue.

The man backed up, apparently well acquainted with the baton.

The guard opened the lock while the two others held Hunter and Litsa by the arms.

Hunter felt his guard release his grip. Saw him move.

The gate opened, and the guard turned to face them.

"Bring them—"

His words were cut short by a bullet slamming into his forehead.

Hunter dropped to his knees and watched as his guard pointed his pistol at the man holding Litsa—and put a bullet into his face.

The guard with the gun removed his mask. "Colonel Hunter, we don't have much time," he said. "My name is Stephens." He pulled a key from his uniform blouse and unlocked the cuffs around Hunter's wrists. "The Resistance is on the move. You need to get these people to the ladder, quickly." He tossed Hunter the handcuff keys. "For her. Now, go. There will be others topside to help you."

With that, the man was gone, disappearing into the shadows.

Hunter quickly unlocked Litsa's cuffs and pulled the gag from her mouth.

"Jarrod!" Litsa screamed.

The man who called Litsa's name tentatively stepped forward, keeping his eyes locked on Hunter.

"It's okay," Litsa said. "He's a friend."

"We need to get these people moving," Hunter said. "There isn't much time."

A loud boom resounded through the complex, and everyone flinched.

"This way," Hunter said, urging them to follow.

Jarrod ran to Litsa, gripped her arms with his strong hands. "I thought you were lost."

Chuck Grossart

"And I, you," she said. "We must follow him. Now."

"Do you trust him?"

Litsa nodded. "With my life."

\*\*\*

Hunter was breathing heavily when he reached the third level. Strung out below him were thirty or so other people, all those awaiting their time in the coffins, now given a second chance at life.

He hoped most of them would survive, but if the gunfire and explosions he was hearing from the upper levels were any indication, not all would.

There was one hell of a firefight going on. And they were climbing right into it.

\*\*\*

Jacques burst into President Carlisle's office. "Sir, we have a situation."

"What is it?" he replied, pulling the IV line from his arm. Blood dripped to the floor.

"What we've always feared, sir. The Resistance has started an armed revolt."

Carlisle stood. "Implement the extermination protocol. Every last one of them."

"Yes, sir."

The Old Ones would kill every single person in the complex who was not one of their own. It was time for a cleansing.

# Chapter 63

Lucas tried not to but passed out on the way down. Sif was right—it *was* like a roller coaster. *A roller coaster from hell,* he thought. He came to just as *Beagle* touched down, and found he couldn't move. Lucas was back in a one-g environment, and he might as well be paralyzed. Here he was, back on terra firma a few miles away from a place that was going to be blown to bits, and he was hopelessly stuck.

"God *damn* you, Sif. You always have to be the hero, don't you?" He was angry with her, furious for putting herself in so much danger without even a second thought.

She mentioned the escape capsule, and maybe—if there was enough time—she could get to it and blast herself away before it was too late.

But time wasn't going to be on her side.

\*\*\*

Stephens made his way to Level Four, and after making sure most of the people in the ladder tunnel at least reached Level Two, he headed toward the labs.

The doors were sealed, but he knew the code. He opened the outer door, then quickly opened the second door, no longer caring if anyone in security control saw him. They were probably too busy with everything else the Resistance was doing to worry about keeping an eye on the lower-level security cameras.

The containment lab was cloaked in shadow, but his prize was just a few feet away, safely tucked away behind a thick pane of Plexiglas.

He was surprised to see Dr. Mattis—one of the Old Ones who caused all of this in the first place—standing outside the glass, staring at the Riy within.

"Step away, Mattis," Stephens said.

Mattis didn't react, as if he hadn't heard a word. Stephens pulled his sidearm and moved closer, repeating his command. "Mattis, step *away*."

Without turning his head, Mattis spoke. "It's really quite a remarkable creature in its own right. Able to survive and flourish in environments where man cannot."

Stephens decided shooting the man would be too merciful. He lowered his weapon and stepped to the containment room controls. He knew he probably wasn't going to make it out of here alive, but it didn't matter. Not anymore. As long as some of his people were able to taste freedom, *real* freedom, for the first time in their lives, then it would all be worth it.

"It wasn't supposed to happen the way it did, you know," Mattis continued, paying no attention to Stephens. "We were experimenting, taking the best qualities of one species and combining it with another to see what could survive, and then those terrible men destroyed the enclosure. All so unfortunate, *so* unfortunate . . ."

Stephens released the locks on the Plexiglas cover. It popped free, just an inch or so.

"All they wanted to do was kill it, but they never saw it for the noble beast it really is, a new species, able to conquer the entire planet. We should be on our knees, praying to it, *worshipping* it."

Stephens hit the button to raise the cover. Mattis backed up, letting it open toward him. Then he stepped close, just a foot away from one of the drones.

"There you are, one of my princes of the day, so beautiful in your perfection . . ."

Stephens could take no more. He hit the lights, bathing the containment chamber and the entire lab in a blinding white light.

The effect on the drones—and the hive—was immediate.

The first drone stepped forward, bumping into Mattis.

As Stephens turned to run, he saw Mattis embrace the thing—like a father opening his arms to a long-lost child—then disappear in a swirling cloud of black mist.

The other drones stumbled out, and the hive, its huge black mass pulsating wildly, slid from the containment chamber.

Stephens ran from the lab, stopping at a comm panel. "This is Stephens, Level Four. Containment breach. The hive is out. I say again, the hive is out."

He turned to run, knowing he bought his people more time to escape, but stopped. Standing before him was one of the drones.

The petals on its chest were peeling back.

Stephens smiled, placed the barrel of his pistol under his chin, and squeezed the trigger.

# Chapter 64

Hunter stepped from the ladder tunnel into a small outbuilding within the Phoenix Complex's fence line. It was early evening. Through a window, he saw the complex security personnel firing at what he assumed was the Resistance. They were firing back.

All at once, the security personnel retreated toward the main entrance, many of them falling as the Resistance continued to fire.

*Are they surrendering?* he wondered.

Behind him, Litsa and her people piled into the small building. They wouldn't all be able to fit in here.

Hunter scanned the courtyard and spied a gaping hole in the perimeter fence.

A way out.

One of the Resistance fighters pointed toward the window and motioned for others to follow him. If these people *weren't* the Resistance, then they were going to be sitting ducks.

As the man approached, he placed his rifle on the ground and raised his hands, motioning for Hunter to come out.

"The rest of you, stay in here," Hunter said. And he opened the door.

"Colonel Hunter, we have to move, now. Get those people out of there and through the fence."

Stephens said there would be help topside, and this must be it. He turned to the group of people packed into the building behind him. "There, through the fence. When you get through the breach, head south-southwest," he said. "And keep running."

Litsa stood by his side as her people streamed from the building's door, racing toward the breach in the fence. "Take them as far as you can, Litsa, until you see *Beagle*," Hunter instructed. "It shouldn't be too far away. Sif will be there, with our other astronaut."

"I'm not leaving without you," she said.

Hunter looked at the man beside her. "You, what's your name?"

"I am Jarrod."

"Jarrod, you're in charge, then. Get them away from here, now."

When he hesitated, Litsa said, "Go, Jarrod, I will follow when I can."

Jarrod nodded once, then took off toward the fence. As he ran, he caught a glint of sunlight from the nearest guard tower. He stopped, saw the rifle scope, and saw where it was aiming. "Litsa! Down now!"

Litsa bent over just as the first bullet slammed into the doorframe behind her, followed by the rifle's crack.

The second shot would follow quickly. Hunter tackled Litsa, rolling across the ground.

A puff of dirt to his right, then another crack.

"Everybody down!" he screamed.

The Resistance forces were quick to react. A hail of automatic weapons fire enveloped the guard tower, which momentarily disappeared in a cloud of concrete dust.

Then, silence.

"Are you okay?" he asked.

Litsa spat the dirt from her mouth. "I am not injured. We must go now."

The last of her people were out of the building and running toward the breach in the fence.

Hunter grabbed Litsa's hand and, together with the remaining members of the Resistance, ran into the wilderness, heading south-southwest.

\*\*\*

President Carlisle sat alone in his office, watching the scene above-ground unfold on a video monitor. He knew the hive had escaped its confines, thanks to the stinking Resistance, and his security forces were forced to turn their attention to it, instead of the escapees.

The animals could be replaced simply enough, he knew. There were still a good many viable females on Level Five, more than enough to replenish their stock. Everyone running through the hole in the fence would be captured again, too. In time. Most would be killed, but some would choose to serve the complex in order to save their lives.

When they brought Lieutenant Colonel Webb back to the Phoenix Complex, though, he would personally shove the tube down the man's throat.

And watch him die.

# Chapter 65

Hunter saw *Beagle* in the distance, her nose sticking up into the sky, small tendrils of smoke curling into the air from burnt vegetation. "There she is," he said, pointing.

"That is your *Beagle* ship?" Litsa asked.

"It is, and the other ships we sent down should be nearby. Come on."

It took them about twenty minutes to reach the landing site. All the while Hunter kept an eye to the sky, wondering when he would see *Resolute* come tearing though the atmosphere, and Litsa kept an eye out for Riy, as the sun was not entirely set yet, and she had no idea how far north they were.

When Hunter reached the ship, he pressed an emergency release lever, popping the exit door. He didn't expect to see Lucas yet, as he was still probably trying to adjust to gravity, but was surprised Sif wasn't outside the ship waiting for them.

He crawled inside. "Sif? Lucas?"

"I'm up here, and I'm too weak to get out of my damn seat."

Hunter crawled up the crew access ladder into the cockpit. He was shocked to see Lucas all by himself. Before he could ask, Lucas answered his question.

"She stayed aboard *Resolute*, Hunter. The nav system failed right before we dropped. She's bringing her in manually."

Hunter's heart sank, then he remembered the escape capsule. "She can use the capsule, then." He didn't like the look on Lucas's face, and he didn't want to ask his next question. "What aren't you telling me, Lucas?"

"It was the main controller that failed, Hunter." Without the controller, there was no other way to bring the ship down. "I'm sorry."

Hunter reached for the radio controls. "*Resolute*, this is *Beagle*. Come in, please. *Resolute*, this is *Beagle*. Do you read?"

"She may not be in range yet," Lucas said softly.

"*Resolute*, this is *Beagle*. Sif, this is Hunter. Talk to me, Sif."

Lucas put his hand on Hunter's arm. "She probably turned it off, Hunter."

"Why the hell would she do that?" he snapped.

"Because she doesn't want to say good-bye."

***

The transmission was choppy, but she could tell who it was.

"—*Beagle*. Sif, this is Hu— Talk to me, Sif."

At least she knew Lucas made it safely down to Earth, and Hunter was there with him.

Her fingers fluttered over the comm button—but she couldn't make herself press it.

*It's better this way*, she thought.

"Outer hull temperature rising rapidly, Commander."

"Copy, Liv." She knew the radio wouldn't work anyway, as soon as the superheated plasma from reentry surrounded the ship. "Time to impact?"

"Time to impact nine minutes, fifty-five seconds. Would you like me to provide an audible countdown?"

Sif laughed. "No, Liv. That won't be necessary. Status of main controller bypass?" Liv was attempting to restore automatic navigation control by finding an alternate path through other equipment.

"Bypass ongoing. Time to estimated completion eleven minutes, five seconds."

Sif sighed. She didn't have that much time.

"Hull temperature still increasing. Will reach critical levels in—"

"Liv complete. I don't really want to know."

Sif watched *Resolute*'s course on her screen, firing the thrusters whenever the ship started to drift off the projected path. It was getting more and more difficult as *Resolute* began to react with Earth's atmosphere.

"Mains are off-line, Commander. Fuel is depleted."

"Copy, Liv."

Her forward velocity was now off the scale, and she would steepen her reentry angle using the thrusters right before the ship would presumably start coming apart. At that point, trying to get out was a nonstarter, as there were only seconds from that point until *Resolute* would impact.

Sif could feel the ship start to buffet. Outside her windows, flashes of light streaked by, orange and red. Soon, that would be all she would see.

And it would be the last thing she would *ever* see.

"—Sif—ome in, Sif—"

"Dammit, Hunter, let it go," she said. "Just let it go."

"Sif, this is Hunter. Pick up your damn mic, Sif." Clear as a bell.

She pressed the comm button. "Hunter, this is Sif. I read you."

She expected some sort of heart-wrenching emotional scene—but that wasn't what she got. "Tell Liv to try bypassing the main controller through the D eight and D nine boards!"

"Liv, bypass the—"

"Liv copied all, will comply. Working."

"Attagirl, Liv! Give me status as soon as you have it."

"Liv will comply."

"Hunter, Liv is giving it a try."

"It might work, Sif, but don't risk your life on it. You need to get the hell out of there."

"And if it doesn't, then Phoenix won't be destroyed. You would do the same thing, Hunter. You might not admit it, but you would."

"Dammit, Sif, I don't want to lose you."

Sif didn't know what to say.

"I want you to get out, Sif. Get your butt in the escape capsule. That's an order."

"I can't do that."

"We'll fight them another way, Sif. We'll do it together—"

Liv's voice. "Negative results with bypass attempt, Commander."

So that was it. "Hunter, no joy. The bypass is a no-go. I'm taking her in myself."

"Sif, please . . ."

The orange glow outside the windows was building, and Sif could hear the growl of static growing in the speaker. There were only a few seconds left until the radio would be worthless.

"Hunter, listen to me. I don't have much time." Sif could feel the tears welling up in her eyes, but she didn't care. "It may not have seemed like it most of the time, but I think you're one of the best pilots and officers I've ever met. This new world needs a leader, and I can't think of anyone better."

"Sif, don't do this."

"You know it has to be this way." She was sobbing now. "Maybe one day you can make me that statue we talked about."

"—Sif—"

"Do it right this time, okay? Don't let them make the same mistakes again." *For me.*

And then, nothing but static.

Sif wiped her eyes with her glove. "All right, Liv, let's put this glorious bitch down right where we need to, okay?"

"Copy, Commander."

The interior of the ship was getting hotter, enough that Sif could feel it through her suit.

"Sixty seconds until thruster pitch-over, Commander."

"Copy, Liv. It's been a pleasure."

"Thank you, Commander."

Outside, Sif could see nothing but the white glare of superheated plasma. The windows were beginning to delaminate and bubble, and before long, they would fail.

The ship was shaking like crazy.

She had only seconds to live.

She thought about her parents. About her dad. She could see him, larger than life, coming home from a deployment and kneeling down to take her in his arms as she ran to him.

"Here I come, Daddy," she said. "I hope you can see this, and you're proud of me. Your little Cate's about to put the hammer down."

She placed her hands on the thruster controls and closed her eyes.

"Nav system online and on automatic, Commander."

"What? *Repeat*, Liv!"

"Nav system on line. Liv has taken control. Thruster pitch-over in thirty-five seconds."

Sif reached for her straps as *Resolute* began to break apart.

# Chapter 66

Hunter could see the glow, high in the sky to the northwest. He didn't want to watch, but he owed Sif at least that much. She was sacrificing her life for him—for *all* of them—and as he glanced at Litsa, he realized Sif was sacrificing herself for all of humanity, as well.

"Is that the other ship?" Litsa asked.

Hunter nodded, unable to speak.

"And Sif, she is still inside?"

This time, he had to speak. "She's making sure the ship hits exactly where it's supposed to, Litsa. She's not getting out."

Litsa turned toward the escapees, *her* people now. "Warriors!" she yelled.

The glow grew brighter in the sky, and larger, as *Resolute* began her fiery descent.

Hunter could see many of them stand, staring up into the sky, their faces proud.

"Hear me!" Litsa yelled as she pointed toward the flaming glow in the sky. "A warrior dies for you today! Urrah!" she yelled, holding her fist high in the sky.

The others did the same. "Urrah!" they yelled in unison. "Urrah! Urrah! Urrah!"

The landscape brightened as *Resolute* fell—the ship burned up, parts of it breaking off, sending sparks and flaming contrails beside it. It flared brighter as the nose thrusters fired, and the ship arced almost straight down.

"You did it, Sif," he said. "You really did it."

They all watched as the huge, flaming mass streaked through the sky, roaring like an enraged lion, and shielded their eyes as it impacted the earth.

The ground shook, and Hunter yelled for everyone to take cover.

As the roar rolled over them and the shock wave hit, Hunter buried his face in the dirt. The new world lost a heroic soul, right when it needed one the most.

All he could see was her smiling face, telling him how great a pilot she was.

And she was right.

He would make sure no one would ever forget what she did here this day, and no one would ever forget the name *Sif*.

He sat up, looked behind him at the billowing mushroom cloud rising into the sky.

Hunter brought himself to attention and snapped a salute in tribute to Commander Caitlyn "Sif" Wagner, United States Navy.

"*Shack*, Navy," he said quietly. "Right on target."

# Epilogue

*Two weeks later*

At final count, fifty-two people escaped the Phoenix Complex: twenty-seven of Litsa's people and twenty-five members of the Resistance. At first the distrust between the two groups was difficult to handle, but Hunter was pleased to see that they were already starting to cooperate.

After dispatching search parties to locate the four cargo landers, they decided to make camp surrounding *Beagle*, which, although still fully operational, sat as a silent monument to all that happened on that day two weeks past. In time, they could use the ship to scout for other habitable places—and possibly other people—as long as she had fuel in her tanks. For now, that was in the future.

*Right* now, they were living for the day.

Hunter saw the flyer overhead on more than one occasion, as there were no high-flying contrails from any other aircraft. Whether or not it was working remained to be seen, but none of the sentries he posted had reported any sign of the Riy. So far.

Maybe they would take *Beagle* south one day, a suborbital hop, just to make sure the things were dead.

---

Litsa's people, not all from the Dak, were proving to be incredibly resourceful. Huts were already raised, built from the available timber, and many people were already forming themselves into job-specific groups. Land was being cleared nearby, where in the spring seeds brought down in the landers would be planted. There were hunters, who scoured the surrounding forests for food, and cooks, who could take a rabbit and turn it into a delicacy over an open fire. Jarrod and Litsa instituted an archery training program, where they taught anyone who was interested how to craft the perfect bow, and how to place an arrow dead center.

It was going to be a struggle, but it was a challenge Hunter relished. After seeing the depravity of the Phoenix Complex, he knew that the real future for humanity *was* out here, in the forests, on the plains, and in the caves. Humanity was getting a do-over, and he prayed they would get it right, this time. Just like Sif wanted.

He glanced to the north and saw the smoke rising from the crater that was once the Phoenix Complex. "We're going to give it our best shot, Sif," he whispered.

"Hunter!" Jarrod yelled. "Come quickly. Lucas calls you."

"Great," Hunter said. "He probably found another poisonous plant he needs to warn me about." With his interest in botany, Lucas was surprisingly helpful spotting those plants to stay away from and finding those most beneficial. "Where is he?" Hunter asked as he walked up to Jarrod.

"He is in the *Beagle* ship. He is very excited."

Hunter jogged over to *Beagle* and poked his head inside the hatch. "What's the crisis, Lucas?"

"It's a beacon, Hunter. I picked up a locator beacon."

Hunter scrambled up the ladder. "Where?"

"It was faint, but I *know* it was from *Orion*. Thirty miles south, bearing one-seven-five degrees."

*Orion. The escape capsule.* Hunter wanted to believe it was true. "Is there any way it could have been released during reentry, and the beacon triggered by the crash?"

"It's not automatic, Hunter. It has to be activated manually."

Hunter grabbed one of their charts and drew a straight line from their current position to the locator beacon. Lucas watched him, smiling.

"Are you ready to go flying, Lucas? Take a short hop or two?" Hunter said, tossing him the chart. Although *Beagle* was designed to make it to orbit and back, she was also capable of short, endo-atmospheric flights.

"I was hoping you'd say that," Lucas said, smiling broadly.

"Good," Hunter replied. "Let's go get her."

# ACKNOWLEDGMENTS

To my wife (and frontline editor), Nessa, who likes nothing more than to curl up with her Kindle, read a book in peace, and not be interrupted by a husband with an annoying habit of sending her every chapter as soon as it's written, I say thank you. I have no idea how you put up with me, but boy am I glad you do.

If one wants to know what it feels like to do a pop-up delivery in a strike fighter, one should ask someone who's done it . . . So, I did. To my old friend Colonel Paul "Sly" Lyman, your help and expertise is much appreciated. If I got anything wrong, Sly, the fault is all mine.

To my underground (literally) "first readers," Frank and Caveman. Your initial feedback and suggestions are always spot-on and valued more than you know. Almost as much as our sanity-saving caption contests.

To Scott Barrie of Cyanotype Book Architects . . . Dude, you did it again. The cover you designed is like a bacon-wrapped jalapeño popper—absolute perfection.

To Jason Kirk and the rest of the 47North team, you have my gratitude for allowing a fat, bald guy the opportunity to tell a story to more people than he ever thought possible. Thank you for your encouragement and guidance, and most of all, thank you for your confidence.

Lastly, I'd like to thank you, my reader, for spending a few hours of your life within the front and back covers of *The Phoenix Descent*. If I was able to capture your interest and take you away to another place for a while, then I did my job, and I truly hope you enjoyed the journey.

You bring the popcorn, and I'll bring the pages.

*Chuck Grossart*
*Bellevue, Nebraska*
*2016*

# AN EXCERPT FROM CHUCK GROSSART'S
## *THE GEMINI EFFECT*

# THE FIRST NIGHT

The extermination of the human race began in a salvage yard.

Under the left rear fender of what remained of a 1962 Chevrolet Nova, to be exact. A rusted shell of what was once called a Chevy II—a "Deuce" to those who loved them—built at the old Kansas City GM Leeds assembly plant during the last week of November 1961. *Wagon Train* was America's favorite TV show in the winter of '61. On the radio, Jimmy Dean's "Big Bad John" replaced Dion's "Runaround Sue" at the top of the Hit Parade. Roger Maris, Mickey Mantle, and the rest of the New York Yankees had won their nineteenth World Series by beating the Cincinnati Reds 13–5 in game five.

The world turned, counting down.

In the weeks and months before Chevy's newest grocery getter rolled off the assembly line, the world witnessed Berlin split in two by concrete barricades and concertina wire, and heard news of a 58-megaton Soviet nuclear device—Царь-бомба, the Tsar Bomb—detonated over the Novaya Zemlya archipelago in the Arctic Ocean. Eleven months later, grainy reconnaissance photos of Soviet missile sites in Cuba would take the world to the brink of nuclear annihilation.

Dallas crowds stood dumbstruck less than two years after the Deuce left the showroom floor, as American innocence slipped away in the back of a '61 Lincoln Continental. A big-eared Texas politician, standing next to a woman in a bloodstained pink Chanel suit, put his hand on a Bible, took the helm of history in his well-washed hands, and slithered full speed ahead toward Southeast Asia to keep all the dominoes from falling.

The Nova was built in a time of war—a cold war. The fear was real then, under the skin, every moment of every day. Like two bullies on the block vying for dominance, a brawl between the opposing forces was a foregone conclusion; it would happen, eventually. Maybe tomorrow. Or even today.

It was an era of calculated risks and strategic brinkmanship by two great powers, each holding a uranium-edged blade to the other's throat. Missiles sat at the ready in buried coffins and silos, armed bombers lined the ramps, and alert crews awaited the Klaxon's scream.

MAD was the acronym of the times: mutually assured destruction, the ultimate catch-22 of the twentieth century. They kill us, we kill them. When the missiles launched and the bombers flew, even the most steadfast warriors on either side knew there'd be no victory parades.

Scientists designed the city-killing bombs, but they'd also built smaller weapons, engineered to be just as deadly, and in some ways, even more destructive. *Virulence* and *infectivity* supplanted *blast* and *radiation* in the killing lexicon. Careful planning and controlled employment of these tiny weapons would render the MAD game obsolete. There'd be a winner, *and* a loser.

The research had been promising—and productive—until it escaped from a clean room.

In a '62 Deuce.

*Chuck Grossart's* The Gemini Effect *is available from 47North.*

# ABOUT THE AUTHOR

*Photo © 2013 Ashley Crawford*

Chuck Grossart lives in Bellevue, Nebraska, with his wife, kids, and usually too many dogs.